# SARAH MASON

# Riding the Line

## Steel Saints MC

First edition

ISBN: 979-8-9992950-0-2

Editing by Dominic Wakeford

This book was professionally typeset on Reedsy.
Find out more at reedsy.com

*For the girls who did it out of order. Who had the babies before the degree, found love in unlikely places, and dared to dream with laundry on the couch and bills on the counter.*

*For the ones still figuring it out, still healing, still building something beautiful from the mess.*

*I see you. I am you. Here's a secret: once you realize you're the only one who decides what makes you happy, there's no going back.*

*This story is for us. The ones who looked at society's two paths and said, "Pass."*

# Chapter 1

The sun was barely up, and I was chasing a cracked-out-of-his-mind Santa-looking dude who shouldn't be able to move this fast. He absolutely reeked—like moldy cheese and cheap alcohol. The smell still burns in my nose from when I first confronted him, and he took off like a rocket. Now, he tore through the streets of Charleston, and I was right behind him, wondering what the heck the guy was on. He skidded to a stop, and I did too.

"I just want the bag!" I yelled at him, hoping he'd toss it down or stay put. But no such luck. He took off again. "Dang it! Give me the bag! I don't care about you!" Harsh, I know. But true. Surely, the guy would run out of juice eventually—he had to.

We got to a back alley intersection. Debating which way to go, he paused. I picked up speed. Dirty Santa seemed to have made a decision. But before he could act on it, a black blur came from the alley to his left and tackled him to the ground. The guy howled pitifully and squirmed on the ground, trying to make his escape.

My partner smirked at me. "You owe me ten bucks. Told ya he would run."

I rolled my eyes. "Fuck off, Shelly, I almost had him anyway."

Her grin widened. "You sound out of breath there, Katie."

I flipped her the bird and returned my attention to Dirty Santa. His eyes were squeezed shut, like he was trying to will us away.

"Look, dude, I was being honest. I really don't care about whatever you're on. Not my district, not my problem. I just need that bag." I pointed to the bright pink My Little Pony bag he clutched to his chest.

He opened one bleary eye and looked me up and down. Shelly let go of him, backing away slowly. Dirty Santa, however, seemed content to stay down. She tried a gentler tone on him, which was ironic since the guy would soon be sporting bruises from her takedown.

"Come on, big guy. That bag isn't your style anyway, right? How about you give us the bag, and we just go our separate ways?"

He seemed to consider this. Still, he said nothing. I was starting to wonder if Dirty Santa even speaks English. Suddenly, he threw the bag at us and took off down the alley.

Back at the squad car, we carefully placed it in an evidence bag. My heart squeezed painfully on seeing the childish scrawl on the back. *Annie.*

Shelly noticed it, too, and asked softly, "Think it'll be the big break?"

I answered honestly, "No, but we've gotta try."

Every single time we thought we'd caught a break on this godforsaken case, we were just led to another dead end. It was beginning to feel like running face-first into a wall, expecting it to be Platform 9 ¾, except, in this world, magic didn't exist, and sometimes little girls didn't make it home.

Anastasia Little disappeared three days ago from her backyard. She was the fifth girl to have gone missing. Five empty bedrooms. Five broken families. Five "Have You Seen This Child?" posters. I hated it. I hated this feeling of powerlessness. We'd got absolutely nothing. We'd turned every stone, been around every corner, and been left empty-handed. Kids don't just disappear. Annie had this backpack with her when she was reported missing. While it would be nice to find something on it, I had a sinking feeling we'd be left with exactly what we had before—a big freaking pile of nothing.

Back at the station, Shelly headed to the lab, and I headed to our war room. Each girl's picture stared at me, details of their kidnappings listed carefully below. Everything was perfect—my own careful handwriting and deliberate organization just how I liked it. Shelly knew I was a stickler for that stuff.

But just then, all the organization in the world wasn't doing us a bit of good.

A knock came at the door, and I turned to see Officer Stanton with three coffees peeking in. I waved him in, and he passed one to me.

"Anything new, Detective McGrady?"

I sipped my coffee and shook my head.

He frowned. "Anything I can do?"

I side-eyed him; he has a crush on Shelly and would scale the side of the Eiffel Tower if she asked him to.

"Detective Vaughn is down at evidence; she'll be back up in a bit."

He blushed crimson, and I went back to staring at the board. I wasn't trying to be a bitch. Really, I wasn't. But just then, I was tired and grimy from my unplanned morning run, and I didn't have the time or energy to play Cupid. Still, I sighed and said, "I'm sorry, it's been a rough morning. Thanks for the coffee; we'll let you know if we need anything else."

He nodded and swiftly left the room.

A few minutes later, I grabbed the coffee Stanton left behind. Shelly was already back at our desk, and I joined her. I prayed to whatever god was in charge of this mess for the lab to come back with literally anything at that point. A speck of dirt, partial print, a hair. Anything.

"Did you tell them to rush it?" I asked, sliding the cup to her.

She nodded. "Let's go over this again."

For the next four hours, she and I pore over everything we've gathered over the past three months.

Kelly MacIntyre, like Anastasia, was taken from her yard. Kelly didn't live with her parents, but with an aunt who had sobbed on my shoulder while I made promises I wasn't sure I could keep.

Mia Huntington was grabbed off her bike in a local park—a blue bike with the training wheels still on it. The tinsel hanging from the bars. The little bell that tinkled in the wind. It haunted my dreams.

Gabriella Santiago had been walking to an ice cream shop down the street with her big brother. Cookies and cream was her favorite flavor. He had gone to the bathroom while waiting for their order. When he came out, she was gone. After calling for and not getting an answer, he ran the whole way home.

Then there was sweet Ruby Johnson, the girl who started it all. Her mother was a hollow shell, her father doing everything he could to keep his wife from drowning in sorrow, while he himself searched tirelessly for her.

They'd been grabbing two girls a month, which meant they would be taking another any day now—and I'd do just about anything to prevent it. Four hours of reliving every detail did nothing except make my heart ache, so we broke for a late lunch. Shelly ordered from a local Chinese place. I was completely lost in thought, almost hypnotized by the fluorescent lights and buzzing from the nearby hallway vending machines, until she cleared her throat pointedly and gestured behind me with a nod. I gave her a questioning frown, and dropped my boots from my desk, before turning around in my chair and coming face to face with Lieutenant Hartwell. Well, more like face to chest.

"Afternoon, sir."

My lieutenant had been in homicide for longer than I'd been a cop, and he looked it. Built like a linebacker with more grey hairs than he should have at his age, and a permanent frown on his lined face, Lieutenant Jason Hartwell played hardball and took cases without progression personally. Unfortunately, this was just such a case. Gosh freaking dang it, and I got caught with my boots on my desk. Literally. This was going to be a fun conversation.

"Detective McGrady, Detective Rameriz—enjoying your break?" He spat the last word like it left a bad taste.

What would he have us do? Starve? I keep that thought to myself.

"Would you like us to order you something?" Shelly offered with a self-deprecating smile, and he turned his frown on her.

I tried to appease him. "Sir, we've been working on the case all morning. We found the backpack, and—"

He leaned past me and riffled through the files scattered on my desk. "And what? Has the lab come back yet?"

I swallowed the anger that came with being interrupted, and Shelly shook her head at me, a silent warning not to say something smart. I gritted my teeth. "No, sir, the lab hasn't gotten back to us yet. We'll find something; I know we will."

Shelly and I were two of his best detectives, despite also being the youngest.

But he shook his head. "No, you won't. Not like this."

He had this look in his eye that I'd never seen before, and it put me on edge. Shelly and I exchanged a glance. He started to leave, then looked over his shoulder at me with a frown. "You coming, McGrady?"

I stood quickly and hurried after him. As he walked out the door, I turned and walked backward, mouthing to my partner, "What is happening?" She shrugged and mouthed back, "Good luck!"

Gee, thanks, pal.

As I followed Hartwell to his office, my mind was racing. Was I getting fired? Demoted? Reassigned to a unit in Alaska? Mailed to Alaska in a box? Hartwell gave me no clues. One of his strides was about three of mine, and I was nearly running to keep up. I hate running. Especially twice in one day. I puffed in irritation and nearly ran smack into him as he abruptly stopped outside his door.

"You keep your mouth shut. No smart shit. No spouting off. You stand there, you listen, you speak when spoken to."

I smiled sweetly and said, "Absolutely." He glared at me, probably doubting my ability to be good. Which was fair, usually, but he'd got my curiosity piqued, so I decided to play nice. For the time being.

He swung the door open and went to stand behind his desk. "Folks, this is Detective McGrady. She's the one I spoke to you about."

It was then that I noticed the four or five other people jammed in the room, and I froze halfway through the door. What in the actual fuck was going on? I looked over each of them, my eyes landing on the FBI jackets and badges, before turning my gaze back to Hartwell.

One of the agents stepped toward me. "Detective, I'm Agent Michael Braxton. And this is Agent Williams," he nodded to a woman about my height who scowled at me like I kicked her puppy, "Agent Bridges," a tall, lanky guy by the desk who gave me a friendly grin, "and Agent Justice." I snorted at the irony, but covered it up with a cough, and looked away from the dark guy holding a briefcase and leaning indifferently against the wall. Agent Williams rolled her eyes, and Hartwell glared at me, but I stared at Braxton, pretending not to notice.

He was cute in a boy-next-door kinda way; his brown eyes were sharp, and he looked me up and down before continuing. "If you choose to accept this assignment, I will be your handler." That brought me back to earth. "Handler?" My voice was sharper than I intended, and Hartwell's glare started to burn holes in my jean jacket.

"Yes, detective. Handler. You've been working that case with the missing girls, correct?" I nodded, and he continued. "I've been working a case, too, and I believe they're connected. Your lieutenant here tells me you're one of the most dedicated detectives he has, and I'm wondering just how far that dedication can go."

Justice handed Braxton a thick file which he held out to me, and Hartwell gave me a nod, which I take as permission to open it.

"The Mafia? You're working a case on the Mafia? And you think they have something to do with my girls?" I thumbed through the file, scanning what I could, since much of the information was redacted.

Agent Bridges stepped forward. "We're looking at one family in particular—the DiAngelos. Most every illegal trade in the U.S. can be traced back to them. Sex trafficking, drug trafficking, weapons trafficking..."

I glanced around the room, wondering if I was being played. "You think they're in South Carolina?"

Agent Justice pulled out another file, this one much smaller, and handed it to me. "We know they are."

Braxton watched closely for my reaction as I opened up the next file, and I swore I felt my heart bottom out. It was a picture of Mia Huntington. Sweet little Mia came from an upper-class family, and was the kind of girl who didn't usually go missing. Mia, who should've been coming home from ballet class on her blue bike right then, just like she was on the day she went missing. I had dedicated her toothless smile to memory. But she wasn't smiling in this picture.

White dress. Pink lips. Mascara. Makeup meant to hide the exhaustion in her eyes. She had clearly been crying. She was only ten, and I felt like I was going to throw up. I didn't even need to flip to the next page. I knew then Mia wasn't coming home. A hot, burning rage filled my gut as my heart shattered for a family that'll never be the same.

I looked up at Braxton, whose eyes had never left me. "What the fuck is this?" I threw the file back at Justice, who caught it, and I stepped toward Braxton. "The DiAngelos did this?"

Braxton nodded. "Them, or one of their cronies."

My hands shook, and I shoved them into my jacket pocket. "What did you mean by handler?"

Braxton exchanged a look with his team, and they came to some sort of silent agreement. He handed me yet another file and I took it gingerly, like this one could burn.

"Meet Nicole Moore. She's not much different from you—just throw in some tight leather and a bad attitude."

I shrugged. "Haven't heard of her."

"That's 'cos she doesn't exist. Yet."

"You've lost me."

"We need someone to go undercover. Deep undercover. It's the only way we have a shot of taking the DiAngelos down. We want that someone to be you."

I blinked at him and had to make a conscious effort to pick my jaw up from the floor.

"I'm not UC-trained. Closest thing to UC I've done is a buy." I looked at Hartwell, who had finally sat down, and back at Braxton. "I am nowhere near ready to infiltrate a high-level group like this."

Williams rolled her eyes again. "Trust me, we know." I debated throwing Hartwell's glass paperweight at her head, as Braxton gave her a hard look.

Justice grunted. "Read the file, detective. We're not asking you to get down and dirty with the DiAngelos. Just one of their buyers, a motorcycle club that has somehow worked its way up into the DiAngelos' web. Their president is tight with them, and that's our way in."

As he spoke, I quickly read the file, and the pieces started to come together.

I looked up at the assembled group. "Tell me how this would work."

Bridges whipped a computer from seemingly out of nowhere and pulled up a Facebook profile. "The background is done. We've already taken care of the cake. All you've got to worry about is the icing. Nicole might as well be real. She's got socials, ex-boyfriends, and an apartment in Georgia, where she was born and raised. Hell, she even has a favorite coffee shop." I leaned closer to the laptop as he took me through her life. "We train you and prep you for a couple weeks—a month, max. Then Kaitlyn McGrady disappears, and Nicole becomes flesh and blood."

I glanced around the room again, chewing on my bottom lip. "I don't get it. Why me? Okay, yeah. I'm like Nicole, whatever that means. And yes, I am familiar with the case. But any cop worth their salt can be briefed on a case and get familiar with it, whether it started out as theirs or not. And you're going to trust a rookie with something this important?"

Braxton nodded like he appreciated the question. "As I said earlier, you and Nicole are already very similar. She's just less..." He seemed to struggle to find the words he was looking for, probably trying not to offend me. We all watched him for a moment, until Hartwell stepped in and said, "She's you without a filter."

Braxton nodded his thanks. "Between that, your familiarity with every aspect of the case, and Jason's personal recommendation, I think you're our best bet. Also, the DiAngelos are a group we've been trying to take down for a while. You won't be the first cop to go undercover, and it has to be someone they don't recognize. What do you think?"

In a truly rare occurrence, I found myself at a loss for words. I gaped at each of them like a fish out of water. "I... I, well. I have no idea. This is a lot to throw at a person."

Williams sighed, and I found myself wondering what would happen if I throat-punched her. "She can't do it. She said it herself, she doesn't have the training. She's not ready for this. And we don't have the time. She'll blow this whole op."

I felt my face flush in anger, and went to tell her exactly where she could shove her opinions, when Hartwell stood up to intervene.

"Now you listen, Agent Williams, Katie here is one of my best. Yes, she's young, but she's eager and quick to learn. She's smart as a whip and would throw herself before a bullet for her partner. If we were to place bets on which cop would have the best shot, Detective McGrady would have my money."

I blinked at him and then blinked some more. He ignored me, of course, but I was floored. Speechless twice in less than ten minutes. For me, that had to be some kind of record.

A knock on the door broke the awkward silence, and a lab tech walked in. She handed a paper to Hartwell and left as quickly as she had come. He looked it over and then handed it to me. It was the lab results from the damn bag, and I stared at it. Negative. No match. Another useless lead. I cursed and felt like setting the report on fire, but instead I crumpled the useless thing in my hand.

I thought of all those little girls, taken from loving families and thrust into their own personal hell. I wondered how long it'd take Shelly and me to bring them the justice they deserve. Everyone else, including Williams' mouthy ass, was silent, watching me struggle. Watching me weigh the pros and cons. Was this something I would die for? I glanced at the report I was holding again. Finally, I looked up at Braxton.

"Okay," I decided, heart pounding. "Whatever it takes. I'm in."

He nodded. "You've got twenty-four hours to make arrangements. Bridges and Justice will help. Then Kaitlyn McGrady is no more, until we bring these bastards to their knees."

# Chapter 2

I tossed another shirt into a box without folding it. The first few boxes, I'd carefully packed each item, being mindful of what was breakable and what wasn't. Then I dropped a decorative vase and the sound of breaking glass was my undoing. I was putting my entire life into a bunch of boxes, like the me packing them would be the same person coming back for them. But that just wasn't the case. Detective Kaitlyn McGrady—decorated cop, straight-A student? She folded her socks, color-coded her closet. Bites her tongue and keeps her head down.

But Nicole Moore? She's a no-nonsense, barely finished high school, hot mess in beat-up sneakers. I had no idea who I was going to be after all of this.

Or when I would be coming home.

I sighed, my eyes wandering around the bare apartment before landing on the shelf by my door and the singular photo I had left out. Me and Shelly, arms around each other and laughing in matching ugly Christmas sweaters at a precinct office party. I wanted so badly to pack it. But that would be super-hard to explain to anyone I met on this op. *Who is that in the picture? Oh, yeah. That's my twin, she's a cop.* Not suspicious at all, right? I sighed again and carefully tucked it in a box with Shelly's address written on the outside.

My badge hung around my neck, and I pulled it out from under my shirt.

For a moment, I stood in the quiet apartment, running my hand over the familiar numbers. Then I tossed it in the box next to the picture. I dialed Shelly's number from memory, but it went to voicemail. I wasn't really sure what to say. Obviously she couldn't know everything, so I kept it short and sweet.

"I'm sending you some of my favorite things to keep hold of until I get back. I can't tell you where I'm going, but I'm okay. I'll be home as soon as I can. Try not to raise too much cane while I'm gone. Love you, girl. Be safe."

I tucked the box under one arm, and shut the door as I left. I didn't bother to lock it—there was nothing in there to take. My mind went back to the past couple of months as I recalled every bit of my training. I'd learned a lot, but becoming Nicky had been complicated.

I made my way to the empty warehouse where we'd set up shop after dropping my box for Shelly off with the doorman, who promised to see it off. I was on autopilot, remembering each detail.

*Two months prior*

It was day three of my training, and I had just started to realize how big this whole thing was. I knelt in front of a simple wooden door held upright by a couple of 2x4s. Braxton thought that something as simple as picking a lock would help me throw away my "good cop" persona and become more like Nicole. I zeroed in on the surprisingly delicate mechanism, more used to kicking in doors than breaking into them.

"Try again." Braxton stood next to me, arms crossed, as I fumbled with the lockpick set. Bridges was on my other side. His tall, lanky form leaned up against a fake door, and he watched as I tried to unlock the door. I was trying to follow his instructions. He had picked a lock like it was nothing. It should be simple, but it wasn't.

"I'm not MacGyver," I muttered, anger and frustration creeping into my voice.

Braxton didn't flinch. "Nope. You're Nicky Moore. She's been doing this stuff since grade school. And she doesn't make excuses."

Bridges glanced between me and Braxton. "Just take your time, do exactly what I showed you."

I wanted to ask him exactly what else I would be doing, but I bit my tongue. Finally, I heard the most beautiful sound. *Click.* The door swung open. I straightened up and wiped thin beads of sweat from my temple with the back of my hand, grinning a little at the small victory. The three of us headed across the dimly lit warehouse, and I played with my newly dyed hair. The red was growing on me, much more vibrant than my natural auburn.

Feeling eyes on me, I glanced over at Braxton.

"You're a quick learner. The first week is never easy," he admitted, before stopping abruptly and turning to me. "Now lose the cop walk."

"The what?"

"Shoulders too straight. Chin up. Calculated steps. You scream law enforcement. You need to move like someone who owns the room. Not like someone who's afraid of getting written up."

I spent the next three hours relearning how to walk. First my sashay was too exaggerated, then it was too understated. *Use your hips. Relax your shoulders. Soften your knees.* Who knew walking was so freaking hard? And all the little things that made me who I was? They had to go, too. We walked through every aspect of Nicky's life until I knew her better than I knew myself, playing out every scenario we could think of. Justice was absolutely delighted when he found out I already knew how to ride a motorcycle from a rebellious phase in college. Secretly, I immediately loved the black and blue Triumph he presented me with—something they'd confiscated from a raid.

After month one, I wanted to scream when their general consensus was that I wasn't ready. I had been busting ass. Of course, the loudest voice advocating for more training was Williams. Katie would've ignored her, so I blamed my new identity when I finally got fed up with her sour ass and decked her. Braxton and Justice had pulled us apart, while Bridges laughed. Her nose was busted, and I felt immensely pleased with the red mark on her cheek that would surely bruise. Detective McGrady would never—but I was getting comfortable with certain aspects of Nicole Moore.

Her devil-may-care attitude, for one.

Still, I decided to buckle down and make the most of the last month. Every now and then, I would find myself wondering about Shelly or Lieutenant Hartwell. I knew that I had to stop thinking like that, but you wouldn't believe how hard it is to just completely erase yourself.

During the final week, Braxton told me their plan for me to integrate myself. There was a biker bar just outside of Atlanta that the Steel Saints frequented. They figured, one way or another, I could catch their attention there. When I kept pushing for exact information, exact instructions, Braxton stopped me.

"Improvise, Katie. Undercover work is ninety percent improv. Your ability to do so will make or break the operation."

That entire week, we fine-tuned Nicky's personality. They took me to a local bar, and took turns critiquing me the next morning. Williams was no longer a part of the case, which was just fine with me. But Braxton, Bridges, and Justice each had a long freaking list of things I needed to work on.

"You hesitated when ordering your drink. Nicole doesn't hesitate. She's in your face, demanding, and knows what she wants."

"But she's also charismatic and charming. Get your drink, charm the bartender, find your in."

"And remember, Katie avoids conflict. She avoids drama. She's a cop, gotta keep her head on straight. Follows the book. Nicky burned the book."

I nodded, feeling kind of lightheaded. I knew that in two days, I would be in Georgia. I had been sleeping in a back room in the warehouse, and after the three of them left, I would be on my own. Braxton had given me the last day to myself—which wasn't much use since I couldn't exactly go out as Nicky, and Katie no longer existed.

I planned to spend the day with an extra-large pizza, an abhorrent amount of Ben and Jerry's, and some *Full House* reruns. In actuality, my pizza got cold and my ice cream melted while *Full House* was distant background noise to my racing thoughts. I was no longer Kaitlyn McGrady. I was Nicole Moore. I was going to avenge those little girls.

And then I would come home.

I hoped.

## Chapter 3

Nicole Moore rolled into Atlanta, Georgia on her Triumph Rocket like the baddest bitch around. I was lucky enough that I already knew how to ride a bike, but this Triumph was by far the nicest thing I'd ever ridden. I was lowkey in love. I pulled up to the Dirty Dogs just as the sun went down, and I sat there, eyeing the various bikes in the lot. This was it. Kaitlyn McGrady was no more—it was time for the new me to own this shit. I would be stupid not to have been nervous. My foot tapped a rhythm on the cracked asphalt.

I was wearing tight black leather pants, worn Vans, and my favorite jean jacket over a crop top that showed just enough skin—an outfit that said, "Yeah, I know I'm hot, but don't touch me." Or at least, that's what I hoped. My red hair was pulled back into a tight and low pony, and I looked like me, except a little bit more reckless and with brown eyes instead of green. "Bad bitch, bad bitch, bad bitch," I muttered to myself, and then I strolled into that dank bar like I owned it.

Immediately, the smell hit me like a slap in the face. Cheap tobacco. Cheaper perfume. Too many people in a warm room. Ew. I scanned the occupants, noting the slight separation between club members, prospects, and patch bunnies, who watch the bikers closely for any sort of invitation. Marking the location of the Steel Saints' leadership, I made my way to the bar and got the attention of the barkeep.

"Whiskey, please. On the rocks."

One thing Nicole and I had in common was our taste in drinks, thankfully. I hated beer; it tasted like piss to me.

Out of the corner of my eye, I saw a few of the bikers watching me, but I pretended not to notice them. This was Steel Saints territory. Not many people just casually stopped in for a drink. Not unless they were looking for trouble. Everyone in here was probably wondering who the heck I was, and what I was doing. I smiled at the barkeep, who slid a glass over to me and eyed me suspiciously before moving down the bar.

I sat there for a while, sipping my drink and wondering what the night would bring. I needed an in, but I had no idea what it might be. I wasn't about to stroll up and proposition myself—I have too much self-respect for that. But I had to do *something* to get their attention. The music thumped through the speakers, a song I wasn't familiar with. I swayed to the beat, nonetheless. When my glass was empty, the barkeep appeared to refill it, and then stomped away again. I'd thought maybe I could get him into some kind of conversation, but the old fart seemed intent on ignoring me for the most part. I frowned, and just then, a skinny guy in prospect leathers sidled up next to me.

"Hey gorgeous, how about I buy your next drink?"

I turned to him, embraced my inner bad bitch, and committed to being all Nicole. Looking him slowly up and down, I brought my eyes back up to his and sneered, "Yeah, no thanks."

His smile dropped briefly, but he adjusted it back on what I'm sure he thought was a charming grin. "Come on, baby, you're new here and all alone. Just one drink won't hurt. I'm Daniel, by the way."

I spun my chair back to the bar. His breath reeked of beer, and his sallow, pockmarked cheeks just weren't doing it for me.

"Again, no thanks."

This time, his smile really dropped, and he put a hand on my shoulder, spinning me back to him. "Fine, you don't want to drink, I got plenty of other things we can do."

I stared at him, remembering I didn't look like a cop and wasn't in familiar territory. Back home, at my favorite haunts, everyone knew me. There? I was at a biker bar and dressed like I was looking for trouble. I guess trouble had come looking for me. Let the games begin.

I slapped his hand away and said, angrily, "I fucking said no. N. O. spells not fucking happening—now back off."

He leaned his face into mine, our noses nearly touching. "I wasn't asking, bitch. You come in here dressed like that and act like you're too good to let a guy buy you a drink. Time someone knocked your ass down a peg."

The alcohol clearly made Dumbass McGee a little too cocky, and a whole lot of angry. I looked him up and down again, the wheels in my head spinning. Over his shoulder, I could see the club watching us, but making no moves to intervene. Assholes. Then I had an idea. Braxton said to improvise, right?

I switched lanes so fast, it'd make a NASCAR driver's head spin. Letting out a small whimper like he'd intimidated me, I pouted and, giving him my biggest puppy-dog eyes, I said, "I'm sorry, please. I just… I'm new and a little scared. You're just so big, you know? I didn't mean it."

I put my hand placatingly on his shoulder. And, thank my lucky stars, the dumb fucker fell for it. Hook, line, and sinker. He grinned and ran a hand down the side of my face. I suppressed the urge to shudder or, better yet, break his fingers, and instead smiled sweetly. "How about you buy us a bottle, and we go outside? You can show me your bike."

He wrapped his arm around my shoulder, and I smiled adoringly at him.

The club had gone back to their business, except for one biker sitting in the corner with his friends. He was big, his bulky frame making the people close to him look small. But, with the light right behind him, I couldn't see much else.

Daniel called for the barkeep, dragging my attention back to him.

"Mike, yo Mike!" The barkeep ambled over. "A bottle of whiskey, bud. I got a thirsty lady here, and I can't leave her hanging, now can I?"

Mike frowned at me, and I had a feeling my little act wasn't fooling him, but I batted my eyelashes innocently. He rolled his eyes and reached for a bottle of Jack behind him, but I stopped him. Shelly once took a fire-breathing class, of all things. Back then, I'd told her it was an insanely useless waste of time. Now the memory sparked an idea.

"Wait, can we get that Old Forester? The 100 proof?"

My dumb new friend hesitated, so I leaned into him. "I've heard it's good and strong… like you."

Mike glared at me, but Dumb-Dumb smiled. "Yeah, only the good stuff."

We headed outside, his hand on my ass, as he guided me to the small group of prospect bikes. His was a decent little Harley, and he leaned up against it, pulling me between his knees. He ran his hands up and down my body, and I fought the urge to knee him in the balls.

"I'm sorry for scaring you back there."

Fucker wasn't sorry, he was just saying what he thought I wanted to hear in the hopes of getting laid, but I played along anyway.

"It's okay, we can start over. My name's Nicole, but everyone calls me Nicky." I wrapped my hands around his neck and pressed my chest into his, watching his eyes darken with lust.

"That's a pretty name for a pretty lady, Nicky. How about we open up that bottle?"

I nodded eagerly, and he handed me the Old Forester. I took a good sip, relishing the burn. As we share the whiskey, I don't miss the way he encourages me to drink more, probably hoping to get me drunk. About halfway through the bottle, I'm buzzed with liquid courage, and poor old Daniel is thoroughly wasted. I thank my Irish heritage which blessed me with the ability to drink like a fish.

I heard the door swing open behind us, and took my cue.

Pretending to be caught in a drunken fall, I wrapped myself around him, throwing myself to the side. His momentum carried us far enough that I ended up next to the bike, and he ended up on the ground. "Oops," I giggled, and he gave me a lopsided grin. He reached for me as I bent forward, probably thinking I was going to help him up. Not today, buddy.

As I bend over, the half-empty whiskey bottle in my hand just so happens to tip enough that its contents pour out over his bike. "Oh no!" I gasped, and Daniel let loose a string of curses. Then I helped him up, and once he was on his feet, I took a cigarette from my pocket.

I lit it, then held it out to him. When he reached for it, I shoved him—hard—into the throng of his buddies who'd gathered behind him. They were probably getting ready to head out for the night; it had gotten pretty late. But, lucky for them, they were just in time for one last show.

I took a couple of steps forward and said, "Hey, Daniel, baby?" He eyed me, not so drunk that he didn't know something wasn't right. "When a lady says no, you should really fucking listen."

With that, I tossed the match right onto the whiskey-soaked leather seat of his Harley and jumped to the side as the 100 proof lit up like the Fourth of July. Fire in the hole, baby.

Daniel hollered like a lunatic and his buddies started running around, intent on getting their bikes away from his. I walked to my bike, wanting to put some distance between myself and the inevitable explosion that'd come once the fire reached the fuel tank. Everyone was pouring out of the bar at this point, and Daniel was still running around like an idiot, kicking dirt on his bike like that would help. I smirked—that Harley was toast. Damn... being Nicole was fun, Kaitlyn would never. I had no idea how exactly this would get me in the club, but I'd figure that out later. They certainly weren't going to forget me anytime soon.

Right as the fuel tank exploded, someone grabbed me by the back of my neck, and steered me to the side of the building. I stopped myself from face-planting into the worn brick and spun around, ready to clock whoever put their hands on me. A hand much bigger than mine caught my fist, and I realized it was the guy who had been watching us from the corner inside.

"You just set my prospect's bike on fire." A worn leather jacket hung off his massive shoulders, and he towered at least a foot over me.

I glared up at him. "He fucking deserved it." I aimed a foot at his balls, which he easily dodged.

"Easy there, Vixen. I'm not saying he didn't."

I glared at him some more, not trusting the easy way he spoke to me—like I was a wild horse, and he was trying to rope me. I went to sidestep him, and he blocked me. I spun to go in the opposite direction, and ran into another dude who had just walked up. I glared at him too, and he grinned at me like he was having fun.

"Mac, your boy's bike is fucking trashed."

I smiled a little at that, and Mac noticed. "Well, Vixen. Danny won't be happy with you."

I turned my attention back to him. "Like I give a shit. And stop calling me that."

He cocked his head at me, dark blue eyes trailing down my body, and I tried not to notice the way a vein jumped along his chiseled jaw. "You're gonna have to answer for that, you know. Can't have people wandering around just thinking it's okay to set shit on fire."

As he talked, he moved closer to me, bringing his face into the light cast by a weak street lamp nearby. I barely held back a gasp because fuck me sideways… Mac must be short for Maverick Mills, the Saints' enforcer. Which meant his buddy was more than likely Dalton Mills, his younger brother and best friend.

Two voices were at war in my head. One was saying *shit, shit, shit*. I was pretty sure that was my voice of reason. But the other voice was whooping because this was exactly what I wanted. I had to get the Saints' attention—and boy, did I have it.

I crossed my arms and squared my body like I was bracing for a hit. "Fine, call the damn cops then. I can tell them it was all an accident. One big misunderstanding." But I already knew there was no way in hell either one of those guys would be calling the local law enforcement—and even if they did, from what I'd been told, the Saints owned half the damn cops anyway.

Mac shook his head at me, and Dalton leaned towards me. "Vixen…" I flipped him off in response to my unwanted nickname, and he grinned again. "We're not exactly the type to call the boys in blue. We like to handle things in-house. Isn't that right, Mac?"

I stayed silent, at war with the fight-or-flight response screaming at me to fucking run. But I knew that if I did, these big-ass idiots would catch me and would probably enjoy the chase. More importantly, I didn't want to run. At least, part of me didn't. I needed this to happen—this was my way in.

While I was lost in thought, Dalton lunged for me. He moved a lot quicker than a man his size should be able to move. He wrapped one muscled arm around my throat and another around my chest, and it suddenly dawned on me that I couldn't get away even if I used every ounce of Academy training I had. So, I did what any girl would do. I turned my head to the side as much as I could, and bit the ever-loving shit out of his bicep.

"Holy motherfucking damnit…" He trailed off in a string of curses, and I clung to his damn arm like a pit bull. I could taste the iron his blood, and it was fucking disgusting.

Then Mac stepped forward and calmly pinched my nose. My eyes widened, and I stared at him, my brown eyes meeting his blue. It was a battle of wills as he cut off my oxygen, and I refused to let go. But the swirling darkness behind my eyes made the decision for me, and I eventually let go of his brother, sucking in lungfuls of air.

Mac chuckled. "You good there, Dalton?"

Dalton swore some more, and I saw the blood running down his arm out of the corner of my eye.

"No, I'm not fucking good, man. Crazy chick bit me if you didn't notice."

I stomped on his foot, and this time, he wasn't having it. His arms tightened around me just enough to make me lightheaded again, and he lifted me off the ground until my toes barely grazed the dirt.

Mac headed off, shaking his head, and Dalton went to follow him. He dragged me past Daniel's blackened bike, the fire now put out. Daniel glared at me with murder in his eyes, the drunken haze burned away by the smoky remnants of his Harley. I smiled at him—albeit a slightly oxygen-deprived one, thanks to Dalton's grip—and his face turned beet-red.

"Stop goading the guy, Vixen," Mac said over his shoulder, and I wonder if he's got eyes in the back of his head or something.

We come to a stop next to a massive red and black Indian that looks like it runs small children over for fun. He pulled out a small bundle of rope from one of the saddlebags, and I started struggling in Dalton's arms.

"Abso-fucking-lutely not, you psychopaths!"

Mac turned to me, and Dalton's chest vibrated with a chuckle. "Ah, come on, you look like the kinda girl who might like being tied up."

I snapped at his arm again, but he was ready for it this time.

"You wish you would ever get the chance to find out, you overgrown Ken doll. And I don't give a damn about being tied up—but I'm not leaving my bike."

Mac and Dalton both paused, the former giving me a surprised look. "Your bike?"

I stopped struggling in Dalton's arms. "That's what I said, isn't it?"

Dalton let go of me and stepped around so he could look at me, his face just as surprised as Mac's.

"You got a bike? Sure it's not your boyfriend's?"

His eyes, a much lighter shade of blue compared to Mac's, shone with humor. In a very mature move, I stuck my tongue out at him. Pointing behind me at my Triumph, I spoke slowly and deliberately, as if talking to children.

"*That* is my bike. Mine. I rode here. On my bike. Which I own. 'Cos girls can ride too. And I am *not* leaving it here."

Mac looked at it, and then back at me. "Why? You afraid someone might set it on fire?" I frowned at him. "Fine. Dalton, get Jackson and a couple of others. You guys flank her, and I swear to God if you somehow manage to lose her... I'll set *your* bikes on fire."

Dalton nodded and jogged off, leaving me alone with Mac. He turned and put the rope back in the bag, evidently deciding I wasn't dumb enough to make a run for it while his back was turned.

I took the opportunity to look him over. A swirl of black ink peeked out of his jacket, and boy, I would be lying if I said he didn't fill those blue jeans nicely. He turned back to me, and I acted like I wasn't just ogling his ass seconds ago.

"Where are you taking me?"

He gave me a look that said I should already know the answer to that question, and I do. We were going to the Steel Saints' clubhouse. That little voice of reason popped back into my head: *shit, shit, shit.* But I smiled at him, because he didn't have a clue that they'd just let the fox into the hen house.

*I'm in, baby.*

# Chapter 4

We pulled into a warehouse around midnight. I spent the entire ride stroking my self-confidence like a skittish cat.

Looking around, I took in the well-lit area. It was surprisingly clean, and "Steel Saints" was printed across the bay door. Other than that, there was nothing to mark what the warehouse was for, but I supposed those two words were warning enough not to come poking around asking questions. Everyone in Atlanta knew who the Saints were.

Dalton pulled in next to me, and I glanced over at him. His bike is a green Harley, about the size of Mac's. Thinking of his brother's massive Indian, I wondered if bike size was related to cock size. I grinned at my own joke, and accidentally giggled out loud, which elicited a funny look.

I scanned the warehouse as I followed dutifully behind Dalton, his buddies flanking me as Mac ordered. The entryway is a big open space, with a couple of dismantled bikes leaning on their kickstands in an area that I assumed is a makeshift garage for repairs and such. There was a pole in the back corner of the room, which I was sure wasn't for supporting the roof, since it had a couple of couches placed around it. I curled my lip in distaste. A mini fridge nearby, and pictures lining one of the walls, completed the relatively boring space.

Dalton glanced over his shoulder at me. "Welcome to our humble abode."

I didn't even spare him a glance.

He took me through a door and motioned for me to stop as he disappeared into the dark— a few seconds later, the lights flickered on. I blinked in surprise. It was a kitchen—a really cute little kitchen. I felt like Alice in Wonderland. From stripper poles in a dusty garage to Rachael Ray's kitchen wasn't what I was expecting. Red gingham valances hung over the windows, and a long dining table sat under a few warmly lit chandeliers. The kitchen itself was all clean stainless steel and granite counters. A fat orange cat snoozed on the island next to a bowl of fruit. I half-expected a chubby grandma to come waddling out of nowhere to whip us up a snack. Dalton grabbed an apple from a nearly empty bowl and made himself comfy at the table, ignoring the dried blood on his arm. His buddies left the same way they came, their job evidently done.

Dalton and I stared at each other for a few moments, him munching on his apple and me just trying to get a read on him. Everything I read about Dalton Mills matched with what I'd seen tonight. A jokester, incredibly intelligent, and fiercely loyal to his brother. He was also, like his brother, ridiculously attractive. But where his brother's good looks were all hard edges and bad-boy menace, Dalton's light blue eyes seemed to laugh at a joke only he could hear, and his wavy blond hair made him look like a surfer boy. Take away the leather jacket and biker boots, and put him in a pair of swim trunks and sandals, and dude would fit right in on a California beach somewhere.

He smiled at me and I looked away, feeling a red flush creep up my neck. Asshole.

"Where's your brother?" I asked, and he quirked an eyebrow at me.

"How do you know Mac's my brother?"

My stomach dropped. Well, fuck me. "Um… well, I dunno. I just assumed you guys were related."

He nodded. "Ah yeah, 'cos we look so much alike."

I swallowed nervously—knowing as well as he did that they looked, at best, distantly related. Those blue eyes assessed me carefully, and I was reminded just how dangerous he is—hell, my throat still hurt from his grip on me earlier that evening.

"You didn't answer my question," I pointed out, and he shrugged.

"He's probably dealing with Daniel's stupid ass."

I frowned in confusion. "What do you mean?"

He got up and brushed past me, throwing the apple core in the trash and grabbing the cat, who gave a disgruntled meow. I watched him cradle the cat like a baby and smiled a little when it started purring like a diesel engine in a semi-truck. At first, I didn't think he was going to answer me, but then he looked up at me.

"Daniel crossed a line tonight. He broke one of Mac's rules, and that's never a good idea."

"What rule is that? Don't let some crazy chick set your shit on fire?" I used air quotes when referring to myself, and he smirked.

"What are you two laughing at?"

I spun around to see Mac, who'd just come through the garage door. I looked over at Dalton, who put the cat back on the counter.

"She just wanted to know where you were. I told her you were dealing with Daniel."

I nodded. "Yeah, even though you haven't told me what rule he broke."

Mac walked over to the chair his brother had recently vacated. The dude was easily six feet tall, but moved with liquid grace. He sat and rested his elbows on his knees, leaning towards me and giving me a look I can't describe. Finally, he said, "He put his hands on you. You told him no, and he didn't listen. In this club, a woman's no is just that. No amount of alcohol in your belly turns that no into a yes. You either have her consent, or you don't. He didn't. I would've ground his ass into the dirt, but I think turning his ride into ash settles the score pretty well."

I gaped at him—that was surprisingly… honorable. And hot. I shoved that last thought down. Far, far down.

"Well, your golden boy sure as shit never asked my permission when he nearly choked me to death. Or does the 'no means no' rule not apply to you two?"

I glanced over at Dalton, who winked at me. "Baby girl, it applies, but it's not really… needed, if you know what I mean. And besides, that was different."

I scoffed, both at his implication that they don't get told no very often and also at his dismissal of his manhandling me.

Mac cleared his throat. "However, your score with me isn't settled."

My gaze swung back over to his. "What score? I didn't do jack shit to you!"

He smiled slowly. Not carefree, like his brother. No, this was all danger. I began to worry my bottom lip, and his eyes tracked the movement.

"Daniel was my prospect. I vouched for him, which means he was mine to teach."

I nodded. "Yeah, I know what it means. So?"

His smile grew bigger. "You ruined his bike. A brand new Harley worth about twenty grand. You got twenty grand in your bank?"

My eyes nearly popped out of my head. Having not bought my Triumph, I had conveniently forgotten just how much a good bike costs. He knew damn well I didn't have twenty grand to my name. I could sell my FBI-paid-for apartment and everything in it, and it wouldn't come close.

"That's what I thought."

I glanced again at Dalton, who seemed to be watching the whole exchange like it was a soap opera. I thought back to our earlier conversation, and tilted my head at him.

"You already said you weren't calling the cops. What happens now?" I was genuinely curious, while trying desperately to ignore my pounding heart. It would help to know if this was going to make or break the op. And my neck.

Mac and Dalton looked at each other. Coming to some sort of silent agreement, Dalton marched over to me and reached into his back pocket. I tensed, which he noticed and said, "Easy there, Vixen, it's just a phone."

Sure enough, he handed me a sleek black device.

"What am I supposed to do with this?"

Mac got up and held the door open. "Go home, Vixen. We'll call you tomorrow once we've figured out what we're gonna do with you."

"Well, that sounds fantastic. I'm sure I'll sleep like a baby. And stop fucking calling me that."

Dalton shook his head at me. "Naw, you're stuck with it. Sleep tight."

I flipped them both off as I walked past Mac, who was still holding the door open. "Make sure you answer when I call."

I stopped, fixing to say something smart, but his dark blue eyes trailed up and down my body, leaving heat like ethanol on fire. I barely suppressed a shiver. As I practically ran out the door, I realized that, technically, I still didn't know their names. Katie did, but not Nicky. So, as much as I really didn't want to, I turned back.

"If I'm going to be working for you, I should probably know your names. Mine's Nicky. So you can stop calling me Vixen."

Dalton winked at me. "You can call me just about anything you want, gorgeous."

I glared at him. "How about dickweed? Or I can spend some time coming up with creative alternatives?"

He laughed. "In that case, you can just stick with Dalton."

I looked over at Maverick, who was still watching me carefully. Looking me up and down, he tilted his head, saying my name like he was savoring it. Testing it out, like a shot of something strong that he's never had before. It sent shivers down my spine. "Maverick, but everyone calls me Mac. Now, go home."

I stared at him for a second, then headed for my bike like my ass was on fire. I was more than ready to get the hell out of there.

Finally back at my apartment, I slipped by the mailroom to check my box. There was a little letter from "Uncle Tommy," who was actually Agent Braxton. The rickety old elevator shook its way to my floor, and gave me enough time to get to the end of Uncle Tommy's messy scrawl. I shoved it in my pocket as I reached 27A, a small place on the first floor. I'd only seen it in pictures, but it wasn't as awful as I'd expected. Clean and neat, with yard sale finds and thrift store furniture. It wasn't much, but until the assignment was done, it was home.

Uncle Tommy had written to welcome me back to Atlanta—Braxton's way of saying congrats on not dying on your first day, I guessed. It also reminded me to keep in touch, and boy did I have an update for him. But now that the adrenaline had worn off, I was so tired I could barely keep my eyes open. I threw my keys and the letter on the counter, kicked off my boots, and stripped as I headed down the hallway. I tossed the bundle of clothes in the corner of my room, and fell into my bed. It's not the soft, cushy one Kaitlyn McGrady had splurged on back in her old apartment, but I was out almost as soon as my head hit the pillow.

When that stupid phone rang the next morning, I groaned and snuggled under the covers I'd evidently crawled under at some point during the night. Those assholes couldn't have given me a full eight hours of sleep? I resisted the urge to throw the damn thing through the window, and climbed out of bed to get it from the pile of laundry I had thrown it into. Pressing it to my ear, I snapped, "What in the fuck? It's the ass crack of dawn!"

I heard a low chuckle on the other end of the line, and Dalton's overly cheerful voice greeted me. "Ah, good morning to you, Vixen—lovely to hear that sweet voice so early. Gets the day started off right, you know?"

I decided that the next time I saw him, I was definitely punching him in the throat. Seemed like a Nicky thing to do. And it'd certainly make Katie feel a lot better, as well.

Sitting back down on my bed, I ran a hand through my hair as he continued. "So, here's the plan. Tony is going to pick you up and bring you back here. So be ready at 10:30. Cool?"

I glanced at the clock on the phone. "Not cool, asshole! It's already past ten. And it's Nicky! Nicky, not Vixen or baby girl or whatever."

I swore I could hear him grin through the phone. "Whatever you say... Vixen." I growled, and he laughed again. "Wear something you won't mind getting dirty. See you soon." Then the twat hung up on me.

Swearing loudly, I stomped to my bathroom and groaned. I looked like an angry, fuzzy red panda. I hadn't taken my makeup off before bed, not being used to wearing any. My mascara and eyeliner had smeared, and my hair looked like I'd stuck my finger in an electrical socket. I glanced at the clock on the wall, swore some more, and started scrubbing at my face as quickly as I could. I found Nicole's potty mouth oddly freeing, and tried to plan my next move. As I got ready, through my sleep-addled brain, I wondered how in the fuck this Tony knew where to pick me up. Someone must have followed me home, and I'd been too tired to notice. Well, that's just fantastic.

I was waiting outside my apartment building with my helmet under my arm when a black Ford F-250 pulled up. The window rolled down, and I found myself looking at a guy who was definitely Italian. Tony, I'd assumed.

"You getting in?" he asked.

I shook my head. "I'm riding my bike."

He raised one eyebrow at me. "Yeah, I doubt that."

I frowned at his tone and spun on my heel towards my bike. It wasn't until I got closer that I saw her leaning in a way she shouldn't be. Some douche had slit my tire while I was sleeping! Probably the same douche who followed me home. That's it, I decided—someone was absolutely getting punched.

I marched back over to Tony and climbed into the truck after throwing my helmet in. Fixing him with my most intimidating glare, I said, "Who slit my damn tire? I want a name!"

He gave me a look that told me he was entirely unimpressed with me. "Lady, you lit a prospect's bike on fire. You're lucky that's all they did to you." Then he turned up the radio and proceeded to completely ignore me as he drove towards the warehouse. I pouted in the passenger seat, deciding maturity was something for after coffee.

The bay door was wide open this time, and the yard was a lot busier. There were a couple of members smoking and pushing each other around. A few other guys were working on the bikes I saw the night before, and there were even a few women wandering around. I took note of everything with a careful eye. Tony parked and climbed out, still not saying a word. I decided the best thing to do was to follow him. As he made his way through the building, a few of the guys greeted him, and one of them stood from where he was kneeling next to a dismantled Indian Scout. He looked at me like he smelled something bad, and I resisted the urge to roll my eyes.

It came as no surprise to see Mac and Dalton both in the kitchen, talking with a few other guys. There was a steaming cup of coffee in Dalton's hands, so I made a beeline straight for Mac instead. They turned to me when I reached them, and I used every ounce of strength in my body to slap the ever-loving shit out of Mac. There was dead silence. Out of the corner of my eye, I saw Tony take that as his cue, and he beat a hasty retreat back into the garage. The rest of the guys followed him, leaving me with just the two brothers.

"You motherfucker! You had me followed?!" My head just barely comes to his chest, so I couldn't get in his face like I wanted to, but that doesn't stop me from being royally pissed off. "And then you had one of your buddies slit my fucking tire?"

I went to shove him, but then he grabbed both my wrists. Before I could blink, he'd spun me around. My hands were behind my back, bent at a painfully awkward angle, and I was shoved up against the wall. I raged, trying to stomp on his damn foot, but while I've got training, he's got brute strength. I threw my head back in an attempt to knock him away, but all he did was take both my wrists in one hand, using the other to grab the back of my neck.

He forced my face into the wall and leaned into me, his mouth at my ear. "Are you fucking done, Vixen?"

I couldn't move if I fucking tried. I was so angry, I could feel my whole body flush with heat, but all I could do was stare daggers into Dalton's soul. He was standing to the side, observing the whole thing with a smirk. Looking like he wished he had popcorn. Assholes. Both of them.

Mac squeezed the back of my neck. "I asked if you were done."

I didn't want to give him the satisfaction, but I know when I've been beaten, so I nodded. He let me go and stepped back as I spun around.

"I've done much worse things to men for much less, Vixen. Don't do that again."

Dalton came up beside him. "Actually, please don't hesitate to ever do that again. That was entertaining as hell. Starts a man's morning better than sex, I think." He pursed his lips like he was thinking. "Well, almost better than sex. Anyways, coffee, anyone?"

I was still pissed as I followed Dalton to the coffee pot; the look on Mac's face could have wilted a spring flower. Dalton refilled his cup and stepped to the side. "Mugs are in the cabinet above the pot."

I quickly filled a cup with the steaming jet-black liquid. I hesitantly opened the fridge in search of cream, and frowned at the almost-empty half-gallon of milk. I grabbed it and then looked around for the sugar, finding it marked on the counter next to the flour and tea canisters. Except all three canisters were empty. I turned to the two men.

Dalton raised an eyebrow at me. "Sugar?"

I nodded grudgingly at him, and he pointed to the cabinet next to the fridge. Who the heck put sugar there? My coffee made, I took a sip and groaned. I can do all things through caffeine which strengthens me—or however that saying goes.

"So, what now?" Mac was still glaring at me, but I ignored him and focused on Dalton.

Dalton glanced at Mac, who didn't seem in any hurry to answer me. He looked between me and his brother, then took a seat at the head of the long table like he did the night before. I sat next to him, and Mac stood behind me and said, "Do you know how to be anything other than a pain in the ass?"

I smiled sweetly at him over my shoulder. "No. Next question."

Mac made some sort of sound that I could have sworn was a growl—as if I needed any more convincing that the guy was unhinged. I sipped my coffee and waited for one of them to break the silence.

Dalton cleared his throat and looked at his brother pointedly, but when Mac made no move to start the conversation, he set his coffee down and said to me, "Mac wasn't exaggerating about how much that bike was worth last night. You'll need to pay that back. And we know exactly how you're going to do it."

I frowned at the bottom of my cup when I realized it was empty, and then jumped when Mac came up behind me with the pot. I stared at him as he filled my cup and then set the milk on the table next to me. I opened my mouth to suggest he see a shrink and get tested for bipolar disorder, but then he said, "You're going to come work for us. Cooking, cleaning, whatever. Eight a.m. to whenever we say you're good. You'll get paid, and a good portion of that will go to paying for that bike. You can do whatever you want with the rest."

I watched him as he came around the table and sat across from me.

"Cooking, cleaning. That's it? Nothing… else?"

Dalton smirked. "Did you want there to be something else?"

I ignored him, and Mac said, "Nothing else."

"Any other options?"

"What do you think?" Dalton said, and at the same time his brother said, "None you would like."

A job inside a job wasn't exactly how I'd pictured this going. But it worked. If I was going to be there every day, it would be the perfect opportunity to keep an eye on things.

"Okay, deal. But no nasty shit, okay?"

Dalton laughed at me. "You're working for a bunch of bikers. Good luck with that."

I sighed and pretended not to notice the way Mac watched my every move as I stood to put my cup in the sink. I turned my back to them to give myself a moment to think. A moment later, I heard the door shut, and when I looked behind me, they were both gone. Discussion over, I guess.

I'd been at this less than three days, and I felt like I was in over my head. But I was in it for the long haul, and that meant becoming a glorified maid for the Steel Saints.

# Chapter 5

I was cleaning the kitchen up when Tony and a couple of his buddies came back in. They were all laughing loudly at something, ruining my moment of peace, and I side-eyed them. Tony was the only one to notice, and he waved me over to the table as they all took a seat. Sighing, I wiped my hands on the dish towel hanging from the stove and said, "What's up, Tony? You need something?"

Tony shook his head. "No, but figured you might want to meet some of the guys. Since you somehow managed to live after smoking Mac."

I frowned, trying to decide if that was a compliment or maybe even a warped attempt at being friendly.

Tony listed off names, and I tried to commit them to memory as best I could—if only for the sake of the case. One of them asked if I could make a bit of late lunch, and I gritted my teeth in response. From detective to making fucking sandwiches for a bunch of leather-clad nitwits. Wonderful. One of them, Luke, must have seen the sour look that crossed my face. He was one of the friendlier ones, but his eyes bore into me as I went over to the massive fridge.

"Oh, what the fuck… hey guys, what do you normally eat for lunch?"

A skinny guy with a crooked nose—Rodney, I think—shrugged. "I dunno, sandwiches or sometimes we'll get pizza delivered."

I held a moldy pack of cheese aloft between two fingers and brandished it at them. "In that case, moldy grilled cheese, anyone? That is, if you have bread?"

They all grimaced at me and looked at each other.

Tony said, "Yeah, I think I speak for everyone when I say no thanks. But sweet of you to offer, really."

"Well, then someone needs to go grocery shopping." I was met with a bunch of blank looks. "Who does the grocery shopping?" More blank looks. "You know what, I'll figure something out, but for now, I think there are some chips in the cabinet."

I looked at the door that leads to the garage, and then at the other door I'd seen a few bikers come in and out of, and chose the latter.

Making my way into a long hallway, I squinted at the sudden change in light. The dim hallway was lined with doors, and I peeked into a few open ones, finding small rooms that made me feel like I was in a motel. The hallway led to a sort of sitting area, which was empty, so I followed another that ended in a set of stairs, and headed down toward the distant sound of a TV. Sure enough, within a few minutes, I found a big room filled with comfy couches and recliners, and one giant flat screen. In one of the recliners sat Dalton who, to my shock, appeared to be reading a book. He looked up as I entered, almost like he sensed the presence of someone new. He smiled at me, put his book down, and got up to greet me.

"Exploring are we, Vixen? Interested in a personal tour?"

I shook my head at him. "No. Well, actually, yes. Just not right now, I have a question." He raised a single eyebrow at me, which I assumed was my all-clear. "Your fridge has old orange juice, moldy cheese, and beer in it. And I think I saw a lemon, or what used to be a lemon."

"That's not a question, Vixen."

"Well, I can't make you guys dinner with that. I already offered Tony and a few other guys a moldy grilled cheese, and they turned me down."

"Rude of them."

I couldn't help but smile a little. "Yeah, so my point is, when I asked them about grocery shopping, I might as well have asked about going to the moon."

He rubbed the back of his neck. "Home etiquette isn't really our thing here, unfortunately. But I can take you to the store if you want."

"Really? I mean, I can handle it myself. I am a big girl."

"Maybe one day, Vixen. But not yet. For now, you get an escort. It's either me, or I can have someone else go with you."

I sighed. "Right, got it. Can we go now?"

He nodded. "Yup, let me grab my jacket and the keys, and I'll meet you outside."

About ten minutes later, Dalton insisted on holding my door open as I climbed into the same truck from earlier that morning. Soon, we were roaring down the highway, and I stared out the window as Dalton turned on the radio. The silence, much to my surprise, wasn't tense or awkward. I turned from the window and tried subtly watching him as he drove with one hand on the wheel, and the other on the center console. After a few minutes, he glanced over at me, and I felt my cheeks redden as he caught me looking.

"It's alright, Vixen. I know I'm pretty."

I scoffed. "Why do you and your brother call me that?"

He glanced at me again, and the light bouncing off the dash made his eyes look like bottomless pools of tropical water.

"It fits. You walked into our bar last night looking like every man's dream. I knew you were trouble the moment I laid my eyes on you. Then you set a prospect's bike on fire, bit me, and spent your entire evening raising hell like you were its queen. We certainly weren't gonna call you Angel."

I raised my chin defiantly. "I'm nobody's angel."

He winked at me. "Don't I know it, baby girl."

My blush came back with a vengeance, and I looked out the window again. He laughed, a low sound that went straight to my core—a feeling I promptly ignored.

At the store, I meandered up and down aisles, at a complete loss on what to grab. It's not like I'd made a list or anything. Dalton followed me and, after our third aisle, said, "Hey Vixen, usually when someone goes grocery shopping, they put things they need in the cart."

"I dunno what to get," I admitted.

He grabbed a box of Frosted Flakes off the shelf and tossed them in the cart. "Get whatever you want. I got the club's card from Mac before we left. It's been a long time since we've had a woman like you in the house. We're long overdue for a stock-up."

"A woman like me?"

"You're not a patch bunny. Women with class don't tend to linger."

"Oh." I pursed my lips and then grabbed a couple other boxes of cereal off the shelf, tossing them in blindly.

We spent the next thirty minutes getting things I thought we'd need. Every time I hesitated, he encouraged me to just buy it so I didn't have to worry about it later. By the time we got to the meat section, the cart was pretty damn full.

I bit my lip. "Dalton, this is going to be a very expensive trip if we get meat."

He shrugged again. "And you're gonna have a bunch of pissed-off bikers if you try and make us go vegetarian. Grab a few steaks, Vixen, and whatever else you want. Don't worry about the cost."

When we got to the truck, he made me get in the cab while he loaded the bed with our haul. I read over the mile-long receipt, wincing at the price at the end. Dalton hadn't even blinked when the cashier read our total, just handed over a shiny black card and gave her a million-watt smile. I'm pretty sure she swooned.

I looked up as Dalton climbed in next to me. "I could've helped with that, you know."

He reached over and patted my thigh in a surprisingly familiar gesture. "Yeah, Vixen, I know. But that's not my style." He sent a quick text, and then we headed back.

He honked as we pulled up in front of the warehouse, and a small herd of bikers came flooding out. They swarmed the truck like ants, and next thing I knew, they'd grabbed all the groceries and headed into the kitchen. This display of chivalry seemed positively medieval, and it threw me off. The file I'd read didn't prepare me for all this. They work with me, putting up all the groceries and following my directions as to where I wanted them, all the while joking around with each other. Occasionally, one of them would hold up an item he found particularly pleasing, and the others would cheer.

As I stood there, watching a bunch of bikers cheering over a bag of mandarin oranges, I realized something that shocked me—they were a family. Maybe a little different and a whole lot of fucked up, but a family all the same. A unit. It was kind of amazing.

When everything had been put away, I couldn't help but smile. I loved the sight of a well-stocked kitchen; it filled me with a sense of peace. What Mac and Dalton didn't know was that I loved to cook, and I was damn good at it too. The kitchen was my happy place. I was less enthused about the cleaning aspect of the job, but I could do this—I think. I glanced at the clock, and noticed it was just past four. A few of the bikers still mingled in the background, but I paid them little mind as I set to work. I wasn't quite sure how many I was cooking for, but from what I'd seen, it would be a full house.

While I was cooking, Mac came in and grabbed a beer from the fridge. He started to walk away, and then stopped. Looking from me to the fridge and then back to me, his brow furrowed. I tossed a pan of sliced veggies and watched him go back to the fridge. Opening it, I heard him say, "Huh." I guess it had taken him a second to comprehend the fridge had suddenly become fully stocked in his absence. He came up to me and leaned on the counter, watching me. I glanced at him with raised eyebrows, but he just sipped his beer.

Finally, I broke the silence. "Can I help you, or are you just trying to become one with the rooster decor?"

To my surprise, he actually laughed. "Am I bothering you, Vixen?"

Sighing, I added some more seasoning to the pan. "No, I'm just not used to being watched. Can you hand me that bowl?"

He slid it towards me, and after throwing the meat that had been marinating into the pan, I covered it and turned off the heat. I moved to the kitchen island, noticing more bikers had made their way into the room. Mac left his spot, grabbed a six-pack from the fridge, and joined them. I made a mental note to add beer to the next grocery list. A lot of beer. I laid out toppings for steak fajitas, and then went on a hunt for plates and bowls. Finally, I holler, "Alright, Saints, come and get it."

I waited for them to come rushing into the kitchen, but they all seemed to be waiting for something. I frowned at Dalton, who was sitting at the table, and he nodded towards the other door, which promptly swung open. Much to my surprise, more people came in—including women and even a couple of kids. One of them, a pretty Hispanic lady with a baby on her hip, smiled at me, her brown eyes open and friendly. I smiled back as another kid came running out from behind her, stopping in front of me.

"Hello!" he said, grinning up at me, a couple of teeth missing and with brown eyes just like his mother's, bright with mischief. "My name is Diego. I'm eight. That's my mom. She said to be nice to you. She said that 'cos my dad and his friends can be dicks sometimes, you would need a friend. What does that mean?"

My jaw dropped, and I looked up at his mom, whose eyes had widened to the size of saucers.

"Diego Jesus Gonzelez, go with your sister and have her make you a plate, or I swear—"

He hurried off and joined a girl who looked to be about fifteen. His mom smiled at me again, this time apologetically.

"I am so sorry—kids sometimes repeat things I really wish they wouldn't. I blame their father. My name is Maria. You may have met my husband, Diego Sr."

I laughed. "Honestly, he just made my day, so it's totally fine. I'm Nicky, it's nice to meet you. And I have no idea if I've met your husband yet. Their faces all kind of blur together."

Maria nodded and shifted the baby on her hip, who chewed on his hand and stared at me with bright eyes.

"Who is this handsome man? Is his name Diego, too?"

"His dad would've loved that but, at risk of inflating his head further, we actually named him Manuel. Everyone calls him Manny." The boy, hearing his name, laughed and waved a slobber-covered fist at me.

Around us, the men start to get up to make their plates now that the women and kids have all gotten theirs. A tall, broad-shouldered duplicate of little Diego came up behind Maria, and kissed her cheek.

"Careful, *mi amor*, she may bite."

She swatted him. "Don't be a *pendejo*. I don't blame the woman. Go, make us both something to eat. It smells delicious."

The guy wandered off, and Maria stepped closer to me. She squeezed my arm and whispered, "To be honest, I think you should've bit Dalton harder. And I would've paid good money to see you set that man-child's bike on fire. I never did like him. I know this is all new and probably more than a little alarming, but most of the guys here are good guys. Stick with us girls, and we'll show you the ropes. We aren't around here too often, but I won't ever pass up the opportunity to not cook." She smiled again before heading to the table where everyone sat in genuine camaraderie. Diego pulled out her chair and took little Manny from her, tossing him in the air, much to the delight of the squealing infant.

As I watched, I sensed someone approaching and turned to see Dalton coming up with two plates of food and a couple of beers tucked under his arm.

"This smells amazing, Vixen. You didn't tell us you could cook."

I shrugged. "You never asked."

He nodded. "I bet there's a lot we don't know about you. Come on, one of these is yours." I blinked at him, and he said, "What? You gotta eat too."

I looked over at the table, and Maria was patting the seat next to her. I stopped Dalton when he went to give me one of the beers. "I'm more of a whiskey girl."

He smiled. "Of course you are," he said, and then took the empty seat next to his brother, who had been watching me the entire time.

Well, this was more than a little unexpected. I soon found any residual tension melting away in the warmth of laughter and conversation around the table. Diego clearly doted on Maria, who fed Manny some of the refried beans I had made. Little Diego seemed intent on wearing his fajitas, and the sister handed him wads of napkins at a time. Several other women had bikers next to them, every single one of them with an arm around each other, or a hand on the knee.

I met the eyes of a blonde woman a few seats down from me, her hand messing with Jackson's hair as he bantered with another guy I hadn't met yet. She gave me an appraising look, her pale eyes neither friendly nor hateful, before returning her attention to her plate.

By the time everyone had had their fill, I was laughing with Maria at some dumb joke Diego had made. She turned to me and said, "Alright, Nicky, I've got to know. What kind of girl shows up to a biker bar in the middle of downtown Atlanta and says, 'Fuck it, I'm setting a bike on fire'?"

I groaned and sipped at the lowball glass of whiskey that had appeared in front of me at some point. "I wasn't planning on it, I swear. I just needed a drink after a long day on the road and—"

Diego held up a hand. "Hey, that leads to my question. Where did you learn to ride?"

I scrambled to remember Nicole's backstory that had been drilled into me. "My brother, actually. I used to beg him to take me riding with him when I was a kid. I guess he got tired of me hanging onto the back of his bike 'cos when I turned sixteen, he gave me my first Triumph. I loved that bike. I might've ridden it a little too hard 'cos one night, I took a corner too fast and—" I make a whoosh sound and mime an explosion with my hands. "When my brother pulled up, I was sitting on the back of the ambo. When he realized I wasn't hurt too bad, he ripped my ass a new one."

"Serves you right!" Dalton hollered from down the table, and I realized everyone had gone quiet to hear my story. "Where's he now?"

I glanced down. "He died a couple of years ago." Maria squeezed my knee, and I looked up at her. "It's alright; I like to think he still rides with me."

Dalton raised his beer. "I'll drink to that." The other bikers raised their drinks, too, and there was a moment of silence before I started clearing empty plates from the table.

As I cleaned, Maria came up to me and handed me a note.

"We're going to head home, honey. Time to put these heathens to bed," she said, looking over at Diego who was holding both boys sleeping soundly, one on each shoulder. Her eyes softened, then she nodded to the piece of paper I'd slipped in my pocket. "That's my number on there. You text me if you need anything. I would offer to stay and help, but Mac told everyone to let you do your job—the overbearing idiot."

I smiled at her. "It's fine, really. Thank you. You're the first friendly face I've met in this place."

She turned to leave. "Eh, don't let them fool you—they're a bunch of softies. But I'm here if you need me. I think we could be friends." She winked at me, slipping her hand into Diego's back pocket as they left.

I kept cleaning until the kitchen was back to its original spotless state, and then rolled my neck, relishing the satisfying pop.

"You keep on surprising me, Vixen."

I jumped and spun around to see Mac—I'd thought I was alone.

"How do you mean?"

He walked over to the trash can and pulled out the full bag, setting it by the door. He didn't answer me, but came over and gently took my wrist. It was slightly bruised from where he had grabbed me earlier, and he frowned in response. For some reason, I felt the need to reassure him.

"It doesn't really hurt. Besides, I did hit you first. And I bit your brother."

He shook his head. "Doesn't matter; bruising women isn't my style." His thumb traced circles over the mark, and while I knew I should pull away, I didn't.

We stood there for a minute until he cleared his throat and backed away. As he headed out the door with the trash bag in hand, I called to him, "You didn't answer me."

He stopped and looked at me over his shoulder. There was a whole world in those dark eyes, a thousand thoughts and feelings flying by in a matter of seconds. But he just turned and left without a word. I stood there, at a loss for words, and then grabbed the whiskey off the shelf and took a shot straight from the bottle. I realized then there was a lot more to Maverick Mills than what I'd read in his file. His gentle touch scared me more than when he was pinning me to a wall and, with that thought, I took another shot.

After finishing up a few jars of overnight oats for an easy breakfast, I began to wonder how I would get home. Perhaps Tony would take me back again? It was getting dark, and I was tired. I labeled the jars carefully, and put them in the fridge. Dalton had put his number in my phone earlier, after taking the one Mac had given me back. I shot off a quick text and sat down next to the same cat from the other night. He'd wandered in from the garage at some point, assuming his spot on the island counter, snoozing away. I'd tried shooing him off, and he'd opened a single baleful eye to glare at me before going back to sleep.

I was in the middle of writing out a meal plan when the door swung up, and Dalton walked in. "Hey Vixen, sorry about that. You can go home whenever you want. Tomorrow I'll have someone show you around the place so you know what you're cleaning. But you're done for today." He rubbed the cat between the ears.

I pointed my pen at the orange tabby. "I don't think it likes me."

"Diesel likes a very select few. Don't take it personal."

I frowned, and Dalton came closer. "You did good for someone who had this whole thing thrown at you. I think you'll fit right in."

I tilted my head at him. "What if I don't want to fit in?"

He brushed a lock of hair behind my ear, and I jerked away in surprise.

"Well, I don't really have an answer for that. We've all gotta find our place."

We stared at each other for a loaded moment, before he picked Diesel up and turned to leave. "Go home, Vixen."

With that, he left me in the kitchen before I could ask him how, exactly, I was supposed to do that. Sighing, I hung my list on the fridge and made my way through the garage to the parking lot. I'd been hoping to find Tony or Jackson or literally anyone I recognized, but there were only a few people still around, none of whom I knew.

As I turned to go back in, my eyes landed on something very familiar, and my mouth fell open. My bike was there by the bay door, my helmet sitting on the seat. The slashed tire had been replaced, and it had clearly been washed. I looked around, but no one made a sound or moved towards me. Too tired to ask questions, I turned the ignition, and the bike roared to life.

As I pulled out of the driveway, I glanced at the hulking building behind me and thought of the two brothers inside, who'd surprised and intrigued me at every turn. Shaking my head, I pushed all thoughts of them away and focused on the cool wind whipping around me as I headed back to my temporary home.

I shouldn't have been this satisfied over groceries and fajita toppings. This wasn't what I trained for. But something about the order, the control of it—it filled a space I didn't know was empty. Still, I'd take chasing leads with Shelly any day.

# Chapter 6

My alarm went off at eight, and I stretched as I reached for my phone. There were only two texts, one from "Uncle Tommy," reminding me about our dinner date on Friday—which was just a chance for me to update him on my progress. Another was from Dalton, letting me know that Maria was going to meet me at the clubhouse at nine to give me a tour. I yawned, then padded towards the kitchen to start the coffee. If I was going to make it through day two, I'd need caffeine.

As the smell of Folgers permeated the apartment, I shuffled through the clothes in my closet. It had been stocked for me, and whoever did it had picked things that helped me fit in my role. I grabbed a Rolling Stones t-shirt and a pair of skinny jeans, then hopped in the shower. By the time I left the bathroom, I felt ready to take on almost anything. I slipped on a pair of Vans and braided my still-wet hair. I had about twenty minutes before I had to go, but I didn't feel very hungry. I flipped on the TV, curled up on the couch, and sipped my coffee, relishing the quiet morning.

Mug washed and all ready to go, I used the number Maria had given me yesterday and shot off a quick text, letting her know I was on my way. I grabbed my earbuds on second thought as I left. Minutes later, I flew out of the parking lot, loving the rumble of my bike between my knees. Turning the corner, I saw Agent Braxton sitting in a business suit at a local coffee shop, looking like any other morning commuter. I shook my head. I didn't know if handlers were usually this hands-on, since I didn't have any other undercover op to compare it to, but the dude was borderline needy.

The clubhouse was about a twenty-minute ride from my apartment, but with morning traffic, it took me about thirty minutes to get there. As I pulled in, Maria stepped out. She must have been watching for me.

"Girl, I love your bike. Sexy *mamacita*," she said, winking at me.

I laughed in response. "Can you ride?"

She shook her head. "Not my thing, to be honest, though I sometimes ride with Diego."

She and I headed toward a side door that circumvented the garage and kitchen areas. Leading me into a small foyer, she made a grand sweeping gesture. "Ta-da, welcome to the home away from home for Steel Saints and company."

I looked around—there was a small table with a few magazines on it, plus a couple of cushy armchairs, a water cooler, and Diesel, who was in the middle of a big stretch. He ambled his way over, his fat orange belly swinging, and then head-butted Maria's leg, looking for pats.

"He likes you?"

She gave me an odd look and scratched the cat under the chin. "Of course. Diesel's a big lover boy."

I frowned. "Dalton told me the opposite. He doesn't seem to like me very much."

She murmured something to Diesel and turned to me. "Dalton is a big, fat liar. Sorry *chica*, but I think he was just trying to make you feel better. I'm sure Diesel will warm up to you." She headed out, leaving the cat and me alone for a moment. We stared at each other until he made a low, rumbling, angry sound, so I flipped him off and head after Maria. It was my first week, and I already had beef with the cat.

Maria led me down a hallway to a small living area that branched off in several directions. She pointed to our right and said, "That's the hallway you'll find yourself in on the way to and from the kitchen or garage."

I nodded. "The one with all the motel rooms."

"An odd but fitting description. So, yeah." She pointed to two other hallways. "Those also have motel rooms. They'll usually be empty. Dalton told me to tell you that all you'll have to do is vacuum, dust, and whatnot in there. Just general upkeep—don't worry about making the beds unless you're told by Bossy Pants One or Two."

I assumed she meant Mac or Dalton, and I laughed.

In the corner was the set of stairs I'd seen last night. Maria noticed me looking at them. "Don't go up, but down is kind of a hangout spot for whoever."

"Bossy Pants is an interesting choice of nickname for my second-in-command, Mrs. Gonzales."

A hulking shape rose from one of the recliners that had its back to us. The darkness had kept him completely obscured. Maria yelped in surprise, and I looked from her to the mystery man and back.

"You must be Nicole Moore. The newest thorn in my side."

The man stepped into the light, giving me my first in-person look at the club president. Silas Greyson was shorter than Mac, but built like a bull. His salt-and-pepper crew cut had a little more salt than pepper, and stubble lined his jaw. He looks me over, his dark eyes hard and unwelcoming.

"So sorry, sir, I didn't see you there."

To break the tension, I said, "Nice to meet you—I'm Nicky."

He hummed. "Hiring you isn't exactly what I would've done if I had been the one to catch you setting bikes on fire. Lucky for you, Maverick was there and not me."

I cleared my throat awkwardly. He stood there for a minute before nodding to Maria, who led us out the way we came.

I turned back to her. "Holy crap, that dude is intense with a capital I."

She giggled nervously. "Yeah, Mr. Greyson is a bit…"

I raised my eyebrows. "Terrifying? Intimidating? Asshole-y?"

I offered up a few other choice adjectives, and she giggled again. "Don't let him hear you say that." Just then, her phone dinged with an incoming text, and she glanced at it with a grimace. "I hate to ditch, Nicky, but I gotta get home to the kids. Hey, you know what? We should go on a girls' date. Shopping, mani-pedis, drink too much and spill dirty secrets—" She wiggled her eyebrows at me suggestively, and I smiled in response.

"I would love that. You let me know when, but go on. Get home to your family. Thank you for showing me around."

She surprised me with a hug, and then headed out towards the kitchen.

I sighed and looked around, not really sure where to start. I decided that I wasn't going to get anywhere until I found some cleaning supplies, so I made my way to the kitchen. Sure enough, under the sink, I find what I need. I grabbed a bucket, a clean washcloth, some Pledge, and a few other odds and ends, and headed back to the motel rooms. I cleaned like my life depended on it for the next couple of hours. Singing along to Nickelback, I tried to force myself to find some sort of enjoyment in a task that felt utterly mundane compared to the job I was used to.

I nearly dropped the bucket when I turned and found Mr. Greyson lurking in the doorway. Pulling my earbuds out, I shove them in my pocket.

"You sure do have a habit of sneaking up on people."

He started towards me, and I had to stop myself from backing up or spraying him with the Windex. I realized that now may be a good time to get some answers, so I said, "I haven't seen you around the club for the past couple of days. Were you out of town?"

He stopped less than a foot from me. "What I do is none of your business, girl."

Okay, so the guy was a douche—no surprise there. But I nodded meekly. "You're right. I'm sorry."

"Sir."

"What?"

"You call me sir, or Mr. Greyson. But you *will* address me properly."

I wanted to call him an asshole, and suggest that maybe he calls me Nicky instead of "girl." Instead, I bit my tongue and said, "Yes, sir."

"Oh, so you can follow directions. Amazing." His tone was bone dry.

"I've done what I've been told since I got here."

"You shouldn't even be here. Maverick must have lost his mind."

"I'm sure he did what he thought was best. *Sir.*" I knew I shouldn't, but I couldn't help but add, "Besides, he's your second-in-command, so wouldn't his state of mind reflect on you?"

Before I could blink, the man backhanded me so fast that I dropped my bucket and stumbled back. Holy shit, that hurt. I placed a hand on my tender cheek and, this time, didn't hide the glare aimed in his direction. He grabbed my hair and pulled my head back, forcing me to look up at him.

"If you want to continue working as some pretty little maid, you will learn your fucking place. Or I can find a job much better suited for a woman like you." His other hand roamed my body, and I couldn't suppress my shudder. He smiled, then abruptly let go before leaving the room.

My cheek wasn't the only thing burning as rage blazed through my body.

Not having much of a choice, I went back to cleaning the rooms but kept my earbuds out in case he decided to show up again. I cursed my temper. As Katie, that fire was something I had grown skilled at restraining. As Nicky, I was clearly growing comfortable with letting it loose. I should have known better than to goad him. His file literally dripped evil. The man was a murderer—he bought and sold people like trinkets, and he had fought his way to the top of this club.

And my dumb ass had to go and sass off.

Mac and Dalton weren't good men, but they weren't anything like that from what little I'd seen so far. How in the hell had those two ended up working for a man like Silas Greyson? Stupid club loyalty bullshit, probably. I stopped scrubbing the bathroom floor and rocked back on my heels, taking a deep breath and reminding myself why I was doing this.

I was just heading to the next room when a hand landed on my shoulder from behind, and I swung my bucket like a weapon as I spun around. Dalton jumped back with a startled, "Whoa!" and I dropped the bucket to the ground with an, "Oh shit!"

He put his hands up and said, "Jesus, Vixen, remind me never to come up behind you ever again." Then his eyes landed on my soon-to-be bruised cheek, and his eyes darkened to a shade of blue not unlike his brother's. "Who the fuck hit you?"

I shook my head. "It doesn't matter. Nothing you can do." I went to grab my bucket off the ground, and he frowned at me.

"Like hell. Who fucking hit you?"

I refused to look at him, pretending to be intently focused on getting everything back into my bucket. Dalton made an angry sound in the back of his throat, and kicked it down the hall, all my cleaning stuff rolling off in different directions. He hauled me up and said, "Vixen, don't make me ask you again. I want a name."

I laughed—part nerves and part anger—and he blinked in surprise. "There is nothing you can fucking do." I enunciated each word carefully. "It was your boss. What are you going to do, Dalton, huh? What can you possibly fucking do to Silas Greyson?"

His frown deepened, and then he swore under his breath. We both knew that I was right, and he wasn't too happy about it. I went after my things, gathering everything up before turning back to him. He just stood there, watching me.

I shook my head at him. "And what does it matter? Why do you even care about what happens to me? We don't know each other. I'm just here to do a job and pay off that stupid Harley. You don't give a damn about me, and I don't give a damn about you."

I marched into the nearest room, and slammed the door behind me.

I slid down the door and buried my head in my hands. I was shaking. I really hoped each day wasn't going to be like this. What was I going to do? And why did telling Dalton that I didn't care about him feel like such a lie? When did his easy smile and quick laugh become something that mattered to me at all? I knew I shouldn't care—that distance was key. It had to be. Seriously, it'd only been three days. I needed to grow up. I had a job to do, and it wasn't being a maid.

Silently, I went through their names in my head. Mia Huntington. Anastasia Little. Gabriella Santiago. Kelly MacIntyre. Ruby Johnson. I said their names over and over until I heard his footsteps disappearing down the hall.

My phone buzzed, and I read the text from Mac: "Lunch was a bust… let's try not to forget dinner by five." Evidently, I was expected to make every meal of the day, no matter how busy I'd been cleaning. Which, to be fair, was the job description of your typical maid, but give a girl a break!

After putting my bucket back under the sink, I grabbed the whiskey off the shelf, and a lowball glass. I downed my first glass and poured another. I'd frozen all the meat out of habit, and with nothing pulled out ahead of time, the only thing that could thaw quickly enough was some kielbasa. I pulled out a few and tossed them in some warm water. I glanced at the clock on the wall as I gathered together pasta, cream, cheese, some sundried tomatoes, and a few other odds and ends. I had about thirty minutes to throw something together for the whole crew.

I found a pot big enough to cook a whole chicken in, with room to spare, and started tossing in ingredients. I put some garlic bread in the oven and made a tossed salad, and by the time five o'clock rolls around, I had a delicious meal all laid out.

One of the guys, Rodney, came in rubbing his hands together. "Oooo baby, what we got today?"

A few other bikers, Jackson and Tony included, followed him into the dining room. I already had a river's worth of beer sitting on the table, and they flocked towards it.

"Hey, Robbie, right? I made a sort of Cajun cheesy pasta with sausage. Sound good?" I tried to be friendly, figuring if I could win over a couple bikers, it would be easier to gather intel.

"Hell yeah, better than some frozen pizza."

The group laughed, and I smiled at them. I continued setting up the island, laying out plates and bowls. As I do so, more guys pour in, including two brothers I'd kind of been hoping wouldn't show for dinner. But Lady Luck was not on my side. Dalton basically ignored me, but Mac stood by the fridge. I pretended not to notice him, but my treacherous body heated under his gaze. Nerves, I told myself, just nerves.

Only a few ladies joined the throng of guys this time, and I smiled again when I saw Maria, who made her way over to me. "Shit girl, wanna come cook for me when you're tired of being here?"

I laughed. "You say that like I'm here willingly." She looked pointedly between me and Mac. "Yeah, I can see how horrible this must be for you.

Two hunks who can't keep their blue eyes off you."

I felt a blush creep up the back of my neck. "They're probably just worried I'll set another bike on fire."

She made a sound of agreement. "Yeah, they don't quite trust you yet. But they don't have my built-in radar. Not their fault."

I glanced at Mac, who'd heard the whole thing, but his face gave nothing away.

There was some silent signal, and everyone started making their plates. This time, Jackson's old lady pulled me into the line with the rest of the women.

"Hi, I'm Holly," she said.

I smiled and replied, "Nicky. But, um… I don't think I'm supposed to be in line."

"Ladies eat first, and those are Mac's rules.  So grab some food."  She handed me a plate and moved down the line.

Maria was already at the table, the seat next to her empty again. I joined her and asked, "What the heck was that about?"

She took another bite of pasta before answering.  "First, this stuff is freaking to die for. Second, that's just Holly. She's a bit… odd. Trust issues galore. But she's good people once she opens up to you. We've been besties since high school. She and Jackson are really good together. They met when we were all kids, and there was a running bet for a while. Would they kill each other, get it out of their system with some hot, angry sex, or settle down?  I am pretty sure I was the only one who put my money on settle down.  And, what do you know, I was right. Shocker. Built. In. Radar." She grabbed a water bottle and took a sip before noticing my expression. "What?"

I started laughing. "Hot, angry sex? Really?"

She joined me, her laugh loud and boisterous. "If you'd seen those two back then, you would get it."

Suddenly Maria fell quiet, as did most of the table. Silas had walked in.

He grabbed a plate of food, and sat in the empty seat next to Mac.  He didn't say a damn thing, and eventually, the conversation around the table resumed. I watched him and noticed him looking up at me, slowly smiling. It was the kind of smile you saw on *See No Evil*, that true crime show Shelly liked to binge-watch. I clenched my fork so hard, a weaker metal would've bent.

Maria grabbed my knee under the table, and I turned to look at her. She shook her head, a silent warning. I glanced over one last time to see him conversing with Mac. Dalton sat across from them, and was making no effort to hide the rage in his eyes as he stared at his boss.

Maria whispered, "Look, I don't know what this is about, but Mr. Greyson isn't the one, Nicky. Most of the guys in here wouldn't touch you, but he took over the club about three years ago—honestly, he terrifies the shit out of me. He should scare you, too. He's bad news, Nicky. Don't push it."

I pushed the last bit of pasta around on my plate, my appetite gone.

"How, Maria? How did he become president?"

Her eyes took on a sadness. "It should've been Mac. But that's not a story for the dinner table. Some other time, I promise."

I looked over again, stealing a brief glance. Dalton was still glaring at Greyson like he could kill him with his bare hands, but then he caught my eye. I grabbed a few nearby plates, and got up, hoping he would follow.

I was bent over the dishwasher when I felt a hand on my lower back. I straightened and found him so close I could smell him—a delicious combination of sweet-smelling motor oil, musk, and leather.

"You're gonna get yourself killed looking at him like that."

The muscle in his neck twitched as he ground his jaw. "You don't have to worry about me, Vixen."

At that moment, I accepted—despite my better judgment—that in a matter of days, I'd come to care for him. I hadn't met a biker I didn't like—other than Daniel and Silas, of course. In the few quiet minutes I'd found for myself, I'd watched them interact with one another. They were more than just some club. They joked and rough-housed, knew each other's families, and I knew by now that when you messed with one man, you messed with them all. They had each other's backs. Which left me even more confused about how in the hell some guy like Silas Greyson had ended up in charge.

"Dalton—" I started, but he interrupted me.

"Don't. I'm serious. For once, just listen. For whatever fucking reason, you're on his shit list, so, for once, just... be a good girl and keep your head down." With that, he walked out the door towards the motel rooms. My eyes followed him, and after he left, they returned to the table.

Both Mac and Greyson were watching me. Greyson said something to Mac, and I saw a vein in his jaw twitch. Our eyes met, and I saw the same anger in Mac's gaze, but his was more tightly leashed than his brother's. I turned back to the dishwasher, busying myself as people started leaving the table and handing their plates to me. But Dalton's words rang in my ears, and I swore I could still feel his hand on my back.

That night, before I climbed into bed, I examined the slight bruise Silas had left. Again, I found myself repeating the girls' names until they were the only thing on my mind. Mia Huntington. Anastasia Little. Gabriella Santiago. Kelly MacIntyre. Ruby Johnson.

I had to remember why I was here.

# Chapter 7

By the end of the second month, I knew each biker by name. I kept the rooms spotless and provided meals three times a day. Lunch was simple, dinner I had yet to make the same thing twice, and I was having fun having a bunch of burly men try something new. Breakfast was something I usually made ahead to give myself more time for cleaning. In the quiet moments, I could almost feel my skin crawl with the need to do something more. Being with Shelly, chasing down leads, busting down doors… that's what I was made for. This domestic housewife shit was about to drive me insane.

On Sundays, I would do a massive brunch spread. A lot of the guys were Christian, and would come back from church half-starved, like praising the Lord took something out of them. They would come roaring in on their bikes, or some of them would bring in their whole families. Bacon, eggs, waffles, muffins, sausage… Rodney had even requested fried chicken once. It was an odd choice for breakfast, but evidently, his mom made it every Sunday when he was a kid. So I added it to the rotation.

Once everyone realized I would take suggestions, the requests came timidly at first, and then it seemed like I had a new one every day. Maria's little boy requested tamales, and I spent half a day cursing the damn things until Maria got wind of it and stepped in. She made it look easy and, at dinner time, my tamales looked like little deformed nuggets next to hers. Still, Diego Sr. and Jr. ate their weight in food that night, so I took it as a victory.

I was cleaning the rooms one day when Maria and Holly came in, hollering like banshees and giggling their asses off. They had raided Mac's "special liquor cabinet" and were evidently quite proud of themselves. Maria opened up her massive mom purse, which held a bottle of black-label bourbon, and Holly had grabbed as many snacks as she could carry from the kitchen. I locked the door, and we spent the next three hours watching *SVU* reruns on the in-room TV. Watching Lieutenant Benson close cases had me wondering if Shelly had been closing any recently. I missed her. Back home, my circle was my badge, my gun, and Shelly. Out here, I was learning what it meant to have friends.

I got a text from Dalton halfway through: "It's adorable that you and your friends think y'all are so slick." Maria and Holly teased me relentlessly, but I was adamant that he was just my boss. I was late with dinner that night, but I regretted not a damn thing.

Day by day, I grew more fond of the Steel Saints crew. And, damn, it made things difficult—an internal war of sorts. I tried to keep an emotional distance. But these guys… they weren't the criminals that the files I had read painted them to be. Yeah, okay—they weren't literal saints. But I had met much worse on the streets of Charleston back home. Men and women who had killed without remorse, or given drugs to children without giving a damn about the lives destroyed. Evil people with no humanity. These guys weren't that. More and more, I found myself joining in on their conversations, laughing at their dumb jokes, and even riding around town with them on club errands.

Dalton was more of a highlight in my days than I was willing to admit. He greeted me almost every morning with a cup of coffee and a smile. When I was cooking in the kitchen, he happily kept me company, telling me stories about his and Mac's childhood, the adventures they'd had as they'd grown, the hearts they'd broken. I did my best to pretend like I wasn't listening. But the dude had a way of making me laugh like no one else. And when I asked him questions or expressed even the slightest interest, the way he smiled at me made me feel things. Things I didn't fully understand. I knew he was just watching me 'cos they didn't quite trust me yet. He even admitted as much, when I pushed him on the subject one day. But still, that didn't stop me from enjoying his company.

Mac was much more distant. Unlike his brother, he made no effort to hide his distrust of me. At first, I didn't think I was ever going to win the guy over. But as time passed, I began to pick up on the little things he would do for me. I complained about being unable to reach the kitchen top shelf, and then the next day, there was a shiny new stepstool by the fridge. One night, I showed Maria my sore and cracked hands from all the cleaning products. Holding a gun did less damage than scrubbing floors with bleach. The next day, there was a pack of rubber gloves in my bucket. Despite riding it back and forth to the clubhouse daily, my bike never needed fuel. Dalton was genuinely clueless when I asked him about it, and that's when I realized—in the background, all the little details… it was Mac.

Always Mac.

I gathered as much intel as I could without raising suspicion. My growing bond with the Saints members made it easier than expected. In a way. Having their trust meant they weren't as careful when talking to me. It also meant that every little tidbit of information I passed to Braxton in my letters to Uncle Tommy felt like a betrayal. But I was just doing my job. Still, while I was meticulous in my letters, I left out details of my growing friendships within the club. That, I told myself, had nothing to do with the DiAngelos and was none of Braxton's business.

I still repeated those girls' names every night before I went to bed, promising myself I would never forget them.

Despite part of my check supposedly going towards Daniel's poor Harley, I was paid well.

About three months in, Maria, Holly, and I planned a girls' outing. I met them at Maria's, an adorable stucco house with a big backyard that had toys littered throughout. Diego Sr. met me outside and opened the garage so I could park my bike off the street. When I walked in, Holly was in the living room playing some game on the TV with little Diego. She greeted me with a smile as I entered. Diego ignored me entirely, completely intent on his game. Jewel, Maria's teenage daughter, lounged on the couch, reading something by John Green.

"Oh good, you're here. My car or Holly's?" Maria said as she came in from the kitchen, holding the baby who she passed to Diego Sr. Manny gurgled and started chewing on the collar of Diego's leather jacket. I cooed at him, and he grinned. Little guy was a carbon copy of his mama, cute as a bug. Diego Jr. started hollering in victory, which earned an irritated look from his sister.

Holly ruffled his hair as she stood. "My car doesn't smell like children. No offense."

Maria shrugged. "Fair. The other day, I found a mummified chicken nugget under Diego's car seat." Holly made a face, and I laughed.

Maria kissed her husband goodbye, and he slapped her rear as she turned to leave.

"Behave yourself, ladies. I don't want to load up the minivan to go on a rescue mission."

Maria winked at him and waltzed out the door without another word.

I turned to him as I shut the door and said, "A maid and two Saints' old ladies. How bad could it possibly be?"

He groaned, while I smiled innocently.

We all piled into Holly's Fusion, and Maria made a show of glancing around the small car. "Hm, I don't know if this is gonna be big enough for all the shopping I have planned," she teased from the passenger seat.

Holly turned towards the local shopping mall and said, "Oh, I don't know about that. You can fit a body in the trunk."

I laughed, and she looked at me in the mirror. "I'm dead serious—no pun intended. I locked Jackson in the trunk once. He had come home wasted, and well, let's just say he never did that again."

Maria and I stared at her, and then our eyes met in the side mirror, and we fell about laughing.

"Girl, that is diabolical," I said.

As we pulled into the mall, Maria rubbed her hands eagerly and then pulled out a list from her pocket. Holly glanced skeptically at it. "What's that?"

Maria brandished it proudly. "My list! I've got us at the coffee shop first, then figured we could stop by Victoria's Secret for a few and swing by Auntie Anne's after for a snack then—"

Like lightning, Holly snatched her list, crumpled it, and threw it out the window where it blew away in the crisp breeze.

Maria made various sounds of protest and looked to me for support; I shrugged at her. "I'm on Holly's side here, sorry girl."

As we all climbed out of the car, Maria turned to glare at me, but her eyes softened when Holly came from the other side and put her arm around Maria's shoulders. "Sorry, honey, but you are not going all 'mom mode' on our day."

Maria sighed, and I linked my arm through hers. "Come on, it's my first shopping trip in Atlanta. Show me how it's done. Oh, and can we please go to HomeGoods? 'Cos I have saved up some serious cash for a new mattress."

Holly frowned. "While a body might fit in my trunk, a mattress sure as shit ain't happening."

"No, but Diego can come get it for you later—or I bet they deliver," Maria said. "Besides, we could use some new bedding in the guest room. Diego got blood all over the sheets. Don't ask."

We headed into the mall, making a beeline for a cute little coffee shop. Five minutes into debating which stores to visit in front of the mall map, I began to wonder if we should have kept Maria's list. Holly dragged us into a photo booth and we made total fools of ourselves behind the curtain. I tucked my copy into my pocket carefully.

Over the next three hours, we raided the shelves in almost every store on the first floor. By the time we made it to the second floor, our arms were already laden with bags.

I finally found my mattress store and, oh sweet heaven, they did deliver. I hated a lumpy mattress. I managed to find one on sale that felt like a cloud. The three of us lay on it until the store kicked us out. When we got to the food court, our bags took up two tables, and I said, "Girls, I think we need to call it quits. There's no way we can carry any more."

Holly winked at me. "I've got a better idea. Grab me some of that crappy pizza, would you? I'll take care of this." Meanwhile Maria headed off to get drinks, and I joined the throng of people by the pizza place.

When I got through the line and back to the table with our food, Maria was already back with three sweet teas.

"Okay, so what's the plan?"

Holly reached for a slice of pizza and nodded towards the escalator. "There's our plan."

I looked over to see three prospects making their way over to us.

"Aw," she said, "Jackson sent one for each of us. Sometimes, I think he might actually be smarter than he looks."

Maria made a general sound of agreement around a mouthful of food.

"Hey, Mrs. Morgan. Jackson said you needed us?" one of the prospects said as they approached us.

Holly waved at all of our bags. "I hope you came in one of the trucks and not your bikes." The prospect nodded, the other two seemingly content to be quiet. One of them winked at me when he caught me looking, and I rolled my eyes. He was cute, but those brown eyes seemed lackluster compared to the blue ones I had found myself preferring lately—though I was loathe to admit it.

"Yes, ma'am, sure did. Wasn't born yesterday. Want us to take all this back to the clubhouse?"

Holly nodded, and the three guys grabbed our bags and left.

Fully sated on greasy pizza, we went through the next stores. Maria went for broke in the bookstore, buying two or three complete sets. "Jewel will go nuts over this stuff," she told me.

I had somehow become her basket after she insisted she didn't need an actual one. In the next store, she put a couple of t-shirts on top of the pile in my arms.

"Her birthday is the weekend after next. Which, by the way, you're totally invited to. She's turning fifteen, and we're throwing her a modernized *quinceañera*. So, literally, everyone is invited." She made a face as we made our way to the front of the store. "Except her dad, of course. Don't need his drama. No sir, no thank you."

I glanced at her, confused. "Diego isn't Jewel's father?"

She shook her head. "He is in every other sense but blood. Her dad... I had a young and dumb moment when I was fifteen. I was so not ready to be a momma, but I stepped up, you know? My girl needed me. But her sperm donor... he's a useless son of a bitch, and always has been. Just took me too long to see it."

Holly appeared behind us. "Who are we talking about?"

"Jesse."

"Oooo, fuck him. I hope he gets run over."

"Literally same. Would make my life so much easier."

I looked between the two. "He's a real piece of work, then?"

Maria nodded. "Just a little," she said, miming the opposite by spreading her arms as wide as they would go.

I squirreled away that nugget of information and said, "I'm going to run back while you finish checking out—I saw something I wanted to grab real quick."

Holly gave me a thumbs up as Maria dug her wallet out of her purse.

I found the book I was looking for pretty quickly. I debated the optics of buying Dalton a gift for all of five seconds before grabbing the worn copy of *The Complete Short Stories of Ernest Hemingway*. He had told me a while back that he loved the classics. I didn't know much about reading, but surely you couldn't get much more classic than a dead guy? I had the clerk wrap it in tissue paper before meeting the girls outside.

We all piled into the car with our bags and headed back to Maria's. It was getting late, and we were all the kind of tired that comes from a long, good day with the people you love. I lounged in the back seat while Holly and Maria bantered up front. My phone buzzed, and I got a text from Dalton letting me know he was having someone bring my things to my apartment.

I typed back, "How will you know what's mine?"

I blushed furiously when he sent back a picture of Holly's red lace nightgown, along with the caption, "While I can't think of anything better than you in this, somehow I feel like it's not your style."

I couldn't resist replying, "Guess you'll never know," then shoved my phone back in my pocket, ignoring the incoming text vibration. I focused on Maria, who was describing Jewel's party in detail.

"So, she wants barbecue and a strawberry chocolate cake. She's already picked out her gown, and Diego found the perfect venue. And you said Jackson can DJ, right?"

Holly nodded. "Yeah, and he's got some old band buddies that are coming, so you'll have live music and all that too."

Maria grinned. "I've been planning this since she turned thirteen. Have you ever been to a *quinceañera*?" she asked me. I shook my head. "You'll love it."

"If you don't mind me asking… you guys all seem to know each other pretty well. When did you first meet?"

Maria and Holly shared a look, one that carried the weight of thousands of memories. Maria turned to me. "Jackson, Dalton, Mac, and Diego were all jocks at my school. Total assholes. Well, not Dalton. And Diego only sometimes. But idiots, you know? I avoided them for the most part. Then this hotshot with a bad attitude moved into a freaking mansion not too far from us. Somehow, she ended up at our school."

Holly took up the story. "I hated Jackson the second I met him. Dude almost ran me over. First day of school, I realized he went there too. Maria kind of made it her mission to keep me from killing him."

"Yeah, and Diego had his hands full dealing with Jackson's temper. Oh, sure—he's all calm and cool now. Didn't used to be that way!"

"Somehow, it all just fell together. I left Jesse after Diego beat him to a pulp. Remind me to tell you *that* story sometime. Eventually, Holly and Jackson worked out their issues."

"We worked out a lot, actually," Holly said, winking at me in the rearview mirror. Maria shook her head, and I grinned.

"What about Mac and Dalton?" I asked.

Holly shrugged. "They were just kind of always there, you know? Mac had always been in charge. The Saints had just gotten up and running. His dad was… well, everyone liked him. And Mrs. Mills, she was like a second mom to me. Towards the end of high school, the five of us were spending every weekend together. At the Mills' or just running around town."

"What happened to them? To their mom and dad?" The car fell deathly quiet, and I realized I had touched on a sore subject. "I'm sorry, I shouldn't have asked—"

Maria interrupted me. "It's okay, *mija*. It's just not our story to tell. Their mom… she was taken too soon. And their dad died shortly after. Doctor said heart attack. Broken heart, I think."

"I miss them. We all do."

I glanced at Holly, surprised by her rare show of emotion.

The rest of the ride was short, but quiet. Even the radio was kept low. When we pulled up in front of Maria's, she and I exited the car after hugging Holly goodbye. Holly drove off quickly while Maria tried to squeeze the life out of me. I felt the need to apologize again. I hadn't realized I was opening old wounds, but Maria shook her head.

"You didn't know. And you should. Maybe one day they will tell you more. But, right now, let's not let it ruin the day. Okay? For the record, I'm so glad you set that bike on fire, girl. If you wouldn't, mine and Holly's dynamic duo would never have become a…" She grasped for the right words.

"Tremendous trio?" I offered with a smile.

She laughed and hugged me harder. "Yes, exactly. Goodnight, *mija*. Drive safe."

I watched her until she was safely inside. Diego had brought my bike out for me when we pulled up. I wasn't sure how, but this new life was becoming more than just a job to me. I didn't want to think about how hard it would be to let it go when it was time.

Once I somehow managed to get my bags secured to my bike, which was no easy task, I headed home.

Back at my apartment, I tossed my keys and helmet on the stand next to the door before kicking off my shoes. Running a hand through my hair to loosen it from the braid it had been in all day, I headed towards the kitchen in search of dinner. That pizza seemed forever ago, and I had the post-shopping munchies. Speaking of, I wondered where my things were.

I'd assumed they would be here by the time I got back. I found some ramen noodles in the cabinet and decided that my missing bags was an issue for full-belly me. While my noodles cooked, I changed into a pair of fuzzy shorts and an old tank top.

Hot cup of noodles in hand, I settled on my worn brown couch before flipping on the TV. I had just settled on my usual *Full House* reruns when there was a knock on the door. I paused, fork halfway to my mouth, and frowned. I'd literally just sat down, for Christ's sake! I briefly contemplated shanking whoever was at the door, casting a sad look at my abandoned dinner.

"This better be important 'cos you just interrupted some serious me time!" I hollered at the door before swinging it open, and then my jaw dropped. Mac was there, leaning against my door, and even more surprisingly, he was laughing at me.

"What are you doing here?"

"Sorry to interrupt your evening, Vixen." Those dark blue eyes roamed over me, taking in the old tank top that showed more than it covered, and the fuzzy shorts with rainbow paw-prints all over them. Said shorts barely covered my ass, and I fought the urge to yank them down.

I spluttered, trying to find a smart response, but then he said, "So red lace isn't your thing. Too bad."

I managed to string my thoughts together enough to say, "I prefer green. And lace isn't worth a damn if you don't have a man with good, rough hands to take it off you."

Holy shit. I was flirting with Maverick Mills. Oh, this was a bad idea. Bad, bad, bad. But my heart wasn't on the same page as my head, and seemed to be in complete control tonight.

My words made his blue eyes turn almost black, and he tilted his head as he ran his hands through his hair. I started chewing on my bottom lip, and he tracked the movement like he had that first night. Searching for anything to break the silence, I looked around, and that's when I noticed the absence of brightly colored bags.

"Wait, if you're here to drop off my stuff… then where is it?"

At that moment, the elevator dinged, and Dalton stepped off it. He was too busy cursing his brother and calling him every name under the sun to notice me at first. But when he dropped my bags to the floor, and some of the heavier ones landed with a light thud, I said, "Hey! Be gentle!"

He turned to me with a grin, and then there was another pair of blue eyes making my knees shake as they lingered on the curves of my body.

"Well, hello, Vixen. Gotta say, this might be better than lace."

I rolled my eyes but smiled. "Like I said, you'll never know."

Mac grunted. "Actually, what you said was that you weren't putting on lace unless you had someone to take it off of you."

Dalton's eyes darkened in a way similar to his brother's, and my breath hitched.

"That a challenge?"

I shook my head vehemently. "No. Nope. Absolutely not. This isn't happening." I stepped into the hallway and bent over to grab my things. "I have a bowl of ramen on the table getting cold, and DJ has probably cracked at least three good jokes by now."

I heard Dalton laugh, and Mac stepped towards me as I straightened up. He was close enough that my chest brushed his, and I wanted so badly to see what he would do if I leaned in and kissed him. How would he taste? Probably better than I could imagine, but I reminded myself I wasn't here to go galivanting with two blue-eyed bikers.

Dalton watched the two of us as his brother tucked a strand of red hair behind my ear. He cupped my jaw and gently brushed my cheek with his thumb. Then suddenly, he stepped back, and I felt his distance like a frigid breeze.

Friends, I reminded myself. Just friends. "Goodnight, Vixen. See you Monday."

Without waiting for his brother, he got on the elevator and left.

Dalton frowned at me, and I shivered. "What are you doing to us, baby girl?" he said, whispering so quietly I barely heard him.

I wasn't about to reply to that—not sure I could, even if I wanted to. Instead, I said, "I got you something while I was out with Maria and Holly today. If you'll come in real quick, I'll dig it out."

Without waiting for an answer, I walked through my apartment, past my cold noodles, to my closed bedroom door, and put everything down. Dalton followed me, quiet for once. I found the small book and handed it to him. He looked from me to it, then started thumbing through it.

"It made me think of you. You said you liked the classics. I'm not really a reader, so I'm not sure what counts as a classic, but I visited his house once, ages ago, and he was evidently a real good author. I figured deceased yet still famous equaled classic?" I realized I was rambling and quickly shut up.

He slipped the book into a pocket on the inside of his jacket, and then startled me by reaching for me. Taking me by the waist, he pulled me close and rested his chin on top of my head before planting a kiss there.

"Vixen, no one's gotten me a gift in a real long time. It's perfect. Thank you." I relaxed into his hold, wrapping my arms around his neck, and for a moment, we just stood there. He pressed one final kiss to my head and then let me go. "I'd better get going. Eat your dinner, get some sleep." He smiled at me, and then was gone—leaving me wondering just exactly how this whole thing was going to turn out.

I didn't know how to stop wanting this. But I also didn't know how to live with it if I ever took the jump. If I let myself fall—if I let myself believe I was a part of the Saints—I wasn't sure I'd find my way back. Every hug, every laugh, every moment was sweet nectar that I knew was poison. And yet, I kept drinking it.

But five little girls were still missing. Maybe even more now, given how long I'd been gone. And here I was, playing house and flirting with men I could never consider an option. I glanced at my noodles, my appetite gone, and fought the urge to throw one of my bags at the TV when the canned laughter from *Full House* filled the room.

# Chapter 8

I spent the next few weeks trying to convince myself that I didn't care about the Mills brothers, and failing miserably. I even tried avoiding them, but that was incredibly hard to do when we were all working in the same building. I confessed my struggle to Maria and Holly, modifying my story so it seemed like it was the thought of sleeping with my bosses that left a bad taste in my mouth. Holly was no help, suggesting I sleep with them both to get it out of my system. She also said that if that didn't work, she knew of at least two good places to hide bodies. Maria was better equipped—she gave me a hug, a box of chocolates, and a bottle of wine.

"*Mija*, sometimes when the *cerebro* and the *corazón* are not on the same page, you need to go somewhere quiet and listen to what they are both saying."

She had no idea just how out of sync they were, though, and my bottom lip quivered, so she just hugged me harder. My stupid, treacherous heart. I guess part of me thought that maybe if I refused to choose between Mac and Dalton, maybe I could trick myself into not caring for either of them.

I received a letter from Uncle Tommy the day after Mac and Dalton stopped by my apartment. Braxton must have seen them, or been told about their visit. His letter cautioned me to keep my head on straight in "such a big city" and to "stay away" from things that could hurt a "sweet girl" like me. I didn't need a decryption key to figure out that he was warning me to remember why I was here, and not to get sidetracked, especially by two ridiculously handsome biker brothers.

I don't know what it was about them that had my heart racing like a middle school girl at her first dance. Dalton, I could kind of understand. The quiet way he would sit in an armchair, reading one of his books, lost in another world. Or maybe it was the way the other guys would come to him for advice, or the way he whistled while he worked on the bikes that came into the shop. I knew he had done bad things. He'd killed people, beaten them. He was suspected of coordinating a robbery that cost a local businessman nearly $1.3 million. But literally nothing I had seen had him looking like the bad guy he had been painted to be.

Mac, on the other hand, was a bigger mystery. I had seen him knock a guy out in one blow for sleeping around on his girl. Which, from the outside, wouldn't seem to be any of Mac's business. But he had these rules which made me wonder if he was as big and bad as he seemed. Like, that first morning when he had pinned me to a wall, holding me so hard I had bruised—the tender way he held my wrist afterwards, and the look on his face when he told me he didn't hurt women. I had watched him run the club his own way when Greyson wasn't around. He wasn't an easy person to report to if you were a Saint, but he was always fair. He had their loyalty simply because they knew that, if their backs were against the wall, Mac would be there no matter what. While Greyson ruled with fear, Mac was just… different.

One day, as I was cleaning up dinner, Dalton came up behind me as everyone left. I told myself that, just this once, we could have some fun. A little fun never hurt anyone, right? When he rested his hand on the small of my back, I grabbed a handful of sudsy bubbles before whipping around and dropping them on his blond head. For a second, he looked stunned and ridiculous. I started laughing, and he smiled at me before joining in. Quick as a flash, he grabbed me by the waist and held me firm before scooping a massive pile of bubbles out of the sink and plopping them on my head. He spun me around as I playfully fought against his hold.

"What the hell are you two doing?"

Mac came in from the side door and frowned at us like we were naughty children. So, I did the only logical thing I could think of—I jumped out of Dalton's arms and grabbed the hose attachment on the sink. Mac had about two seconds to comprehend what I was fixing to do. He raised his hands like he could fend off the spray. A pointless maneuver. With a wink, I doused him completely, and he just stood there, dripping wet. His brother and I looked at each other, then back at him—dead silence. Then Dalton started roaring with laughter.

"She got you damn good. About time someone pulled one over you."

He was still laughing when, in two long strides, Mac was next to me and grabbed the hose.

Dalton's eyes widened. "Now wait a damn minute..." he said as he backed up, but his brother had already squeezed the nozzle.

This time, I started laughing hysterically at the sight of them. Hair dripping wet, shirts clinging to their bodies in a way any woman would appreciate. It was like an impromptu wet t-shirt contest. Dalton eyed me, and the two brothers shared a look. I realized, too late, that they had silently joined forces and bolted for the nearest door. As I rounded the island, Dalton swooped in and grabbed me again. Much like the night we first met, he lifted me off the ground and carried me back to his brother. Mac stood by the sink, nozzle in hand. Dalton held me tight, and I squealed as Mac absolutely doused me in water. When he finally turned it off, I was wet from head to toe.

When I shivered, it was more from the way Mac looked at me than the temperature. My wet shirt clung to my body like a second skin, highlighting every curve. Dalton held me to his chest, my back pressed against him, and I couldn't resist leaning into him. I don't know what had gotten into me. Maybe I was getting a bit too comfortable being Nicky? I was going to settle on blaming the whiskey I'd had with dinner.

But the sheer strength of the man holding me took my breath away; I could feel it in the hard planes of his body. He ran his hands down my sides, following every curve until they landed on my hips and squeezed. I bit my lip and looked back at him over my shoulder, still blaming the whiskey for the fire I could feel in my core.

I knew he wanted me just as badly as I wanted him. I could feel it. When I looked back at his brother, Mac's eyes had darkened—something I had come to learn meant he was allowing himself to give in, just a bit, to the way he felt for me. He had put the nozzle back in the sink at some point and was leaning against the counter, watching us. It was the whiskey, I told myself, as I rubbed against Dalton, who made a deep, groaning sound in the back of his throat. Mac licked his lips, his eyes never leaving mine as Dalton's hands gripped my hips in a vise, pulling me as close to him as possible. His head dipped to nip my ear, and I couldn't hold back my moan.

Just the whiskey…

Suddenly, the door to the motel rooms swung open, and Milo, one of the Saints, came in. I jumped away from Dalton like I had been electrocuted. Whiskey or no whiskey, the spell was broken. Milo looked like a kid who had been caught with his hand in the cookie jar, and he averted his gaze to look at anything besides the three soaking-wet adults he had just walked in on.

"Hey, boss, I was looking for you, but it's really not that important now that I think about it." He finally got up the courage to look up at said boss, and when his eyes met Mac's, he went deathly pale. Mac was practically staring holes into the poor man's soul.

"I'm gonna go,." I said, before bolting out of the door as quickly as my feet could carry me. I was fixing to freeze my ass off on the ride home, but that was hardly the first thing on my list of problems. What the fuck had I been thinking? This wasn't me. It couldn't be me.

"Vixen, no. Come on, just wait a minute," Dalton protested as I headed for my bike, but I didn't stop.

He followed me into the garage, and I glanced over my shoulder. Milo and Mac had followed as well. *Keep going. Stop looking back.* As I grabbed my helmet and keys from by the door, I heard Dalton lay into poor Milo.

"You idiot, you sure know how to ruin a good thing, don't you?"

I spun my tires, gravel flying, as I pulled out of the parking lot.

When I got back into my apartment, I slammed the door behind me and threw myself down on my couch. I screamed into a pillow and cursed my lot in life. I was a cop, a good cop. I was here to do a job. Who's to say those two would even spare the real me a glance? I was such an idiot. What did I expect—that I could just have a casual fling, leave, and never look back? I wasn't that kind of girl. What was I going to do? No amount of whiskey could explain away the way I felt tonight. I wanted to talk to someone so badly, bare my soul until it stopped hurting so much. But as I lay there, clinging to a pillow, I felt a tear slide down my cheek, and I realized that it wasn't my soul that was ripping in two.

It was my heart.

For the next three days, I hid at home—like a coward. I ignored every text and call from Mac and Dalton. I pleaded with Holly and Maria to leave me alone. But, like any good friends, that just wasn't something they could do. On day four, they showed up at my door around noon with several pints of ice cream, and two bottles of wine. I hadn't showered, had barely slept, and I vaguely recalled the handful of Cheerios I had snacked on at some point last night.

"Oh *mija*, look at you, you poor thing," Maria said, as Holly added, "Damn girl, you look like shit."

I must have given them a pitiful look because, in a flurry of movement, they both rushed in and guided me to the couch. Maria sat down with me while Holly went towards the kitchen.

"We heard what happened between you, Dalton, and Mac."

"And we've heard that you haven't been answering their calls. Mac is going insane—he's been biting everyone's heads off. Dalton looks like… well, he looks even worse than you."

This morsel of information came from Holly, who had come back from the kitchen with a couple of wine glasses.

Maria shook her head. "Jackson and Diego somehow convinced them to stay put and let us come to you. So, here we are. We should've come sooner. What is going on? Those two… they have walls. I should know. They don't let just anyone in. After everything they've been through… this is killing them."

I looked between these two women, both of whom cared for me deeply in their own way. I felt the moment my own walls crumbled, and I started sobbing. Without a word, they enveloped me in a hug, one on each side of me. They didn't push me to talk. Didn't do anything other than hold me as I cried like a baby. Every doubt. Every fear. Every uncertainty since I had started this assignment was finally let loose—like a dam bursting open, giving in to the pressure at its cracks.

I couldn't tell them what was going on in my head. I couldn't ask if they thought I was failing those little girls. I couldn't ask them if I was betraying who I was. I couldn't tell them the turmoil my heart was in, and why. But I could cry. I could let myself feel. So, I did.

For the next several hours, we sat on that couch until the pain started to fade. They told me stories between bites of pizza that had been delivered shortly after their arrival, and spoons of half-melted ice cream. Holly told me about her messed-up childhood, how Jackson healed a part of her that had been broken for so long, she had forgotten what it felt like to be whole. Maria reminisced about growing up with Diego, and how long it took both of them to finally admit their feelings for each other.

We laughed, cried, and drank more wine until the sun set in the sky.

When they finally said goodbye, I felt about ten pounds lighter. After one last group hug by the door, they headed towards the elevator as I stood in the doorway watching them leave.

Maria turned to me before they got on. "Whatever it is, it'll be okay. We're here for you, *chica*."

I smiled at her and hoped she was right.

As I was getting ready for bed, I texted Mac and Dalton: "I'm okay, it's okay. I just needed time. I'll see you tomorrow." Then I silenced my phone and went to sleep.

The next day, I pulled into the clubhouse parking lot around 7:30. I was determined to make a big breakfast, having missed the last four days of work. But when I walked into the kitchen, Dalton was waiting for me. Before I could speak, he covered the ground between us and wrapped his arms around me.

"Baby girl, don't ever ghost me like that again. I'm sorry. I'm so sorry. I didn't mean to spook you or upset you—whatever I did, tell me, and I'll never do it again."

I stepped back and gently grabbed his face between my hands. "Dalton," I said, trying to calm him. "Dalton, stop. You didn't do anything." His blue eyes were damn near frantic. This wasn't the kind of fear that came from a bruised ego or romantic fallout—this was something deeper. More painful. Darker.

I had been told his dad had died of a heart attack. Or a broken heart, right after their mother died. After doing a little digging on my part, I learned that it had been Dalton who found his father in the garage, his body cold. It had been Dalton who had tried to support his brother through the abrupt change in leadership and, months later, after a supply run had gone bad, it had been Dalton who had woken up from injuries of his own to find his brother in a coma.

In one way or another, people kept leaving him. It had broken a part of him. The sudden understand came crashing down on me and, in a second, I understood. I had been a cop long enough to recognize a trauma response.

He shook his head, dismissing my words and dislodging my hands. His breath came rapidly, and I realized he was about two seconds away from a panic attack. I stepped towards him and wrapped my arms around him. Holding him like he held me. I stood on my tiptoes and tucked my head into his neck, wishing he wasn't so damn tall.

"It's okay. I'm fine. *We're* fine. Just breathe. I'm here now."

Slowly but surely, I felt the tension leave his body, and he embraced me again. We stood there for a minute, and he rested his chin on the top of my head.

Finally, he took a step back, and I looked up at him. He pressed a kiss to my forehead and gave me a sad smile. "I'll let you get to work, Vixen. I need to talk to Mac."

With that, he headed towards the motel rooms. I also knew a retreat when I saw one. I wanted to stop him, realizing I wasn't the only fucked-up one reeling from this mess.

After the door closed behind him, I got to work making breakfast. I settled on one of my favorites—homemade quiche. Shelly used to make it for me whenever we had camped out at each other's places, working a case or celebrating a closed one. She made one with bacon, ham, spinach, tomatoes, cheese, and onion. I swear I could eat the whole thing. And I could use a little piece of home right now. With three of those in the oven, I added eggs to the growing list of groceries. I went to the store twice a month, and it was getting close to time. A few of the guys had been adding things they wanted on there, too, in my absence.

I sipped at my coffee and went through the cabinets. I wondered if I could ask Mac for a chest freezer. A local butcher sold whole cows, and while I didn't mind grocery-store meat, it had nothing on something straight from the source.

Maria and Holly had helped me create a text group with almost all of the guys on it, so I checked on the quiche and sent out, "Breakfast will be done in about ten. If you want anything else from the store, get it on the list by the end of the day."

My text was met with a flurry of smiley faces and thumbs-up emojis.

They started pouring into the dining room as I was pulling the quiches out of the oven to cool. Two of the guys, Rodney and Clint, came up behind me, and I turned to them. Rodney surprised me with a hug, and Clint, one of the older bikers, pressed a kiss on my cheek. Clint was kind of like the grandpa of the group; a lot of the guys called him Pops.

"What was that for?" I asked with a smile.

Rodney shrugged and shoved his hands in his pockets. "We were all kind of worried about you."

Clint leaned over the stove, sniffing at breakfast, and said, "You can't just disappear like that, sweetheart. Mac and Dalton were ornery bastards these past few days, and it wasn't just your cooking that they missed…"

I shooed him away from the stove. "Oh, it was just Mac and Dalton that missed me then?" I teased.

Clint grunted and wagged a finger at me. "You gave us all quite the scare. You're a part of the family now."

Before I could respond, he and Rodney both rejoined their friends at the table. I cut the quiche up and started making plates. There was some leftover fruit salad in the fridge that was a day shy of turning, so I grabbed that and served it next to the quiche.

"Alright, everyone, come grab a plate."

I stepped back and made room for the throng of hungry people. I smiled a little as I watched them, realizing I had missed this more than I cared to admit. Dalton came through the door, and when our eyes met, I grinned at him. He winked at me, and that simple gesture let me know everything was alright. There was no sign of Mac, though. I kept an eye on the door, waiting for him, but Dalton came up beside me.

"He's not coming, Vixen." I frowned, then glanced at the door again, and he rubbed my back. "Just give him time."

I nodded, and stepped forward to grab two plates. I handed one to him and took the other to the side. Grabbing a pen and a Sharpie, I wrapped the plate in Saran wrap, then wrote "Mac's" on it before sticking it in the fridge.

After breakfast, I rinsed off the dishes and handed them to Dalton, who put them in the dishwasher. He came up behind me, kissed me on the neck, and said, "I've gotta get going, Vixen. Got something I need to do."

I leaned into him and said, "You got my head all twisted around, you know that?"

He wrapped an arm around my waist. "The feeling's mutual, but we'll talk later, okay? I'll see you tomorrow." He pressed another kiss to the spot he seemed to favor, and I hummed my pleasure. I had pushed all my doubts firmly to the back of my mind. For now.

I gathered my cleaning bucket and headed towards the rooms. I had a single earbud in, listening to music yet trying to stay alert. When I heard the door open behind me, I turned, worried Silas had come back from wherever he disappeared to all the time. Instead, it was Mac leaning against the doorframe. The way he was looking at me made me feel about ten inches tall.

"Mac, hi. Is everything okay?"

I watched as he clenched his jaw so hard I thought it was bound to break.

He took a step toward me, and I took a step back.

"Mac?"

He still didn't say a word—just stepped into the small room with me, then turned and locked the door behind him.

"Okay, you're freaking me out. What are you doing?"

"Four fucking days." He took a step towards me with each word. "You just vanished for four fucking days. And you ask me if everything is okay?"

He wasn't shouting; his voice was so low and deadly calm that I didn't dare take my eyes off him. I thought back to Dalton's reaction when he had first seen me. This was also a trauma response, just one on an entirely different end of the spectrum.

I did my best to keep my voice smooth and gentle. "Mac, please, let me explain. I was scared, okay?"

He laughed, but it was a sound completely devoid of humor. "*You* were scared? And how exactly did you think I felt, how Dalton felt? The only fucking reason we didn't come after you is because your girlfriends stopped us. But, please. Tell me how scared you were."

I'd never seen him like this. This raw. This wasn't just anger—it was grief, twisted into fury. The only way he knew how to be. I remembered a little of what Maria had told me—losing his mother, then his dad, before being expected to jump into leadership like Superman. No time for grief. No time for pain. Mac hadn't been allowed to fall apart. The club needed him. He'd been barely twenty, and they expected so much from him. And when he finally did break—when someone put a pipe to his skull and left him in a coma—he woke up to find Silas wearing the crown. Ever since, Mac had clung to control like it was armor. Armor that protected his brother. His club. Himself. But lately… he had started to let his control slip. Started to let me in. And I had run away. I had burned his trust like it didn't cost him everything to give it in the first place.

I shook my head. "Mac, please. Don't be like this." I reached for him, but he grabbed my wrist and yanked me towards him. I fell against his chest and said, "Jesus, Mac, I thought you said you didn't hurt women. What the fuck was that?"

He made an angry sound and grabbed my jaw. He tilted my head back until I was looking into a pair of the stormiest blue eyes I had ever seen.

"Vixen, I'm not trying to hurt you. But you damn sure keep hurting me."

"That's stupid—I haven't done a thing to you!" I protested, and he stared down at me.

"Not all wounds can be seen."

I blinked at him and whispered, "Mac, I never meant to hurt you. I just needed space."

He traced my jawline with his thumb, then rubbed circles on my cheek. "Four days, Vixen. You were killing me for four days."

I leaned into his touch and then stiffened in surprise when he leaned in and kissed me.

He tasted like mint and smoke, and I found myself relaxing into him. He kissed me slowly, like he was savoring the feel of my lips on his. I tucked my hands into the back pocket of his jeans, and pulled him closer to me. When he groaned, I shivered, and he wrapped his hands in my hair. He bit my lip gently, and I opened to him as he deepened the kiss. He groaned again and then pulled away.

"You're gonna be the death of me, Vixen."

I kissed him once more, just a whisper of a touch, relishing the feel of his five o'clock shadow.

"I don't want to be," I said quietly, and rested my forehead against his chest. But I already was, or would be. However, in that moment—standing in his arms—I found myself not caring so much. As selfish as that made me.

His phone started to ring, and he pulled it out of his jacket, still holding me to his side with his other arm. "Mills." A few seconds later, he rolled his eyes. "Yes, sir, I'll get it done." He ground his jaw again, and I kissed the tense muscles there.

"Greyson?" I asked.

He nodded. "Fucker is coming back to town."

As much as I hated to do it, I pressed gently for any information I could get. "Where does he run off to all the time?"

He sighed. "Our supplier. Bunch of scumbags I wouldn't share a fucking urinal with. But he thinks… well, honestly, I don't know what he's thinking. He's an idiot."

"An idiot who is somehow your boss. How did that happen, Mac?"

He looked down at me and pulled me into him. "Another time, Vixen. I'll see you at dinner—Greyson needs me to take care of something, and I won't make it to lunch."

He kissed me goodbye, and I watched him go, trying to ignore the voice of reason screaming in the back of my mind.

# Chapter 9

Over the next couple of weeks, Dalton showered me with affection. The usual morning coffee he greeted me with was now accompanied by a kiss. Mac was a bit more reserved, finding me in the quiet hours when I was alone. He interrupted my cleaning frequently, stealing kisses in darkened rooms. I was damn near giddy with happiness, even if at night that same happiness was the thing that kept me from sleeping. Maria and Holly teased me relentlessly, but I learned to roll with it.

One morning, as I walked to my bike to head to work, Dalton surprised me at the door of my apartment building. He held an empty saddlebag aloft, and I gave him a questioning look. He tossed the bag to me. "Pack for a weekend, Vixen. We're going on a trip, no work for you. Meet me by the bikes."

He winked at me before turning to leave, and I hollered at his retreating back, "Wait, what am I packing for?" He smiled at me over his shoulder but, of course, didn't bother answering me.

Back in my apartment, I grabbed some spare clothes and shoved them in the bag. I hesitated before also tossing in some lingerie Holly had made me buy the last time we went shopping. Switching out of my Vans, I slipped on my boots and a heavier jacket better suited for the road. I texted Maria and Holly in our group chat, letting them know I would be gone for the next couple of days with Dalton. Holly replied with a winking emoji and an eggplant next to a donut. I blushed crimson but laughed at her antics. Maria sent, "Don't do anything I wouldn't do."

I grabbed the loaded saddlebag and slung it over my shoulders before heading back down to meet Dalton.

Dalton whistled as I walked toward him, and I rolled my eyes. "You saw me literally not even twenty minutes ago." He grabbed my hips and pulled me into him. I was still holding my helmet and bag, but I wrapped my free arm around his neck. He kissed me deeply, and I ran my hand through the hair on the back of his head. When he pushed the kiss further, I opened for him eagerly and moaned.

He sighed into my mouth and pulled away. "We better get going, Vixen, otherwise I may just take you right back up to your place."

I leaned into him, nipped at his ear, and whispered, "I might just let you." I heard him swear as I sashayed over to my bike. "Where are we going, by the way?" I asked as I secured the saddlebag to the back of my Triumph.

He just smiled before swinging his leg over and starting a Roadster I hadn't seen before.

"Whose bike is that?"

He gave the throttle a little gas, and the engine purred. "I've got more than one bike, babe. But I only got the one girl." He gave me a cheesy grin.

I laughed. "Oh yeah? She know you're here?"

Shrugging, he said, "Probably. Not much gets by her; she's pretty damn smart. Now, please shut that beautiful mouth and follow me."

I gave him a mock salute and followed his bike out of the lot.

We drove for an hour before stopping to get a bite to eat. The waitress at the diner flirted openly with Dalton. I shot daggers at her until he switched seats to one next to me, and wrapped an arm around my shoulders. She turned bright red and stomped away with a huff. He kissed me on the cheek and whispered, "I kinda like you jealous." He paid, and when we got back to our bikes, I kissed him like a woman starved. Someone hollered at us to get a room, and we broke apart laughing.

We drove for another hour, the air getting cooler and cleaner the longer we rode. We were riding along Lake Sinclair when he turned onto a gravel road. My mind was racing with questions, wondering where we were when he stopped in front of a beautiful cabin right on the edge of the water. It was shielded by cedar and oak trees, had massive bay windows along the side, and a long path that led down to where the water lapped gently at the shore. It was absolutely stunning.

Dalton parked his bike under a carport, and I pulled in beside him. "Where are we?"

With an arm around my waist, he led me to the front door. "Welcome to the Mills cabin, Vixen. This has been in my family long as I can remember. Mac and I made some updates when we got it." He unlocked the door and swung it open, gently pushing me inside. I turned full circle, taking in the sweeping staircase, the deer antler chandelier, and the warm golden wood around us. "What do you think?"

I turned to him, smiling so big it hurt my cheeks. "Can I see the kitchen?"

He laughed. "Yeah, baby, you can see the kitchen. You can go wherever you want. Come on."

He led me down a hallway with a large sitting room off one side. Opening up a Dutch door, he stepped back to let me in. The kitchen was just as stunning as the rest of the house, and I ran my hand along the grey marble countertops with gold inlay. Over the sink was a huge window overlooking the lake, and the dining room had a large sliding glass door that opened onto a patio.

I turned to Dalton who was watching me carefully, waiting for my reaction. When he smiled at me tentatively, I ran to him and jumped into his arms. He caught me easily and said, "So you like it?"

I kissed him. "Baby, I love it. It's absolutely perfect. It's all ours for the weekend?"

He carried me over to the counter and sat me down, running his hands down my thighs and squeezing my calves. "Just you and me, Vixen."

A little voice in the back of my head told me this wasn't a good idea, but I shoved it away. Just for the weekend, I told myself, and my heart was all too eager to accept what my brain knew was a lie.

Dalton went to grab the bags from our bikes while I roamed the lower half of the house. Each room was just as stunning as the next. The sun sparkled off the lake as it sank lower in the sky, filling the house with a beautiful evening light. I stepped outside and walked down the path to the dock that bobbed peacefully in the water. Before I could think better of it, I took my boots and socks off, then rolled up my pant legs and dangled my legs off the dock. The water was soothing, and the peaceful silence was utter bliss.

I sat there, face tilted towards the sky as I basked in the warmth of the evening. I didn't even hear Dalton come outside until he stepped on the dock and it wobbled under his weight. I smiled at him over my shoulder, and he sat next to me. Leaning into him, I said, "I don't think I've seen a place so perfect." He made a general sound of agreement, and we sat there together until the sun touched the horizon.

Eventually he stood up, pulling me up with him. "Come on, I'll make us dinner." I gave him a look, and he pushed me playfully. "Yes, Vixen, I can cook." He grabbed my boots, and I followed him inside.

I sat on one of the barstools at the kitchen island, watching him while he made our dinner, sipping the whiskey and Coke he had made me, and laughing at the stories he told me. I wasn't prepared when he asked me about my childhood. I knew Nicky's backstory, but I didn't want to tell him that one. I wanted him to know the real me—Katie. Not some made-up cover story. I decided that a little truth wouldn't hurt, and I blended my story with Nicky's as best I could. The closer we became, the more lying to him hurt like a knife twisting in my chest.

He didn't notice my inner turmoil as I told him about growing up in South Carolina, weaving my elaborate story like a con artist. I was beyond grateful for the change in subject when he carried two plates to the patio, leaving me to grab drinks. We didn't say much as we ate—I was watching the sunset as I savored one of the best rib eyes in my life.

When I looked back at him, he was watching me closely, and I smiled nervously. "What?"

But he just grinned back and reached for my hand. We sat there until the moon rose in the sky, and I shivered—at which point, he insisted we go inside.

"Come on, Vixen, let me show you your room."

I followed him up the stairs, realizing he hadn't intended on us sleeping together in one room. I didn't say anything about it, not wanting to come off as needy or worse, but I was surprised. The room he showed me was easily half the size of my apartment, with a massive en suite bathroom.

He pulled me to him before I went in. "I'll be in the office, just down the hall. Third door on the left. Go ahead and get settled in. Should have everything you need." He squeezed my waist, but I stopped him when he stepped back, standing on tiptoes to press my lips to his.

The kiss was burning hot and excruciatingly slow. I nipped gently at his lower lip, running my tongue over the spot, until I felt him smile against me. He wedged a knee between my legs, and I rubbed against him, relishing the delicious friction. I tousled the hair at the base of his neck between my fingers, pulling him closer to me in a way that made him moan. Hands on my hips, dragging me closer, until there wasn't an inch between us. Like we couldn't get close enough. When I finally pulled away, I was panting a little, and his eyes were hooded. I smiled softly before reaching for my door and watched him walk away, enjoying the view—and hungry for what was to come.

The bed was ridiculous, and I was instantly in love. I plopped down on the cloud-like mattress and lay there for a minute, my mind racing. Taking the DiAngelos down was still important to me, but the Mills brothers were… unexpected. Even more surprising were my feelings for them, and I wasn't quite sure what to do with them. I had tried staying away, but my body responded to them in a way that was completely foreign to me. It was like an addiction.

In short, the whole situation was fucked.

I groaned and dragged myself up, deciding to check out the rest of the room, specifically the bathroom. I all but jumped for joy when I saw the tub big enough to fit a small family in, and the jets lining the sides of it. My apartment had a tub that barely came up to my knees when I was standing, and I wasn't entirely sure a ten-year-old could stretch out fully in it. This tub was heaven, and I needed a slice immediately. I went back to my bags, pulling out some pajamas. I found the bathroom cabinets fully stocked with everything a girl could need.

Turning on the tub, I filled it with some delicious-smelling lavender vanilla bath salts and soap. As the tub filled up with bubbles, the whole bathroom started smelling like a bakery. I stripped eagerly, pressed the button for the jets, and slid into the hot water with a groan. At first, the burn was almost too much, but once my body adjusted, I could practically feel every sore muscle and knot easing itself out. I decided that if I were to die right in this moment, I would do so in total bliss.

I sat there, enjoying my bath, until the water started to cool. A fuzzy robe and a pair of house slippers were neatly stored in the same cabinet I had found my bath things in. Slipping those over my PJs, I grabbed my phone and took a picture of the bathroom and bedroom. Sending both to the girls, I also texted Uncle Tommy to let him know where I was—I didn't say with whom, even though I bet he already knew. I tossed my phone on the bed, determined to ignore it, lest I receive an unwelcome response from Braxton.

When I found the office, the room was dark except for a couple of lamps. Dalton sat in an armchair, under one of the lamps, reading. I leaned against a nearby bookcase, smiling at the sight of him. He was a big man for the chair, but he looked completely at ease. His heavy boots were propped up on a footrest, and his black leather jacket was draped across the back of the chair.

I wasn't even sure he had heard me come in, but then he said, "Like what you see, baby girl?" My smile grew wider, and he looked up at me with a grin of his own. "Come here."

My smile became seductive as I walked towards him.

He kicked the footrest to the side and watched me saunter to him. When I was within grabbing distance, he dropped his book to the floor with a thud and pulled me until I stood between his legs, looking down at him. His eyes never left mine as he untied the robe until it fell open, revealing my shirt that ended at my belly button, and the shorts that didn't even cover my ass. They were the same shorts I had been wearing when he and Mac had come to my apartment, and I had packed them deliberately, remembering the hungry way he had looked at me in them.

Before I could think better of it, I straddled his lap and leaned in to nuzzle his neck, loving the smell of him. The expensive, sweet-smelling oil he used on his bikes, combined with the scent of warm leather and musk, wrapped up in one delicious package. His hands roamed my body freely, and I shivered under his touch. I sat up, arching into him as his hands found my breasts under my shirt and tugged at my sensitive nipples. I could feel him under me, his hardness pressing into my core, and I groaned, "Dalton," as I rubbed against him. He pressed his face into my chest, biting me through my shirt, and I moaned. I felt his cock twitch in response.

"Baby girl, the things I want to do to you… What I would give to feel that pretty pussy squeeze my cock as you come."

I moaned again as his words filled me with a heat unlike anything I had felt before.

Suddenly, he stood, picking me up and carrying me to the nearby desk. He laid me gently on it and then kissed me. I opened for him eagerly, completely lost to the lust that filled my body. When he leaned back, I could see the same feelings reflected back in those bright blue eyes.

"Vixen, baby, if we do this, you're mine, and I am yours. There's no going back, so be sure you want this."

I felt the briefest flicker of doubt, a small voice in the back of my mind wondering if he would feel the same if he knew the truth about me. But selfishly, I didn't care at that moment. All I knew was how badly I wanted this man.

"Let me hear you say it, gorgeous. I need you to say it."

His hand traveled down my stomach until he found the mound between my thighs, and he pressed there. His blue eyes searched mine, a heat in them, as he rubbed me through my shorts, and I couldn't help but buck at the sensation.

"Dalton, baby, please… for the love of God, yes, please."

His smile was nothing like the carefree one I usually saw. This one was all sex and sin and full of promise.

"I've been waiting for the day I would finally get to hear you beg for me,

Vixen."

He pulled off my shorts, and the second he lowered his face between my legs, I saw stars. Hands braced on my thighs, the man ate me out like I was a five-star feast, and he was starving. He kept me pinned on the table, tongue swiping through my folds. He gently dragged his teeth over my clit, then blew cold air over the warm wetness. I bucked again, and I felt his rumble of pleasure in my core.

I wasn't sure how long I lay on that desk, how many times he licked and sucked and nibbled every inch of the sensitive skin between my thighs. When I came, I screamed his name and ground mercilessly against his face, one hand wrapped in his hair. His tongue circled my clit one last time before he put two fingers inside of me and stood up, leaning in to kiss me. I could taste myself on his lips, and he watched me as he worked me with his fingers. I swear I could feel the calluses on his hands, as he rubbed the heel of his palm against my clit and slid another finger into me.

When my eyes closed as a second orgasm built, he used his other hand to grab my throat. "Look at me, Vixen. Look at me when you come."

I was helpless to do anything but obey and screamed his name like a confession dragged from my lips.

Somehow, he managed to wrangle a third orgasm out of me, and by that point, my bath was rendered obsolete. I was covered in a fine sheen of sweat, and he hadn't even put his cock in me, though I had all but begged for it. When I was not much more than a trembling mess, he picked me up and carried me back to the chair. I was sore, in a completely delicious way. I curled up in his lap, resting my head under his chin. He grabbed his jacket and used it as a makeshift blanket.

At some point, I must have fallen asleep because the next thing I knew, I was waking up in my bed. I was snuggled under the covers, the moon lighting up the room just enough to see my bags on the dresser and my phone on my nightstand.

I reached for it, noting the missed call from Uncle Tommy and the messages from Maria and Holly. It was almost four a.m. I lay there, hoping to go back to sleep, but I couldn't despite the immensely comfy bed. I crawled from underneath the sheets and rolled my neck before padding into the hallway. I wasn't quite sure which room was Dalton's, but I was determined to find it. The first door I opened looked like a cleaning closet with linens and various supplies. The second and third doors led to sparsely decorated bedrooms. The fourth, a small bathroom. I grumbled, sleepy and growing irritated.

But the fifth door yielded something more interesting.

The curtain was drawn over the window, but the dim light from the hallway enabled me to see enough. I glanced around before going in. Navy blue bedding covered a neatly made bed as big as mine. The furniture was a rich oak, and the carpet under my feet was plush. I walked over to the dresser and picked up one of the photographs on it. I realized this must be Mac's room, and I looked over the picture of two young boys holding each other and laughing. The familiar mess of blond hair next to the equally familiar black hair, slicked back even then.

I put the picture down with the rest of them. A smiling older woman, I assumed was their mother. A sunset over the dock I had been sitting on last night. A group of bikes outside the familiar clubhouse. Part of me wanted to look around, but a bigger part just wanted to go back to sleep. So, with one last look around, I quietly shut the door and went to the one next to it. This room was decorated in a forest green, but had a sleeping figure in the bed.

As quiet as I could, unsure if I would be welcome, I slipped under the sheets and lay next to Dalton. I hardly dared to breathe, though I longed to touch him. Suddenly, he rolled towards me and, in one smooth motion, pulled me into him. I twisted until my back was flush with his chest, and he held me tight.

"You're not as sneaky as you think, Vixen."

I whispered back, "I wasn't sure you would want me here."

He pressed a kiss against my bare shoulder, where my top had slipped down. "Baby girl, you are always welcome in my bed. Now, go to sleep. You'll need your energy for tomorrow."

I was asleep before I even registered his words.

When I woke up again, the sunlight was fighting its way through the thick curtains, and a nearby clock told me it was just past nine. Dalton was still asleep—he had rolled over onto his back at some point—and I smiled when I realized the comforter was tented to a rather impressive height over his groin. Deciding I was already in it this far, I used every ounce of stealth in my body to slide deeper under the sheets. He groaned like he was waking up when I pulled down his shorts, but a quick peek told me he was still asleep. His cock was fully erect, the veins in it making my pussy practically weep. I was dying to know how he felt inside of me, but first, I wanted to give him a little bit of the pleasure he had given me in the office.

He twitched when I slid my lips over him, and I relaxed my throat as much as I could until I reached his base. Mouth wrapped around him, I licked him from the tip down, and began to suck like I was trying to drag his soul out. His hips bucked, and this time, when he groaned, he said, "Damnit, Vixen, holy fuck…"

I smiled around him and didn't hold back—taking him into my mouth like I wanted to wreck him with the same hunger he stirred in me. He flipped the covers back and fisted his hand in my hair. I peered up at him through my lashes and dragged my teeth gently up the shaft before licking the precum off the tip, and sucking him back down to the base.

"Just like that, baby girl, let me see those pretty lips work."

I loved it when his pretty boy persona slipped—the man who gave me orders in bed was a man used to being in charge. To having his orders obeyed. I moaned, knowing he would feel the vibration, and wrapped my hand around the base of his cock as I bobbed my head up and down with zeal.

He came with a shout, shooting down my throat, and I nearly choked. The grip he had on my head was almost painful as he held me where he wanted me, and I fucking loved it. When he was done, he leaned up and grabbed my waist, pulling me onto him. He flipped us both until I was underneath him, and kissed me with a hunger that I readily responded to. He pressed his knee between my thighs, and I ground against it, desperate for release from the pressure building inside my core. I reached for him and found him already hard again—wrapping my hand around him, I tried to guide his cock towards my entrance.

He stopped me, grabbing my wrist and pinning me to the sheets. "You better be sure about this, baby girl."

I bucked impatiently against him, and he smirked at me. "Damnit, Dalton… I'm sure."

That was all he needed to hear. With one hard thrust, he was seated deep inside me, and I shouted with pleasure. He wasn't gentle, or slow. No, he fit himself inside me like he had already decided it was home. He didn't just fuck me. He worshipped my body. Hand around my throat for more control. Nibbling sensitive skin. Pinching my breasts. Thumbing my clit as he pounded into me. Pulling my hair and whispering things in my ear.

Over the next couple of hours, I lost count of how many times he made me come. Until then, I had considered myself a lucky girl to finish more than once. But Dalton introduced me to positions I had never even thought of. It was hot. It was rough. It was dirty. And I loved everything about it.

Afterward, we lay there in each other's arms. He had gotten a warm washcloth and cleaned me up, something no one had ever done before. I was blissfully spent and very glad to be on the pill. His seed had spilled out onto my thighs. It hadn't bothered me—I trusted him to be clean, and he had felt the same. As he ran the damp cloth across my thighs, I felt him hesitate. That's when I realized… *Shit.* There were just some things you couldn't cover up.

Like a fucking bullet wound.

He traced the spot just above my pelvic bone. Shelly and I had busted a drug dealer who had been lacing his goods with fentanyl. When we cornered him, he got off a couple shots. I still remember the sudden, burning pain before I hit the ground. Shelly fired two rounds into his chest, then ran to my side. It wasn't a mortal wound, but it hurt like hell.

My heart raced, trying to explain away the scar.

"That's a bullet wound, Vixen." He lifted his head to meet my eyes, and I swallowed.

"Yes."

He raised an eyebrow, and I looked away.

"Who was shooting at you, baby girl?"

"Just the wrong place, wrong time. I'm sorry. It's a bad memory. Can we talk about something else?"

He looked at me for a second, and I prayed he wouldn't see through the lie. Then he kissed the slightly raised mark, finished cleaning my legs, and lay next to me. I thanked my lucky stars he believed me.

And cursed every one of them for having to lie to a man who deserved the truth.

One evening after dinner, I decided to go for a swim in the lake. To my delight, Dalton had packed me a swimsuit and I changed eagerly before diving into the cool waters. I swam for a bit, before flipping onto my back and floating.  I could hear the crickets and feel the breeze as it caressed my exposed belly. For the first time in days—hell, maybe weeks—I wasn't thinking about reports or missing girls or what name I was supposed to answer to.

I was just… here.

Movement out of the corner of my eye had me glancing over at the dock, and I found Dalton watching me, his arms crossed and a soft, small smile on his face.

"You gonna stand there like a creeper or are you going to join?"

He tilted his head at me. "Depends. I kind of like just watching you."

Slowly, my eyes never leaving his, I reached up around my neck and untied my top. I pulled it off and held it in the air. Like waving a red flag at a bull. "Just watching, huh?"

His grin widened. Slow, wicked. I slipped under the surface and swam closer to the dock. When I came up for air, I was much closer, and he was crouching by the edge. With a sharp look in his eyes and his elbows on his knees, he looked like a predator. Ready to leap.

I reached under the surface, wiggled out of the bottoms, and with a flick of my wrist, tossed them onto the dock. They landed with a wet slap at his feet.

"Oops," I said, blinking up at him innocently.

"You're gonna kill me, Vixen."

"Better men have tried," I said, treading water.

"True," he said, his voice suddenly quiet. "But none of them were you."

I froze. Just for a second. Because somewhere underneath the teasing, I heard it—the truth. The pain. I ducked back beneath the water, my heart hammering, and when I came up again, he was gone from the edge. A second later, I heard the splash behind me. I didn't turn around. I just smiled and let him come to me. A moment later, strong arms wrapped around my waist from behind. He pulled me gently against him, bare skin sliding against mine beneath the surface, his lips brushing the curve of my shoulder.

"You really know how to test a man's self-control," he murmured, voice low and rough in my ear.

"Pretty sure we left self-control back at the cabin," I whispered, tilting my head so he could kiss the line of my throat. He chuckled softly, and I felt the rumble of it against my back. His hands wandered—slowly, reverently— down my arms, over my hips, across the small of my back. Touches that weren't rushed or greedy, just… intentional. Like he was memorizing the feel of me. I turned in his arms, wrapping my legs around his waist as our lips met. The kiss was slow, deep, hungry in the way quiet moments always are—the kind that doesn't need an audience or a bed, just breath and water and want.

He held me like I was something precious, our bodies weightless in the lake, but tethered to each other by the ache that had been building between us for weeks. He shifted us, swimming toward the dock with me still wrapped around him. The water lapped against us as he carried me, the sun casting fire across the ripples. When we reached the dock, he lifted me like I weighed nothing and set me gently on the warm wood, then pulled himself up beside me. The air kissed our wet skin as we fell together, tangled limbs, beating hearts, slick and shimmering under the golden sky.

He hovered over me, brushing damp strands of hair from my face, his expression open in a way I hadn't seen before.

"I don't think I've ever wanted someone the way I want you."

I reached up, touched his cheek, and let my thumb trace the curve of his lips. "I tried fighting it, you know. You did, too. Let's make the giving in, the wait, worth it."

The rest of the world faded. The trees, the lake, the danger waiting back in town. For a while, there was only the heat of his skin, the soft press of lips on mine, the sunset wrapping us in gold. This wasn't the rough, burning passion that had consumed us inside the cabin. The water had washed away the fear. The hesitation. The lies.

He made love to me like I was his goddess, and he was my priest.

When the stars took the sky and we finally went inside, we curled up in front of the fireplace, bare and warm and *real.*

We didn't talk.

We didn't need to.

On Sunday, before we left, we were standing on the pier again. I sat between his legs, leaning against his back. He whispered in my ear, "I'm damn glad I met you. This is the happiest I've been in a long, long time, Vixen."

I thought about those words over and over as we rode home, and I discovered what it felt like to feel your heart burst and break at the same time. Would he forgive me when he found out the truth?

# Chapter 10

Dalton walked me to the door of my apartment on Sunday night. We lingered there, neither of us eager to end the magic of the weekend.

"Thank you for this weekend, Dalton. I'll never forget it."

No matter what happened—even when I returned to Charleston, even when they would come to hate me—I would cherish these moments.

The stabbing sadness in my heart must have been evident on my face because his brow furrowed. "We'll do it again, Vixen. I promise. Whenever you want, just say the word."

I smiled at him, and he cupped my cheek. If only that were the reason for the hurt, if only he could make it go away so easily. He kissed me softly, and I couldn't help but lean into his touch. I had become truly addicted to the taste of him.

I jumped about ten feet in the air when my door swung violently open, and he moved in front of me protectively. But it was just Holly and Maria, whooping like a couple of children.

"It's about damn time, really. I was starting to wonder if you were ever gonna make a move. Slacker," Holly said, shoulder-bumped Dalton.

He protested, "She sets bikes on fire. I wasn't about to make another unwanted pass at the pretty, crazy lady."

I feigned innocence. "Hey, I'm right here, you know!"

He winked at me, and Maria stepped into the hallway, a glass of wine in one hand, and with the other, shooed him towards the elevator. "Go on, move it. I need some tea to go with this Chardonnay."

He shook his head and, with one final kiss, headed for the elevator. I sighed when he disappeared from sight, and Holly pulled me into my apartment. "Girl, you are pistol-whipped!"

I took the glass of wine she offered as she sipped on her own. "Y'all, now isn't really the time for a powwow. I'm tired! Plus, it's almost seven at night!"

Maria curled up on my couch while Holly claimed the single armchair. Patting the empty seat next to her, Maria smiled at me. "*Hermana*, I done ordered us a couple of pizzas. Do you know how long it's been since we've had some in-house romance? You will not deprive me of this."

I groaned. "Pizza?"

My resolve began to crumble, and Holly's keen eyes zoned in like a bird of prey. "Pizza… supreme, add pineapple, stuffed crust." She wiggled her fingers at me, and I plopped dramatically on the couch next to Maria, almost spilling my wine. They had ordered my favorite, the extortionists.

"I hope it gets here soon."

Maria squealed and leaned towards me. "Girl, spill. Where have you even been?"

I held up my hands. "Hold up, if I spill, you guys gotta do the same." I still had a job to do—I had to remember that. Part of me was feeling like I had a lot to make up for after the events of the weekend.

Holly raised an eyebrow. "What do you want to know?"

"Everything. Why isn't Mac in charge? Where does Greyson run off to? Who the Saints are, who they want to be. I want to know everything about…"

I hesitated, and Maria placed an encouraging hand on my knee. "Tell us, *hermana*."

I looked up at her, fighting the tears that suddenly came to my eyes. "I want to know everything about the men I think I may be falling for," I whispered.

Maria placed her glass on the coffee table, and threw her arms around me. "It's overdue. We'll tell you everything we know—since those boys are taking their sweet time about it."

Holly crossed her legs, settling further into the armchair. "And that's a lot of shit too. Good thing we ordered two pizzas."

I grabbed the afghan off the back of the couch, and wrapped myself in it. I truly did want to know more about Dalton and Mac. After the weekend, I knew my feelings for Dalton went way past friends with benefits. As for Mac, I really thought there could be something there. However, I wasn't completely honest about my reasons for wanting this information. And embarking on this latest betrayal against the two women I had grown to love like sisters made me feel like absolute trash—the lowest of the low.

"So what do you want to know first?"

"Mm, I dunno. Maybe why Mac isn't in charge when he clearly should be? Greyson is an ass, he's never there, yet he wears the pres patch?"

Holly and Maria exchanged a glance before Maria said, "Girl, now that's a story. See, Mac and Dalton's old man was the president. Which should've made Mac next in line. But remember when we said their mom passed away? Afterwards, their dad just… checked out, you know? He stayed home. Barely ate, drank himself stupid. It wasn't Hannah's time. She was the glue that held everyone together. She didn't take crap from anyone, and her boys adored her."

I hadn't read much about their mom, and curiosity got the better of me. "How did she die?"

Holly looked down, but not before I saw the tear slide down her cheek. "It was two years ago. Jackson and I had just moved in together. She was shopping for a housewarming gift—for me of all people—and someone gunned her down. We never did find out who." She took a deep, shuddering breath. "She didn't deserve that. I mean, no one does, but certainly not Hannah. I'm sure I've said it before, but she was like a mom to me."

My heart broke for the two men who had their mother stolen from them, and broke even more when I realized they might as well have lost two parents that day from what I'd heard.

"Wait, so Greyson just stepped in after she died?"

Maria shook her head. "Not quite. Like I said, their dad wasn't able to move on. So, Mac stepped in for a time. Greyson was just a member of the Saints at that point. No one really liked him, but we all tolerated him 'cos he and Mr. Mills grew up together. One day, Mac took him and a few other Saints on a supply run. Diego and Jackson were there. Next thing I know, I'm getting a call from the hospital. There had been a gunfight. I had never been so scared in my life. I was pregnant with Diego Jr. at the time. When I got to the hospital, the place was swarming with cops. Jackson was in surgery but doing okay, and I found Diego pacing outside Mac's room with his arm in a sling. Mac was in a coma, and they weren't sure when—or if—he would wake up."

The thought of Mac hurt made it harder to breathe than I cared to admit. To hide the tremor in my hand, I took a sip of wine.

Just then, the doorbell rang, and Holly got up to get our pizzas. Maria was quiet, seemingly lost in her memories, but when Holly got back we all grabbed a slice, forgoing plates. After a few moments, she continued.

"Greyson was there, too. He had taken a bullet to the shoulder, and another went through his side. But, somehow, he made all the cops and questions just *poof.*" She mimed that last word with her hands, and took a sip of wine. "Next thing we knew, he was giving orders while Mac was in that coma. The Saints… well, let's just say I begged Diego to leave after a few months under Greyson's charge. He started messing around with this one guy, Alexander DiAngelo. I met the guy once—an absolute douche, and he scared the shit out of me."

"But Mac woke up, what, about six months ago, right? Why didn't he take the reins back?" That was another piece of the puzzle that the file I had been given didn't cover.

Holly grabbed another piece of pizza and said, "Trust me, we would all like to know."

Maria was quiet again, and I glanced at her. She seemed determined to look anywhere but at me or Holly all of a sudden.

Holly noticed, too. "You know, don't you? You know why. Figures— you've been mixed in with this group a lot longer than I have."

Maria shook her head vehemently and bit her lip. "I'm really not supposed to say."

Holly threw a piece of crust at her head. "Girl, we're your bestie! Isn't that right, Nicky?"

I made a general sound of agreement around a mouthful of food.

Maria sighed. "Fine. But you didn't hear this from me. I only know 'cos Diego is shit with secrets when he's had tequila."

Holly winked and said, "Pinky promise," holding up her pinky finger. I followed suit.

"Well, supposedly, Dalton was there that night, too. I mean, wherever Mac went, Dalton followed. Greyson evidently pulled Mac out of the line of fire when he got hit, and saved Dalton too. They owe him a life debt. So, Greyson cashed in. Mac and Dalton could basically do whatever they wanted, as long as it didn't interfere with Greyson's business with the DiAngelo family. And he got to keep the pres patch."

Holly said, "That's some low, dirty shit. I *knew* I didn't like that fucker. I'll just add it to my list of reasons."

I chewed the inside of my cheek, head spinning with everything I had learned. It made sense. I wondered how much it must kill Mac and Dalton inside. The club they grew up in, the club their dad ran, handed over to a slimebag of a man all because he was in the right place at the right time...

"That's a lot of shit for a girl to process."

Holly held up the empty wine bottle. "More wine?"

I checked the time on my phone, and was surprised to see we had been talking for almost two hours. "I'm tired, y'all, it's been a long weekend. Without much sleep." I winked at my friends, who groaned.

Maria said, "Now wait a damn minute, I spilled all the tea, but you didn't even give us a drop."

I all but dragged them to the door, but couldn't not give them anything in return. "Dalton took me to their cabin out by Lake Sinclair. The man is... very talented with his hands, tongue, and other appendages. We swam in the lake, went to the bedroom, ate some food, went to the bedroom, he demolished me in a game of Scrabble, then we went to the bedroom. You get the drift."

Maria and Holly groaned again, but I insisted I needed sleep. God's honest truth, I was exhausted. I hugged them both goodbye, but as I went to shut the door, Holly stopped me.

"Okay, just one question. Was it always the bedroom or did you 'see' other areas of the house?" She used air quotations and swayed her hips suggestively. Maria laughed, and I couldn't help but smile as I felt a blush creep up my neck. A blush that Holly, of course, noticed.

"You dirty dog, you."

I rolled my eyes and shoved her out the door, but I couldn't keep the smile off my face. I watched them until they were in the elevator and Maria shouted, "Love you!" as the doors closed.

Little things like that had me realizing I was going to be picking pieces of my heart off the floor for the rest of my life.

The next morning, I pulled into the clubhouse, my Triumph sputtering to a stop. I had barely gotten her started this morning, and she had acted funny the whole way here. I looked around before settling on Bobby, one of the guys who usually lingered around the garage tinkering on something or another.

"Hey, can you do me a favor?"

He got up from the couch as I approached, untangling himself from some girl.

"What's up, Nicky?"

I tossed him my keys, which he caught easily. "Something's wrong with my baby. Can you check it out for me? Please?"

He grinned, showing off a missing bottom tooth. "Are you kidding? I've been wanting to get my hands on that bike since the day you first pulled in."

I thanked him, warning him to be gentle with her, before heading into the kitchen to start breakfast.

A few of the guys were hanging out by the coffee pot, and they greeted me with nods and hellos. Rodney was there, and poured me a cup which I happily took. Part of me wondered where Dalton was, since he was usually my morning caffeine supplier. I settled on something easy for breakfast, pulling out some biscuits I'd made and frozen. With those in the oven, I got to work on some sausage gravy. As I was cooking, my phone rang.

"This is Nicky."

"Vixen, I need you to come upstairs."

"Mac?"

"Upstairs. There are three doors. Knock on the one at the end of the hall. Now." Then the grump hung up on me.

Wow, he was in a great mood. I grumbled and then turned to Rodney who was still lingering by the coffee pot. "Here, you can finish this."

His eyes widened. "I can't cook!"

I pulled up a recipe for sausage gravy on my phone and then texted it to him. "There. You can read, right? You got this, big guy. Mac wants me."

He gaped at me, and I patted him on the back reassuringly as I left. Glancing over my shoulder as I opened the door, I found him scrolling on his phone with his brow furrowed as he mouthed what I assumed were the directions I had sent him.

I made my way down the hall, towards the stairs I had been told to never go up. The short hallway at the top was dark, except for a light coming from under the closed door at the end of the hall. Hesitantly, I knocked on it. It swung open with force, and I yelped in surprise when I was pulled inside. Mac had me by the wrist as he slammed the door shut, then he pushed me up against the wall. Pinning my hands above my head with one hand, he grabbed my chin in the other and kissed me like it was the only thing that could keep him alive. It was demanding, and rough. His lips exerted an almost bruising pressure on mine, but my body responded almost before my mind could catch up with what was happening.

He wedged his knee between my legs, pushing my thighs apart and rubbing me through my jeans. Kissing down my jawline, then to my neck, he growled, and I was unable to stifle my moan. One big hand moved to my breast, pushing up my shirt. He grabbed my nipple, twisting it painfully. I whimpered, but he soothed the hurt when he wrapped his mouth around it. He sucked and nibbled on my breast until I was panting. Suddenly he stepped back, leaving me a weak-kneed mess, grabbing at the wall for support. His eyes were wild, and he ran a hand through his hair. He started to pace the small room, and I took a wobbly step towards him.

"Mac, talk to me. What's going on?"

He didn't answer me but sat down on a bed. I looked around the room for the first time, realizing I was in a more lived-in version of the motel rooms below us. The furniture was nicer, and there were a couple pictures on the wall. Slowly, like I was approaching a bear, I moved to the bed and sat next to him.

"Not that I'm complaining, but… what was that, Mac?"

He laughed mirthlessly. "You were with my brother all weekend, Vixen."

I blinked at him. I wasn't exactly a vanilla girl. Threesomes weren't a novelty to me, and I wasn't really the exclusive type. In the whole host of problems I was dealing with, it hadn't even occurred to me that I might come between the two brothers. I felt incredibly stupid.

They didn't exactly seem like the vanilla kind either, so I was trying to figure out where he was coming from. "Have you guys ever, um, shared a girl before?"

He rolled his eyes at me. "This is different."

"So, you have?" He gave me a hard side-eye, then a gruff nod. "Right… so what's the issue?"

He startled me again when he stood up like a bottle rocket taking off. I had no idea how the guy moved so fast, and so smoothly. He was like a tiger or something. He walked over to the window. "Like I said, this is different."

I tossed my hands up in frustration. "Yeah, you said, but you keep leaving out the *how* part."

He turned back to me and, in two huge strides, he was on top of me again. He pushed me back into the bed where I fell with a huff. Then he was leaning over me, an arm on either side. A part of me realized this the first time I had seen him without his jacket on, and I ached to trace the black swirls of ink that went up his arms and around his neck and chest. Preferably with my tongue. He must have seen the look in my eyes, and his darkened in response.

His next words brought me back to earth with a shock.

"How many times did my brother make you come, Vixen? How many times did that pussy shudder around his cock? How many times did you scream his name?"

His filthy words left me speechless, and for a moment, I just stared at him with my mouth open. Then it hit me. "Oh for fuck's sake, you're jealous. Aren't you?" He glared at me, and I knew I had my answer.

We stared at each other for a minute, until I decided I'd had enough of being pinned. I wrapped my legs around his waist, and used his weight to flip us. It wasn't easy, but thank you Academy training—though I doubted very much my instructor had this particular situation in mind when he taught us this move.

Mac stared up at me in shock, but I ignored the look. "You have nothing to be jealous of." His look of shock morphed into one of disbelief. So I said fuck it, and upped the ante. Placing my hands on his chest, I rolled my hips on his groin, and almost immediately, I felt him harden underneath me. He grabbed my hips, stilling me, so I leaned down and nibbled on his ear. I licked the swirl of black ink there, and couldn't help smiling in satisfaction when I heard him groan.

"Vixen, sit up." His voice was all gruff command, and it sent shivers down my spine as I complied.

He was still hard as a rock, but I just sat there, staring into his eyes. While his brothers' were the color of the sea as it crashed into shore, Mac's were the color you would find closer to the sea floor. So dark, so full of secrets. His thumbs started rubbing a bruising pattern on my thigh. I was starting to realize I really liked the kind of pain this man put me in.

"Mac, I'm not choosing between you and your brother. I just can't. Maybe that makes me greedy, but it is what it is. But, for as long as you want me, you've got me."

He frowned. "That's what I'm afraid of, Vixen. What if I never stop wanting you?"

I opened my mouth to reply, when a screeching alarm sounded throughout the whole building. That's when I realized I smelled smoke.

"Oh fuck me!" I shouted as I jumped off Mac and ran out the door, down the stairs.

Mac was hot on my heels as I yanked the door to the kitchen open to see

Rodney running around with a pan that was literally on fire. He looked completely panicked, and waved the pan around, which only succeeded in dumping the flaming contents on the floor. A few of his buddies stood at the table, more than a couple of them laughing.

Mac grabbed the fire extinguisher off the wall and put out the flames, then fixed the laughing Saints with a hard glare that quickly shut them up. I marched over to Rodney and snatched the pan out of his hand. I hadn't realized he was wearing an oven mitt and cried out in pain when my hand met the hot metal, dropping it to the floor. I swore viciously, turning to the sink and running my red palm under the cold water.

"Rodney, what in the actual fuck, dude? It was gravy. Never in my life have I ever heard of someone setting gravy on fire. Like, how?" I fixed him with a withering look, keeping my hand under the faucet.

Rodney looked like a kicked puppy. "I told you I couldn't cook," he muttered.

I sighed as Mac walked over to me. The look he gave Rodney probably could've started another fire. I hissed when Mac gently rubbed my hand—it wasn't a bad burn, but it fucking hurt.

Just then, Dalton and Clint walked in. Clint propped open the door, hollering for a couple of the guys in the garage, telling them it was all hands on deck to clean up the mess. Dalton's eyes met mine as his brother cradled my burnt hand.

"Well shit, Vixen. You didn't have to start another fire to get my attention."

I frowned at him. "This one isn't on me, thank you very much."

He grabbed a first aid kit from under the sink and sat at the table. I went to sit next to him, but Mac sat in my chair and dragged me onto his knee. I sat there, keenly aware of the other guys in the room watching me sit on their boss's lap while the boss's brother spread burn cream on my hand.

Dalton wrapped my hand in a clean, white bandage. "Alright, baby girl. Don't get that wet."

I smiled like a love-drunk teenager at him, and he gave me a funny look. "What?"

I shrugged, leaning back into Mac's chest.

"I dunno, I just figured you wouldn't call me that as much when we weren't alone."

I felt Mac's chest vibrate as he grumbled, and I smacked him in the thigh without turning to look at him. I was having none of that jealous shit. I had enough problems as it was.

Dalton smirked at his brother, and then looked at me. "You're mine. Well, ours. I think we've made that pretty clear, Vixen."

For the rest of the day, I didn't leave Mac's room other than to make lunch and, later, dinner. The upstairs area was evidently where Mac and Dalton lived, having sold their family home after their dad passed. They kept the cabin, but everything else… Too many memories, I guessed.

They pretty much left me to it, coming in to check on me now and then but refusing to let me clean despite my insistence that my hand was fine. Mac dropped me off at home that night because my bike evidently needed more work than I thought.

If it weren't for the haze of happiness I was in, I probably would've noticed the figure in the dark corner of my apartment before locking the door behind me.

# Chapter 11

I headed toward the kitchen, craving something sweet to chase the leftover adrenaline from the day. But something made me stop. The hair on the back of my neck stood up, and a chill went down my spine. I glanced around my apartment. Nothing. But the darkness weighed on me.

Frowning, I went over by the stove where a pan I had cleaned this morning sat. I made a show of looking in the cabinet for snacks. I hadn't seen anything, but every cell in my body knew something wasn't right. A cop's instincts were what kept them alive. I trusted mine, and right now? Red flags. Which is why I was almost prepared for the figure that came lunging out of the shadows.

Almost. But not quite.

I grabbed the pan. A swing and a miss as the figure went low, tackling me to the ground. I hit my shoulder hard and used my bad hand to brace myself. "Fuck!" I hissed as the pain from my burned palm shot up my arm. But I didn't have time to dwell.

He was on me in a second, hands closing around my throat like a vise. My vision blurred at the edges as I thrashed, groping blindly for the pan I'd dropped. There. I grabbed it, swinging it as hard as I could and knocking him in the head. He fell to the side with a curse.

*That voice. I knew that voice.*

I scrambled to my feet and, hurrying over to the light switches on the wall of the kitchen, I flipped every one of those suckers on. My apartment lit up like Las Vegas. My eyes adjusted to the light, and immediately I recognized my attacker.

Daniel was blinking hard, trying to force his eyes to acclimate to the sudden onslaught of light. I had left my phone on the coffee table, where I had first tossed it when I came inside. I cursed myself for not paying attention, for being so slack. I had let my guard down. I just hoped it wouldn't get me killed.

Turning, I ran to the living room, but Daniel's dumb ass was a lot quicker than I gave him credit for. He grabbed me by my ponytail and yanked as hard as he could. I cried out, stumbling but managing to keep my footing. We circled each other.

"Surprised to see me?"

"Surprised that you're this fucking stupid," I snarled. "Would've thought you had learned your lesson when I set your damn Harley on fire."

"Fuck you, bitch. You ruined my fucking life. What the fuck am I supposed to do now? No bike, no leather. I was *this* close to becoming a Saint, this fucking close and you ruined everything!"

"Maybe you should learn to listen, then. You did it to yourself."

He lunged for me, and I darted to the side. I was still lightheaded from him choking me, and my reflexes weren't as good as they'd been a few months ago. I had a rigorous workout routine as a cop—one I hadn't thought to keep up, and now regretted.

When he pulled out a knife from under his jacket, I eyed it warily as he brandished it at me.

"I'm going to make you wish you had said yes, bitch. We could've had some fun. But, now I'm going to make you beg."

I glared at him. "You fucking wish."

This time, when he lunged, I wasn't quick enough. A trail of blood bloomed across my stomach as the long blade sliced through my thin top. The cut was deep, and it burned like hell. I tried again to make my way to my coffee table, to my phone, but he kept blocking me. I knew under my couch, I had stashed a knife of my own. I had to get there. I grabbed a decorative box off a nearby shelf—it wasn't much, but it was heavy. Wistfully, I thought of the 9mm I carried when I had my badge.

He darted forward again, leaning low like last time, and I sidestepped, bringing the box corner down with all the force I could muster onto his back. It broke apart with a resounding crack, and I cursed the stupid, useless thing. But it did the trick.

"Fucking cunt!" he hollered.

I remembered then that Braxton had told me they had ensured the apartments nearest to me were kept empty. Something about safety, and them being good for surveillance. I thought about how closely he watched me, and I prayed someone was watching now.

My blood was soaking my shirt, making me dizzy. I stumbled, and Daniel smiled. *Remember your training. Go low.* Lunging for his knees, I managed to knock us both to the ground. Hoping I stunned him, I crawled desperately for the couch. Fuck, I was so close. I felt him grab my ankle and yank me back towards him. I screamed, in rage and in pain, kicking him in the face. A sickening crunch. His nose instantly spurted blood, but he recovered quickly. I didn't withdraw my leg quick enough, and his face was twisted with a sick kind of joy when he stabbed me in the thigh.

I had been shot before. Punched in the face. Knocked around. I was a cop—I could take a certain amount of abuse. But everyone had their limit, and I was quickly reaching mine. He pinned me to the ground, digging his knee into the wound on my leg, and I couldn't help the strangled cry that tore from my throat. His nose was definitely broken, and I took a little bit of solace in that. And, from the looks of where my pan had caught him, he would be sporting a black eye tomorrow, too. But at this point, I was more concerned about making sure I saw tomorrow at all.

I thought of Shelly—what I would give for some backup now.

Once again, I found myself underneath him with his hand wrapped around my throat. His knife toyed with the buttons on my shirt and I clawed at his face, getting in a few good swipes before he pressed the blade to my throat.

"Stop fighting me, damnit."

I laughed drily. "As if."

My laughter just pissed him off more, and he drove the blade into my shoulder. Between the wound on my stomach, the wound on my leg, and now this… I had to do something, or I was going to die here.

He moved his legs to pin my arms down and cut my top open. A sadistic gleam was in his eye when he said, "What if I cut your heart out and left it for them to find?"

My eyes widened, and he grinned at me. I wasn't sure if by "them" he meant he knew who I really was, or if he meant Mac and Dalton. Either way, the thought terrified me. Oh, God—everything hurt like hell.

Using every ounce of training I had, every ounce of fight left in me, I pulled my arm out from under him. The sudden movement threw him off balance, giving me just enough time to grab the switchblade from under the couch.

It was a small blade, and I was quickly losing strength, but when he turned to me, I jammed it into his side as hard as I could. He roared and fell backwards, clutching at the handle protruding from under his ribs. I rolled, crying out from the pain that being on my stomach put on my injuries. I only had seconds. I grabbed my phone, which was thankfully on the edge of the table. I had barely hit the buttons for a redial when Daniel stomped over and kicked me as hard as he could. The phone went flying and I screamed in agony. He picked me up, dragging me to the couch.

He leaned down. "Now that you're a bit more relaxed, why don't you and I have some fun?"

I screamed again, and again, fighting with every ounce of fading strength I had.

Images flashed in my mind.

The precinct. Faded flooring and flickering fluorescents.

My old apartment, only marginally less dingy than this one.

Laughing at the dinner table with the people I had grown to care for.

The look in Mac's eyes when he would let his guard down.

Dalton's easy smile and the way he held me as we watched the sun rise.

I could hear Shelly singing off-tune to an old Shania Twain song.

Through all of that, I felt his hands on me. When he bit me, I didn't even flinch. He dragged the blade across my collarbone, the scratch offering up small beads of blood. I wanted to fight. Scream. Something.

But all I could do was give in to the black.

*

*Maverick*

I was almost back to the clubhouse when my phone rang. When I had dropped Vixen off at the door, she had kissed me goodbye. Confident, and sexy as sin, she had put those red lips on mine like she owned them. Little did she know she owned damn near every part of me. She consumed my thoughts. Her laugh, her smile, the sway in her hips when she walked. The way she commandeered the kitchen at meal time. She was a wildfire from the moment we met, and damn if I didn't relish the burn.

Like my thoughts had summoned her, it was her name on my screen. I answered after the third or fourth ring, determined to maintain the air of indifference I tried keeping up around her. I was sure she saw right through me—but can't blame a man for trying.

"What now, Vixen?" I frowned when that drawl of hers didn't immediately come through the other end. "Vixen?"

Silence.

I was fixing to hang up, thinking she had accidentally dialed me, when a sound straight from my nightmares shattered the evening around me. She was screaming. I could hear the fear and pain in her voice. I recognized the sound because I had heard it dragged from the mouths of more men than I could count. It wasn't something I was proud of, but I knew the sound of terror by heart. Hearing it from her? For the first time in a very long time, I felt weakened by fear. I could barely think past the all-consuming desperation to get to her.

I jerked the steering wheel as hard as I could, the truck leaving marks as I U-turned into oncoming traffic. It was late enough that the streets were almost empty, but a few horns blared at me all the same. I ignored them, desperate to catch any sound coming from that phone. I could only catch the occasional whimper, and the sound of another man's voice. I muted it so whoever it was couldn't hear me. Pressing the pedal to the floor and urging the big truck to go as fast as it could, I sent up a prayer to a god I wasn't sure I still believed in.

"Hold on, baby. Just hold on. I'm coming."

I grabbed my club phone and dialed the number from memory.

"Hey, big brother. I'm guessing since you're calling me, you didn't get lucky tonight. Gosh, you must be feeling left out—"

I snapped, "Shut the fuck up and listen. Someone's in Vixen's apartment. She was screaming. I turned around, but I don't know what I'm walking into." Dead silence, "Dalton?"

Then I heard the jangle of keys and the slamming of a door.

"I'm still here." Gone was the light and carefree tone most people were used to. This was the sound that many of our enemies heard right before they died. "I'll be there in ten. Jackson! Diego! With me. Now."

The call disconnected, and I threw it to the side.

My wheels jumped the curb as I turned back into her shitty apartment building. I knew Dalton would be there soon, but I wasn't waiting. I grabbed my gun from under the seat and ran inside. I didn't stop running as I checked the clip. The movements were familiar to me. Something I could do in my sleep. Forgoing the elevator, I took the stairs three at a time. When I stepped out onto her floor, I kept my steps light. Nothing to break the silence that clung to the stale air around me. I took the safety off as I ran to the woman who had somehow found her way into my heart.

When I got to the door, I strained to hear any sound. Unable to make anything out, I opened the door as quietly and as smoothly as I could. The door, thankfully, eased open without even a squeak. When I peered into the room, I saw fucking red. My vision tunneled. Daniel Hall stood in front of my Vixen, who was passed out on the couch. I took in the blood seeping from several wounds, and the bite marks on her breasts and neck. Fucking animal was unzipping his pants. I didn't even hesitate as I stormed into the tiny apartment.

Daniel turned to me, shock and horror on his face when he realized who was now in the room. Fucking fool. I closed the distance between him and me in seconds. My hand closed around his throat, and I tossed him against the wall like a rag doll. He fell there, the impact knocking him out. I didn't spare him another glance as I leaned over her limp body. She didn't stir. Nothing. Her chest rose and fell. Barely.

I heard Dalton in the hall hollering for me, and I yelled back, "It's clear! Get the fuck in here!"

I kneeled on the couch, holding her face between my hands. She had three stab wounds, and the couch was soaked red beneath her.

"Baby girl, I need you to wake up. Come on, Vixen, wake up." I grabbed a blanket off the couch and pressed it to her stomach. That son of a bitch had sliced her open. So much red. I couldn't breathe, couldn't think, couldn't see beyond the woman in front of me. "You're stronger than this. Let me see those beautiful brown eyes."

*Please. Please open your eyes.*

"Oh my fucking God, no," Dalton said as he ran into the apartment, barely glancing at the prone figure still by the wall. He felt for a pulse. "She's alive, but barely. We gotta go, Mac. Now."

I scooped her up in my arms as carefully and quickly as I could. She might as well have been a doll. Rodney, Jackson, and Diego stood in the hallway. Their eyes widened when they saw my Vixen.

Diego turned sheet white. "Holy fuck, this is gonna kill Maria."

Dalton glared at him. "This isn't gonna fucking kill anyone, except him." He pointed behind us at Daniel, who had begun to stir. "Take him to the shed. Make him comfortable."

The shed was where we took men when we wanted information out of them. My three best men knew exactly where it was, and what to do when they got Daniel there.

My truck was still idling in the parking lot, their bikes scattered by the door. I handed Nicky over to Dalton before climbing into the back seat of the Ford, turning to grab her back from him. The bleeding was slowing down, and I had seen enough men die from blood loss to know that wasn't a good thing. I cradled her in my arms, and Dalton jumped in the front. He peeled out into the streets, heading to the nearest hospital.

"How is she?" he asked, glancing in the rearview mirror, his eyes heavy with worry and fear. He looked so much like our mother, and the thought of her was like a bullet to the chest. I couldn't face burying another woman I loved. I couldn't fucking do it. I ran my hand down the side of my Vixen's face. She had been so vibrant just an hour ago. Now her pale skin stood out in stark contrast against the black leather of the seats.

"Not fucking good. She's lost a lot of blood."

I saw the muscles in his jaw clench as he focused on the road, bobbing in and out of the late-night traffic.

"Are those actual fucking bite marks?"

I just nodded, and he swore. In the distance, I could see the lights of the hospital. "Come on, gorgeous, hold on for me just a bit longer." I placed my fingers just under her chin, and my heart fucking bottomed out. "Dalton, I can't find a pulse. She's not breathing!"

*Not again. Please, not again.*

"No, no, no," I muttered, and minutes later Dalton skidded to a stop outside the ER entrance. He screamed for help and ran to help me get her out of the truck. I slid her along the seat as gently as I could, until Dalton was able to lift her in his arms. A few nurses ran out as he turned with her limp body, and I heard one of them yell, "Oh my God, someone page the trauma team and get me a gurney."

There was a rush of movement, and more staff running out of the hospital as pagers went wild. Dalton laid her on the gurney that was wheeled out, and we ran with them as they rushed her inside. The team swarming around her worked to get a pulse, and a couple of people forced me and Dalton out of the room.

"Clear!"

Her body jerked, and I fought to keep myself upright.

"Increase charge to 200. Clear!"

She jerked. We waited. My breath came ragged.

"I've got a pulse!"

Dalton's eyes were wild with rage, fear, and uncertainty. Being this helpless wasn't a feeling either of us were used to. It had only happened twice before. I ran my hands through my hair, pacing just outside of the room while also trying to stay out of everyone's way.

They padded her wounds, doing their best to staunch any further blood flow, and wheeled her out of the room and down the hallway.

I reached for her. "You fight, Vixen. Don't you dare leave me."

Dalton was on the other side, running alongside the gurney just as I was, his eyes never leaving her bruised and battered face. Another nurse grabbed my arm, pulling me away from her. Dalton shook off the nurse pulling him away, and looked frantically after the gurney that was quickly leaving our sight.

"Sir, you need to stay here. I'm sorry, but you need to let us work."

Sitting in that too-bright waiting room, I had never seen my brother look so damn lost—except when we lost our mother. Part of me itched to get my hands on the son of a bitch who caused this whole mess. I should've killed him when I had the chance. But another, bigger part of me ached so badly from not being at her side, that I thought I would die if I left the hospital. The woman made me irrational. I clung to the memory of her smile and the taste of her lips on mine like a drowning man.

"She'll pull through. Our girl's a fighter, Mac. And once we know what the fuck is going on, once she's in the clear, we are gonna make that fucker wish he had never been born."

I was silent but nodded my agreement. Dalton's voice was raspy from shouting, and I knew he needed the reassurance, but right now, that just wasn't something I could offer. His own words sounded like he was trying to convince himself more than me. I glanced over at him, my eyes landing on the small bite mark on his bicep. She had scarred him when she bit him, clamping down so hard it left a permanent mark.

Dalton's eyes followed mine, and a small smile lifted the corner of his mouth. "See, she's a fighter."

Just then, the doors opened and Jackson came in, Maria and Holly hot on his heels. Maria's face was tear-streaked and puffy from crying. Holly's face was damn near unreadable except for her eyes, which darted between Dalton and me, and then around the lobby in an absolute panic. She clung to Jackson's hand, and Maria threw herself at me.

"Diego stayed home with the babies. Jackson picked me up. What the fuck is happening, Maverick? Who did this? She's gonna be okay, right?"

Dalton stood and pulled Maria into his arms, rubbing a soothing pattern up and down her back. His eyes met mine over the top of her head, and I shook my head, at a loss for words.

A nurse hurried over from the desk. "Visiting hours were over at 8:30, everyone. You don't have to go home, but you can't stay here."

Dalton and Maria started protesting at once, and the poor nurse stepped back. Clearly, she wasn't prepared for the combined onslaught of a six-foot-tall biker and a small Latina mom. I didn't blame her. Holly was still glued to Jackson's side, and he had his arm protectively around her in a way that hurt me physically. When she stepped towards the nurse, the woman gave her a wary look. The poor lady was probably overworked, underpaid, and exhausted. I knew it all too well—my mom had been a nurse before she met my dad.

Holly silenced Maria with a hand on her friend's arm and Dalton with a look. She had become the picture of calm, taking control while the rest of us searched for a foothold.

"Listen, ma'am. We're not trying to be rude. But our friend was just brought in with a stab wound—"

"Three."

All eyes turned to me, and I cleared my throat awkwardly. "She was stabbed three times." I didn't mention all the tiny cuts—the wounds I felt as clearly as if they were my own.

Maria started crying again, and Holly's voice shook a little when she corrected herself, "Our friend was brought in with three stab wounds. We just want an update before leaving." The nurse hesitated, and Holly continued, pointing at me. "The pediatric wing at this hospital was named after his mother, and paid for by me. I don't like throwing our weight around, but damnit, just let us stay here until we know what happened. That girl…" her voice cracked again, "she means a lot to all of us."

Sometimes, it was easy to forget that Holly was rich, but I would be more than grateful if it had helped us gain a little favor.

The nurse looked between our small group, taking in our miserable expressions. Dalton was hunched over next to me like he could curl in on himself and make the pain stop. I guessed yelling at the nurse took the last little bit of fight out of him, and to be honest, I wasn't feeling like much of a hotshot myself.

Finally, the nurse sighed. "Okay, but you can't wait here. This area is for visitors, during the day. And for emergency room patients. The lobby on the main floor, next to the gift shop, is open all hours. You're welcome to wait there."

About three hours later, a doctor came down to find us and a few other Saints scattered around the lobby. We all stood when he approached, his face grim.

"I'm told that you folks would like an update on… I'm sorry. She didn't have ID on her. Are you family?"

Holly shook her head. "Her name is Nicky. And we're the only family she's got."

The doctor seemed to consider this and then said, "Alright, I'll do my best to explain everything—perhaps you would like to sit down?" When none of us moved, he pressed on. "Your friend suffered extensive trauma to her pectineus muscle," he said, pointing to a spot on his inner thigh, "and her deltoid." He indicated a place on his shoulder.

"Muscular damage such as this, while obviously not desirable, is reparable. The wound on her upper abdomen was our main cause for concern. We performed a CT scan which confirmed internal bleeding. The knife entered through the upper abdomen, just beneath the ribcage, penetrating her liver and gallbladder. The damage to her liver was extensive." He paused. "She went into cardiac arrest during surgery due to blood loss, but we were able to resuscitate her."

Maria ran over to a nearby trash can and threw up, and Holly was deathly pale. Dalton's breath came hard and fast, and I felt like I had been hit by a truck which had backed up and run me over again, just for good measure. Maria rejoined the group, looking green, and Holly embraced her. They stood there, clinging to each other for support.

Dalton finally broke the silence. "So, she's going to be okay?"

The doctor hesitated. "Unfortunately, that is up to her. She also had a partial shoulder subluxation, meaning her shoulder was just barely in her socket. A concussion, and then there's the bite wounds. We've done all we can for now. Her liver has been repaired, but we had to remove her gallbladder entirely. Her shoulder has been put back into place, and she is on medication as a precaution against brain bleeds and swelling, as well as to reduce any fever or infection. I wish I could tell you more."

After speaking with the doctor, Maria begged to see Nicky, but her pleas fell on deaf ears. A few people left after we had gotten the update, but several of us stayed. We looked like one sorry bunch. Jackson sat on a bench, and Holly curled beside him, resting her head on his lap. When he leaned down and whispered something in her ear, she turned her face until it was hidden from view, but her body shook with silent sobs.

Maria stepped away to call Diego, and I heard him tell her that his mother was on the way to watch the kids, and he would be there as soon as he could. Dalton and I sat in one of the many small and uncomfortable plastic chairs, and neither of us said a word.

Maria came over and sat next to me. "Diego is going to bring you a shirt. She'll be okay."

I hadn't even noticed the blood covering me. Her blood. I just nodded my thanks, but all I could think about was how I never had the guts to tell her how I felt.

<h1 style="text-align:center">Chapter 12</h1>

I woke to the sound of a very annoying beeping. The unfamiliar room was dark, and I looked around to get my bearings. Now that I was awake, my whole body ached, and I shuddered as I remembered why. Daniel, in my apartment. The glint of a knife. My blood, a shocking red against the grey carpet. My heart pounded in my chest, and the stupid beeping machine, which I assumed was a heart monitor of sorts, started beeping faster. I took a few calming breaths, but then I saw Mac and Dalton. The panic still hummed under my skin, but the sight of them… it quieted the noise, just for a second.

My boys.

Mac was asleep in a tiny chair by my shoulder, his arm stretched out on the bed with his hand inches from mine. His head lolled at an awkward angle. He must have fallen asleep while holding my hand, an unexpectedly sweet gesture. Dalton was in another chair, this one only slightly bigger, by my feet. His back was to me, and he faced the door like he was on guard duty. But he had his hand on my ankle, and from his vague outline, I could see that he was reading. The spine of the book was just about discernible from where I lay. My heart cracked open when I realized it was the Hemingway stories I'd bought him. I tried smiling again, but felt my lips crack.

"The world breaks everyone," I rasped, my voice little more than a breath, "and afterward, many are strong at the broken places." I wasn't even sure he could hear me. I hadn't understood everything I'd read, not really—but that line had buried itself in my chest and made a home there. I hadn't read it for me. I'd read it for him. Maybe I hadn't understood Hemingway. But I was starting to understand *him.*

Mac lurched to his feet, immediately adopting a defensive position, while he tried to figure out what had woken him. I laughed, or tried to. I sounded more like a cat hacking up a hairball, and I found out that laughing hurt like being stabbed all over again. Dalton came up beside me as Mac leaned over, his eyes desperately searching mine. I could see the fear and the worry in his dark blue eyes, and both he and his brother were sporting some serious under-eye bags.

Dalton smoothed my hair back from my face, and I leaned into his touch. "There's our girl. How are you feeling, Vixen?"

Mac pressed a button on the wall. "Someone should be here soon, baby."

I smiled at him. "Oh, so it's baby now? Careful, I might start thinking you care about me."

When neither he nor his brother laughed, I looked between the two of them. They looked about as bad as I felt. Rough stubble lined their jaws, their hair was a mess, and their clothes were rumpled.

I went to sit up and couldn't stop myself yelping as the wound across my stomach pulled tight. There was an excruciating throbbing across my abdomen as well, and it radiated from my side. Dalton immediately reached for me, a strong hand on my back. Mac grabbed my hand.

"Tell us what you need."

Oh my God, it hurt unlike anything I had felt before. It made me think of the first time I'd gotten shot. I panted. "Help me sit up, I can't stand lying down like this."

Mac sat on the bed next to me, pulling me into his chest and letting me use him for support, while Dalton gathered every pillow he could find and arranged them behind me. With a press of a button, he raised the back half of the bed until it was more chair-like.

Tears blurred my vision by the time I relaxed back into the pillows and I whimpered—despite their gentleness, every small bump just really fucking hurt. Mac scooted his giant frame further into the small bed, squeezing himself next to me. I pressed up against his side, and he put his arm around me when I buried my face in his shirt. Dalton was rubbing my back soothingly and I tried desperately to focus on anything but the agony racking my body. I didn't even bother looking up at the knock on the door.

A sweet, female voice said, "Well, good morning everyone. Isn't this a nice surprise?"

I wanted to tell her that I very much disagreed with her choice of words, but I didn't dare move. The throbbing was finally starting to subside, and I was afraid it would come back if I so much as looked at her. I heard her fiddle around with the machine around me, and then felt her mess with the IV in my hand.

"Alright, I've paged the doctor, and he should be here soon—but right now, I need to get some vitals." The room was dead silent, and I opened one eye to see her looking at Mac expectantly. "Sir, that means you need to move. Please."

He didn't, his arm still around my shoulders.

I sighed, wincing as I turned to her. I held my stomach like I could possibly keep a hold on the pain, but the pressure made the knife wound hurt as well.

"It's alright, I'm okay. Let the nice lady do her job."

Mac frowned at me, and I did my best to give him a reassuring smile. He grumbled as he went to go stand by his brother's side. The two of them stood at the side of the room in an identical stance—their arms crossed, their legs shoulder-width apart. My own personal guards. I winked at them, trying to get them to relax. No such luck.

"You have some good friends," the nurse said, giving me a friendly grin. She turned on a small overhead light, and opened my shirt to look at my stomach. There was a neat row of stitches that stretched from one side to the other, another small set on my shoulder and, judging from the itchiness in my leg, probably another set there.

I was Frankenstein's monster.

"Any itchiness, soreness, fevers, or chills?" I gave her an incredulous look and she patted my knee. "I meant around the suture sites, dear. Any soreness there specifically?" She had clearly been doing this a long time, reading me like a book.

"My leg itches like there's something crawling in my skin, and my stomach feels tight when I move, but other than that, nothing."

She nodded. "Good, that's to be expected. The itchiness is from your body trying to build new tissue, bridging the gap between one side to the other. That tightness is just proof that it's working away. Now, I'm sure you're wondering why it feels like someone scooped out your insides with a rusty spoon?"

"I have a few questions, actually."

"Absolutely. The doctor is on his way, and he'll be able to answer everything. Right now, I'm going to go find you a few extra pillows, and something to drink. Just water, for now, until you're cleared for other fluids. I'll be right back."

She shut the door gently behind her, and I looked at the two men who had never taken their eyes off me.

"It was bad, huh?"

Dalton suddenly found the ceiling tiles very interesting, blinking furiously and refusing to look back at me. Mac's voice, usually so calm and cool, was ragged as he said, "You died in my arms. Then again on the table. These past three days, watching you fight to live while I could do nothing but… sit here. Just fucking sitting here and praying to a god I barely believe in, hoping you would come back to me."

I stared at him. "Three days? I was out for three days?"

Before he could respond, the doctor came bustling into the room and flipped on the light, absolutely blinding me. The same nurse from earlier followed, putting a pitcher of water and some pillows on the counter.

"Alright, gentlemen, why don't you wait in the lobby while I have a talk with my patient?"

They both looked at the doctor, but didn't budge.

"It's okay," I reassured the doctor. "They can stay, I don't mind."

The doctor looked between the three of us and sighed. "In that case, let's get started."

He walked me through the details of my condition when I got to the hospital, which could be summed in a few words—really, really fucking bad. As he talked, I ran my hands over my body, noting the bruises that were in the shape of teeth and the wounds that would scar. More for my collection. I could almost feel the ghost of hateful hands on me. I started shaking, realizing just how close I had been to dying. Before he could finish with the whole recovery how-to, I jumped to my feet—or tried to. I must have blacked out before my feet even hit the ground, because the next thing I knew, I was back in bed.

I don't know if it was seeing myself in the light for the first time, or the clinical way the doctor spoke, or just the trauma of the whole thing hitting me at once, but I started sobbing. Each broken gasp for air sent a lightning strike of pain through my entire body, making me cry even harder. Mac and Dalton were damn near frantic, the doctor yelling at them to calm down, which I'm sure only made it worse. When Dalton reached for me, I couldn't help but flinch. I barely registered the flash of hurt across his face. Over their shoulders, my eyes met the nurse's, and with one look, she understood.

"Enough, everyone. All of you, out. Dr. Jaques, respectfully, that includes you. Ms. Moore needs a moment to herself."

Mac and Dalton protested, but she fixed them with an unwaveringly stern look.

"You may wait in the hallway. Surely you can see all this yelling and hovering isn't what she needs right now?"

My sobs had dissolved into hiccups, and I was hunched in on myself, trying to pretend the pain away. Mac looked at me, and Dalton took a step back, giving me space.

"Vixen, baby?"

I couldn't look at them.

"Please, please go."

Like kicked puppies, they finally left the room, and I watched them through a small window as they disappeared down the hallway. I vaguely heard the doctor instruct the nurse to let him know when I was ready to go over everything else. Then it was just me and her in the room. She approached me slowly. Her voice was gentle and soothing.

"Oh, sweet girl. You've been through so much, but you don't have to be so strong. It's okay to cry."

I did so, burying my head in my hands. She came up beside me, and didn't try to touch me but said, "You woke up not even an hour ago, honey. Your body has barely had time to process the amount of pain you must be in. Then some stranger comes in and tells you how he had to cut you open to keep you from dying. And all from a man putting his hands on you when he had no business to. I'm sure you must feel overwhelmed."

I hesitated to admit it but somehow, it felt like she—out of all people—would understand.

"I hadn't seen the bite marks before. I didn't realize, I had no idea—can I ask, he didn't..." I could barely get the damn word out, afraid of the answer. "Did he rape me?"

"No—your friends made damn sure of that."

I bet they did. I wondered what had happened to Daniel after Mac and Dalton found me, then I realized I really didn't care.

"I feel so fucking filthy," I whispered.

"If you want, I can help you shower. We'll have to be careful with your stitches. Dr. Jaques approved some pain relief. Would you like to wait for that before then? Otherwise, I won't lie, it's not going to feel good."

"No, I don't want to wait. Please, just help me get up."

I had never felt so weak. It took me approximately ten years just to stand, and even then, I leaned heavily on her. She took my weight like a champ. The bathroom looked miles away. Step by agonizing step, we shuffled our way there.

"I'm Nurse Humphrey, by the way. But you can call me Stella—all my friends do."

I smiled at her as best I could through the haze of pain that I was beginning to realize was going to be my new normal for a while. My legs shook. My breath came fast. My head swam. I zeroed in on the far wall, trying to think of anything but the pain.

When we finally got to the bathroom, a thin sheen of sweat coated my body, and I was panting. It made my abdomen hurt, so I found myself whimpering in between the wheezing for breath. Stella murmured reassuring words, and I didn't give a damn as she helped me undress. I was sure she had seen much worse in her years as a trauma nurse than my naked body. I was grateful for the thin hospital gown, not even wanting to think about how hard it would be to remove actual clothes. Stella was an angel, her touch feather-light as she helped me in the shower.

She was right—the shower was anything but comfortable. But I felt infinitely better, washing the last remnants of that asshole down the drain. I sat in the little white chair as she made me feel a bit more whole. When she helped me back into bed, she gave me a glass of water and some white pills that I hoped were the strongest painkiller this side of the moon.

"I'll have someone from the cafeteria bring you something to eat. Just something light, some broth. If you can keep that down and want more, just let me know. But you need to eat something with that medicine I just gave you—otherwise you'll be tasting colors."

I smiled at her. "I think I love you."

She patted my knee, tucking me into bed. Stella had pulled out all the stops to make me comfortable, even braiding my wet hair. "Would you like me to send your friends in?"

I nodded. "Please."

I lay back against the pillows, closing my eyes. That was the most exhausting shower of my life. A piercing shriek broke the silence, and my eyes flew open just as Maria all but skidded to a stop next to my bed. She reached for me before hugging herself, realizing that touching me might not be the best idea. Her hands twitched like she itched to hug me. Holly was right behind her, a rare smile on her face.

Maria bounced on her toes. "Oh, I want to hug you so damn bad, girl!"

I grinned at her. "I appreciate it, but please don't. You may actually finish me off."

Her face fell, and she shook her head. "No, *hermana*, no death jokes from you for a long while. My heart can't take it."

Holly sat on the bed at my feet. "You scared the shit out of all of us, Nicky."

"Maybe next time I should set the dude on fire, and not the bike."

Holly smiled at me. "Now *there's* an idea."

Maria dragged the chair Mac had been sitting in closer to me. "How are you holding up?"

I gave her a shaky smile. "It's hit or miss, not gonna lie. One second I'm fine; the next, I am an absolute fucking mess. Plus, a doctor was digging around in my stomach and took a souvenir, so… yeah."

"You almost died. I would wheel you down to the psychiatric ward if you weren't kinda messed up in the head for a bit," she replied.

"If it helps, there's no doubt in anyone's mind that you have those two boys wrapped around your pretty little finger. They spent almost every hour right next to you. The doctors and nurses all but dragged them out at the end of the night," Holly added.

I was about to ask them if they knew what happened to Daniel, but there was a knock on the door. I fought to keep the shock off my face when I looked up and saw Agent Braxton in a white doctor's coat. Agent Williams stood beside him, dressed like the world's grumpiest nurse.

"Excuse me, ladies, but we need to run some more tests on the patient." Braxton lied with practiced ease, and he smiled at Holly and Maria as they assured me they would be back later, before leaving the room.

As soon as they were gone, Braxton's smile disappeared. Williams shut the door and closed all the blinds. Braxton came up beside the bed and made a show out of looking over the monitor, and I hated that I couldn't do much more than lie there. Finally, he broke the heavy silence.

"What the fuck are you doing, McGrady?"

I blinked at him. "Excuse me?" I had expected condolences. Sympathy. Reassurance. Being admonished hadn't even crossed my mind, and his tone raised my hackles.

"You've been on the assignment for a little over eight months. So far, and correct me if I'm wrong, you've been treating it like a fucking vacation. Going shopping with your new girlfriends, doing God knows what with your new boy toys, and strutting around the damn clubhouse like you own the place. Yet, you've given us fucking nothing."

His words were all venom and ice. I felt the tendrils of rage curl in my gut, and it took conscious effort to keep my voice even. "A vacation? Are you fucking serious? Have you lost your fucking mind? Do you not see where we are at?"

His eyes flashed, and we glared at each other.

"Williams, meet me at the car," he said.

She had been watching the whole exchange with rapt attention, and her eyes jerked to him in shock. "Sir?"

He didn't look at her. "The car. I'll meet you there in a few minutes."

She scoffed in disbelief and stomped out, slamming the door behind her.

Braxton leaned over me, and I once more cursed the fact that I couldn't move. "What are you doing with the Mills brothers?"

I raised my chin. "Nothing." My voice was calm as the lie left my lips—I was embracing my inner Nicky.

"I thought we put you under to gather intel on the DiAngelos."

"You did, and I am. I am telling you everything I know, but it was you who told me this wasn't going to be a quick and easy job."

"You are getting awful close with Ms. Gonzalez and Ms. Morgan."

"They're good people."

"Have you forgotten why you're here?"

"Is this an interrogation?"

"Should it be?"

"Fuck you. I'm giving everything I've got to this assignment. You've got more details about the Steel Saints and Silas Greyson than you've ever had before. The Saints aren't the way into the DiAngelos family—Silas Greyson is. I've made that clear in every report I've given you."

"Remember who you're speaking to, detective. I am your handler; this is my job. You're getting too close to the Saints. I'm pulling you out."

I stared at him. "Like hell you are! I'm already in it this far, and I'm not stopping until the job is done."

"Can I trust you to keep your distance?"

"Of course."

He finally paused, still leaning over me. I wanted to tell him to fuck off, but that was more of a Nicole move than it was something Katie would do. He startled me when he laid his hand on mine. "I've been watching you closely, Katie. You're getting in pretty deep. I don't want you getting hurt."

I pulled my hand out from under his. "I am literally in a hospital, Agent Braxton. But I signed up for this. I knew there were risks. I'm fine—or I will be. You don't need to worry about me. You trained me for this, remember?"

A glimmer of displeasure crossed his face when I pulled away from him. "You are not Nicole. Remember that."

I couldn't help but defend my alter-ego. "Nicole isn't a bad person. She's a lot like me. That's why you chose me for this job. Like Lieutenant Hartwell said all those months ago, she and I aren't much different."

"I want you to double your reports, and remember, I'm always nearby. You got one more chance at this. You end up at the hospital again, you're done. And stay away from the Mills brothers."

I glared at him—the only thing stopping me from hitting him with the IV pole was my inability to lift it. Hell, if I could've made it to the bathroom without assistance, I might've decked him with the call button just for fun.

"Are handlers usually this hands-on? I thought there was supposed to be a certain level of trust."

He didn't answer me when he opened the door, but he turned to me just as he went to shut it back behind him. "Caring about the detective under my command isn't a crime. Get some rest, McGrady."

# Chapter 13

I spent almost a month in that damn hospital. Nurse Stella became one of my new favorite people. Even when she was off duty, she made sure I was taken care of. Mac and Dalton doted on me, handling me with careful tenderness and seeing to my every need. When a nurse wasn't readily available, Dalton helped me shower—every touch a sweet reverence to my battered body.

Mac, while less distant than I had grown accustomed to, was still emotionally disconnected from me. But he held my hand during every uncomfortable test and glowered at the doctors like it was their fault for doing their job. In his own way, through the walls around his heart, I could tell he cared fiercely, and I loved him deeply for it.

I was elated to finally be moved out of the ICU. One day, shortly after my lunch had been brought in, my door swung open to a flood of people. Rodney, his brother Robbie, Clint, Jackson, Diego, Tony, and a bunch of other Saints poured in. I greeted them all by name, smiling so big my face hurt. They came bearing flowers, chocolates, and even a couple of hand-drawn get-well-soon cards from their kids, which I absolutely cherished. It made me realize I had come to consider many of them family, a fact that had me sobbing into Nurse Stella's arms later that night. She and a select few staff had been informed of my real identity. For the first time in months, I had someone to talk to, and she was a wonderful listener.

One day, after a particular grueling physical therapy session, Clint came in toting a massive stuffed fox and handed it over, looking very proud of himself.

"I know those two call you Vixen, so I hunted everywhere for that thing."

I gave the old man the best hug I could manage, and a big kiss on the cheek despite the grumble that came from Mac. "I absolutely love it."

Clint's face turned cherry red, and I heard Rodney tease him about not being used to sweet words from a pretty girl.

Those two visited me regularly, complaining about each other's cooking. They had started taking turns, and the general consensus was that Robbie couldn't boil water without ruining it, while the only thing Cliff knew how to cook was burgers. Big shocker there. Mac kept a careful eye on me during their visits, and anytime I showed any sign of being tired, he would kick them out fast as a blink.

Maria and Holly were also regulars. The day before I was released, Maria handed me a key and announced, "You're staying with me until you can find a new place. One closer to the clubhouse, and closer to all of us."

"And one with less blood-red décor," Holly joked. Maria frowned at her, but I laughed. You could always count on Holly for inappropriate jokes.

"Anyways," Maria said, "you'll also still need help getting around for a bit. Google says it'll be a month or two before you can stand on your own without it feeling like knives in your belly."

I grimaced—I'd read the same and wasn't thrilled about it. Still, I protested, "You have three kids, Maria. I don't want to burden you and Diego further."

"Number one, you won't be a burden. Number two, Holly has a fuck ton of stairs at her place. She and I have already talked about it—you're staying with me."

"Oh, well, if you two have made plans, it would be remiss of me to stand in your way."

Maria smiled, and Holly winked at me. "Exactly. So, it's settled then. Maria and I are going to her place to get your room ready. It's currently a mix of bike parts and broken toys. Mac said he would drop you off tomorrow as soon as you are released."

The night before I was to be freed from this hellscape, I sat alone in the too-still room. There was no laughter, no Maria telling Jewel to knock it off, no Dalton bickering with Mac over who brought better snacks, no Rodney yelling about cafeteria food. Just me, a dimmed overhead light, and a silence that left too much room for my thoughts. Molly the Fox sat on the chair beside my bed, a bright orange absurdity with a pink ribbon tied crookedly around her neck. My hand brushed over her soft fur, and I felt the sting behind my eyes come back with a vengeance.

But this time, it wasn't my physical pain that made me feel so hopeless.

Before the tears could fall, the door creaked open. Stella didn't say anything, just glided in with that calm, sure presence that never felt like an intrusion. She glanced around like she expected the room to still be full, then looked at me with a knowing tilt of her head. She didn't ask if I was okay. She just walked over, fluffed a few pillows, and straightened Molly's crooked bow. Her fingers were so gentle with it—like she knew that even fixing a stuffed fox meant something tonight. Then she looked at me and said, "Wanna talk about it?"

I opened my mouth to lie. To say I was fine. To default to the half-truths that had become second nature. But Stella knew the truth. She knew who I was. She had seen me act as Nicky, knowing I was Katie. If anyone would understand, it was her. This was my first chance in months to just… stop. Stop pretending. Stop lying. Stop being so fucking alone. So, even though I knew the risks, I swallowed hard and said, "I'm in love with two men."

Honestly, I didn't know where to start, so I just went with the first words that popped into my head. Stella's eyebrows raised a touch, but she didn't say anything—just sat on the edge of the bed and waited.

"I know I'm not supposed to be. Like, I went through all this training and I have this mission. I know the rules. I know it's reckless. I know that when this is all over, I'm going to lose them both. And I may even lose my job." I looked down at my bandaged hand, fingers curled slightly from the stiffness. "But I can't help it. I thought I was solid as Katie. That I could keep my distance. Keep my focus. But somewhere along the line, I stopped pretending to be Nicky… and just started being her. I still want to take down the bad guys, but now I want more."

The tears came, slow and hot. I hated crying, and I'd been doing a hell of a lot of it lately. But Stella didn't flinch. She reached out and took my hand in both of hers, thumbs brushing lightly over my skin. It was like a dam had broken inside of me. I told her everything. How the club wasn't full of monsters and mobsters, like I thought. The little inside jokes, the conversations at the dinner table, the way they were with each other.

I told her about Dalton, the first time I knew I was in love with him. How I thought Mac had hated me, keeping me at a distance. But when I realized the distance was just to keep the people he loved safe, I saw past his tough exterior to the heart of a really good man—and I found myself falling for him, too.

Stella just sat and listened, not saying a word until I was done.

"I get it," she said quietly. "Sometimes we put on a mask… and then realize the mask fits better than we ever expected. Doesn't mean the person behind it isn't real. Just means you were more than one thing all along."

I laughed—a broken, bitter sound. "Katie folds her socks and color-codes her closet. Nicky burns motorcycles and tells mobsters to go fuck themselves. How the hell am I both? They're from two different worlds."

"Are they?" she said simply. "Maybe, on the surface, they don't look the same. But, if you dig a little bit deeper, you might find more similarities than you expected. At least from what I have seen."

I couldn't look at her. "They love her. Nicky. The version of me that's bold and reckless and free. And when they find out who I am—what I've been doing—they'll hate me."

Stella squeezed my hand. "Maybe. Maybe not. But loving someone… really loving someone? Means you love the heart, not just the name. And I've seen the way those two look at you. That's not something that disappears overnight. It's not going to be easy, but love always does find a way."

I let out a shaky breath. "I'm just so tired of lying."

"Then don't. At least not right now. Right here with me, you don't have to be anyone but you."

It wasn't a fix. It wasn't a promise. But it was a moment. One of the first in months where I wasn't acting, wasn't pretending, wasn't undercover. I had known that the job was going to throw some curveballs, but I was drowning in the lies I told. Sitting next to this kind woman with her gentle hands and wise words, I could just be human. Neither Katie nor Nicky, but a person. Broken, bruised, and scared... but finally, quietly, seen.

The next morning, Dr. Jaques gave me a fat stack of papers with aftercare instructions. What to do and not to do during recovery. Mac and Dalton, of course, were right by my side, and listened intently to every word. They asked a million questions, and finally, I asked them to shut the hell up so I could go home. Dalton tried to convince me to use a wheelchair, so I threw my stack of papers at him. I still moved like that turtle from *Kung Fu Panda*, with none of the grace, but like hell was I using a wheelchair.

Dalton sat with me in the back of the truck on the way over to Maria's. I was sore, but excited as hell to get out of there.

"What are you two going to do with yourselves now that I'm not bedridden? Guard dog duty is over for you."

Dalton gently pulled me to his chest and kissed the top of my head. "Don't worry about us, Vixen. You focus on getting better, and then I can think of plenty of things for us to do." He winked suggestively, and I felt my neck turn red. I met Mac's eyes in the rearview mirror and blushed harder when he smiled at me.

We pulled up outside Maria's, and Dalton helped me out while Diego Jr. ran towards us. Maria stood on the porch with Manny on her hip and Diego Sr. at her side. Little Diego was yammering on a million miles an hour, and I didn't pay much attention until he grabbed my hand and started pulling me toward the house.

"Come on, Aunt Nicky!"

I gaped at him and then at Maria, who shrugged and smiled at me. I smiled back—I kind of liked the sound of Aunt Nicky.

Mac and Dalton followed me to the porch. While Maria, the kids, and I all went inside, the two of them stayed outside with Jackson. I cast a curious glance over my shoulder at the three men who were speaking in a hushed whisper.

"Aunt Nicky, look what I made for you!" Diego said, dragging my attention to a giant "Welcome" banner that hung from the ceiling. It was decorated in pink glitter, shedding on the floor in a shiny pink mess that I knew Maria was *thrilled* about.

I couldn't bend to give the boy a hug, so instead I ruffled his mess of brown hair. "I love it, buddy." He gave me a toothy grin and ran off down the hallway.

I turned to Maria. "Girl, that is a lot of glitter."

She groaned. "Don't get me started on that. He found a bunch of leftover decor from Jewel's *quinceañera*. By the time I got wind of it, Jewel had happily supplied all the glitter."

The teenager in question was sitting in the living room but came into the kitchen as we talked. She giggled. "Sorry, momma. *No arrepentirse de nada.*"

Maria scowled at her daughter. "*Por eso mismo vas a tener que limpiarlo.* And no Spanish while Nicky is here."

Jewel protested—both the glitter punishment and her mother's forbidding Spanish.

"You don't have to do that, Maria. I don't care what language y'all speak. I'm a guest here."

But Maria was having none of it. She fixed Jewel with a stern stare which sent the girl stomping towards the living room in a huff, and then turned that stare on me, so I decided to keep my mouth shut on the matter. Maria put Manny in a high chair while she worked in the kitchen. I offered to help her, but she practically laughed in my face.

"I didn't realize you had healed overnight!" I rolled my eyes as she brandished a spoon at me. "The doctor said take it easy, remember."

I sighed but took a seat at the table. The guys came in from off the porch, and Manny threw a baby puff at his dad.

"Vixen giving you a hard time already, Maria?" Dalton said, giving her a friendly hug.

She laughed. "I don't think your girl knows the meaning of take it easy or sit still. Might have to tie her down."

Dalton's sexy grin was intoxicating, and my attention was so focused on him that I didn't notice Mac coming up behind me until I felt his breath on my ear.

"Bet you'd like that, wouldn't you, Vixen?"

I turned so red I thought I would set the chair on fire and turned to give him an admonishing look, reminiscent of the one Maria had given Jewel and me a moment ago. But he just smirked at me.

Diego was pretending he hadn't heard us, and Maria turned back to the pot on the stove with a wink at me.

Mac headed for the door and said, "Alright, Vixen. We gotta get going. Keep your phone on you."

I stood at the table, legs just a little bit shaky, and Dalton kissed me, then followed his brother out. Mac nodded at Diego, who nodded back— probably some secret male agreement. He started to leave, but then stopped. He turned around and looked at me. I gave him a curious look, head skewed to the side like a confused puppy. Suddenly, he was in front of me again. He cupped the back of my head, tilting my face up and towards his, then he captured my lips with his.

This wasn't the chaste kiss Dalton had just given me. This was heat and danger, and it made me forget everyone else in the room. I was vaguely aware of Diego covering baby Manny's eyes. Mac nipped my lip, and my heart felt like it would beat its way out of my chest. Then Maria cleared her throat and broke the spell. Mac moved his hand from where it had been wrapped in my hair until it cupped my cheek. I leaned into his touch and smiled at him. He pressed his forehead against mine and said, "Be good, Vixen."

Dalton chuckled, then shook his head as he shoulder-bumped his brother on their way out the door.

Maria cleared her throat again, and I turned to look at her. "What?" I said innocently. Diego picked up Manny, and beat a hasty retreat towards the living room.

"Girl!" Maria smirked at me. "I've never seen him like that. Not with anyone. Not even in high school."

"What was he like?"

She tilted her head. "Mac was pretty much the same. Calm, quiet, yet somehow still in charge. Dalton was a total man-ho. They've both matured, obviously. But you do something to them, Nicky. Holy shit, wait 'til I tell Holly you about turned my kitchen into an episode of *Pasión de Gavilanes*."

I groaned and threw a dish towel at her as she hummed the theme song, swaying her ample hips to the imaginary beat.

Diego came from the hallway, dragging a bin of toys as best he could. "Aunt Nicky, wanna play?"

As if I could turn him down.

"Absolutely I do, handsome man. But you're gonna have to play on the table 'cos Aunt Nicky can't move too well, okay?" Look at me, talking in third person and shit.

Diego gave his mother a quizzical look, and she said, "You can play with toys on the table only when Aunt Nicky is here, and they better be cleared off for dinner."

The little boy nodded eagerly before handing me a few action figures and climbing into the chair next to me.

Diego and I played while his mom cooked. Diego Sr. would come into the kitchen every now and then, on the hunt for a snack for the baby and stealing kisses from his wife. It was a sweet, domestic scene, and I found myself completely at peace—despite the fact that Diego kept brutally killing my action figure. So far, I had been murdered by a T. rex, a bomber, and a Barbie. He was thrilled every time I went down dramatically, groaning and moaning and playing along.

"Alright, *mi familia*, dinner is ready. Everyone, come wash your hands!"

Jewel sauntered into the kitchen with Manny in her arms. "You said no Spanish, Mom. Just saying."

She dragged the high chair over to the table and secured Manny in it before taking the seat across from me. Diego busied himself clearing the toys from the table, while his dad set out plates and silverware. Jewel and I just sat there, her staring at me—man, the kid should take up detective work. I squirmed in my seat. Was this a normal teenager thing? Because her brown eyes were staring into my soul.

"Sorry I missed your party, by the way," I said, trying to break the ice.

She shrugged. "You were almost dead. Would've totally ruined the mood."

Well, alrighty then.

Maria set down a massive platter of chicken drenched in some sort of brown sauce. The smell was enough to send me to heaven. Next to it, she put a big bowl of yellow rice and then some sort of corn dish that had peppers and black beans in it. I was practically drooling when Maria sat next to me and said, "I hope you like *mole*."

I shrugged. "I have no idea what that is, but it smells divine. Definitely better than hospital food."

Over the next hour, I ate my weight in food while listening to the Gonzales family banter and chat. They were a rambunctious group—even little Manny occasionally shouting baby nonsense while his mom fed him a mixture of baby food and little bits off her plate. Jewel and her stepdad were locked in an intense debate about her book budget. She had evidently exceeded it for the month, and was expertly negotiating for more. Maria brought out some *tres leches* cake for dessert, and I was pretty sure I could've taken the whole thing to my room and been a happy woman.

"Girl, you need to show me how to make all this. I'm afraid my skills are decidedly centered on American cuisine. This is some of the best food I've ever had."

Maria shrugged my compliment off, but smiled broadly. "You made those delicious fajitas that first night, remember? And then those tamales my son suckered you into making."

"Girl, my tamales probably haunt the dreams of your *abuela*."

She had told me about her grandma more times than I can count. The woman was evidently a force to be reckoned with, old school and no nonsense. But she had loved Maria fiercely, and had a penchant for taking in lost souls—a trait her beloved granddaughter had clearly inherited.

Maria laughed at me, and even Diego Sr. cracked a smile. "You're not wrong there, Nicole. That woman scared the shit out of me."

Maria threw a napkin at him, and he winked at her. Handing the baby a piece of chicken to gnaw on, she said, "She would've loved you, you know. I'll have to show you some pictures while you're here."

I took a sip of my water. "I would love that."

When dinner was over, my offer to help clean up was promptly dismissed. No surprise there. I played with Manny at the dining room table while they got everything put away. Despite my insistence that I was fine, Maria was adamant that I let her help me stand. Secretly, I was grateful for the help. My pain meds were starting to wear off, and the damn things were probably in my room which seemed incredibly far away.

We moved to the living room, Maria fussing around me like a mother hen. When I was settled in the oversized recliner, she tossed a blanket on my lap, and squashed pillows around me. I couldn't move too well, but the bracing from the pillows helped ease the pain, so I didn't complain. Jewel and Diego Jr. played with Manny on the floor. Diego Sr. came up next to me with a glass of milk and my pills.

"Oh, you're the best."

"Thank Maria—I think she's got a notification set up on her phone for your meds."

She was sitting on the couch but heard him and replied, "Well, of course I do. You've got a crap ton of them. Not that I need it, really. When they start wearing off, you can try and hide it, but it's written all over your face."

Her husband joined her on the couch, and she curled up next to him. He wrapped an arm protectively around her, pulling her in close.

Diego climbed up next to his dad and laid his head on his father's lap. "Momma, can we watch *Lion King*?"

Jewel sat next to Maria and leaned into her. "The second one, not the first one. We've seen that one hundreds of times."

Diego and Maria looked at me, and I shrugged. "No complaints here."

The baby was playing on his little mat with all of his toys, but laughed when "One of Us" started to play.

Halfway through the movie, in between dozing off, I found myself watching the little family gathered on the couch. Maria had picked up Manny at some point, and the little boy was fast asleep in his momma's arms. Diego had one arm around his son, who was still lying on his lap, and the other around Maria. Maria leaned against him, and Jewel was sharing a blanket with her mom.

They were the perfect picture, and I couldn't help but stare. I hadn't really ever thought about starting a family before—wearing white, walking down the aisle, and all that jazz was the last thing on my mind. But they were so comfortable, so relaxed with each other. So secure in their love, that nothing else mattered. It hit me all of a sudden how much I wanted that. And, even though I knew it was completely illogical, I let myself imagine having it with my boys.

Maybe… a baby with auburn hair and blue eyes.

But one day, they would discover my lies, and any feelings they had for me would vanish. Still, for now, a girl could dream.

When the movie was over, Maria and Diego untangled themselves from the children who had fallen asleep on them. Jewel woke up, then yawned and stretched. She kissed her parents goodnight, surprised me with a hug, and then went upstairs to her room. Diego took the baby from Maria so she could stand without risking waking him. She took Manny back, cooing to him when he fretted. She rocked him in her arms while Diego scooped his son up into his arms. Diego followed Jewel upstairs, while Maria went down the hall to Manny's room. A little while later, as I started dozing off again in my chair, Maria came up behind and gently squeezed my good shoulder.

"You okay?" she asked.

I nodded. "Absolutely. You have such a beautiful family."

Her smile was wistful. "I got really lucky with Diego. He's one of the good ones."

When Diego came back downstairs from putting his son to bed, he offered his arm so I could stand without too much trouble. Maria had made up the guest room for me, and the bed looked delightfully inviting—especially compared to the hospital bed I had been sleeping in. My giant stuffed fox, Molly, was there amongst the pillows. Maria fussed around us as Diego helped me climb into bed.

After he left the two of us alone, Maria said, "Are you comfy? Do you have enough pillows? Blankets? All set?"

I shook my head at her. "I'm fine, Mom—promise. I'm a big girl."

She leaned forward and gently hugged me. "You almost died, Nicky. I am allowed to be a mother hen for a bit."

I hugged her back as best I could. "It'll take more than some asshole with a micropenis to take me out."

She laughed and said, "You're damn right. Goodnight, *hermana*. Sleep tight."

Shutting the door behind her, I was left in almost total darkness. I had become used to the light and noise at the hospital, and this was a welcome change. The only thing I missed was the two men at my bedside who had been keeping me company.

Their absence left me antsy, and I reached for my phone on the nightstand, grimacing at the stretching movement. I debated which one to text for a minute, and then decided to just create a group chat between all of us. I giggled to myself as I titled it, "Threesome?" They must have gotten the notification, because my phone pinged instantly with a message from Dalton.

"Excuse me?"

Another ping, a message from Mac. "WTF?"

I sent back the angel emoji, along with a question mark.

"You know exactly what you're doing, ma'am."

"Oh, so it's ma'am now?"

"Don't make me come over there."

"What are you going to do? Break into Maria's house?"

"Try me."

Mac rejoined the conversation. "I want to know what's up with the group name."

"Nothing's up," I sent back.

"Vixen…"

"Mac."

"Dalton. There, now it sounds like AA."

I laughed and snuggled deeper under the covers. "I can change it to something more vanilla for you two. Didn't realize you were so delicate."

"What about our weekend together said delicate?"

"As soon as you're better, I'll show you just how delicate I am."

"Maybe you both need to prove me wrong, then. Have you seriously never shared a woman?"

Three dots appeared, showing Dalton texting a reply, but he must have deleted it, so Mac replied, "This is different, Vixen."

"You've said that. But I disagree."

"Baby girl, fucking some patch bunny isn't the same as being with you."

I bit my lip, aware I was treading dangerous waters. "Agreed. It's better."

"Where's this coming from, gorgeous?"

Mac calling me that made me feel like a love-struck teenager. Every dang time. "IDK, I'm just lying here in bed, and I've gotten so used to having you guys next to me, it's hard to fall asleep. So my mind is doing its thing. Plus, I haven't had sex in over a month."

"And your horny little mind just went straight to a threesome?"

"Come on, Dalton, tell me that the three of us and a weekend away at the cabin doesn't sound like heaven?"

"I'm not knocking that."

"Mac?"

"You're seriously asking me this right now?"

"Yes?"

I could practically hear the man's sigh.

"Vixen, I'm not sharing you the first time I get you naked."

"Can't say I blame him, baby girl."

"I'm a selfish bastard."

"You're my selfish bastard."

"Damn right."

"I'm yours too, baby girl. You've got both of us. Don't doubt that."

A sudden wave of sadness hit me—that little voice in the back of my mind wondering if they would feel the same if they knew the truth.

"I'm gonna hit the sack, y'all. Goodnight."

"Goodnight, gorgeous."

"Goodnight, Vixen."

# Chapter 14

Agent Braxton agreed to let me find a new apartment—meaning picking one off a list they'd already wired to hell and back. Maria and Holly had more fun apartment-hunting than I did, but we finally settled on a cute little one-bedroom townhouse about ten minutes from the clubhouse. A bunch of the guys volunteered to help me move furniture, which was an unexpected kindness. The only things I brought from my old place were my beloved mattress, the TV, and all the kitchen necessities. Everything else, I found at local thrift stores and auctions.

Mac and Dalton kept trying to pay for my furniture, which pissed me off.

"I'm perfectly capable of buying my own shit, thank you very much. And besides, how does that make me look—my bosses buying me expensive shit? What about how it makes you look?"

Mac seemed offended. "Why the fuck would we care how it makes us look?"

Dalton shrugged and gave me a crooked smile. "If anyone's got a problem with me helping out my girl, they are more than welcome to say that to my face." He said the words like a cocky challenge.

I rolled my eyes and said sarcastically, "And they say chivalry is dead."

"Excuse me, where are you wanting this stuff?"

I turned my attention to the delivery driver and his coworker who were waiting at the end of the driveway. "Sorry, yeah. The table set goes in the living room, right when you walk in. Same with the rug. But the highboy goes up the stairs, in the hallway."

I hadn't planned on spending a lot of time, energy, or money on furniture shopping. I knew this was a temporary home, mine only as long as I was on assignment. But, encouraged by Maria and Holly, I hit the antique furniture store and kind of went nuts. I couldn't resist the gorgeous, honey-oak coffee table with the matching side tables for my living room. And the highboy would make the perfect place for sheets and towels and such. Maybe I could find a way to bring it with me when all this was said and done? If anything was gonna survive the fallout from when the truth hit the ground, it would be the furniture.

I followed the delivery guys inside, Mac and Dalton right behind me. I had the two of them help put away my plates and pots and such while I scrounged for a snack. Maria and Holly had promised to stop by later with wine and pizza to properly break in the new place. I was still sore, but it was a much more tolerable pain. I would always have those ugly scars to remind me of that night. Sometimes, I would have nightmares so vivid, I would wake up in a cold sweat. The second night it happened, I couldn't go back to sleep—staring into the dark corners of my room at Maria's, flinching at the sounds of people driving past the house.

So, I called Dalton.

Not ten minutes afterwards, I about pissed myself when he crawled through the window like a lunatic. I had a good mind to chew his ass out for practically breaking into my friend's home, but I was such a mess. He crawled into bed next to me, pulling me to his chest, and not the least bit bothered by the sweat coating my body. He held me until I stopped trembling, and he made me promise to always call him when I had a night terror, no matter what. With him tracing small, comforting circles on my back, I fell asleep in the comfort and safety of his arms.

Maria nearly had a coronary when he followed me into the kitchen the next morning.

"Anything else, ma'am?"

The delivery driver brought me back to the present and was looking expectantly at me.

"No, everything looks great. Thank you." I tipped them both, and sent them on their way. I sat at the table with an apple, a jar of peanut butter, and a spoon. Dalton sat next to me, giving my lunch a funny look. I brandished my spoon at him. "Don't you dare judge me."

He held up his hands in surrender and said, "Wouldn't dream of it."

Mac stood behind me, gently rubbing my shoulders and working the tender muscles there. "How are you holding up, Vixen?"

I shrugged. "So so. Better if you keep doing that."

He bent down, kissing my neck and sending shivers up my spine. The three of us hadn't really talked about the whole threesome thing since that night, but no one had changed the group chat name. Plus, the two brothers made no effort to hide their affection when it was all three of us. I, for one, was loving it.

Dalton's phone rang, and his brow furrowed when he looked at it. "It's Silas. The hell is he calling me for and not you?"

The question was directed at his brother, who answered, "No idea. Put it on speaker."

My eyebrows probably disappeared into my hairline, realizing I was about to be privy to a conversation between my boys and my target for the first time.

"Where the fuck are you?"

Dalton's eyes narrowed to slits at Greyson's tone. "In town. What's up?"

"Where's your brother?"

Dalton looked at Mac, giving him a signal to continue. "He's with me. Something wrong?"

"You fucking tell me."

Mac stopped rubbing my shoulders and walked over next to his brother. "We haven't heard anything, Silas. Want to key us in?"

"That's what I fucking get, letting a couple of boys run my club."

Mac's voice was deadly. "My *father's* club, actually."

Dalton was gripping the phone so hard, I was surprised the thing wasn't cracking.

"Your father is dead, boy. And you're about to be, if you don't get over to the clubhouse in the next twenty minutes. The DiAngelos are up in arms over that last shipment, saying they were missing some guns or some shit."

"Be careful how you talk about our father. You're only in fucking charge because Mac lets you be."

I had never heard Dalton sound so angry.

Silas laughed on the other end of the phone. "You keep telling yourself that, son."

Dalton opened his mouth, but Mac shook his head, stopping him.

"You've got twenty minutes. Both of you had better be here. And give that sweet little thing you're probably with my love."

With that, Silas hung up, and Dalton threw the phone against the wall. Mac's eyes were almost black, and Dalton was pacing beside the table. I nibbled on a spoonful of peanut butter, watching them.

"Who the fuck does he think he is?"

"Easy, brother. He won't be here forever."

"He needs to go, Mac. He's ruining the Saints. Dad would be ashamed."

"I know."

"You said it was short-term, Maverick. That this shit with the DiAngelos wouldn't last."

"Damnit, Dalton—I know."

The two men stared at each other, and seemed to have forgotten I was even there.

"I hate to interrupt… but what's going on? What's crawled up his ass?"

"Shit, Vixen. You shouldn't have had to hear all that."

"But I did. So what's up?"

Dalton dragged a hand down his face. "What do you know about the DiAngelos?"

Mac gave him a warning look, which he ignored.

I shrugged, feigning nonchalance. "Not much," I lied.

"Silas is in deep with them—God only knows why. That's where he goes all the fucking time. He's like their little pet or some shit. I kinda think they just keep him around for entertainment. Anyway, it works. 'Cos when he's gone, Mac and I can do what needs done. As long as we keep the DiAngelos supplied, we can do whatever we want."

"Supplied with what?" I did my best to keep my voice light, my eyes fixed on Dalton. I wanted to know this as Nicky, if it meant being able to support them. But, as Katie, I *needed* to know.

"Guns, drugs—black market shit. They get that, Silas stays over there, and everyone is happy. Silas only ever comes back when he feels like waving his dick in everyone's face, or when something's gone wrong. Like now."

"Speaking of," Mac interrupted, "we need to go. Don't want to keep the *boss* waiting."

I stood, putting my peanut butter back on the table. I stepped into Mac, running my hands through his hair before running them down his neck to his arms. His eyes were still a blue so dark, they were like a bottomless sea. A sure sign he was either stressed, angry, or both.

I grabbed his wrists and pulled his arms around me. "You'll figure it out. Whatever else, you're a good leader, Mac. Your people like and respect you. That's all that matters." I leaned up on my tiptoes and kissed him, licking his lower lip until he opened to me with a groan. His hands tightened on my waist, before sliding down to my ass. I wrapped my arms back around his neck, and moaned into his mouth.

"Um, excuse me. My pants are getting tight. I thought we had somewhere to be?"

I smiled over Mac's shoulder at Dalton, who was indeed sporting an impressive hard-on.

"You're just jealous."

I stepped away from Mac and he smacked me on the ass as I walked over to his brother. I was really starting to like this two-for-one deal. Dalton picked me up and set me on the table in one smooth move. I wrapped my legs around him, pressing my core against his length. He tilted my head back with one hand, and kissed me as deeply as his brother had. With the other, he slipped his hand under my t-shirt and wrapped it around my breast. He made a sound of pleasure when he realized I wasn't wearing a bra. He rolled my nipple between his fingers, and I whimpered at the delicious mix of pleasure and pain.

"We're going to be late." Mac's voice was thick and low.

I broke away from Dalton, who gave me a crooked grin. "Look who's jealous now."

I ran my eyes over Mac, who was also incredibly hard. Ugh, I absolutely didn't want them to leave. Stupid Silas.

Dalton kissed me on the neck on his way out the door. "I'll talk to you later, Vixen, baby." Before Mac could follow him, I grabbed his hand, and he raised an eyebrow at me. Not giving myself a chance to overthink it, I cupped Mac's cock in my hand over his jeans. I gripped him firmly, teasing him and feeling him growing even bigger in my hand.

"I like to think I'm a patient woman, but I'm growing cobwebs down there. When are you going to give me what I want, Mac?"

He stepped away from me, and I was disappointed until he moved behind me and pressed himself against my ass. He reached around me and tucked his hand into the waistband of my sweats. I was holding my breath, which I released in a moan when he slid his palm over my opening. I leaned back against him, letting my head loll against his shoulder.

"Is this what you've been wanting, gorgeous?" He slid two fingers between my lips. "So wet for me, Vixen."

I shivered, my knees fighting to keep me upright. He rubbed small, tight circles over my clit and I bucked in his hold. Fuck me, that felt good.

"You've been healing, Vixen." He slipped a finger inside of me. "When I fuck you for the first time, I don't want to be gentle." He slipped another finger inside of me, and I was practically panting. He pumped his fingers in and out of me, and I ground against him. "When I fuck you, I want to slam my cock into you and shake the fucking bed. When you come, I want to feel this pretty little pussy squeeze my cock so hard as you shatter around me."

I whimpered as he put another finger inside of me. "Fuck, Mac, baby, please…"

"Do you want to come for me, Vixen? Is this what you need, gorgeous?"

His relentless pace got faster, his three fingers working my pussy with expertise. I was so fucking close, and when I told him as much, he used his other hand to squeeze my breast.

"Come for me, gorgeous. I want you to coat my fingers in your sweet juices. Come for me, Vixen."

I shouted as I came, my pussy gushing as he worked me through one of the best orgasms of my life. I was a trembling mess, and that was just from the man's fingers. When he slid his fingers out of me, they made a thick, wet sound, and he pushed them into my mouth. I sucked on them greedily and he said, "That's my girl. Soon, Vixen, soon."

He kissed me goodbye, despite my doing my best to make him stay. I watched out the window as he walked towards his brother, who was leaning against the truck. Dalton gave Mac a knowing smirk, and Mac shoved him, nearly knocking Dalton on his ass. I couldn't help but laugh at their antics. Before climbing into the passenger side, Dalton turned back to where I stood in the window, and he winked at me. My thighs were still damp from my release, and damn if I didn't want more. I watched them drive away, and then headed back to the kitchen.

Halfway there, I froze. My eyes found the potted fern in the corner of the living room. The fern with a mic hidden in the dirt.

*Holy fucking shit.*

What had I been thinking? How had I forgotten?

They heard that. Heard me. My heart beat a frantic pattern in my chest.

As my mind raced, I came to a sudden realization—an understanding with myself. They were already judging me. Braxton knew I was becoming more involved than I should be. He had warned me to stay away in that hospital room. I was walking a fine line. But, at some point, I stopped caring. I told myself that the mission didn't include celibacy. And, as long as it didn't keep me from doing my job, I was allowed a little fun. At least that's what I told myself. I eyed the hidden device again, chewing on my bottom lip. I shook my head, as if I could dislodge the pesky worries by doing so, and continued towards the kitchen.

After putting up my peanut butter, I headed upstairs to my bedroom. I figured if I was going to make this house a home, I would start here and work my way through. I started unpacking boxes, hanging and folding clothes with music blaring from the Bluetooth speaker I had connected my phone to. With all my clothes put away, I grabbed the box with my new shoe rack in it, and sat on the floor. It was relatively easy to put together, and I tucked it into the back of my closet. I had pried a board loose in the back, stashing a few things there. The bedroom was a decent size, with two windows that brought in lots of natural light—with one over the bed and one facing the small yard. The closet was twice as big as the one in my old apartment, and Mac had mounted a TV in my room for me.

I made my way into the hallway, a small space at the top of the stairs with my bedroom at one end, and the main bathroom at the other. I was a little disappointed not to have a connecting bathroom, but had decided to deal with it. The bathroom didn't have a tub, but a super-nice shower and a vanity with plenty of room for getting ready in the morning. It also had a distinctly musty smell, so I turned my attention to cleaning it until it shone.

I decided that I was going to have to replace the blinding, and very unflattering, fluorescents as soon as possible. I had found a turtle-themed bathroom set online, and with it, the room was now properly decked out. Dalton had found me a bunch of little turtle figurines at a local yard sale, and had looked incredibly amused when I squealed in delight. I freaking love turtles, man.

Just as I was coming down the stairs, the doorbell rang and I opened it up to find Maria and Holly. Maria was loaded down with bags, looking like a pack mule, and Holly was balancing three pizzas and two very large bottles of Chardonnay. Maria rushed in and threw everything down on the living room floor with a huff, and Holly swept past her into the kitchen.

"Oh, this is so cute! I hate to admit it, but you might have been right about this place."

I followed Holly into the kitchen, and Maria followed me. "Thanks? I think?"

Holly laughed at me. "No, I'm serious. It's very homey. In a good way."

I had decorated the kitchen in various shades of blue, mainly due to all my pots and pans being blue already. The cheap white vinyl countertop and the old wooden cabinets weren't exactly appealing to the eye, so I had thrown a blue valance on the window over the sink, and bought a new blue coffee pot. The table Mac had sat me on not even three hours ago had a pretty runner with blue flowers on it. There was a sliding glass door that led to the backyard, and I'd hurriedly ripped down the ugly-as-sin Venetian blinds that had hung over it. The kitchen towel hanging from the oven made me giggle. It read "When in doubt, pull out," and had a picture of some half-burnt bread on it.

Maria grabbed a slice of the pizza Holly had set on the table. "What else needs done?"

I shrugged. "Not much. If those were the towels and stuff that you brought, we can put those up. Finish getting the living room situated."

Holly was munching on a piece of pizza as well. "Wait 'til you see the bed set I picked out for you. Your old one looked like you got it from a homeless man." Maria gave her a look, and Holly added, "No offense. But you'll like it, promise."

I grabbed some glasses from the cabinets and poured us each a glass of wine, then I turned my music back on, and the three of us got to work. Maria took all the tags off my new linens, throwing them in the wash before helping Holly move furniture in the living room. We finished the first bottle by the time the dryer dinged, and were goofing off more than we were being productive.

They teased me relentlessly about my relationship with Mac and Dalton, pressing me for details. I was reluctant to give too much away, but when Holly asked if they were good in bed, I blushed about five different shades of red, and she howled with laughter. I was growing to love these two women dearly. When I was with them, I could forget all about being Detective McGrady—a rule-follower and all-around good girl. Instead, I was all Nicole—someone unafraid to voice her opinion, doing so often and unapologetically.

And someone, to my surprise, I really enjoyed being.

I watched from the doorway as Jackson and Diego pulled up. Maria had one glass too many and Holly, who was doing her best to support her but who had also had more than her fair share of wine, was stumbling next to her. The two men helped their partners into the back of Maria's minivan, and Diego waved to me as they pulled away. I, for one, was very pleasantly buzzed and not feeling up to climbing the stairs just yet. So, I slowly made my way over to the couch, and threw myself rather ungracefully down. I snuggled into the plush cushions, loving the chenille fabric of my new sofa.

My phone buzzed with an incoming text and I rolled over onto my side as I read the message from Dalton on our group chat.

"I've got good news and bad news, Vixen."

"Bad news—it's all bad fucking news," Mac added.

"It is not. Just ignore him."

"Fuck you."

"Rude."

I raised my eyebrows—whatever had gone down with Greyson had left Mac in a very bad mood.

"Sorry to interrupt the love-fest, but what's up?"

"What do you want first?"

"Um… good news?"

"There is none."

"Shut up, Mac. Good news, baby girl, is you get to take my credit card and go get three dresses for you and your friends."

"Maria and Holly?"

"No, Rodney and Clint. Yes, Maria and Holly."

I chewed on my bottom lip as I began to worry, but replied, "Smart ass. What's the bad news?"

"Silas has some fucking dinner planned for the DiAngelos. Somehow, he said you've caught his eye and he wants you there."

"Actually, what he said was that he couldn't wait to get his hands on what had me and Dalton so pussy-whipped. I tried to put my fist through his face, but my idiot brother stopped me."

That surprised me. Usually, Mac was the cool-headed, steadfast leader.

Another text from Dalton: "Mac, shut the fuck up. I wanted to bust his ass too, but we both know that's not an option. Yet."

The little active light by Mac's name in the chat went from green to grey, signaling he had logged off, and then Dalton called me.

"Sorry, baby girl. He's been drinking, more than he usually does."

"It's okay. Is he good?"

"Neither of us are, to be honest. The thought of you having to spend more than five minutes in the same room as Silas or the DiAngelos makes both of us sick. We tried talking him out of it, but it got nasty."

"Shit, I'm sorry."

"You have absolutely nothing to be sorry for."

"When's the dinner?"

"Friday night. You'll need a formal evening gown. And I haven't talked to Diego or Jackson yet, but I want them and your friends there. Safety in numbers and all that."

"I don't want to put them in danger, Dalton. You said the DiAngelos are going to be there?"

"There won't be any danger, Vixen. No one is stupid enough to lay a hand on a Saints' old lady—not even the DiAngelos."

"Old lady? You mean—"

"Yeah, Vixen. I had this whole plan to take you for another weekend at the cabin but... I love you. I know it's only been a few months—"

"Almost a year."

"Mm, almost a year. But I do love you. And I won't let anything hurt you."

"Well then, looks like I have to go shopping. Dress like a proper old lady."

The words made me giddy.

"You'll look stunning in whatever you wear, but I'm serious about using my card. Now, it's getting late and you have to be at work in the morning. I have a couple more calls to make, and I need to go check on Mac. He doesn't get like this often but... well, he already thinks he failed you once. Honestly, we both did. But try and get some sleep, babe."

"You guys didn't fail me. I'll see you in the morning. And Dalton?"

"Yeah, Vixen?"

"I love you, too."

I could practically hear the smile in his voice when he hung up. When I went to bed that night, I was practically floating. My cute new fox bed set, courtesy of Holly, was heavenly and soft, but I'm not sure I would have even noticed if it was uncomfortable. Dalton loved me and, while I knew it was the most unreasonable, most unrealistic, and possibly the stupidest thing ever… I loved him too. God help me.

But I was too busy riding the high to worry about what the future would bring. At least for now.

# Chapter 15

Maria, Holly, and I made plans to go out on Wednesday to look for dresses. The days at work leading up to it were painful. Greyson was lingering around like a bad smell. Mac was alternating between being a total grouch and an absolute drama queen. Dalton was my rock, and also the one hiding the whiskey from his brother. The first time he told me he loved me in front of Maria and Holly, they were standing behind him and made a scene of cheering. He had winked at me and left me to deal with my ridiculous friends.

Holly had somehow managed to get us last-minute appointments at a swanky dress shop in town. We'd been required to send in our measurements prior, and Holly assured Maria and me that Donni knew what he was doing. She also told us that we were going to love Donni, but pulling up outside the gorgeous brick building with ivy crawling up the sides, I was more than a little apprehensive. The place screamed money. Dalton had tried giving me his heavy credit card, but when I had refused it, he had given it to Holly who was more than happy to take it.

Maria's cheeks were flushed—a sure sign she was excited—and she linked her arm with mine as Holly ushered us into the building. The door rang with a sweet chime as it shut behind us, and not even ten seconds later, a large man in black slacks and a silk purple button-down came hurrying towards us.

"*Amore mio!*" He embraced Holly and kissed her cheeks. "How I have missed you! And you brought friends!"

The man I assumed was Donni turned to Maria and me, still standing behind the door. He embraced us each in turn. "*Bellissima, assolutamente bellissima.* Yes, yes this is going to be wonderful." He was loud and exuberant, smelling of expensive cologne, and his thick Italian accent made him just a little hard to understand. His bald head was so shiny, I could practically see my reflection in it.

"So, um… how do you know Holly?"

Before he could answer, another, much slimmer, man came from the back carrying a tray holding champagne flutes. "Donatello, please do tell me you did not forget their refreshments?"

"My apologies, *il mio amato marito.* I was so eager to greet them, I am afraid it slipped my mind. But I see you already took care of it. *Dove sarei senza di te?* I was just getting ready to tell them about Antonio."

Maria had grabbed a flute off the offered tray, but paused before raising it to her lips. "Wait… you're Tony's family!"

I glanced between her and the two men. "Wait, Tony Tony? Like big, butch, black leather, Tony?"

Donni laughed, "Ah yes, the one and only. He is my nephew."

Holly headed towards a sitting area that had white cushioned chairs fanned out around a giant mirror. "Donni and Lorenzo are the classy ones, clearly."

They beamed at her, and I decided that Holly had been right—disliking the two men would've been like hating on a puppy. Maria and I sat next to Holly, while Donni and Lorenzo disappeared behind a large velvet curtain. I eyed the incredibly expensive-looking gowns that surrounded us—elegant white wedding dresses on one side of the room, and evening gowns in various shades and colors on the other.

"Oh, here they come. Y'all are going to love this. Donni designs all the dresses in here, and Lorenzo makes them. Honestly, they are total goals. They adore each other, and there's no better place for a gown than here. All their dresses are exclusive to this shop."

I raised my eyebrows. "Sounds expensive." I jerked backward and about fell out of my chair when a piece of plastic unexpectedly hit me in the face. Holly had flicked Dalton's credit card at me. She and Maria cackled while I resituated myself, and gave them both dirty looks.

Point taken.

Maria opened her mouth, probably to say something smart, but was interrupted by the reappearance of Donni and Lorenzo. Donni was pulling one dress rack and pushing another, while Lorenzo followed behind with yet another rack. Oh boy. Each of us had a cart stop in front of us, and I gaped at the row of dresses in front of me. This was gonna take all day.

Donni clapped his hands together, cheeks bright red and eyes bright. "*Signoras*, you have each sent me your measurements. *Che meravigliosa varietà.*"

Lorenzo nodded in agreement, though I had absolutely no idea what he was saying. And measurements? I hadn't sent anything. One of the boys, maybe?

Donni continued, making a grand sweeping gesture to the dresses before us. The two men acted like the world was their stage—all dramatic exuberance that was hard not to get swept up in.

"Here at DL Designs, we pride ourselves on making dresses for all—not just the slim."

Lorenzo nodded even more enthusiastically. "*Snello non è l'unica forma di bellezza.*"

Maria, Holly, and I exchanged glances. Italian was a beautiful language, but outside of "*signora*" and "*sì*" I was out of my depth.

Lorenzo kept our glasses full as we spent the next several hours trying on dresses. After the fourth or fifth dress, he went to the back room and came back with a bountiful charcuterie board loaded with cheese, meats, crackers, and even fruit and nuts. Donni had put on a pair of glasses at some point and would, every now and then, make suggestions on styling the dress or would ask Lorenzo about taking in a few inches here or there.

I couldn't lie—being pampered like that was a blast.

Lorenzo had left in search of bottled water, and Donni had run off proclaiming he had the perfect dresses for us. After giving us each some water and insisting we drink it, Lorenzo joined his husband in a far corner, and they talked in a hushed whisper. A few minutes later, they came back up to us as we were debating which one to go with.

Lorenzo shook his head. "No, no. You ladies have looked absolutely lovely in these gowns. How could you not? We made them!" He winked at us, then continued, "But these are the ones. *Perfetto.*"

Donni handed us each a gown wrapped in a protective cloth.

Holly's was a sweeping red gown with an open back and off-the-shoulder sweetheart neckline. She ran her hand down the glimmering material and smiled. "Oh yeah, this is it. Donni, you've been holding out on us." She hurried off to try it on.

Maria held hers out for me to see, and I nodded in approval. It was a gold sequined mermaid gown, with a deep V that would plummet down her chest and probably give Diego a heart attack.

I carefully pulled the protective sleeve from my gown, and Lorenzo winked at me. "Holly mentioned you had affections for two certain bikers we know. I thought this a fitting color."

The dress I was holding was, without a doubt, the most beautiful and elegant thing I had ever seen. I was instantly in love. It was a deep, midnight blue chiffon with cap sleeves that would leave most of my arm bare, and each side was split from the mid-thigh down. The Queen Anne neckline would show just the right amount of cleavage, and the bodice was decorated with fine, silver beads in a leaf pattern. Holly came out of the dressing room looking like a Hollywood star in the floor-length sheath dress. We smiled when our eyes met, and she ushered me to the dressing room.

When I walked out, I felt like a queen. Maria was resplendent in her dress, every sinful curve highlighted by the clinging fabric. She gasped, and Holly feigned swooning, when I walked towards them. I rolled my eyes at their dramatics. The three of us stood arm in arm in front of the floor-length mirrors, and damn if we weren't a sight to see. Donni wolf-whistled and Lorenzo jabbed him with an elbow.

Holly looked at them through the mirror. "We'll take them. I think I love you two."

When their point of sale system cheerfully dinged with the total, I just about died. Holly and Maria assured me Dalton wouldn't even blink at the price tag, and I couldn't help but wonder how on earth a biker could be so damn rich. How many figurative pies did the Saints have their fingers in and, more importantly, what kind?

Maria dropped me off at my place, and I waved them goodbye as they drove away. Unlocking the door, I hung my dress from the banister and headed into the kitchen, kicking my shoes off as I went. Unbraiding my hair from the disheveled mess it had become, I ran my hands through it until it was mostly smooth. I made my way over to the counter, and calmly pulled a knife from the block. Then I threw it with every ounce of strength I had at the dark figure sitting at my table.

When he dodged the blade, just barely, I shrieked in surprise and flipped on a light.

Mac looked at the blade embedded in the wall behind him, and then at me with a raised eyebrow. "Where the hell did you learn to throw a blade like that?"

I did the only thing that I knew would distract him from an answer I couldn't give him—I freaked the fuck out.

"Oh my God, what the fuck are you doing? I was fucking attacked by a rando in my apartment not even five months ago! Are you crazy?! Sitting in the damn dark, lurking like some serial killer!"

He stood quickly. "Shit, Vixen. I'm sorry, I wasn't even thinking about that. I should've turned on the light or waited outside, but I just wanted to see you. Fuck." He ran a hand through his hair, and then reached for me.

I buried my face in my hands and tried to breathe. One, I had almost skewered the man I loved. Two, I had defended myself a little too well. I tensed when Mac wrapped his arms around me, but he pulled me close, whispering soothing words and desperate apologies in my ear. When I finally started to relax, I looked up at him.

"Have you not heard of a little thing called texting? Or calling? Carrier pigeons?"

His mouth quirked up in an amused, crooked grin, and I found myself staring at his lips.

"Carrier pigeon?" he teased.

I shoved him, but he didn't budge. "Anything is better than scaring the ever-loving shit out of me."

He kissed the top of my head. "I know, Vixen. I will be more careful, promise." I stepped away from him and frowned at the knife. His gaze followed mine, and I swear he chuckled. "Go upstairs, gorgeous. Take a shower, relax, and I'll be up in a bit."

I raised a single eyebrow at him. "You sure?"

He shooed me towards the stairs, spanking me on the ass as I walked away. I laughed, and ran upstairs before he could get me again. I grabbed my dress on the way up, and shut myself in my bedroom. I stashed the gown in the far back corner of my closet, then grabbed a pair of pajamas. Just as my hand closed on the knob, I hesitated. Mac was here for a reason, and I was no virgin. I finally, *finally*, had this man all to myself, and nothing else to do. Fuck the fuzzy pants—this called for lace. After making the switch, I headed to the bathroom.

I took my sweet time in the shower, relishing the hot water soothing away the aches and pains that, unfortunately, came with adulthood and recovery. I paused when I heard a knock on the door as I was toweling off, but Mac hollered, "Got it!"

I ripped the tag off the bundle of lace, stuffing it deep inside the trash can. Twisting my hair in a messy knot on top of my head, I surveyed my reflection. The dark green lacy nightgown had two thin straps holding it in place over my breasts, which were threatening to spill out of the top. The bottom barely covered my ass, and the satin material clung to my curves. I wasn't nearly as voluptuous as Maria, but I could still make heads turn when I tried.

I poked my head out the door and looked around for Mac, but I could still hear him fiddling around downstairs. Before I could second-guess myself, I headed downstairs, trying to do that sexy down-the-stars walk I had seen on some of Maria's favorite telenovelas. Instead, I felt like an absolute idiot and nearly broke an ankle. Sigh. As I rounded the corner, I could hear the faucet running. It was now or never. I really hoped I hadn't read the situation wrong.

I decided to go for the casual approach and leaned against the wall, watching him at the sink before saying, "Thank you for cleaning up the mess."

"Vixen, I thought I told you to wait—" He turned as he spoke, and seemed to lose his train of thought when he caught sight of me. "Fuck me."

Well, that's the plan.

I batted my eyelashes innocently. "What?"

Dark blue eyes roamed my body, and I swear I felt them like the sweetest of heat on my skin. I smiled at him, and his returning smile was all sinful promise.

"I thought you said lace isn't worth the time if you don't have a good man with rough hands to take it off you."

"Mm, I did say that. I'm surprised you remember. So, I guess that begs the question…"

He took a step closer to me. "What question is that, Vixen?"

"Do I have a good man to take it off of me?"

He closed the distance between us with liquid grace, picked me up, and carried me to the counter. His hands nearly encompassed my thighs, and I wrapped my legs around his waist, using them to pull him closer to me. He pressed his face into my neck, kissing the sweet spot there and nibbling at the tender skin. He ran his hands over my nightgown, a ravenous look in his eyes.

"I don't know about *good*, Vixen, but I can tell you the chances of this little thing you've got on surviving the night aren't all that high."

"Ruin it, baby," I whispered, and then I slid my hands under his shirt and caressed the hard ridges of his abdomen, wishing I could trace the tattoos I knew were there. "Ruin me."

That was all the encouragement he needed. He bunched the material in his hands and ripped it with one smooth movement. My poor gown—still, I had a feeling I wasn't going to miss it too much. His hands cupped my breasts, and he pressed his knee against my center. I ground against it, but he withdrew despite my protests.

"No, Vixen. Tonight, you're going to listen to me. You're going to take exactly what I give you. Understood?"

I stared at him. I had never been with someone so dominant, but I wasn't unfamiliar with the dynamic. His words were turning me on, and I had a feeling if he started talking dirty to me, I was going to come undone. I had been lost in thought when he sharply twisted my nipple, and I gasped from the pain.

"Understood, Vixen?"

"Fuck, yes. Understood." I looked up at him through lowered lashes. "Sir."

His blue eyes blazed like fire. I knew he would like that.

He moved his hands, wrapping one in my still-wet hair and moving the other to my inner thigh. He pulled on my hair until my head tilted back, my neck completely exposed to him. I already knew what the man could do with just his fingers, and I was fucking starving for more.

"The things I want to do to you…" He started kissing my neck again, and when he dragged his teeth across my skin, I moaned.

He leaned back, untangling his hand from my hair and spreading my legs further apart. "Mac," I whimpered. For the love of all things holy, this man was taking his sweet fucking time.

"You want to come, gorgeous?"

I touched myself, desperate for the contact. "Yes, sir."

His gaze followed my hand as it left a trail through the wetness between my thighs. Just as I started teasing my clit, he grabbed my hand and brought it to his mouth, licking the arousal off my fingers. He groaned, a deep, guttural sound, and replaced my hand with his own.

Using the rough pad of his thumb, he rubbed punishing circles on my clit, and I thrust my hips into his touch. When I closed my eyes, he paused and said, "Keep them open, Vixen. I want to see you come."

I licked my lips but opened my eyes to meet his as he slammed three fingers inside of me. Gasping at the sudden intrusion, I shivered in anticipation. Last time, he had worked me up to three but, shit, I wasn't complaining. He worked the sweet spot inside of me, rubbing and twisting and pumping in and out of my pussy. I was so fucking close, I began to pant.

He eased another finger inside of me, stretching me so deliciously, and I threw my head back in ecstasy. "Please, baby, oh God." He bit my exposed neck and I screamed his name as I shattered around his fingers. He didn't stop moving, and I could hear the sounds of him working me through my high.

"Fuck, Vixen. Just like that, baby. Come undone for me. Such a good girl."

He removed his fingers and held them to my lips like last time. After I licked them clean, he tossed the ruined nightgown to the side, and I didn't hesitate before taking his shirt off of him. I leant forward, tracing the swirls of black ink that run across his chiseled stomach and up his neck. Before I could undo his pants, he picked me up, and the cool metal of his belt buckle pressed right against my vagina.

"I'm not done with you yet, Vixen."

I smiled at him. "Better fucking not be."

If he was anything like his brother, I was in for a long night, and I was perfectly okay with that. I tried to get down and walk, but he refused to let me go, carrying me up the stairs into my bedroom. He laid us down on the bed, and kissed my bare stomach.

His grin was an easy, carefree one that I had never seen before, and I instantly loved it. The second his lips met mine, we lost ourselves in each other, losing all track of time. He was all over me, his hands roaming and squeezing and teasing every inch of my skin. I threaded his thick, black hair in my hands, pulling him closer and locking my legs around his hips. When he untangled himself from me, it was to kiss his way down my throat over my breasts and stomach, and to the apex of my thighs. He bit me again, then soothed away the pain I was beginning to crave with a kiss.

"I've been wanting to do this for months, Vixen."

Before I could speak, he licked my pussy and I cried out. When I looked down at him, he said, "I've been dying to know how you taste." I looked down, watching as he pushed his tongue inside of me, and I couldn't stop the tremble in my legs if I'd tried. He withdrew, and I moaned, but he squeezed my hip. "Even fucking better than anything I could've imagined." Then he buried his face there, and I was utterly helpless to the absolute skill this man possessed.

When I thought back to his brother doing the same, the thought just turned me on even more. I reached for Mac, pushing my pussy into his face in a desperate search for my climax. He growled in approval, fucking me with his tongue and raking his teeth along my sensitive lips. When he sucked on my clit, I came so hard and fast, I fucking saw stars. I thrashed against his face and he didn't let up, grabbing my hips to hold me in place as he swallowed every drop of cum gushing from my cunt. He consumed me in every way, and I was in heaven.

I was still riding my high when I heard the jingle of his belt buckle. I opened bleary eyes, watching him take his jeans off to reveal a cock thickly lined with veins and so hard I was sure it hurt. He pulled a condom out of his pocket, but I shook my head. I wanted to feel him bare inside me, like I had with Dalton.

"Babe, I'm clean and I'm on the pill. I trust you. For the love of God, I need to feel you inside me."

He hesitated, and I could see the shadow of uncertainty across his face. I leaned up and reached for him, wrapping my hand around his dick, and licking the droplets of precum off of him. He moaned, and I pumped my hand a little harder.

When he finally gave in, he grabbed my hips and threw me back into the bed, flipping me over onto my stomach in the same motion. He pulled my ass into the air, and I wiggled it teasingly.

"Fuck me, Mac. I won't break."

His grip on my hips became almost punishing, and I spread my legs, flattening my chest on the pillows to give him better access. When he guided his dick to my entrance, I whimpered and rubbed myself against his tip. He stilled me and then slammed into me so hard, my legs nearly gave out.

He kept me upright, one arm wrapped around my waist, using the other hand to grab my hair. He pulled my head back, arching me into a position that had his cock ramming inside so deep, I forgot how to breathe. I was screaming with each violent thrust, and his primal grunts were hot as hell. It was incredibly rough, bordering on painful, and it was some of the best sex in my life. Who knew I would like a little pain with my pleasure so much? Evidently, he did.

The sounds of sex filled the room, and his hand moved from my hair to my throat. He pulled me into an almost sitting position, and as he fucked me, he whispered dirty things in my ear. "Such a good fucking girl, such a perfect little pussy for my cock. Do you like the way I fuck you, Vixen? Do you like the way I stretch your sweet, tight cunt?"

He squeezed my throat tight enough that my vision started to black out, and I felt it the moment he came inside of me. He growled in my ear, and jerked his hips as his cum shot out of him in spurts. He released my throat, and as the oxygen rushed back into me, I shattered around him. My body wasn't mine anymore as I hit the fucking stars and kept going.

Still, he murmured into my ear, "That's my girl. Come for me, Vixen. Give it all to me, gorgeous. Fucking hell, you're stunning. See how your pussy weeps for me."

I was a shaking, soaking wet mess when he laid us down on the bed with his half-soft cock still inside of me. He pulled me to him, my back flush with his chest, and held me until my senses returned. My pussy was sore as hell, but my God, I regretted not a damn thing. He got out of bed and, when I protested, he kissed my forehead.

"I'll be right back, gorgeous."

I frowned but, true to his word, he was back no more than five minutes later with a wet washcloth and a glass of water.

He babied me into a sitting position and insisted I drink. I did so as he spread my legs again and gently, reverently cleaned me with the warm, wet cloth. Just like his brother had. He kissed the inside of my thigh, tossed the washcloth in my laundry bin, and pulled me close to him again as he sat back down. I set the glass on the nightstand and curled into him. The thumping of his heartbeat was becoming my new favorite sound, drowning out the little voice in the back of my mind telling me this was a bad idea. He grabbed the blanket from the foot of my bed and wrapped it around us and, for a few minutes, we sat in a peaceful silence.

That was, until my stomach growled loudly.

"What happened to that snack you promised me?" I quipped, and I felt his chest vibrate with a chuckle.

"It's probably sitting on the counter getting cold."

I looked up at him. "Well, do you think you can go get it? I'm not entirely sure my legs work yet."

He made a sound that was all male satisfaction, and I smiled. He didn't bother getting dressed as he left the room, and I found myself with an excellent view of his really nice ass. He glanced over his shoulder at me before heading down the stairs, and caught me staring unabashedly.

"Like what you see, Vixen?"

I couldn't wipe the smile off my face even if I'd tried. "I've made it pretty damn clear I do. However… I'd love to see if I like the way you taste as much as I like the way you look."

He winked at me before heading down the stairs. I stretched and eased myself under my comforter, feeling properly used and perfectly content. My phone was still sitting on the nightstand, and I reached for it. I took a picture of Mac's discarded pants and sent it to Maria and Holly. Their response was immediate, and I was laughing when Mac came back in. He was carrying a massive Taco Bell bag, and I showed him the string of texts when he crawled under the covers with me. Much to my surprise, he took my phone and sent them a picture of the two of us in bed.

"Sorry, ladies, I'm stealing her for tonight."

I was digging through the Taco Bell bag when he shut off my phone and tossed it to the side. Sometimes, I marveled at how well Mac knew me. Burritos, even cold ones, were top-notch post-sex food.

We sat there talking most of the night, munching on chips and telling each other stories. I hated not being able to be entirely truthful with him, but I weaved my past with Nicole's as best I could. It was oddly reminiscent of my time in the cabin with Dalton. I found myself less and less able to lie to them.

At some point, Mac started talking about his past—nothing too detailed, just quiet pieces slipped between sips of soda and stolen bites of burrito. I wasn't sure when his walls had come down, but I was quickly realizing that the man behind the armor might be one of my favorite people. He apologized for how cold he'd been when we first met, his voice rough with the kind of regret that doesn't come easy. And as he spoke, I could feel the edges of old scars beneath every word. Someone had hurt him once—maybe more than once. And here he was, handing me trust like it wasn't the most precious thing he had left. It wrecked something in me to know that I was going to break it. That this fragile, impossible thing between us couldn't survive the weight of my lies. But I buried the guilt—deep—and let myself drown in what he was finally willing to give.

Sometime around three in the morning, after he had finally fallen asleep, I ran my hand down the side of his face. The room was quiet except for the soft hum of the ceiling fan and Mac's slow, even breathing. He lay next to me, one arm heavy across my stomach, his chest rising and falling against my side. His skin was warm. His heartbeat steady. We'd finally crossed the line we'd both been circling for months. And it had been... God, it had been everything.

I should have felt peace. Or at least the kind of sleepy bliss you see in the movies. But instead, I stared up at the ceiling, my mind spinning like a storm. There was a mic in the corner and in the air vent and, in the silence, I felt them like a heavy presence. Wired by Bridges. Monitored by Braxton. I had spent ages pretending not to care. That I could do what I wanted with my body. That I was entitled to this. To *them*. That as long as I did my job, nobody would question what I did with my nights. Or who I spent them with.

But I knew that wasn't true.

Braxton wasn't just suspicious anymore—he was watching. Listening. Judging. A quiet part of me called it jealousy. And soon I'd have to sit across from him again. Another debrief in another nondescript van or diner booth. Would he bring it up? Would he say my name the way he did when he pretended it was about the mission and not control?

Would they fire me? Maybe. Not because I slept with someone, I didn't think. But because I cared. Because I wasn't pretending anymore. Because *Nicky* had stopped being a mask, and started being real. Real enough to fall in love with two men who should've been nothing more than just part of the mission. Instead, they had somehow become part of me. I shifted slightly, trying not to wake Mac who murmured something in his sleep, and tightened his grip on me. My throat closed. God, I was in so much trouble.

Would I do it again? My gaze flicked back to the vent. Yeah. Yeah, I would. I hadn't planned on this. The love I felt for these two took my breath away. I knew it was going to kill me to walk away. But denying my feelings, distancing myself from them… that would've taken a strength I'm not even sure Hercules possessed.

Braxton be damned. Let them listen. I was going to love them even if it killed me.

# Chapter 16

Mac and I barely left the bedroom all day Thursday. At some point later in the evening, he got a call from Silas which brought our love fest to a tragic end. When he went to put his shirt back on, I stopped him and did something I had been dying to do—trailing my tongue along every line of ink, tasting and savoring every inch of his toned abdomen. It got us both so hot and bothered, he bent me over the dining room table and fucked me so hard we left marks on the floor from the table scooting across the floor.

I kissed him goodbye and watched him leave until his bike disappeared from view. I headed for the shower, but stopped when I got into the bathroom. At some point, he had braced me up against the shower wall and held me while I bounced on his cock. When I came, I had pulled on the shower curtain which came crashing down around us. He had promised to fix it before leaving but, big shock, we had gotten distracted. I grinned and went to grab my phone from the bedroom. I snapped a picture of the fallen rod and sent it to our group chat before fixing it myself.

After my shower, I checked my messages for their reply and laughed.

Dalton had said, "Gee, wonder how that happened."

To which Mac replied, "I'll give you two guesses. Try not to be too jealous."

Feeling sexier and more desired than I had ever felt in my life, I took a picture of myself in the mirror and sent it back to them along with the message, "Jealousy has no place here, boys."

"Fuck, brother. When did we get so damn lucky?"

"I'm not looking a gift horse in the mouth."

"Are you calling me a horse, Mac?"

"I'm not into zoophilia, gorgeous."

"Ew!"

"That's nasty, dude."

"She asked."

"I definitely did not. Anyways... When did you two accept I wasn't choosing?"

"If we had tried making you choose, what would you have done?"

I didn't hesitate. "Quit you both cold turkey. All or nothing. I wouldn't come between you guys."

"But you would happily *come* between us. What do you think, Dalton? One of us in her pussy, while the other fucks that dirty mouth?"

"I think I'm supposed to be paying attention in this dumb-as-hell meeting and instead I'm now trying to think of toothless grandmas and puppies with broken legs."

I was confused, but his comment quickly made sense when he sent a picture of his jeans tenting underneath a table.

"See what you do to us, Vixen?"

"Fuck, I just left and I'm ready to go back."

The two of them proceeded to fill my phone with the things they wanted to do to me, and I decided the first opportunity I got, I was going to have them both. Fuck it all. After a while, I lied and told them I was going to sleep, before immediately calling Holly and Maria in a group FaceTime.

Maria squealed. "Girl! First Dalton, now Maverick! Holy shit, you're nuts."

Holly winked at me, lounging in her bed in one of Jackson's shirts. "You, my darling Nicky, are officially my favorite slut."

"In the words of the great Dorothy, you are the queen of Slutdom. Long live the queen."

I cackled. "I absolutely am not. I just have a... voracious appetite."

"Okay but—and I don't even know if I am allowed to ask this as a married woman—how are they?"

"Fuck, I'm married and I don't give a damn. You didn't tell us squat about Dalton, now you've spent the day with Maverick. Girl, you need to spill!"

I bit my lip. "Well, let's just say that it was more than adequate. And the house is fully, and I mean fully, broken in."

Holly choked on the Coke she was sipping, and Maria snorted with laughter. Jackson walked into the frame and asked, "What are y'all talking about?"

Holly smirked at him. "How good your bosses are in bed."

He looked at her and then back at us on the small screen, and back at her. "Right, on that note... I'm out." Dude practically ran out of the room, and we all howled.

"Oh hey, by the way," Holly set her drink down and leaned forward, "I hired a girl I know to do our hair and makeup. She'll be at my place around two, I think. Bring your dresses and we can all get ready here."

"Why do I feel like the prized pig being led to auction?" I joked half-heartedly.

Maria bit her lip at the same time Holly said, "Um, 'cos you kind of are?"

Maria tsked. "I mean, it's not that bad."

"Have you guys met the DiAngelos?"

"Once."

"I've only met the youngest brother. He's not an asshole like the rest of them, but that probably has something to do with the fact that he's Diego Jr.'s age."

"So, it's bad?"

"Honestly, they probably don't even know you exist. From what Jackson was telling me, it's Greyson that's the issue. Probably 'cos Dalton and Maverick can't, or won't, hide how they feel. Some kind of power trip thing or something, maybe? He wants what they have."

Holly's words weren't exactly reassuring, but Maria added, "Not only will Mac and Dalton be there, but so will we. Including Diego and Jackson. Trust me, no one is fucking with us."

I told them about the first time Greyson had gotten me alone, and Maria visibly cringed.

Holly's hazel eyes narrowed to near slits. "That asshole! Putting your hands on you like that!" Holly said.

Maria glanced to the side. "You're not the only one. He likes trying to take things that aren't his. He was super-touchy with me when Mac was in that coma and Diego was at the hospital every day. But it all stopped after I had Diego Jr."

I cursed the screen preventing me from hugging my friends. "Listen, it'll be fine. Power in numbers and all that. Greyson is an ass, but we got this. We're going to go there, looking fine as hell, eat all the hors d'oeuvres, and drink too much champagne."

"Then we're going to go home and get railed by our fine-ass men!" Holly raised her Coke in a mock toast and I grinned.

Maria clapped her hands. "Hell yeah, I'll drink to that!"

My phone pinged low battery and since it was getting late, I bid my girls goodbye and hung up. I lay in bed after plugging the thing in, missing Mac's presence and Dalton's voice.

I was finally meeting the DiAngelos, the whole reason for this charade. Tomorrow, I had to get as much information about them as possible without raising suspicion—or creating any more hostility than necessary.

At some point, I fell into a fitful sleep, and I woke up around ten feeling like crap. Mac had told me not to worry about coming in today, so I was surprised when my phone showed a missed call. I tried calling him back, but the call went straight to voicemail. A couple of minutes later, a text from him came through: "It's all good, Vixen. I'm in with Silas right now but I'll talk to you later."

I stretched and then headed into the bathroom. After washing my face, I tossed back a couple of ibuprofen and headed downstairs for a late breakfast.

With a plate of eggs and toast in one hand, and a cup of coffee in the other, I made myself comfy on the couch before flipping on the TV. I loved these quiet mornings alone. Or, at least, I used to. Now I found myself wishing I had company. Blue-eyed company, to be exact. I sighed and started a letter to Uncle Tommy while sipping on my coffee. In between bites of egg, I told him about the dinner with the DiAngelos. I also added that, from everything I had seen, the Mills brothers and a vast majority of the club had no desire to be affiliated with the family. I guess, in the back of my mind, I was hoping to prove that the men I loved weren't the bad guys.

I busied myself around the house, wiping down counters and cleaning my bedroom and bathroom until a honk outside startled me. Opening the door, I discovered Maria idling at the end of the driveway in her minivan. I walked out to her, not bothering to put shoes on, as she rolled the window down.

"Girl, what are you doing? I thought we were meeting at Holly's?"

She shrugged. "Your place is on my way and, besides, do you really want to try and figure out how to strap a gown with shoes and shit to the back of a bike?"

I eyed my Triumph, sitting at the front of my drive. She had a point.

"Alright, let me get my shoes on and I'll be right back." A few minutes later, I had everything I needed and tossed it into the back of her car. "Who's watching the kids?"

"Diego's *mamà* has them until tomorrow night. I'm kind of excited—he and I haven't had a lot of alone time lately."

I listened as she told me about the most recent drama with her ex on the way to Holly's. It had been really messing with Jewel's head, and I hated it for the poor kid. But I reassured Maria that she wasn't to blame. Just because she slept with the dude didn't make her responsible for all his bad decisions. Holly's place was about five minutes from mine, a swanky-looking Georgian that could've fit two of my townhouse inside.

"So, like… how rich is Holly?"

Maria gave me a look like she couldn't believe I was asking, since the answer was staring us right in the face.

It was around one, which meant we had about an hour before the lady Holly hired would be here. Jackson was out, evidently taking care of some last-minute things with Diego, Mac, and Dalton, so it was just us girls. I liked how close the four men were. After all, Jackson had been one of the guys to follow me to the clubhouse that first night.

Holly was in sweats and one of her husband's t-shirts, and I teased her as she opened up the door. "What, no butler?"

She scoffed at me. "Had to fire the last one for sleeping with one of the maids."

I stared at her, and after a few seconds, she started laughing. "I'm teasing, Nicky. I don't like people enough to have a bunch of servants or whatever running around."

With that, Maria and I followed her up the stairs to what I had assumed was a spare bedroom but actually just turned out to be a giant closet. Oh, so the girl was *rich* rich. I glanced at her when she wasn't looking. Holly wore jeans and faded rock-n-roll t-shirts. I think I'd only ever seen her in the same two pairs of shoes. It made sense, when I thought about it. She could always get us spots at some of the best restaurants, had all these connections, and could call in all these favors—I just never put two and two together. Now, staring at the massive array of clothes, I wondered about this other side of my friend I hadn't seen, or paid attention to, before.

The three of us took turns helping each other into our gowns so we would be ready when the makeup artist got here. Holly laid out a pair of gold and diamond pendant earrings to go with her red gown, and then showed off this gorgeous bangle she had found. It was a golden snake with ruby eyes that rested its head on the top of her hand and wound its way up her arm.

I held it up to the light. "Christ, Holly. This is fucking beautiful! It's perfect for you, too!"

She smiled at me. "I'm not normally one for the glamorous and shiny, but I couldn't resist it. I got something for you guys, too!"

She handed Maria and me each a box with a pretty white bow on top.

Maria opened hers and immediately started talking animatedly in Spanish, something she did when she was incredibly excited. I marveled at the golden diadem she held aloft as she raved, though neither Holly nor I had a clue what she was saying. It was a delicate weaving of several gold bands, and a single teardrop diamond hung from the center. It would, quite literally, be the cherry on top of her outfit. She switched to English and looked over at me. "Nicky, open yours!"

I did so eagerly and, for a moment, I just stared at it. I wasn't really sure what it was, or even how to wear it, but I could tell it was incredibly expensive and so beautiful it took my breath away. I clenched my jaw, trying to fight back tears, and looked up at Holly who was watching me carefully.

"I had it custom-made. It goes around your thigh and hangs down the outside of your leg. I thought it would look beautiful with your dress since it had those splits in the sides."

I started crying in earnest, and they both hurried to me—together, we all just looked at the marvel I was holding in my hand.

Several strings of tiny sapphires hung from a band of dark, blue velvet. They fell almost to my knee, where they gathered into one singular band from which a tiny, silver fox dangled. Words couldn't describe how absolutely beautiful it was. They were still hugging me when Holly said, "Maria helped design it. But we've been friends for over a year now. You've become someone we can rely on, someone we trust. You're auntie to Maria's kids, you put up with my shit. You're my best friend—Maria's too. And now Mac and Dalton are head over heels for you. We're not letting you go. This is just... our way of saying welcome to the family."

I started sobbing. They had no idea that I wasn't some girl born and raised in Georgia. That my name wasn't really Nicole. I mean, yeah—Nicole and I had our similarities. But she wasn't me. And I wanted so very, very badly to tell them the truth. I had grown to love them both, just as I found myself deeply in love with Mac and Dalton. I hated it, but I had to see it through. Once I brought the DiAngelos down, I would tell them the truth. And I would pray to whatever god was in charge that they would be able to forgive me.

I was drying my eyes when the doorbell rang and Holly's dog, Hugo, went ape shit. She hollered at him, "Oh sure, Maria and Nicky pull up and not a peep out of you, but suddenly you're all attack, kill. Useless mutt."

Her terse words would've been mildly alarming to an outsider, but I was fairly confident she would kill for that dog. We followed her to the top of the stairs, where we were met by Hugo who was still howling, but stopped once he realized we were there. He turned his attention to getting pets, and when Maria turned away from him, trying to avoid getting hair on her dress, he turned his soulful and sad eyes on me.

I knelt carefully and scratched the basset hound's ears, and his whole butt wiggled. Hugo was about as bright as a box of rocks, but was the sweetest dog and utterly devoted to Holly.

Holly came back upstairs with a team of people behind her and Maria said, "Holly, I thought you said makeup artist. As in singular."

Before Holly could answer, a girl with bright pink hair held out her hand. "Hi, I'm Morgan. I'm pretty fucking awesome, but I am *not* Wonder Woman. No way could I get all three of you ready in time on my own. So I brought a few more Amazonian warriors, if you will."

I instantly liked her open and friendly demeanor.

We each got assigned three people—one for hair, one for makeup, and even one for nails. My team consisted of a lady named Zoe, her twin sister named Chloe, and a guy named James. Everyone had come prepared—Chloe was toting a makeup and hair suitcase thing the size of a small motorcycle. James tried talking me into some crazy bejeweled nail idea, but I really wanted to keep it simple. We met halfway, me agreeing to a few silver embellishments on my thumb and ring fingers, and him agreeing not to turn my hands into a disco ball. Over at Holly's chair, Morgan showed her an eyeshadow palette while another woman applied French tip acrylics. Maria had her head tipped back as a slender guy applied rouge to her full cheeks.

We sat in those chairs for almost four hours, the team of cosmeticians working at the speed of light to get us ready. The dinner started at seven, and we were cutting it fine. When we finally got up, the three of us stood in front of the small wall of mirrors in Holly's closet room. A couple of the people gathered behind us wolf-whistled, and a few others cheered. We made a damn striking group. Holly's red dress brought out the hazel in her eyes, Maria's golden brown skin seemed to be literally glowing, and me? Well, I just couldn't stop staring at the fox dangling on my thigh.

A horn honked downstairs, and we exchanged puzzled looks. Having gotten all packed up, Morgan and her team followed us down to the entryway. A sleek, black limousine waited out front, and Maria clapped her hands in delight. I looked at Holly, who shrugged.

"Wasn't me."

Morgan was loading up the cargo vans, and they all waved goodbye as they pulled past the limo. Just then, my phone dinged cheerfully. It was Mac, on our group chat.

"Enjoy the ride. We'll see you soon, gorgeous."

"It was my idea, by the way," Dalton said.

"Bullshit."

"Totally was. Love you, baby. Get here quick and save me from these lunatics."

I laughed and showed Maria and Holly the string of texts. Maria twirled, the sequins on her dress catching the last of the evening light, making her look like a diamond.

The driver climbed out and opened the door for us. "Good evening, ladies. My name is Nicholas, and I will be your driver tonight. I hope the car is stocked to your liking. It is about a twenty-minute drive to our destination."

Careful so as not to wrinkle our dresses or mess up our hair and makeup, the three of us piled into the car.

"Where even is the party or dinner or whatever it is?" I asked.

"It's less a party and more of a chance for Greyson to show everyone how big and bad he is with his buddies. But it's at this hotel downtown. He usually rents the lower ballroom. It's not half-bad as long as you ignore like eighty percent of the people in there. The bar is open, the food is free."

I groaned, and Maria patted my knee reassuringly.

Holly held up a bottle of tequila in triumph, and I eyed it. I needed to keep my wits about me, but one shot wouldn't hurt, right? Holly drank straight from the bottle and then passed it to Maria, who took a swig and passed it to me.

Fuck it. "Here's to liquid courage and best friends."

They cheered, and I took a long swallow, then another for good measure.

Holly laughed. "Easy, killer—I know you're nervous, but I think your boy toys would kill us if you showed up drunk."

Maria chortled at that.

I rolled my eyes and threw a fancy cloth napkin at them.

We nibbled on the cheese and crackers, took a couple more sips of tequila, and bantered about our lives as old ladies. I was doing my best to calm my nerves. I had my girls with me, and I looked fine as hell. Plus, I got to spend the evening on the arms of the men I loved. I was going to shove my quickly growing mountain of issues into the back of my mind, and just worry about having fun and getting as much information about the DiAngelos as possible.

That's all that mattered.

# Chapter 17

When we pulled up outside the hotel, Holly took one last shot and said, "Fuck. Here we go."

Maria and I shared an apprehensive look. Despite all our bravado, I think we were all a bit nervous. However, when I caught a glimpse of the entrance, the butterflies in my stomach practically caught on fire.

Holly whistled and Maria said, "*Dios mio*, we are some lucky as hell women."

Diego was wearing a white suit that would've made most men look like a backstreet pimp, but had him looking like the sugar daddy every woman in Atlanta might wish for. Jackson, meanwhile, was in a black three-piece suit with a red tie, looking like a prince of Hell.

And my guys? Well, my guys had me wanting to forget the party altogether. I mean, seriously. We should have just left then and there. Dalton and Mac were both wearing light grey suits with dark blue ties. Mac's hair was slicked back, and Dalton was leaning up against a marble baluster. He stepped forward next to his brother when our driver stopped the limo.

Holly was the first to climb out, her dress pooling on the ground around her, and a slow smile crept across Jackson's face. She twirled for him, and he grabbed her by the waist mid-spin, kissing her for all the world to see. Maria was behind Holly, and the lights from the hotel bounced off her dress. She looked like an angel, and Diego's face said he was more than willing to worship. For a second, nerves paralyzed me. This was a much bigger event than I had thought, and I had no idea what waited inside. I wasn't even armed—a 9 mm would sure feel good on my thigh right about now.

Taking a deep breath, I stepped out behind my friends and my eyes immediately found Mac's.

His smile erased every single doubt in my mind, and his gaze seemed to devour me.

Dalton whistled low and said, "Damn baby girl, how am I supposed to concentrate tonight?"

Mac stepped behind me, wrapping his arms around my waist and kissing my neck. I leaned into him as he whispered into my ear, "I've never seen anything so beautiful."

Dalton pulled me from his brother, and gave my hips a gentle squeeze. I tilted my head up toward him and he said, "You, my love, never cease to amaze me."

His kiss was sweet and chaste but still Maria teased, "Geez you two, get a room."

I blushed crimson when Holly said, "Just make sure the bed is big enough for three."

Jackson looked positively scandalized, and Diego shook his head. As he did so, a stray breeze caught the flap of his jacket, and my breath caught. He was fucking armed. I scanned Jackson, only then noticing the bump in his waistline at the small of his back. One quick glance confirmed that both Mac and Dalton were also carrying. I suddenly felt an even stronger desire for a weapon of my own.

Unfortunately, if anything went sideways tonight, I would have to rely on the guys to protect me and my friends. While I was used to having a partner, I had never had or needed a savior—and the feeling was not a good one. Especially after my run-in with Daniel.

I did my best to brush the thought from my mind as Mac and Dalton came up on either side of me. I placed my hands on the crooks of their arms as they escorted me inside, and I couldn't resist stretching up to press a kiss to their respective jaws. Dalton's familiar, comforting scent fused with Mac's sinfully delicious musk made me feel weak in the knees.

Silas was waiting just inside with a guy about the same age. If Silas' presence wasn't enough to raise the hairs on the back of my neck, this guy was. He had cold, cruel eyes and something about him had every instinct inside of me warning me not to turn my back.

I must have tensed up, because Dalton placed his hand on top of mine and murmured comforting words, while Mac pressed a kiss to the top of my head. "Easy, Vixen. We've got you. No setting bikes on fire tonight, gorgeous. Let me and Dalton take care of everything."

I nodded, giving them both a shaky smile. Holly and Jackson were right behind us, Maria and Diego right behind them. Strength in numbers. It was going to be okay. I forced myself to look at Silas, and his cool, grey eyes leered at me. Fucking gag. We came to a stop in front of him, and he practically ignored the men at my side.

"Good evening, Ms. Moore. I'm so glad you could make it. You look good enough to eat." His gaze lingered on my chest before raking over my body in a way he had no right to. His language was much more formal than usual, obviously posturing for his buddy.

I felt like throwing up in my mouth. This time, it was me that felt both Mac and Dalton tense. Before they could say anything, I said, "Thanks for the invite. Though I didn't really have a choice."

"Of course you had a choice, girl. You just wouldn't have liked the other option." I glared at him and he smirked at me. "Nicole, meet Luca DiAngelo. Luca, this is the one I was talking about. I told you she had both my best men pussy-whipped."

I was pretty sure Dalton was clenching his fist hard enough to break, and the vein that jumped in Mac's jaw looked like it was about to pop.

"Watch how you fucking talk about her, Silas. You have the title, but you do not have their loyalty."

My eyes flew to Mac, the blatant threat hanging heavy in the air, and Silas' neck turned beet-red. Luca watched the whole exchange with cool amusement. If memory served, he was one of the four men at the head of the DiAngelo mess. The one who dealt in women and children—treating them like cattle—and the thought of Silas even mentioning me by name made me sick.

If anyone was responsible for my missing girls, it was him.

I dragged my eyes from Luca and tugged on Mac. "Come on, he's not worth your fucking time. Not yet. Let him live in his grand delusion a little longer."

Silas swore, calling me a bitch and a few other things to boot, so I had to practically drag the brothers to where our friends were waiting by the staircase. Together, the seven of us descended to the ballroom below. We hadn't even been there for thirty minutes, and already tensions were high. This was going to be just fantastic.

The ballroom was decorated in deep purple, and a few waiters roamed around, carrying trays of champagne flutes. I grabbed one, as did Holly and Maria. The guys, however, didn't touch the alcohol.

"Anyone else feel like Barney threw up in here?"

Maria choked on her drink and Holly laughed. "Barney, as in the mildly traumatizing dinosaur? Yes, absolutely."

Maria frowned. "Wait, how was it traumatizing? I loved Barney!"

Diego and Jackson shared an amused glance over their heads.

Holly sipped her champagne. "Girl, that fucker was creepy as hell."

"I used to have nightmares as a boy about that damned thing coming into my room at night."

All eyes swung to Dalton and he shrugged, unashamed by the admission. I bit my lip to keep from laughing but he noticed, of course, and winked at me, causing me to snort in a very unladylike fashion.

I turned my attention to Mac, who was scanning the room. "Did you have nightmares about a chubby, purple dinosaur?"

Mac shook his head vehemently. "Of course not." He put a hand on the small of my back, guiding me towards a table in the corner. Our friends followed and he said, loudly enough for them to hear, "But I did have beef with the Cheshire Cat. How the fuck did that thing end up in a children's movie?"

Diego wrapped his hand in Maria's. "Flying monkeys, man. My mom used to take me to the zoo all the time as a kid. After I watched that damn movie, she couldn't take me anywhere near the ape exhibit without me freaking out. She said I was, like, twelve before I got over it."

Maria threw her head back laughing. "Oh my God, I remember your mom telling me about that. I didn't realize you were still scared of them when we met. I would've totally used that."

He spanked her, and she yelped, swearing at him in Spanish and blushing furiously.

As we all sat down at the table, everyone looked at Jackson, who threw his hands up. "I got nothing. I guess I was just a braver kid than all you weirdos."

Holly leaned over and kissed him before giving him an angelic smile and then said to us, "Actually, on our first date, I discovered the man was deathly afraid of dolls. I, of course, had no idea and thought I was giving him a truly wonderful gift when I put fifty of them in his bedroom."

Jackson rolled his eyes. "Yeah, I had to sleep in my living room for over a week. Dolls are creepy, man. Anyone who has seen a horror movie knows they're bad news!"

A waiter came over to see if we needed anything, and Mac ordered me a whiskey without me even having to ask. I placed my hand on his thigh under the table, and on my other side, Dalton was fiddling with the fox charm on my leg. Maria was teasing Diego relentlessly about his fear of flying monkeys. Holly and Jackson had their heads bent, foreheads almost touching as they whispered to each other.

Scanning the room, I noted the location of every DiAngelo I knew in the room. There were a lot of them, and I chewed my bottom lip.

Dalton squeezed my thigh. "What's on your mind, Vixen?"

I shook my head but turned to him. Maybe now was a good time for answers.

"I was just wondering how Silas got involved with the Saints. And how he got the Saints involved with the DiAngelos. I mean, I know all about how he became president of the club. Which, by the way, is horse shit. But, I don't know much outside of that."

Dalton exchanged a look with Mac, who nodded. Dalton reclined in his chair, stretching with his hands behind his head. Mac placed his hand on mine on the table, his thumb rubbing circles on the back of my hand. Taking a sip of his drink, Dalton said, "Silas showed up about ten years ago. Mac and I were just punk-ass teenagers; I was barely sixteen. Our dad took Silas under his wing, for whatever reason. At first, everything was great. Silas was like a second dad to us.

"And then our mom… she went out shopping one day. Holly and Jackson had just started dating. This was five years ago, but I remember it like it was yesterday. The whole club was just different then. We were all hanging out, just playing cards and shooting the shit. My dad got the call first. She was bleeding out on the streets; she knew she was dying. But her priority was just telling us she loved us one more time. By the time EMS got there, it was too late. DOA.

"She'd been gunned down in the street like a common dog. But she was the heart and soul of this place. Her and my dad started the Saints. It did something to us. It killed my dad. We buried him barely any time after Mom. Silas was there the whole time, a refuge in our storm if you will. He carried our mom's casket to the grave, and then our dad's. Mac took over but—"

"I wasn't ready."

I realized the whole table had been listening when everyone looked to Mac, whose words had been so quiet we could barely hear him over the rest of the room.

"I wanted to be. But, to be honest, I was still a kid. I had no fucking idea what I was doing." His eyes were haunted and I leaned into him. "What happened next… That night, that fucking coma. When I woke up, Silas was different. I was even less fit to lead, and he saved my life. Saved Dalton's life. It seemed like the only logical solution at the time. By the time I realized I sold my soul to the fucking devil, club rules prevented me from taking it back."

"I don't get it," I said, looking at them all in turn. "Once you realized he was a Class A asshole, why couldn't you just kick him out?"

To my surprise, it was Jackson who answered. "It doesn't work like that, Nicky. Clubs, especially one as big as ours, operate on an honor system. There's a strict set of rules. We have our own laws and procedures and shit. Even to kick out a prospect like Daniel for some dumb shit, it takes more than just one guy saying fuck it. There's a voting system."

Diego nodded, his arm wrapped around Maria who was playing with her wedding ring. "When we voted on Silas taking over, the vast majority of us just assumed it was temporary. Shocker, Silas had other plans. He had a few people in place. And to replace a president, even a temp one, you have to have a majority vote. He's got enough pull that we haven't been able to vote him out."

"That's bullshit."

Holly and Maria nodded in agreement with me, and Dalton smiled at me.

"We'll figure it out, Vixen. Mac and I have a plan."

"But in the meantime, you have to play ball with groups like the DiAngelos."

"We have our ways, gorgeous. What did you think all those motel rooms were for?"

I gave Mac a confused look, and Dalton leaned forward. "What we say cannot leave this table."

His words were a stark wake-up call, and I looked at the ground. I was a fucking traitor, and the words burned when they left my lips.

"Of course not."

"The motel rooms aren't just for bikers and their families who need a place to stay. What Silas doesn't know is that we use them as a refuge for people trying to get away from the DiAngelos. Victims of sexual assault, families of people who cheated them in some way, people who just want an out. We stash them at the clubhouse, use our connections to build them a new life. New names, new identity, new everything."

I gaped at Dalton and then looked up at Mac, who had his arm around my shoulders. A glance over at the other side of the table revealed they all knew about this. Not a single surprised face.

"You guys save them?"

Holly flagged down a server for a drink refill and said, "We try. We can't save them all, but we try. Silas is going to get his one day, Nicky. Don't doubt that."

I couldn't believe it. I needed names—names of the people they've saved. I could use this to get pardons when I brought the DiAngelos down, if pardons were even necessary. I was elated. I knew my men and my friends were good people, but now I had proof. Leaning forward, I pulled Dalton by his collar until his lips met mine. Kissing him deeply, I heard someone clear their throat, but I wasn't quite done. Turning, I met Mac's lips with my own and he made a deep, guttural sound of appreciation.

Another, louder sound of someone clearing their throat came, and I reluctantly drew away from Mac. He was watching me carefully, a crooked smile on his face, while Dalton looked like a kid in a candy shop.

"I love you two so much. Please don't ever forget that."

"I'm sure the hotel has rooms available if you three need to disappear for a bit…"

Jackson's voice was light and teasing, and Holly quirked an eyebrow at me in amusement. Diego coughed, trying to hide a laugh, and Maria smacked him in the shoulder.

Dalton returned his hand to my thigh, once again playing with the charm there. "If we leave now, we aren't coming back."

I blushed and leaned back into Mac's side. Suddenly, microphone feedback pierced the air, and I winced. Looking over to the stage, I saw Silas and four DiAngelos in front of a podium. I swallowed thickly. I knew exactly who those men were. One, of course, was Luca DiAngelo. Next to him was Armand DiAngelo, king of the gun trade. Then there was Michael DiAngelo, who dealt and made more drugs than you would find in a Walgreens. And lastly, worst of all, was Robert DiAngelo. He oversaw it all. If evil were ever to take a human form and walk the earth, it would look a hell of a lot like him.

"Everyone, settle down now. Here we gather to celebrate the best partnership Georgia has ever seen."

Silas sure did think a lot of himself, pompous asshole. Luca seemed to agree, his lip curling as he watched Silas, and even Michael rolled his eyes.

Robert surveyed the room like he couldn't believe he had been dragged here.

Silas was oblivious and continued, "Almost five years ago, the Steel Saints and the DiAngelo family joined rank. The Saints are no longer some back-alley group of crooked boy scouts."

I scowled at the description, my face reflected around the table, and I felt Mac tense up from where I still leaned against him.

"Robert and I have big plans, everyone."

Silas surveyed the room—a mix of dirty politicians, cops, and lawyers, as well as a few other Saints. I committed every single one of their faces to memory. Other than my table, everyone was here willingly and took part in the whole DiAngelo mess to line their pockets. Bunch of scumbags.

Silas droned on for a few more minutes about his big plans, without ever really saying what those plans were. It was boring as hell, but when he was done, a flurry of wait staff came out of a side door pushing carts of plates covered by shiny silver domes.

I sat up, and Holly murmured, "Saved by the bell," as the wait staff set plates of food in front of every chair.

The seats quickly filled, and the room was mostly quiet besides the sound of silverware on plates. The whole thing was a stuffy, oppressive affair, but at least the food was good. Our glasses were never empty, and I just watched and listened, taking in as much as I could of everything around me. Three tables down, Silas sat with the heads of the DiAngelo family. I barely paid attention to the easygoing banter at my own table, wishing we were closer to Silas.

When I glanced towards them again, I about dropped my bite of roast chicken when I met the grey eyes of Luca and Robert DiAngelo. Robert's face was a mask but Luca smirked at me, his smile cold and cruel.

"Vixen?" Dalton leaned forward, placing his hand over mine where it rested on the table, and squeezed to get my attention.

"Yeah, sorry. What did I miss?"

Six pairs of concerned eyes watched me—they must have been trying to get my attention for a hot minute.

Maria's gentle, brown eyes searched my face. "Everything okay, *mija*?"

"Yeah, it's just… every time I look up, someone at that damn table is staring over here. And, just a second ago, fucking Luca was looking at me like a piece of meat."

Mac's eyes flew to the table in question, looking ready to get up and beat a DiAngelo to a pulp. Dalton gripped my hand so tightly it almost hurt. I hurried to reassure them both. "It's okay, really. I'm fine. I just… I really hate those sons of bitches." Holly's hazel eyes assessed me, and I smiled at all my friends. "I'm fine. Let's just try and have a good time tonight, okay?"

About an hour later, as the evening was winding down and I had danced until my feet hurt, I was making my way to the bathroom. Dalton and Mac had taken turns twirling me around the dance floor and, despite the weight of the evening, I was actually having a lot of fun. Even Maria, Holly, and I had danced to a fun beat none of us knew. Every now and then, I would catch wind of some new tidbit of information from an overheard conversation that I squirreled away. I'd just disentangled myself from Dalton's arms as he pressed a kiss into my neck, and everyone was gathering their things from the table. I, however, was feeling the effects of too much whiskey and water, and needed to find a bathroom as soon as possible.

The nearest bathroom was set down a long hallway, just outside the ballroom. Out of fucking nowhere, Silas appeared at my side. He grabbed me by my elbow and said, "Good evening, Ms. Moore. You and I need to talk." His mouth was near my ear, and I could smell and feel his hot breath. His grip was unforgiving.

I snarled at him, "Mac and Dalton are waiting for me."

He twisted my arm, and I forced myself not to wince as he pulled me into a darkened room.

"They can keep fucking waiting."

I yanked myself out of his group, stumbling away from him. "What do you want?"

"We've talked about this. You will address me with respect."

"I only give respect to those who have earned it."

I was expecting his backhand, and dodged it easily.

"You little cunt. I knew you were trouble the second I laid eyes on you."

I wished I was armed so damn bad. But Mac and Dalton weren't even five minutes away. They had been my heroes once before—if I took too long, they would come looking for me.

"What do you want?" I repeated.

Silas just stared at me and finally said, "I want to see the look on your face when you realize I wasn't the one who wanted to speak with you."

Then he turned and left, and for a minute, I was confused as hell.

Then, from a dark corner behind me, a low voice said, "Alone at last."

My heart just about burst out of my chest, and I spun around—not an easy feat in heels. Luca was watching me, so still and silent that I hadn't even noticed him when Silas had dragged me in here. Two quick strides, and he was on me.

Luca wrapped his hand around my throat and backed me into the nearest wall. He was so quick, I didn't even have time to yell.

"You have been giving Silas some trouble. Trouble, trouble, trouble." The room was dark, but those steel-grey eyes would haunt my dreams. He leaned in, and I shuddered as he dragged his nose down my cheek and my neck. "A woman like you could make me some serious money. What do you think? $200 a night, $300 and anything goes?"

I gagged at the thought, and then the motherfucker licked me. Without hesitation, I kneed him in the balls with every ounce of strength I had. He roared, his hands going to cover his junk, and I ran for the door.

"Remember our conversation, bitch. Keep pushing. I'll always have a place for you."

He let me go, much to my surprise. I didn't stop running until I ran into Dalton coming out of the ballroom.

He stopped me. "Woah, baby, woah. Easy, Vixen. What the hell is going on? What's wrong?" His blue eyes searched my face, and Mac came up beside him, scanning the hallway behind me for threats. Dalton wrapped his arms around me, and I relaxed against him, trying to get myself under control. Mac made as if to go down the hallway, but I stopped him.

"No, don't. Please, I just want to go home. My home, not the clubhouse. Let's end the night on a positive note. Okay? For me?"

Dalton rubbed his hands up and down my bare arms. He and his brother exchanged a look over my head. Eventually, they both nodded.

Mac moved to right behind me, sandwiching me between the two of them. He kissed the top of my head. "Home it is."

Maria, Holly, Jackson, and Diego were waiting by the limo which was idling by the door. We all climbed in after I reassured them I was fine. I joked I still had to pee and all, but begged them to leave it be. They did, and as we pulled away, I clung to the cell phone I had stolen out of Luca's suit pocket. I couldn't help but smile.

DiAngelos, zero. Me, one.

# Chapter 18

The limousine driver dropped off everyone at their door. Mac, Dalton, and I were the last to get out. I was eager to forget my interaction with Luca and Silas, and even more eager to put that cellphone somewhere safe until I could get it to Braxton. They headed to the kitchen, but stopped when they noticed I wasn't following them. Dalton reached for me, pulling me into a kiss. I stepped back, turning to Mac and kissing him too.

I'd had threesomes before, but something about the anticipation of this one made butterflies swarm my stomach. Still, there was something I had to do first.

I walked towards the staircase, tossing a smile over my shoulder at them. "I'm going to die if I don't get out of this dress. I'll be in the bathroom."

Dalton winked at me. "Don't get too comfortable, Vixen."

Mac disappeared into the kitchen, and I could hear him rummaging around. I pulled off my heels, heading for the bathroom. I had a Ziploc baggie full of pads, and a waterproof travel bag for makeup. I washed my makeup off real quick, then dumped the pads haphazardly in one of the drawers, tossing the phone in there after powering the thing off. I tucked the baggie into the makeup baggie, then dug around I found the sewing kit I had put in there.

Just as I sat on the toilet, there was a knock on the door, and I realized I had been in here for a hot minute.

"Um, yeah? What's up?"

It was Mac who answered, "You good, Vixen?"

"Yeah, babe. I'm going to hop in the shower really quick. Why don't you and Dalton hang out in the bedroom? And can one of you bring me some PJs?"

This time it was Dalton. "You won't be needing PJs." Then came a dull thud. Dalton cursed, and I realized Mac must have pushed his brother into the wall. I couldn't help but smile.

"Play nicely, you two. You'll both get turns. I'll be out in a few minutes."

I heard them walk away, then struggled out of my dress. There was only one tiny zipper, and the gown was unforgivingly tight. I banged my elbow on the counter, cursed, and after a few minutes, was finally standing naked and triumphant in a pile of blue. I frowned when I realized I should've just asked one of them to help me, but brushed the thought to the side.

The shower was big enough for me to sit on the edge opposite the shower head and not get too wet with it on. I perched there and started sewing the edges of the makeup bag up. I kept the thread tight, doing my best to ensure the phone was as secure as possible in the bag. I leaned out of the shower, tossed the phone in the back of the toilet, and rinsed off quickly.

I paused before opening the bathroom door, briefly considering the repercussions of sleeping with the two brothers. They didn't even know the real me, but I knew and loved them. I wanted to be with them, and damn it if that didn't make me the most selfish person alive. I shoved the annoying bitch that was my voice of reason way to the back of my mind, and wrapped myself in a robe.

I was instantly grateful for my king bed, because there was no fucking way the three of us were going to fit on my old mattress. Mac was sitting on the edge of the bed, and those dark blue eyes I had grown so fond of watched me closely as I walked closer. Dalton was sitting at the back, leaning against the headboard with his hands behind his head and his white button-down opened to reveal his defined chest and abdomen. The smile he gave me was cocky. Having both their eyes on me at the same time sent a jolt of electricity straight to my core.

I bit my lip, and Mac stood up, walking towards me.

"Look at me, Vixen."

I turned my attention away from his brother and back to him. He cupped my jaw, his thumb on my chin as he tilted my head back, forcing me to look up at him as we stood chest to chest.

"You sure about this, gorgeous?"

I tucked my hands into his back pocket, eager to get as close as possible. There were just too many clothes between us.

"I'm positive, Maverick Mills. I'm yours, as long as you want me."

His hand moved from my chin to my robe, sliding it open and running his hands around my waist. He kissed my neck and I groaned, peeking over his shoulder to see Dalton who had leaned forward, propping his elbows on his knees. He looked ready to pounce, and I smiled at him.

"Don't be a hog, Mac. Bring our girl over here."

I yelped in surprise when Mac suddenly grabbed my ass, picking me up. He carried me over to the bed, dropping me down next to Dalton who leaned over me. His lips captured mine in a searing kiss, and I moaned into his mouth. He cupped my breast in his hand, rubbing circles over my nipples as I arched into his touch. I reached up, running my hands across his stomach and down to his belt. I unbuckled his pants and reached down past his boxers. When I wrapped my hand around his cock, it jumped in response. He groaned.

I loved the way I affected them. Just as much as they affected me.

Dalton trailed kisses down my jaw, over my neck, and to my chest where he captured a taut nipple in his mouth. I whimpered as he lavished the peak with his tongue, sucking and licking and raking his teeth over the sensitive flesh. I began to pump my fist around his cock, but he moved out of reach, and I whimpered again. His hand was suddenly between my legs, and he trailed a finger through my slick folds. He released my nipple with a pop and turned to Mac with a grin.

"She's fucking soaked, man."

My eyes flew open, and I turned my head to find Mac standing just behind me. He had discarded his shirt and pants, and was leaning up against the wall in just his boxers, which were impressively tented. His eyes were almost black as he bent down on the bed next to me.

Wrapping a hand around my throat, he kissed me and bit my lip before leaning up and looking at his brother, who still had his hand on my pussy. "Make her come, Dalton." He grabbed both my wrists and pinned them above my head with the hand not on my throat. "I wanna hear her scream, brother."

My eyes flicked between the two men on either side of me, and I swear the fire in my belly could've set the bed ablaze.

Dalton removed his hand from between my legs, and I protested, but Mac bent low, whispering in my ear to hush. I was so focused on him and the alternating pressure he was putting on my neck that I didn't see what Dalton had moved to do.

Suddenly, my whole body about came off the bed and I cried out, "Oh my fucking God, yes!" I looked down at Dalton, who had licked my pussy from top to bottom before biting my clit. He winked at me before disappearing between my thighs.

I thrashed and Mac crooned into my ear, still gripping my wrists with one hand and my throat with the other. "Such a good fucking girl. Do you like how my brother eats your pussy, Vixen? Are you going to let me fuck that soaking wet cunt when he's done?" I whimpered and tried to free my hands from my Mac's grip, but he nipped my ear. "No, gorgeous. You're staying right fucking here. Just take it—come for us, baby."

Dalton licked and sucked my pussy like it was a mission he had trained for all his life. He slipped his tongue inside of me, and used his thumb to rub my clit.

"Yes, baby, yes. Please, Dalton, baby, I am so fucking close." I rubbed my pussy in his face as best I could, and his groan vibrated through my body.

Mac moved closer to me, squeezing tighter on my throat and murmuring words that would make the devil blush in my ear. I screamed when I came, very glad I didn't have any close neighbors—the pleasure was almost blindingly painful. I tried twisting away from Dalton, but he laid his arms across my waist, pinning me in place and continuing to suck my soul from my body as I came.

I whimpered when he finally moved away, and Mac leaned back, finally letting my wrists and throat go. Dalton kissed me, and our tongues clashed as I savored the taste of myself on his tongue. He pulled away, and said, "That's my girl."

I didn't even have time to respond before Mac grabbed my hips and flipped me over onto my belly. A glance over my shoulder showed him pulling his boxers off, his dick jutting out and I eyed it, longing to run my tongue over the thick veins.

Dalton grabbed my chin, gentler than his brother, and turned me back to him. I watched him as he also stripped off his boxers, licking my lips at the sight of him. Just as hard and thick as his brother, looking every bit as delicious.

"Remember that morning at the cabin? When I filled that pretty little mouth with my cum?"

Mac grabbed my hips, pulling my ass into the air as he planted kisses down my spine. He fisted his hand in my hair, pulling my head back. I moaned, "Fuck, Mac. Please, for the love of God, fuck me. Someone fuck me."

Both of them chuckled, and I sent glares in their direction.

"Hear that, Dalton? Our Vixen is begging."

Mac spread my legs, rubbing the tip of his cock across my soaking wet opening, and I whimpered, "Please."

Dalton fisted himself, and precum leaked out of the tip of his cock. I licked my lips, my eyes flitting back and forth between the two men. He pressed the tip of his dick against my mouth, but when I opened it to take him, he withdrew, and I swore, which made them both laugh again.

"Assholes."

Dalton ran his finger down my jaw, and Mac pulled my head further back. I was arched perfectly, ass up high enough that Mac could bury himself deep inside me, and my head far enough back that Dalton could hit the back of my throat with his cock.

Dalton pressed his tip against my lips once more. This time, I moaned but kept my mouth closed, and a shudder ran through me as Mac rubbed his cock up and down my vagina, spreading my cum all over my pussy. They must have exchanged some unspoken signal because they slammed their cocks into me at the same time—I would've collapsed against the bed if it hadn't been for Mac holding me up.

Dalton's hand replaced Mac's on the back of my head, pulling on my hair for leverage, groaning as he thrust his cock in my mouth. "Open up for me, Vixen. Relax your jaw, you can take all of me."

I did my best to follow his directions, and I could feel the tip of his cock brushing the back of my throat. Tears ran down my cheeks, and he threw his head back in absolute rapture.

Meanwhile, Mac was slamming his cock into me from behind. The hot, slapping sound of skin on skin and the sweet, musky smell of sex began to permeate the room. I couldn't see him, but he kept his grip tight on my hips.

"That's it, gorgeous. See how you were made for us. This fucking pussy is so damn tight. Look at how that dirty mouth takes my brother's cock. How does it feel to have us both deep inside you? You're gonna be fucking filled with cum, Vixen. This sweet little cunt is fucking dripping."

His filthy words had shivers racing down my spine, and I moaned around Dalton's cock.

The pleasure was building like a tsunami in my gut, the light in the room fading to black, and my head fucking spinning. It hurt so fucking good, and I couldn't stop it when my body started to shake. Dalton groaned and began to fuck my mouth even harder. Mac also picked up the pace, thrusting into my pussy so fast and hard, the whole bed began to move from the wall. As Dalton pounded into me, he shoved me back onto Mac's cock, and as Mac slammed his hips into me, I was pushed forward, taking Dalton so deep I couldn't breathe.

"Fuck, I am going to come, baby girl."

I blinked bleary eyes up at Dalton when he said that, and Mac growled behind me. He spanked my ass, and I almost fell into Dalton who came with a shout, shooting hot cum down my throat. I swallowed every single drop as his cock jerked inside my mouth. He stepped back, breathing heavily, and watched as Mac continued to fuck me. He spanked me again, and I screamed, the combination of pain and pleasure so addicting I prayed it would never end. He pulled my head and I sat back, leaning against his chest, and he bit the spot where my neck turned into my shoulder.

"Mac, Dalton, baby, yes, please, oh God, yes! Yes, baby, yes!"

I shattered around Mac's cock, coming so hard my vision went black, and I felt Mac pulse inside of me as he roared and filled me with his cum.

I felt Mac's cock twitch, and still he didn't stop moving. He fucked me through my orgasm, and it seemed like it would never end. I realized I was crying, and I panted as my vision swam. Mac held me close, laying me down on the bed as he pulled his cock out of me. I closed my eyes and reached for Dalton, who sat next to me, and pulled my head into his lap. I kissed his inner thigh, and he smiled down at me—smoothing my hair with one hand, and gently rubbing my breast with the other.

My eyes shot open when I caught on to what Mac was doing.

"No, God. I can't. I can't come again. You're going to fucking break me."

I tried squirming away, but Dalton held me in place as Mac ran his tongue around my entrance. He licked every single drop of cum off of me, and rubbed his nose through my slit.

"Fucking hell, Vixen. I love the smell of you."

Then he grabbed my thighs and began sucking on my incredibly sensitive clit, and I cried out, "Mac, please."

He stopped and looked up at me. "We can't let you go to sleep dirty, Vixen. Now, be a good girl and lie back while I eat this pussy."

And how the fuck could a girl say no to that?

I lounged in Dalton's lap, his still half-hard cock mere inches from my face. He caressed my breast with one rough hand, running his thumb over my nipple over and over again. He pulled at the pink nub and I gasped, then shouted as pleasure overtook me once again as Mac slid his tongue deep inside me. He licked my inner walls and I moaned, then reached up and grabbed Dalton's cock.

He jerked in surprise, but I began twisting and rubbing his dick up and down until he was fully hard again. My spit hadn't dried on him yet, and he threw his head back against the wall. "Yes, Vixen. Just like that."

Mac looked up and saw what I was doing to his brother. He grinned and went back to eating my pussy like it was his favorite meal. I thrashed against him as he buried his face in me, and kept jerking my fist up and down his brother's cock. Dalton and I came at the same time, hot spurts of cum shooting over my hand, and I screamed yet again. This time, my voice was noticeably hoarse. Dalton leaned over me, kissing me and whispering in my ear how much he loved me.

Mac fell onto the bed on his knees, and I watched as he pumped his own hard cock. My eyes never left his as he came with a groan, spreading his thick white seed all over my stomach. He sat back on his heels, surveying the mess we had made. The bed was crooked. The sheets were a crumpled mess. His brother's cum dripped over my shoulder and chest, while Mac's cum covered my stomach.

We were all covered in a fine sheen of sweat, and I teased, "What was that about not letting me go to bed messy?"

Mac smiled at me, and I felt the low rumble of Dalton's chuckle. Dalton gently lifted my head off his lap, and I protested as he stood up, but he hushed me. Mac left the room, and a few seconds later, I heard the shower turn on. Dalton bent down, picking me up bridal-style in his arms, and carried me to the bathroom. He set me down, and I leaned heavily on Mac, my legs practically jello.

Mac helped me in the shower and, almost reverently, he scrubbed me from head to toe after squeezing my shower gel on a cloth. I whimpered when he ran the cloth between my legs, my pussy so achingly sore I was sure I would be walking funny for weeks. He kissed the same spot where he had bitten me earlier and crooned into my ear, "Such a good girl, Vixen. I love you."

It was the first time I had heard those words from him, though he showed me every day, and I wrapped my arms around his neck, pressing my head into his neck and whispering, "I love you too."

He dried me off and, despite my protests, he carried me back to the bedroom.

Dalton had changed the sheets, and put his boxers back on. Mac put me next to him before climbing in on the other side, dragging the comforter over all three of us. I snuggled between the two men, tangling my legs with Dalton's and lying on Mac's chest. I was clean and warm, and perfectly exhausted.

For a minute, I let the peace of the moment wash over me, and I basked in the wonder of it. Between the two men I loved, one running his hands through my hair, and the other rubbing a soothing hand up and down my leg, I was deliriously happy.

Before I knew it, I was fast asleep.

# Chapter 19

The following Monday, I took the day off. Though the job had become less like work and more like taking care of my family and getting paid for it, I still felt the need to ask permission. Mac and Dalton both gave me funny looks when I made the request, but they sent me on my way with a kiss and, in Mac's case, a spank on the ass.

I pulled into a cute little lunch spot about an hour outside of Atlanta on my Triumph. My bike got some odd looks from a bunch of guys, which turned into judgmental ones as soon as their eyes landed on me.

I ignored them all, and I realized that once upon a time, Kaitlyn McGrady would've been more than a little bothered by what people thought of her. I guess Nicole was rubbing off on me. I kinda liked it.

I sat at a corner table, and ordered a sweet tea while I waited for company. I had Luca's phone tucked safely in my jacket pocket, and my knee bounced faster the longer I waited, my nerves getting the better of me. About twenty minutes later, just as I went to check my phone, a hand on my shoulder made me turn.

Braxton stood over me, in jeans and a t-shirt, which was a stark contrast to his usual suit. "Afternoon, Nicole."

I gave him a brief smile as he sat across from me.

"Your last letter left much to the imagination."

I glanced around and slid the wrapped phone to him as subtly as possible.

He glanced at it before giving me a questioning look.

"I found this. I think it'll be everything you've ever wanted."

"Is this what I think it is?"

"I took it for a test drive, if you will. It's got all the latest games."

Braxton tucked the phone into his pocket as a waiter made his way over to the table. We both ordered lunch and, while we waited, I told him what I had learned about the club. As I talked, I realized that, subconsciously, I was painting the people I loved in a rosy light.

Maria, the sweetheart who took every lost soul under her wing.

Holly, the fiery loudmouth with a heart of gold.

And my boys. Dalton, the one who stayed up late helping kids with math homework. The one who loved working on the bikes, who made people laugh when they were at their lowest. And Mac. Big, gruff, and often standoffish, but on the inside, just a man with a taped-up heart.

Good people.

*My* people.

At some point, I realized Braxton had all but stopped paying attention to my brief. When he reached for my hand, I was startled enough that I didn't immediately withdraw. He looked at me, an unfamiliar look in his eyes.

"I'm worried about you."

I finally withdrew my hand. "I'm fine."

He shook his head and reached for me again, and this time, the look I gave him was utterly baffled. "Katie, you're getting in too deep. I should've made you come home the second you landed in the hospital. I've been watching you ever since, and this isn't going to end well for you. Watching… and listening."

I tucked my hands in my lap. "What the fuck are you talking about?" But I already knew.

Braxton was clearly becoming agitated, and our food sat in front of us, getting cold. He leaned forward. "Do I need to elaborate? I've heard every breathless moan. Every fucking word whispered in the dark. I know what you sound like when he makes you come. I know Dalton calls you 'baby girl' when he's buried inside you." His eyes were practically burning holes into me. "You are too fucking close. You've become *her.*"

The silence between us turned sharp and electric. I couldn't stop the cold shiver that worked its way up my spine. The way he looked at me—it wasn't just anger or betrayal. It was something else. Something possessive. It scared the shit out of me.

"Braxton…" I started carefully, but he cut me off.

"I gave you space. I backed off. I trusted you to keep your head. But you've fallen so far into this role that you don't even *want* to come up for air. This," he said, patting his pocket, "will help. But, damn it, can't you see what I am trying to say?"

I scoffed. "No, not fucking really. Who I sleep with is none of your business. Clearly, I'm still doing my job."

He slammed his hands down on the table, and I jumped. He was acting unhinged, and I hushed him as he began to speak, but he ignored me. "I… I've come to care for you. Watching you this past year. I know you better than they ever will. And now I have to stand by while you spread your legs for some bikers?"

I brought my hands back to the table, clenching the silverware so hard my knuckles were white. "Excuse me? You're my boss, but you don't own me."

"Oh, but *they* do?" He wouldn't look at me. Finally, his eyes met mine, and he lifted his chin. "I'm just trying to keep you safe, detective."

I blinked and then blinked again. He couldn't be serious. Did he actually think this was justified? Maybe I was a hypocrite, but this crossed a line.

"I want a new handler."

"You don't mean that."

It took everything in me not to stand up and shout. I leaned forward and enunciated every word. "You think I'm kidding? You've been going off about how I'm too close, how I'm too attached. It's you! You're the problem! And yeah, I am sleeping with a couple of bikers. But they have names. And the job description didn't include celibacy."

He glared at me. "Don't tell me you actually have feelings for them?"

"None of your damn business." I lifted my chin, knowing he already knew the answer to that question. "Listen, they are good men. And my love life is of no business of yours unless it interferes with my mission—which it doesn't."

"That's where you're wrong."

"No, that's where *you're* wrong. And why I want another damn handler."

"So, if it came down to it… a shoot-out between us and them, you would have our backs?"

"I would have the backs of the good guys. Everything I've seen says we're on the same side."

"We follow the law. They don't."

"They saved my fucking life, Braxton. They stopped Daniel. They brought me to the hospital. They sat by my bed. Where were you when I was bleeding out on that floor? Were you watching then? Watching as I fought to stay alive? What would you have done if he had raped me, agent?"

Raising my voice, I spat the last word and earned a few curious looks from the nearby tables.

"Katie, it's not that simple—"

I cut him off. "It really is, though. I'm here today because they cared more about me than your damn agency." I stood up to walk away, and Braxton stood with me, grabbing my arm and pulling me to him.

"I love you. The real you. The one that they don't even know exists. I've been by your side even if you couldn't see me for over a year. Why can't you see what I am trying to say?"

Yet again, I pulled myself away from him, and started to head for my bike. "I don't mean to be a bitch, but it's not reciprocated. Not to mention a huge conflict of interest."

*Hypocrite*, a little voice whispered inside my head. But I shoved it to the side. I was ready to go, leaving my uneaten lunch on the table. "I want a new handler, Braxton. Hope the phone helps."

I ignored his protests as he followed me, swung a leg over my bike, and rode away.

I was still fuming when I got back to the clubhouse. Originally, I had planned on taking the whole day off, but if I went home, I knew I would do nothing but sit there and stew in my anger. Plus, I hadn't even had a chance to eat. So, I busied myself in the kitchen. My mind was still racing, reeling at Braxton's sheer audacity. I mumbled a few choice curses. I felt stupid. I had known that my relationship with the two brothers would have repercussions, but I'd been living in a wonderful bubble of bliss. And denial. Braxton had just popped it.

"Damn, Vixen, I think you killed it."

I startled, turning to look at Dalton, who had walked in and was watching me. I looked back at the tomato I had been cutting, which was eviscerated into mush. Shit. I dropped the knife and ran my hands through my red hair, which was free of its usual braid, and gnawed on my bottom lip. I kept my focus on the poor tomato, even though I heard him walk towards me. He placed a gentle hand on my hip, and turned me to him. Using his thumb, he freed my lip from between my teeth, and ran his hand along my jaw.

"What's wrong, baby girl? I thought you were taking the day off?" Those clear blue eyes I loved searched my face, and I reluctantly looked up at him, shaking my head. He frowned and pulled me closer to him. "No ma'am, you're not getting off that easy. Talk to me, Nicky."

I sighed and buried my face in his shoulder, allowing his familiar scent to envelop me like a comforting blanket. He seemed to sense my need to just be held, and wrapped his arms around me.

After a few moments, he whispered, "Talk to me, Vixen. Let me help."

"You can't. I can't." I muttered the words into his jacket; it was a miracle he heard me.

He ran his hands down my back. "Why not?"

Resting my chin on his shoulder, I trapped my lip between my teeth again, worrying the sensitive skin. He took a step back, and I looked up at him.

"I want to tell you, but I can't. Not yet. I'm sorry."

He played with my hair, running his hands through it. I knew I would never stop enjoying the way that man touched me like he couldn't get enough. I closed my eyes, enjoying the sensation even while guilt threatened to tear me apart.

I expected him to protest or push harder for answers, but instead, he simply kissed my forehead and said, "Whenever you're ready, I'm here."

I opened my eyes, willing myself not to cry, and just drank in the sight of him. This would be so much easier if he was an asshole. If I didn't love him. He and his brother both. I was so fucked.

Would they hate me?

Would they ever forgive me?

Would they regret every moment, every touch, every kiss?

My racing thoughts were interrupted by the dinging of the oven, letting me know it was preheated. I kissed him, then returned my attention to the mess behind me.

"I do want to tell you," I whispered, but I don't think he heard me.

As I finished putting the final touches on the chicken parmesan I was making, he went and grabbed two glasses and a bottle of whiskey. Leaning against the counter, he sipped on his drink and watched me. With dinner in the oven, I reached for my glass that he had poured for me. I leaned next to him, and for a few moments, we just stood in silence. He had opened his mouth to say something when his brother walked in, grabbed himself a glass, and poured a generous measure.

Something was upsetting Mac—I could see it in the way that muscle along his jaw jumped because he was grinding his teeth.

He leaned against the counter across from Dalton and me. His eyes ran over my body like a drowning man searching for a lifebuoy. I cocked my head at him, silently asking him what was on his mind. Dalton's eyes flicked between his brother and me, sipping at his whiskey and waiting for the conversation to start. After a minute, Mac finally spoke.

"Dalton and I are heading out soon, Vixen."

I frowned at him. "What for?"

I glanced at Dalton, who didn't seem phased by the news, and kept his eyes on his brother.

"Silas and Luca are moving a shipment. A big one. I need you to get the motel rooms ready. Clean sheets, make sure all the lights work, spotless. I'll talk to Holly and Maria before we head out; they've helped before. And—" he hesitated, looking between me and his brother and the floor. Those blue eyes troubled like a stormy sea. "Grab some kids' toys. Girls' toys. Put those in a few rooms, too."

It took everything in me to keep my jaw from dropping. I'd learned at that awful dinner that the motel rooms were often used for victims of sex trafficking—the few women they could get away from the DiAngelos without too much fuss. And I knew, from my training, that Luca DiAngelo traded in women like a cowboy did cattle. But kids' toys? That could only mean one thing… Children weren't easy to sneak out; their freedom did not come cheap. As much as it disgusted me, I knew that children brought in the most money for scumbags like the DiAngelos.

Why would Dalton and Mac risk everything they've been working toward?

Unless they had finally decided that enough was enough.

Unless this marked the beginning of the end, and they were ready to give Silas the boot.

I looked over at Mac, who was watching me carefully. I knew that if I were to give any sign, any hint of discomfort, he would have someone else do my job. When I squared my shoulders and lifted my jaw, the faint glint of approval I saw in his eyes made me want to preen like a love bird. I ignored the oven when it dinged and walked over to Mac instead. Wrapping my arms around his waist as best I could, I stood on tiptoes and kissed his stubbled jaw. I was faintly aware of Dalton pulling dinner out of the oven, and setting it on the counter. Mac pulled me into him and, when he leaned in for a kiss, I opened for him eagerly. I loved the taste of this man—a delicious combination of coffee and whiskey and mint. I pulled away from the kiss reluctantly and stepped back, looking between the two men I had grown to love despite my best efforts not to.

"Please promise me you'll be careful."

"We've done this a hundred times, baby girl."

I shot Dalton an admonishing look. "Don't do that. Don't lie to me. This is different. You know it, I know it, Mac knows it…"

He flashed me a crooked, apologetic smile, and glanced at his brother who said, "You're right, gorgeous. This is different."

"I told you those killer instincts were going to be trouble. We can't keep her in the dark forever."

I nodded, agreeing with Dalton. Part of me wanted the full story so I could protect them as best I could, while another part wanted it so I could do my job.

"What he said. Don't you trust me?"

*You shouldn't. But I want you to.* I kept that part to myself.

Mac ran a hand through his hair. "It's not that, Vixen. We're just trying to protect you. This is messy. Club business always is."

"I don't need protecting. I don't mind messy." I was still standing between the two of them, but Dalton came closer, and ran a tender thumb along my jaw.

"We know, baby girl."

My eyes searched his, which don't give anything away.

I frowned. "Then tell me."

Dalton brought me to him, stealing a kiss that I pulled away from with a huff. "Tell me," I demand.

But another look between Dalton and Mac said I'd already gotten all the information I was going to get tonight. I scoffed, and stomped over to the fridge. Pulling out a couple big bags of salad mix, I turned my back to them and distracted myself by focusing on a salad to go with my chicken. I could feel them watching me.

"When do you leave?"

They both answered, "Tonight."

That gave me pause, and I froze for a second before asking, "And when will you be back?"

"Tomorrow."

I knew that if I were to have turned around, they'd be standing side by side. My dark prince and my knight in shining armor. Different, yet so similar. There wasn't a thing I could do to keep them from going. And what kind of person would I be if I even asked them to? They were saving lives. Innocent lives. They had to go.

"Please," I whispered, "please just be careful. Come back to me. Promise me that."

My words were met with silence, then strong hands wrapped around my waist, turning me around. I found myself sandwiched between the two men, who had moved closer to me. Dalton had his thumbs hooked through two of the belt loops on my jeans.

Mac took my hand, tracing soothing circles over my palm. "I don't make promises I can't keep, gorgeous. What Dalton and I do is dangerous. Being a part of this club is dangerous. But I can promise you that there are very few forces on this earth that would have the capability of stopping me from coming home to you." He brought my hand to his lips. "Very fucking few."

I leaned my head back against Dalton's shoulder. "I love you both so fucking much. Just be careful, okay? I… I don't deserve this. Us."

Out of the corner of my eye, I saw Dalton open his mouth to protest, but I pressed my head back into his neck and he quieted. "One day you'll understand. But, for now, let's just eat. You two need food and rest before you go."

Without another word, I disentangled myself from between the two of them. Mac sent out a text and, a few minutes later, more of the club came pouring in.

Rodney shot me a wink. "I thought we were doomed to my cooking or something."

I laughed, but it felt a little forced, and I took a step back for the flood of people helping themselves to a plate before taking their seats at the table.

I don't see Maria or Holly, and Dalton noticed my questioning look. "They're at home, Vixen. Jackson and Diego are going with us."

That made sense—they were probably cashing in on some much-needed family time. I sat between Mac and Dalton, and was quiet throughout dinner. Dalton bantered back and forth with a few of his friends, his hand never leaving my thigh under the table. Mac, meanwhile, was sipping a whiskey, leaning back in his chair, and just watching everything around him.

When he caught me looking at him for the millionth time, he leaned towards me and pressed a kiss to that sweet spot between my neck and shoulder. "Just breathe, gorgeous." He whispered the words into my ear, making me shiver.

Instead of everyone just leaving after the meal was over, like normal, every person at the table helped clean up. The mood was somehow more somber, as if everyone knew something was going down. I found myself watching Dalton and Mac. They had left on plenty of these so-called errands, and I'd grown used to coming to find rooms empty but clearly freshly slept in. They were here, and then gone again. For their safety, and ours.

But this time, there were kids involved. This was a greater risk. They couldn't travel to the safehouses alone—they were more valuable to the DiAngelos.

I couldn't help but think this would all be a hell of a lot easier if my dumb ass hadn't fallen in love with the Mills brothers. I glanced over at the men in question, aware that it's too late to go back now. Nor would I, even if I could. I was just going to have to trust that they knew what they were doing, and wouldn't do anything stupid in their determination to bring Silas down.

# Chapter 20

After dinner was cleaned up, the two of them disappeared to make final arrangements, and I headed to the rooms to see what needed to be done. As I was straightening up the bed in one room, a knock on the door had me turning to find Maria standing with a mountain of toys and stuffed animals in her arms. Seeing my friend preparing for this like I was, somehow made it more real.

She smiled at me, but there was a shadow in her eyes that wasn't usually there.

"Hey, *chica*. Wanna help put these out?"

I reached for a fluffy pink bunny and ran my hand over the soft velvet ears, setting it on the bed before following Maria to the other rooms.

"You're worried," I stated plainly, making sure the room was practically spotless.

Maria busied herself setting a couple of toy trucks on the dresser, seemingly determined to position them just right. But then she sighed and turned to me. "I'm trying to pretend this is just like any other trip they've taken."

"But it's not, is it?"

She didn't bother to answer, just walked to the next room with me right behind her. We repeated the same actions there—me, fiddling with the bed, and her carefully placing a couple of Barbie dolls on the nightstand. She held one of the Barbies up and said, "It's kids, Nicky. They've never messed with kids. And I fucking hate myself for wishing they would just… not risk it. Not go after the people who need them most. But—" She broke off, and her lower lip wobbled. "I don't want to bury my husband, or tell *our* children that their daddy isn't coming home. This is so much more dangerous. Does that make me selfish? I don't know." A tear slid down her cheek, and as I moved closer to her, I noticed the puffy redness under her makeup.

"You are the least selfish person I know," I said, hugging my friend as best I could around the armful of toys she still carried. She sniffled. "I know I am still kind of new at this. You've watched Diego leave on I don't know how many assignments or missions or whatever you want to call them. But you've watched him come home too, right? Every time. Him and Jackson, Mac, and Dalton. They're really good at this. We just gotta stick together and hold the fort down until they get back."

My words sounded braver than I felt in that moment, but earned me a watery smile.

"You are damn right. Our boys are lean, mean fighting machines."

I looked up to find Holly lingering in the hallway just outside the door. She smiled at me when our eyes met but, like Maria's and I'm sure my own, there was a shadow of worry on her face.

Not usually a touchy person, she still leaned in to hug us both and said, "It'll be okay. It always is. We'll get this stuff set up for the kids, give 'em some see-ya-later loving, and then go steal Mac's good whiskey and find a place to hide away for the night."

I winked at her. "I know where he keeps the best stuff. And where Dalton keeps his favorite snacks."

Maria chuckled, and Holly grabbed the toys from her. "Then we better get this done quick."

We finished prepping the rooms—setting out toys, fluffing pillows, wiping down every surface like our lives depended on it—then headed downstairs. The lounge was unusually quiet, just the guys huddled around a table in the back, whispering over a blueprint that stretched from edge to edge. I scanned it quickly, trying to find a name or location or anything, but the paper was frustratingly blank other than the outlines of walls and doors. Frowning at it, I let Dalton pull me into him and switched my focus to the people gathered around the table. Maria sat on Diego's knee, his hand reassuringly placed on the small of her back. Holly stood behind Jackson, her arm draped over his shoulder as she leaned over him. He reached up to hold her hand, and I smiled a little when she intertwined her fingers with his.

I leaned further into Dalton, and he pressed a kiss on top of my head. Part of me was still torn between duty and desire, but I was starting to accept that my love for them wasn't something I could control. No matter how heavy it made my badge feel. I just hoped like hell they could find a way to forgive me when this was all said and done. Mac stood across from his brother, and he rolled up the blueprint before taking a seat. Words weren't necessary—he said everything he needed to say with the way his eyes seemed to devour me. I smiled at him and, for a minute, the room was quiet. For once, the room was empty except for our group.

I broke the silence almost reluctantly. "Is it just you four going?"

Mac nodded. "Small groups get in and out faster and quieter."

I knew that from my own experiences. But I also knew there was safety in numbers. "Can I ask a question?" I glanced at Dalton, then back at Mac, who gestured for me to continue. "One, you're obviously doing this to bring down Silas, right? But also the DiAngelos? And save some kids? But somehow not get arrested yourselves? With no military training, or any other training to speak of?"

Dalton pulled me closer to him. "That was a lot of questions, Vixen."

I frowned. I needed the details for reasons they couldn't know, but I was also freaking worried about the idiots. Honestly, I had no idea how they hadn't been arrested or killed yet.

Before I could open my mouth again, Dalton said, "I was wondering when you would start speaking up. I could see those wheels turning in your head every other time we've left."

Jackson spoke up. "I was a Marine, actually. Eons ago."

I cocked my head at him. "Really? How old are you?"

"I'm 32—I joined right out of high school. I was no G.I. Joe, but I knew enough, and was good enough, that I could teach these guys everything I was taught. It's worked out pretty well for us. And it's nice knowing that the guys who have my back aren't complete idiots."

Diego threw a book at Jackson, who caught it with the hand that wasn't still holding Holly's. I felt Dalton chuckle, and even Mac grinned a little.

"Also, we never kill. That's a no-go." I switched my attention back to Dalton, then glanced at Maria and Holly who seemed unfazed by the conversation, like they already knew all of this. Which, to be fair, they probably did. "We go in, we disable, we leave. Then a local precinct gets a nice little anonymous call, and finds a bunch of lowlifes all gift-wrapped for them."

I blinked, then pulled a chair over to sit down as I processed what I'd heard. I'd been told that the Steel Saints were a bunch of gun-toting, drug-running, bloodthirsty criminals. After barely any time with them, I'd realized this wasn't true outside of Silas and his merry band of assholes. I learned that not only were they not the villains the FBI had painted them to be, they were inherently good. I couldn't deny that it made me love them all the more. They weren't literal saints—and maybe they were still shy of being heroes—but they were men who risked their lives to make the world a better place. Totally unprotected by a badge or title. To me, that not only counted for something—but was everything.

"You see why we love them?" Holly gave me a knowing look. "Do we want to tie them down to the nearest radiator every time they leave? Absolutely. But who would we be to stop them from following their hearts and making this world a little bit less of a hellhole?" She leaned forward to kiss Jackson, and he turned his head so his lips could meet hers.

I couldn't help but yearn for that kind of love, that kind of devotion, but I wasn't sure if that was ever going to be in the cards for me. Dalton cracked some joke to ease the tension, and I tried to relax to the sound of their familiar banter.

After a bit, I excused myself and headed towards the bathroom. I saw Mac get up and follow me, but I pretended not to notice until we were alone. In the hallway, I turned to him and he grabbed me by the hips as I tilted my face up for a kiss. His lips were warm and welcoming, the kiss slow and sweet. Loving him was like diving in the world's deepest pool, and if I never came up for air… well, what a lovely way to go.

Reluctantly, I pulled back, and I searched those blue eyes for the answers I knew I could always find there. We both had fought so hard not to fall in love. But, in the end, it turned out walls were just not something our two hearts were willing to have between us.

"You okay?" I whispered softly, wrapping my hands around his neck. He was easily a foot taller than me, so it was a bit of a stretch. I leaned into his touch as one hand caressed my cheek.

"Mm, it's almost midnight. About time to get going. We wanna get there just before dawn."

"Element of surprise. And Silas will be there? The DiAngelos? You're sure?"

He nodded. "We've combed over the intel more times than I can count. Every 't' crossed, every 'i' dotted. We're sure."

I glanced over at the clock on the wall. It was just past 11:30 p.m. I chewed on my bottom lip, lost in nervous thought, until his thumb pulled it from between my teeth.

"Don't worry, gorgeous. We'll be home soon enough."

I sighed and leaned into him, my face pressed into the leather of his jacket. We stood there, arms around each other for a minute, before I broke the embrace with a smile.

"I would happily stand here in this hallway forever with you, but then I'm afraid I would pee myself. I didn't come out here just for hugs."

Mac's laugh was one of my favorite sounds. Deep and warm, and incredibly rare. I treasured it like gold. I kissed him again before all but running to the bathroom. Once inside, I pulled out my phone and tried to figure out how in the hell I was supposed to contact anyone. I had stomped off from my meeting with Braxton, and now I wasn't sure what would happen if I texted "Uncle Tommy." I still didn't want to talk to the asshole, so I sent a tentative text: "Aunt Lucy?" It was a Hail Mary, so I was surprised when I got a quick response.

"Hi, sweetie!"

"Is Uncle Tommy there?" I frowned at the phone, fully willing to dunk the thing in the water tank behind the toilet if I got any other answer besides no.

"Sorry, dear. He's gone to town to get his head together."

I had no choice but to trust that this person was, in fact, not Uncle Tommy masquerading as Aunt Lucy. I was so ready to be over with this shit. All the damn lies and pretending. I sent off a flurry of texts, hoping like hell Aunt Lucy would understand what I was saying without actually saying anything, in case the club members or, worse, one of the boys got ahold of my phone. After a few minutes, I was starting to think she wasn't going to respond. Then her reply came through: "Sounds like fun! Let me know how it goes. Love you!"

A knock on the door almost made me fall off the toilet.

"Nicky?" Maria's voice was tentative. "You okay in there?"

"Maybe she fell in."

I could hear the smirk in Holly's voice, and I smiled. I rubbed under my eyes furiously, reddening the area and blinking furiously. A quick glance in the mirror confirmed I looked like I'd been crying. I opened the door and made my voice hoarse. "Sorry guys, I just needed a minute."

Maria immediately embraced me, and I suddenly felt like a piece of crap. Holly awkwardly patted me on the back.

Maria didn't let go of me, saying, "I thought I was supposed to be the crier!"

I hugged her tight and stepped back. "I'm fine. Really."

Holly cleared her throat. "I know none of us want to do it. But it's time to send off our valiant knights." Maria and I gave her an odd look, and Holly shrugged, "I was trying to lighten the mood by being funny. Ha ha."

I snorted, and Maria pursed her lips to keep from laughing, her eyes twinkling. I followed the two of them outside to where the guys were waiting by a black cargo van with tinted windows. They all had body armor on, and were armed to the teeth. I about tripped over my feet when I noticed what was on each of their chests—no fucking way could it be that easy.

"Are those body cams?" I asked as we got closer, and Dalton turned to me, an eyebrow raised.

"Yes?"

I grinned, unable to hold back the thrill that gave me, and everyone gave me an odd look. Dalton glanced at his brother, who was fiddling with the straps of his kevlar.

"Are you just really, really happy that we're recording this epic Silas takedown for posterity? Or do you just like cameras? 'Cos if it's the latter, I got plenty of ideas for later." He winked at me, and Mac gave him an admonishing look.

Luckily, I was saved from needing to explain my excitement by a squeal from Maria as Diego picked her up and spun her around. Setting her back down, they stood with their heads pressed together, and spoke to each other in whispered Spanish.

Holly was fussing over Jackson's gun and vest, checking the straps and little minor details that, as a cop, I knew could mean a man's survival or death. I was surprised she knew them too, but she moved over everything with a quiet efficiency. When she stood, I heard her say to him, "Don't be a dumbass. Get in, get out, and get your ass home in one piece."

He smirked at her, and gave a mock salute. "Yes, ma'am." She swatted the back of his head, and he looked at her like she hung the moon and stars.

Dalton had gotten into the back of the van, and was doing a last-minute equipment check. Mac stood to the side, watching over everyone. I walked over to him, and pressed a kiss to his cheek. He looked down at me with a soft smile, and I couldn't help but say, "I would beg you to stay, but I don't think it'll work. So, I'll just settle for knowing you got this all together."

Dalton climbed back out and stood next to me after pressing a kiss to my other cheek. He and his brother shared a look, before Mac said, "You know we do, Vixen. It'll be fine. This is it. We get Silas, we get a piece of shit DiAngelo or two, we come back to you."

"And we all lived happily ever after. The end," Dalton added with a wink.

I frowned at him, but glanced at the body cam again. This camera, if they did it right, could mean the end of everything. Fuck. I looked between the two men I loved, but was sidetracked by Diego climbing into the driver's seat and Jackson walking up beside us.

"I hate to end the party, but we got to go if we want to get there on time."

I started to chew my lip again, but Mac's hand darted out to stop me. He pulled me in for a kiss, and I tried to memorize his taste.

"Hey, don't be a hog. I need some of that good luck loving, too." I turned with a half-smile, and found myself in Dalton's waiting arms. "I love you, Vixen."

My smile suddenly felt heavier, my heart sadder—for more reasons than I could count. "I love you, too. Be careful."

He kissed me goodbye, then climbed back into the van into the vacant seat beside his brother. He gave me one final wink before Jackson slid the door closed, and climbed into the passenger seat next to Diego. Maria, Holly, and I watched the van disappear down the road.

Maria sighed, and Holly said, "Yup. This still really fucking sucks."

# Chapter 21

*Maverick*

I wasn't used to having someone worth coming home to—it was a feeling a guy could get used to. Dalton fiddled with one of the computers in the van, and I glanced between him and the woman we both loved as her figure got smaller out the window. Feeling my eyes on him, he glanced up, and raised his eyebrows as if to ask a question. I shook my head, and he gave me a knowing smirk.

"Thinking about her?"

*Always*, I wanted to say, but instead just nodded towards the computer he had been messing with. "Everything good?"

Unphased by my lack of response, he nodded and said, "If shit doesn't go sideways, we should be home in time for dinner. Everybody good for one last run-through?" Diego turned the radio down, and Jackson spun around as I ran us through the plan.

"Alright, so the compound is roughly three hours out—deep in the woods, off a private road owned by one of the DiAngelo shell companies. Intel said it was a temporary holding site, a place to stash victims before transporting them out of the country. We know from past experience the place is gonna be set up with a defense perimeter better than the fucking White House. As per usual, Dalton is in charge of hacking into their security system. Then it's get in, take down who we can, find Silas and his buddies, and get those kids out safe. No one dies, no alarms, no screw-ups. Get the evidence, get the kids, get out. Good?" I met the eyes of the three men I trusted most, as they each nodded their consent. "Then let's get this shit done and get home."

We hit just after three a.m.

I watched my brother's back as, with the press of a few buttons, he disabled their entire system. "Comms check, everybody copy? Cams on?" Once I had confirmation, I headed towards the front door. There were no guards posted outside—they relied too heavily on technology that could be easily hacked. Inside, it was dim, with only a few lowlights in the hallway. Most of the lackeys were either asleep or half-alert—fucking perfect for us.

Room by room, we moved. Zip ties. Chloroform. One by one, guards dropped. Those dumb enough to resist were handled easily enough. Within fifteen minutes, the whole first level was secure, and not one of us had more than a busted lip or bruised cheek. We hadn't found any kids, just a fuck ton of drugs. I led us to the basement door, and waited for Diego to pick the lock. Glancing at my team, I knew I wasn't the only one preparing for the nightmares we were sure to find below. We had done this more times than I could count, but never with children.

The basement door swung open with a creak. A small, flickering light over the stairs illuminated the space just enough to see the mold on the walls. The air was humid and stale, and you could hear whimpers coming from below. I heard Dalton mutter a few curses and, out of the corner of my eye, I saw Diego cross himself. We were fixing to walk into Hell. With Jackson being more experienced than I was, I moved aside to allow him to lead us down the rickety staircase. His steps were silent, and he moved like a ghost. Making our way into the room below, we were met with the first set of cages.

Wide, fearful eyes peeked out from beneath unkempt hair, raggedy clothes hanging off thin frames. Boys and girls, ranging from five to fifteen. I genuinely felt sick. These kids… God only knew what they'd been through, or where they had come from. The hell they'd seen. Rage, hot and burning, made its way through my chest. I was dimly aware of Diego and Dalton approaching the cells. When the first chain fell off the door, several of the kids started crying and whimpering in utter terror.

My brother spoke soft, gentle words. "It's okay. Don't be afraid. We're going to get you out of here. You're safe now." Diego translated in Spanish, just to ensure the message got to as many of them as it could.

They made their way through the next five cells, each as full as the next. Slowly, the kids began to move towards Jackson and me. Jackson knelt, holding his hand out to a little boy who looked about eight or nine. The kid eyed him, distrust and fear in his brown eyes, before hesitantly taking Jackson's outstretched hand. I looked around. There were easily thirty kids here—luckily we had arranged to have more vans waiting to take them back.

I nodded at Jackson. "You know what to do—get them out of here. Dalton and I will catch up."

I watched as Jackson and Diego shepherded the children up the stairs towards freedom. It was time for my brother and me to go see about getting a dog put down.

The upper level of the house had three rooms, padded for sound suppression. Two were bedrooms, and I didn't even let myself think about that. The third was an office with a thick steel door. Were they even aware that their time was up? Dalton bypassed the numerical code lock on the door with ease, and we drew the guns that had been kept holstered at our hips. The office smelled like money and rot, like old wood and even older sins.

Silas stood next to Luca and Michael DiAngelo—they were arguing over something on a laptop. We had caught them completely off guard, three identical looks of shock on their face.

"Hands up—back away from the computer," I said, pointing my gun dead center at Silas.

Michael, the only one armed out of the three of them, reached for his gun, but Dalton trained his Glock on him and said, "Please just give me a fucking reason."

Luca sneered, "I didn't realize the fucking Boy Scouts made house calls."

I ignored him, never looking away from Silas, who was glaring at me with undisguised hate. "Y'all are through. This little operation you got going? Dragging the Saints through the mud? It's fucking done."

This time it was Michael who guffawed. "Silas was right. You're a whole other level of delusional. What exactly are you going to do? Kill us?"

Dalton handed me his gun, and I trained both weapons on the group of scumbags in front of me as he moved closer. "Are you gonna be good and stay still, or are you going to make this fun for me?"

"Don't shoot. It's me, boss. Rodney met us halfway, I came back to help."

I glanced over my shoulder to see Jackson making his way into the room, his gun drawn. I nodded my thanks and returned my attention to where Dalton had grabbed some zip ties from his pocket. Michael was first, and I could see in his eyes that he wanted to fight. Jackson could see it too, and he moved in without me having to say a word. A gun to his temple made the son of a bitch real compliant, and he swore vehemently when Dalton notched the ties so they cut off his circulation.

Luca was next and, quick as the snake he is, he jammed his elbow into Dalton's face. Dalton's nose instantly broke, and my brother grabbed Luca by the back of his head, slamming the man's face into the desk and knocking him flat. Luca crumpled on the ground, while Dalton calmly secured him despite the blood flow. Ignoring Michael's threats and outrage, Dalton grinned at me as he approached Silas who, much to my surprise, had remained quiet this entire time. His eyes were still trained on me. Something about the way he looked at me raised red flags, like the motherfucker still had cards to play.

Dalton pushed him to the ground, and still the fucker glared at me like he had the upper hand.

The three of us ransacked the room. Anything incriminating was placed in a neat pile on the desk, just to make it extra easy for the Feds that would be here in a few hours. I took my body cam off its holster on my chest, and placed it on top of the files. Jackson checked the ties on their arms and legs, kicked Silas in the ribs for good measure, and then moved to lead us outside. It was time to go home.

But a cold, low laugh stopped us. Silas must have finally lost what was left of his mind. I ignored him, but then he said, "You really think this is how it ends? You two back in charge of the Saints, some sort of happy little fairytale with that red-headed bitch?"

Our backs were to him, but Dalton and I looked at each other. That son of a bitch really didn't know when to shut the fuck up.

"No, we're not really the fairytale type. But the truth finally coming out? That feels damn good. The thought of what they'll do to you in prison gives me fuzzy feelings."

Dalton tossed the words over his shoulder, and I glanced behind me to see Silas' neck turn red like it did when he was pissed.

"You want the truth, boy? I'll tell you the fucking truth," Silas said. "Your whore of a mother was going to expose everything. I had plans, plans to bring the Saints out of the fucking gutter. I was going to make something of the club. I had it all worked out, then that bitch found out I was working with the DiAngelos. So, I handled it." His voice was smug and cruel. Jackson froze by the door, and I spun on my heel. In a few quick steps, I marched over to Silas and grabbed him by the collar, lifting him up. Dalton was hot on my heels.

"What the fuck do you mean you handled it? You hired someone to kill my mother?" I nearly choked on the words.

Silas' face was inches from mine, but he smirked. "No, you idiot. I pulled the trigger myself."

I saw fucking red, and before I could even fully process what I was doing, I threw him against the wall. For a moment he lay there, but then he struggled into a sitting position and leered at us.

Dalton had been frozen beside me, but now he muttered, "You were family." The look in his eyes was a blend of devastation and wrath. At some point, Luca had woken up and the DiAngelo brothers were watching the whole thing with a sadistic glee.

"I did what I had to do for the club," Silas spat. "Your mother would've torn everything apart. No way was she going to let the DiAngelos near us. I couldn't let that opportunity, all that money, go to waste. I did what I had to do."

"Our father was your best friend! He called you his brother, you bastard."

"He was weak, and so was she. He saved me from having to kill him too when his heart gave out. You two were fucking children—it should've been me put in charge."

I took a glass paperweight off the desk and threw it at the wall next to his head. Silas flinched but said, "I watched as you struggled to do what was necessary. It was like trying to watch a dog learn to bite. Pathetic. It should've been me!"

Suddenly, it clicked in my head, and I knew the words were true before they even left my lips. "It was you. That night in the warehouse. That bad intel. You set us up."

He rolled his eyes. "Obviously. Couldn't let your ass die though—had to have someone who could control your brother. You had to give me the control. And you did. You laid everything in my lap. Pathetic. But exactly what I needed to happen."

"You saved my life just so you could take everything." My hand twitched—I wanted so badly to draw my gun and shoot that traitor in the head.

For me.

For my dad.

For my sweet mother, who'd never done a cruel thing in her life.

Silas took everything from us.

Out of the corner of my eye, I saw Jackson take a step closer, his eyes like stone. Dalton seemed lost to the pain. It took everything in me not to end it, but I had a woman waiting for me back home, and that body cam was still recording. If I killed him, my head was going to roll just like theirs. I turned to head for the door and said to Jackson, "I've heard enough. Shut them up."

Out in the hallway, I stood with Dalton and dialed the number I had memorized. While the phone rang, I asked him, "You good?"

His answering laugh was dry and humorless. "Not even fucking remotely. I'll be better when we get back to her. Don't ask me any more dumb shit until she's in my arms."

Fair enough. A voice finally sounded on the other end of the phone—some detective on the case whose name I hadn't bothered memorizing.

"I'm fixing to make your day. No names, no questions. And don't even bother trying to trace the call. You'll find two high-ranking members of the DiAngelo family restrained inside a house at the coordinates I'm sending. Along with several of their goons, all restrained but, for the most part, unharmed. You'll also find physical evidence inside to make your case airtight, including body cam footage that covers every inch of what my people found inside. There were children in the holding cells in the basement. They're safe, and I'll make sure they're cared for. That's all you need to know. You're welcome."

I disconnected the call mid-question, and looked at the time before dropping the phone on the floor and stomping on it.

Jackson joined us in the hallway, and the three of us made our way out of that hellhole. A team would come through after we left and remove any evidence of us having been there.

Diego could sense something was wrong the second we got back to the van. "What happened?"

I shook my head. "Nothing that affects what happened here today. Just… let's get home. Then debrief." Diego glanced at Jackson, who shook his head. A subtle sign not to press me. Dalton sat with his head pressed against the side of the van, face to the roof and eyes closed. I climbed in across from and, a few minutes later, we were headed home.

*

I surveyed the scene in front of me. Three vans had pulled up about thirty minutes ago, and my heart bottomed out when the doors opened to reveal children inside. All wrapped in soft blankets, all looking like they were seeing the light of day for the first time in years. The light of hope. Medics were waiting. Volunteers too. People who didn't ask questions. They approached the vans, and coaxed the kids out with steady hands and warm hearts. I wasn't a crier, but I couldn't deny the tears in my eyes. My boys did this—they saved these kids. If that wasn't enough to make a girl fall in love, then I don't know what would.

I was so distracted watching the team of volunteers take care of the survivors that I almost missed Mac and Dalton's van pulling in. A second later, Holly joined me. Maria had already gone home to the kids, but I had sent her a text when the other vans got here so she was already on her way. Jackson got out first, and Holly immediately headed towards him. I saw her pause, and then she was reaching for him, her eyes scanning his face before pressing a kiss to his lips and resting her forehead against his. His hands were trembling as they came to rest on her back, probably from the adrenaline.

My heart was in my chest. I had never been the one waiting at home before. I was the one charging in, saving the day. This whole time had been about forcing myself to breathe, to stay calm. I zoned in on the sight of the van door opening. Mac stepped out, and it felt like my whole world exhaled a sigh of relief. I covered the distance between us as quickly as I could without running. My eyes scanned every inch of him. He looked tired—no, beyond tired. Blood on his sleeve, dirty jeans, and his walls were up—his face hard, and almost unreadable. But he was home. Alive. For the moment, that was all I cared about.

He waited for me to get to him, and I threw my arms around him before he could even say a word. He didn't resist, his arms coming around me and holding me in a way he never had before. Like he needed to know I was there. A drowning man, and I was his lighthouse.

"You're okay," I whispered, "you're okay."

I wasn't sure who I was trying to convince. When I leaned back to look at him, I could see a million feelings in those blue eyes. But mostly I saw pain. Not the kind that would come from a right hook or stray bullet like I feared. No, this was the deep emotional pain that came from the soul. He definitely wasn't okay.

Dalton climbed out of the van next, a stiffness to him that made his usual fluid movements almost jerky. His nose was broken, but other than that, he was fine. Physically. His jaw was locked, and when his eyes met mine, they were far away despite the small smile he tried and failed to give me.

"Dalton—" I reached for him but, to my surprise, he stepped back. Away from me.

"Not now, Vixen. I need a minute."

I felt like a rug had been pulled from underneath me. He turned and headed back to the clubhouse, shoulders rigid. As he disappeared inside, Maria's car pulled up and she ran out almost before it was parked. Diego caught her in his arms. There was tension in him, too.

Something was wrong. Not just mission-went-sideways wrong. Deeper. Really, really wrong. I turned back to Mac, questions on my lips, but he pulled away. Stepping around me, he raised his voice for everyone to hear and said, "I need to talk to everyone. Inside."

I reached for him again. "Baby? What happened?" He looked down at me and, for a second, his mask fell away, and I saw the storm in those blue eyes. The grief. The betrayal. The pain.

Holly and Jackson came to stand next to me as I watched one of the men I loved head inside. The pair were hand in hand, but Holly reached for me, giving my hand a gentle squeeze before letting go. Maria and Diego were as close as two people could get and still walk in a straight line. We followed them inside, and found everyone in the garage heading into the kitchen. Pretty much every member of the club crammed into the room.

Dalton was nowhere to be seen, but Mac leaned against the counter, waiting for everyone to get situated. After the room quieted down, he looked up from the drink he was sipping. His eyes met mine before scanning the room.

You could've heard a pin drop when he finally said, "I know many of you were fond of my mother. Pretty much all of you, really. Which is why I feel you deserve to know the truth." He paused, seeming to gather some inner strength. "Silas Greyson killed her. He gunned her down in the streets."

I tried not to react, not visibly. I had never met the woman. Never seen the love she had for this club and everyone in it. Never got to witness the relationship she had with her sons. To me, she was a story. A cherished memory, wrapped in hurt. But for them, for Mac and Dalton, she had once been everything to them. I never looked away from him, barely registering the gasps and whispers and looks of horror. Maria started to cry, while

Holly looked ready to burn everything to the ground.

Mac continued, "Silas had been planning to work with the DiAngelos before my dad died. My mother found out and, knowing she would expose him, he…" Mac swallowed, his eyes flicking to mine again and then away. "He said he pulled the trigger himself."

Holly made a sound of strangled rage, and Jackson placed his hand on the back of her neck as if to calm her. Maria sank into Diego, who held her close. I watched Mac struggle to stay standing on the foundation of everything he thought he knew as it crumbled beneath him. I hadn't liked Silas from the moment I met him. Now, I had never loathed a man more violently.

The room came alive with whispers, and Mac let it go on for a moment before saying, "There's more. The ambush… the one that nearly killed me. That was Silas, too. He fed us the bad intel."

Several of the guys stood up at that, and the whispers turned to shouts. I had a feeling that if Silas were to magically walk in right then, he wouldn't last a second. And part of me wished he would.

One question sounded above the rest. "Why? Why would he do that?"

Mac took a sip of his drink, taking his time swallowing. "He said I was in the way. That I had to be sidelined so he could take over the club. And when he pulled me out, saved my life… he did it so I would owe him. So I would give him what he wanted—the club."

His words were briefly met with silence, and then Patrick—one of Silas' buddies—stood up and said, "And we're just supposed to believe you?"

In one quick, smooth motion, Mac threw his drink at Patrick's head. The man dodged it, and the glass shattered on the wall behind him. Before a fight could start, Mac waded through the mess of people and stood in front of Patrick. "Get the fuck out of my club."

Patrick, who looked about two seconds away from pissing himself, was stupid enough to say, "It's not your club. You're not the pres, and you can't just kick me out."

Mac never looked away, and Jackson rose to his feet. "I motion for an emergency club meeting. All members present to vote on presidency and this son of a bitch's patch."

Diego didn't move, but said loudly enough for everyone to hear, "I second that motion."

Mac turned away from Patrick, and Jackson moved to stand next to his friend. "All those in favor of Maverick Mills for presidency, say aye—those not in favor, say nay."

A resounding "aye" filled the room.

"All those in favor of every bastard who said nay to get the fuck out and not come back, say aye."

An even louder "aye" rang out, this time accompanied by cheering. For a moment, pride filled my chest until I remembered who I really was. But I pushed that all aside to watch Mac take the mantle he had always been meant to have. Jackson, Diego, Rodney, and several others I had grown fond of began pushing Silas' supporters out the door—both literally and figuratively. It should've been a great victory, but the man who should've looked like he was on top of the world just appeared lost. I stood, and he looked over at me as I made my way through the crowd.

He blamed himself for everything. I could see it on his face, and it broke my heart. "Mac, baby," I said, just loud enough for him to hear, placing a hand on his arm and willing him to open up to me. "This is not your fault."

That muscle in his jaw flexed like it did when he was upset. "I handed him everything, Vixen."

"You trusted a man who was your father's best friend. Someone you once called family. That's not weakness—that's not your fault. That's just being human."

"He killed her. He might as well have killed my father. He almost killed me. He destroyed everything this club stood for. You should've seen the look on Dalton's face. I didn't stop him."

"No," I said, my voice firm but gentle, "he did this, not you. Your brother knows that. And your parents wouldn't blame you either, I just know it. You can't punish yourself for not seeing through him sooner. You did what you could as soon as you realized what was going on. You rescued all those people."

He didn't answer, but I could see him slowly start to accept what I was saying. The tightness was leaving his eyes, and when he looked at me, I knew he was going to be okay. Now for the other Mills brother...

"Where's Dalton?"

Mac gestured with his chin towards the back of the clubhouse, where their rooms were. "Processing."

"I should go to him."

"He needs you more than he knows, gorgeous. We both do." He kissed me and then pushed me gently towards the door. "Go."

# Chapter 22

I headed towards Dalton on heavy feet. The motel rooms I passed were filled with children, sleeping or snacking or just huddled together for comfort. They seemed to finally realize they were safe, but I knew they would never be the same. I glanced in a few of the rooms, searching again for a familiar face. But, unfortunately, I didn't see any signs of the girls who had started this whole thing.

I made my way up the back stairs, not really sure what I would find. The hallway was dark, except for a sliver of light peeking out from underneath his door. I knocked, then pushed the door open. Dalton sat on the edge of his bed, head in his hands. "Hey, you. Thought you might need some company."

His voice was quiet, rough. The charming, funny man I knew was hidden under a river of pain. A pain I felt as strongly as if it were my own.

"Not sure what I need right now."

I walked over to him, and knelt between his knees. Reaching up, I held his face between my hands and coaxed him to look at me. "You're not alone, Dalton. I'm here. It's okay."

"How could I not see it? Why didn't we do something sooner?"

"Baby, those kinds of questions are only good for stirring up ghosts. They don't do anything for the living. You survived. You took it back. And now you will rebuild."

He leaned into my touch, just barely. A sort of surrender. Then he surged forward, wrapping his arms around me and picking me up. He turned us both around, laying me in the bed and hovering over me. I ran my hands down his back as he buried his face in my hair.

One last time, I told myself. He needed me just as much as I needed him. One last time. I held him close to me, letting the silence fill all the places words couldn't reach. When he leaned back and his lips found mine, I kissed him eagerly. At first, it was a desperate, aching need for each other. But the desire soon heated the moment beyond something sweet.

When his tongue swept across my lips, I opened for him and wrapped my legs around his waist. He devoured the taste of me as I began to move, rubbing myself on the hardened length of him I could feel through his jeans. He kissed a trail down my jaw and over my throat, before pausing at my collarbone. He sat up, reaching for his shirt, but I stopped him, wanting to do it myself. Words weren't needed as I slowly peeled his shirt from his tanned skin, as if I could lift the weight from his shoulders with every button undone. I ran my hands down his chest to the top of his pants, and unbuttoned those too.

When I moved to take my own clothes off, he grabbed my hands in one of his and leaned down to whisper in my ear, "My turn, baby girl."

He undressed me carefully, his hands leaving hot trails of desire over every inch of my skin. Throwing my pants to the side, he kissed my thigh and spread my legs with something akin to reverence. Lowering his head, he blew softly across my exposed pussy, and I moaned at the sensation. Looking up at me, he sucked my clit into his mouth and I bucked as pleasure ransacked my body. His tongue lavished my most sensitive spot as his fingers spread my lips and swirled in the wetness he found there. Making a deep, guttural sound of approval, Dalton finally broke eye contact as he devoted his full attention to eating me out like I was his last meal.

I bucked again, and he moved an arm across my hips to pin me in place. His tongue pushed inside of me, licking my inner walls, and the man tongue-fucked me until my legs shook.

"Dalton, oh my fucking God, baby…"

My eyes rolled back in my head when he gently nipped at my clit, sucking it back into his mouth and moving his fingers back inside of me. He pushed another finger inside of me, stretching me deliciously, and looked up at me. His eyes were hooded with desire, and I whimpered when he pushed a third finger into my pussy, and started stroking my G-spot.

"Such a good girl. Come for me, Vixen. I want to watch you shatter."

His filthy words were always my undoing, and this time was no different. My whole body locked up, nearly lifting me off the bed as I came with a shout. The whole clubhouse must have heard me scream his name.

When I relaxed back into the pillows, he pulled his fingers out and held them to my lips. Dutifully, I sucked them clean before he began playing with my tits. His rubbing his calloused thumb over my nipple had the pink flesh completely erect, and I cried out again when he pinched it. I ran my hands through his hair, guiding his lips closer to mine, needing to taste him. Taste us. He kissed me with none of the ferocity he had shown my pussy, instead taking his time and savoring me. With one quick, hard thrust, his cock was inside me and he swallowed the whimper that escaped me. He pushed himself up over me, and I grabbed his hips as he fucked me. He moved inside me like he was chasing something he'd lost long ago, and I met him with everything I had left. It wasn't about release—it was about remembering we were alive.

I felt another orgasm build inside me, a fire burning deep in me. His eyes closed in ecstasy as he increased his pace even more. We moved together like it was the only thing keeping us from unraveling. He moved one hand to my sore, swollen clit again and tweaked it just right. I shattered around him, and he yelled as he pumped his seed inside me. The ride was a long one, and he collapsed on top of me. When we had both made it back down to earth, he rolled so we were both on our sides.

I held him as the broken parts became whole. And, though he didn't know it, he held me while the whole parts broke.

I twisted until I was on my back, reclined against the headrest. His head was on my lap, and I played with his hair. Soon enough, he fell asleep—the exhaustion finally taking hold of him. I watched him sleep until footsteps made me look up, and I found Mac quietly making his way towards us. I smiled softly, and patted the bed next to me. He took off his shirt, leaving it in his wake, and crawled into bed. He pulled the rumpled blankets behind him as he lay down, and I helped him to cover me and his brother. He lay back against the pillows, and tangled his legs with mine.

"You okay?" I whispered.

"Better now."

One hand still wrapped in Dalton's hair, I reached for Mac with my other. I began to hum softly, a song my mother had sung to me when I was young. Dalton began to snore softly, and eventually his brother fell asleep too.

I was tired, but my mind was racing too quickly to even consider rest. I stared at the ceiling, tears burning my eyes. This was it. The mission was over. With what the boys had left behind, there was nothing left for me to bring to the table. The good guys had won. Yet, here I was, feeling like I had lost not only the battle, but the war.

My cover, the story I had been living for a year—it was unraveling as they slept blissfully unaware. Men I loved. Men I had betrayed. The tears ran fast down my face. But I refused to make a sound, not risking waking them. They needed the rest, needed peace. And when that call came, I would give that to them, even though it would sting at first. I would walk away, and leave this all behind. I would pray they would find a way to forgive me, and that I would learn to forgive myself.

At some point, I must have fallen asleep and I blinked, trying to figure out what had woken me. That's when I registered the buzzing in my back pocket. The boys stirred and, as gently as I could, I extracted myself from the bed before making my way to the hallway where I answered the call from an unknown number. My hands were shaking, and I couldn't deny the dread in my heart.

"Hello?"

"Hello, detective."

"Lieutenant Hartwell?" I was surprised to hear my old boss's voice on the other end of the line. He was not who I'd been expecting.

"It's over, Katie. Time to come home."

"Home… to South Carolina?"

"You did well, detective. The DiAngelos have been dismantled and, from what we have been told, several children have been rescued. DiAngelo trade deals are collapsing all over the country. It's good work."

"What about—" I cleared my throat, forcing myself to sound calm, "what about everyone here? The Steel Saints?"

"Say your goodbyes, but it's time. Debriefing is eight a.m. Monday."

"Copy."

"See you then."

"Yes, sir."

The line went dead, and I bit back a sob. Almost blindly, I stumbled back into the bedroom and into Dalton's bathroom. Quietly shutting the door behind me, I turned to face the mirror. Nicole Moore stared back at me. But Nicole was a lie. And Katie… Katie had fallen in love. I sank down, letting the cold tile embrace me like an old friend. I had been so stupid. I knew this day was coming. I had told myself over and over again that developing feelings was a bad move. But the heart wants what the heart wants. And now it felt like mine was shattering all over the bathroom floor.

After an eternity, I came out of the bathroom and a voice said, "You okay, Vixen?"

I startled and looked over at Mac, who had woken up at some point. I gave him a smile, hoping he couldn't see my tear tracks in the dark. "I'm fine, handsome. Go back to sleep. All my stuff is in your room, so I'm going to take a shower real quick. Then I'll be back." I nearly choked on the words, but walked over to him and leaned down to give him a kiss. "I love you."

He reached up, caressing my cheek. "I love you too, gorgeous."

I practically ran out of the room. When I got to Mac's, I headed straight for the nightstand where I knew he kept a notepad and pen. I held the pen over the paper, at a complete loss for what to even say. What words could possibly convey the sorrow I felt, and how much I loved them. My tears fell faster, splattering on the paper. The scratch of pen on paper was the only sound I could hear in the still of quickly approaching night. I had no need for any of the clothes here, so I didn't bother to grab them.

On my way out of the room, I stopped and stared at the picture of Mac, Dalton, and me with our bikes. I bit my lip and, before I could change my mind, took the picture from the frame and tucked it into my pocket. One last glance behind me and, fully aware I was taking the coward's way out, I headed to what had once been my home. On top of Mac's dresser was the tear-stained paper I had left behind. The only words written were a desperate plea.

"Please forgive me."

I stood in the doorway for one final heartbeat, breathing in the smell of motor oil and cologne—everything I loved was in this room. And everything I could no longer have.

I tried to turn off every thought as I walked past members of the club. People, good people, I had come to know and care for like family over the past year. If they sensed something was wrong, they didn't say anything. Rodney asked me if I wanted a drink, to celebrate the new leadership. I couldn't even say no—I just pretended like I hadn't heard him.

I found my Triumph where I had left it. Breaking every speed limit, I headed to the cute little house I had made my home. Every memory hit like a knife the second I crossed the threshold. I pried the loose board in the back of the closet away from the others to get my passport, secondary phone, and spare cash out. I had more than enough for a ticket home. I shoved it all into a bag and used the phone Dalton had given me to order an Uber to the airport.

Katie didn't ride motorcycles.

When I threw the phone on the bed, my eyes landed on the giant stuffed fox, and I froze. Shaking my head, tears yet again blurring my eyes, I forced myself to turn away. But I stopped by the mall strip picture sitting on my dresser. Sandwiched between Maria and Holly, my happy and carefree smile wasn't fake. I tucked that next to the other picture in my pocket.

In the back of the Uber, I texted a number I knew by heart, and hoped she wouldn't hate me too much. Shelly, my former best friend and old partner. I wasn't really sure what—if anything—they'd told her, but I knew when I got back to South Carolina, I was going to need a friend, not to mention a ride.

After a brief back and forth, her insisting I prove I was who I said I was, she readily agreed to meet me there.

"Girl, I have so much to tell you! Right after I beat the shit out of you for just pulling some Oompa Loompa shit."

Shelly's metaphors had never made sense, but the chuckle that escaped me was a raspy surprise.

"I'll see you soon."

She sent back a flurry of emojis, and I steeled myself for the beginning of the end.

# Chapter 23



*Maverick*

I reached across the sheets, finding nothing but emptiness. The bed was cold, and early morning light softly illuminated the room. I blinked, rubbing the sleep from my eyes, and called out, "Vixen?" My voice was still rough, and I cleared my throat before calling out again, "Dalton?"

For a moment, I felt weird. Grown ass man sharing a bed with his brother. But it didn't matter, didn't count when she lay between us. I sat up and stretched, relishing the pop in my back. The door to the bathroom was open, and I could see that it was also empty. They must be downstairs.

Grabbing my shirt off the floor, I pulled it over my head as I made my way down the hall and past the motel rooms, greeting a few shell-shocked kids on my way. To my surprise, a few of them actually responded with hesitant smiles. If I knew her at all, Nicky was probably whipping them up one of the best breakfasts they would ever have in their lives. I hope she made waffles. I fucking loved her waffles. I yawned as I pushed the kitchen door open and found my brother pouring a cup of coffee, barefoot and dressed just in a pair of shorts.

"Nicky come down with you?"

"I thought she was with you?"

He gave me an odd look. "She wasn't in bed when I got up. I assumed she" was in the shower or something."

Unease tightened my gut, and I turned to head back upstairs. Dalton followed, leaving his mug on the counter.

"She's probably just in the shower. If we go barging in there, she's gonna throw something sharp or heavy at us."

"No, 'cos when she woke me up last night, she told me she was going to shower before coming back to bed. So, either she's taking the world's longest, and coldest, shower or—"

"Something's wrong."

I took the stairs two at a time, heading straight for my room. I checked the bathroom and wasn't surprised to find it empty. Where had she gone?

Dalton appeared in the doorway. "Anything?"

I started to shake my head, and then I saw the carefully folded note on my pillow. "My boys" was written on the top in a familiar hand, and somehow I knew the second I opened that note, my world was never going to be the same.

I felt Dalton move closer, his eyes on that slip of paper too. "Not it," he murmured.

I held the note so that we could both see what was written inside, but was shocked when I read the three simple words, surrounded by what I assumed were dried tears.

"Please forgive me."

Forgive her. For what? What the fuck was going on? What had she done? Where was our girl? I looked up at Dalton and saw every question I had reflected in his eyes. He looked from the note she had left to me, and back at the note.

"What the actual fuck is this, Mac? What is going on?"

I shook my head. "I don't know. But we are damn sure going to find out."

I let the paper fall onto the bed like it burned my hands, and turned to leave. I froze when I realized the picture on the wall was now just an empty frame.

*This just keeps getting better.*

On our bikes, we drove like men possessed, flying around every corner until we skidded to a stop outside Nicky's house. Her beloved Triumph was parked out front. The front door was locked, but we both had a key. I was on edge as we made our way inside, Dalton as equally tense, but not a thing was out of place. Together, we headed upstairs to her room which looked the same as it had the last time we were here. Dalton pushed past me, then stopped dead in front of the open closet. I followed, looking inside to see what had made my brother look like his world just stopped.

And then mine stopped, too.

One of the boards on the back wall had been pried loose. Inside was a small compartment that had clearly been used to house God only knows what. Now, it sat empty.

"She was hiding something."

I glanced at Dalton. No shit, brother. I turned from the closet and its lack of answers. It wasn't until my second scan of the room that I noticed the phone on the bed. I said nothing, but Dalton saw it too.

"That's the one I gave her."

We shared a glance.

"I'll call Jackson, you call Diego. Call fucking everyone. We have to find her."

We searched for two days.

I don't remember the last time I slept. Dalton only ate the food Maria forced on him. Jackson and Diego were running down every favor, hunting for every scrap of intel they could find. We scoured the fucking earth for her. But she had vanished, like some sort of ghost.

On the second night, I found Holly consoling a weeping Maria. The two of them had busied themselves getting the rescued kids moved on, but there were only a handful of kids left, and plenty of space freed up for unwanted thoughts.

I ransacked my brain for any mention of a place she would go. Dalton even drove down to check the lake house. She wouldn't just leave us, I told myself. Not Nicky, not Vixen. At night, lying in bed wide awake and staring at the ceiling, I retraced every memory of her. From the second she had walked into the local bar like she owned it, I had watched her. I knew she was trouble before she even set that piece of shit's bike on fire, before she swung on me. She had been a spitfire, and Dalton's nickname for her just stuck no matter how hard she tried to shake it off. I tried like hell to fight it, but it was like she was the other half of me. I couldn't stop loving her even if I had tried.

And damn if I didn't try.

Monday morning dawned grey and ugly. Rain was pouring down, and there was no sound of her bustling around in the kitchen. Dalton sat at the counter, staring at a cup of coffee that was quickly growing cold in front of him. He glanced at me when I walked in, but didn't say a word. I poured my own cup and sat next to him.

After a few moments of silence, he asked, "When do we stop looking?"

I looked at him. Part of me wanted to yell, to berate him for wanting to give up. But I didn't. He was just saying the same thing I had been thinking. I sighed, but didn't answer, opting to sip at my coffee instead.

Our not-so-peaceful morning was shattered when Jackson blew into the room like his ass was on fire. Holly was behind him, hollering at him to slow down, but he didn't seem to hear her. He disappeared towards the motel rooms, and Holly stood in the kitchen with a scowl on her face and her hands on her hips.

"What's up with him?" I asked.

"Wish I fucking knew," she scoffed.

A few minutes later, Jackson came back, and the three of us watched him with equal expressions of bafflement as he lugged one of the small TVs into the kitchen and plugged it in. "Y'all need to see this. I just got word."

He plugged the TV in and began furiously flipping through channels before settling on a news station.

I opened my mouth to ask him what the fuck was going on, but then a familiar face had me snapping my jaw shut. Nicky stood on stage behind the news anchor, except gone was the vibrant red hair and brown eyes. In place of her usual jeans and faded t-shirt, she wore a crisp police uniform, with auburn hair tied in a tight bun at the nape of her neck, and a thin smile on her face—like she had been dragged on the stage against her will. But I would recognize the woman I loved anywhere.

Dalton stood slowly, creeping closer to the monitor like he might spook it, and I gestured at Jackson to turn it up.

"… undercover for over a year under the alias Nicole Moore, Detective McGrady is credited with gathering critical evidence leading to the arrest of multiple high-ranking members of the DiAngelo family. Detective McGrady had reportedly been working on a related case when the FBI's Organized Crime Task Force enlisted her assistance. Now, it's our understanding that you've never done an undercover operation of this magnitude—is that correct, detective?"

Nicky's—or whoever she was—eyes flicked from the anchor to the camera and back again before a man standing next to her gently guided her forward. She gave the microphone shoved in her face a dirty look and cleared her throat. "Um… yeah, that's right. My lieutenant here," she gestured at the man who had prodded her forward, "recommended me for the case. I'm still adjusting to my old life, this life. But it was an opportunity I couldn't turn down, and I wouldn't change anything that happened even if I could."

"Absolutely—still, it must be hard returning home after over a year away. But you took down some really bad people. That must feel good."

"Well, yeah. But I didn't do it alone. There are a few really brave men and women who did some really great things. Honestly, it's them we should be thanking. They're the heroes, not me."

The anchor gave her a confused look, and you could've heard a pin drop in the room as Detective McGrady was ushered off stage by her supposed boss.

I wondered what her real name was. No wonder we couldn't fucking find her—Nicole Moore had never fucking existed. She was a lie. She wasn't ours. She never had been. She was a pretty little thing who had come for one thing and one thing only. She left in the night because she had come to do a job and, once the job was done, what reason would she possibly have to stay?

Certainly not me. She had gotten what she wanted from me.

I remembered her fight with Daniel. The blood. The panic. The way she clawed her way back from the edge like she'd done it before. She was a fighter—I always knew that. But maybe if I hadn't been so consumed by the fear of losing her, I would've seen it for what it was. Tactical. Trained. Controlled, even in chaos. Not just instinct. Not just survival. She fought like someone who had fought before. And I didn't see it, didn't want to see it. Because loving her had already blinded me.

I couldn't move. Holly began to laugh, a completely unhinged and lost sound. "A cop. Holy fucking shit, she's a cop. She fucking lied to us. She *lied* to us." Her voice cracked, and Jackson reached for her, but she took a staggering step back—like the thought of physical touch pained her.

I ran my hands through my hair, and glanced at my brother. Dalton hadn't said a word. He just stood there—stone still. But I saw it. That shift in his expression. Like something was cracking open inside him. Not loud. Not sudden. Just the kind of break that happens after too much pressure on old glass.

"Dalton," I said, to get his attention. To get him to look away from the screen that just shattered our reality. He looked at me, and I'd never forget the way his face looked in that moment. Rage and grief all twisted up in a way that made my stomach churn.

"She lied," he said, almost to himself, "right to my face."

"Brother—"

"She said it was a stray bullet. Wrong place, wrong time."

I blinked. "What?"

"There's a scar. On her hip. Did you notice? It's small. But I knew what it was. I touched it. I asked. I wanted to protect her from whoever had hurt her." His voice was shaking now, teeth clenched. "And she fed me some bullshit story, and I bought it. Because I wanted to. Because I—" He cut himself off, turning away, fists clenched at his sides.

I stepped toward him. "She threw a knife at me once." Everyone looked at me. "It was right after Daniel, and I wasn't thinking. Just wanted to surprise her. She walked in like she didn't see me. Next thing I knew, I felt the breeze on my cheek as I barely dodged the knife she threw. She was so calm, the throw was so precise. But she started freaking out, and I dropped it. I should've questioned her. But all I could think about was calming her down. There were signs. We missed them."

Dalton laughed bitterly. "I loved her. She said she loved me. I believed her."

"We all did."

He didn't answer, just dropped into the nearest chair like he'd been hit. "Doesn't make it hurt less," he whispered.

I glanced back at the TV, but I didn't see anything as images and sounds instead played in my mind. The fire in her eyes the first night we met. The way she said my name. That soft smile she gave me when we were in a room full of people, the one that narrowed my entire world down to just her. I had been a fool to trust her. And an even bigger one to love her.

I couldn't stand being in that damned room for another minute. Grabbing my keys out of my jacket, I pulled on the worn leather as I all but ran out the door. Trying to forget every time she had put my jacket on.

The house was too quiet. I wasn't really sure what brought me here. I had just gotten on my bike and next thing I knew, I pulled up outside a familiar door. Stepping inside, I locked the door behind me more out of habit than need. She wasn't here. But the scent of her still clung to the walls—vanilla, lavender, and something warm. I stood by the door, chest tight, heart thudding like it was waiting for a fight.

I didn't know what I was looking for. Closure? Another letter? A fucking explanation? Something—anything—that said this wasn't just a job to her. That it wasn't all one long, elaborate lie. That she had meant it. Meant every touch. Every word. Every look. But the silence screamed at me. I closed my eyes like I could will her back—will back what we had.

I moved to the kitchen, opened a drawer. Just silverware. Moved to the bookshelf. Ran my fingers over the spines. Hemingway. A worn paperback with a cracked spine and a folded page—the same book she'd given Dalton. I froze. It was a stark reminder that I wasn't the only one she had betrayed. My brother was back at the clubhouse, and I left him to deal with everything alone. But I wanted answers. Needed them. So I kept looking.

The moment came sudden. I bumped the potted fern in the corner with my boot. The thing had already begun to wilt, and I paused to spare it a glance. But then something shifted in the soil. I stilled completely. Leaned down. Moved the leaves aside. A sliver of black plastic, barely visible. A mic. A fucking mic. My blood ran cold as I pried it free.

And then the next twenty minutes disappeared in a blur of rage and pain.

I ripped apart every inch of the apartment. Yanking books off shelves. Tearing through drawers. Dragging the mattress from the frame. I pulled down the vent cover, hands shaking so bad it took three tries. Another mic. And another. Five in total, laid out like sins on the coffee table. I sat on the couch. Barely able to move. To think. I just stared at them. Breathing like I'd run miles.

Nothing had been sacred.

Every word, every laugh, every moan… *recorded*. Every whisper against her skin. Every fucking heartbeat. Just a part of her mission.

"Goddamn you," I muttered, voice raw. "Goddamn you, woman."

I slammed my fist into the table before me, the mics jumping from the impact. Before I could stop myself, I rose and threw the whole table against the wall. Still, it wasn't enough. Not nearly. I sank back onto the couch, elbows on my knees, and buried my face in my hands.

"I loved you," I whispered to no one. "I fucking loved you."

*

After the debriefing, I had been all but been dragged to a surprise interview with a local news station. I had protested, using every excuse in the book to get out of it. My pleas fell on deaf ears. So, there I was. In my crisp, carefully pressed uniform. Lieutenant Hartwell had thought to surprise me with it. My hair back to its true auburn, my eyes no longer brown but a vivid green. I had hesitated to take out my contacts, to redo my hair.

But I wasn't her anymore. I had to.

I couldn't help but tug uncomfortably at my sleeves. Part of me longed for a certain someone's black leather jacket. Or my comfy slip-on sneakers. I was zoned out when the news anchor turned to me, asking a question I'd barely registered. Lieutenant Hartwell gently nudged me forward. I had once been proud of my badge, but now it felt like it was going to drag me down. When the lady kept talking about me like I had personally brought down the DiAngelos, I felt physically sick.

"They're the heroes, not me," I'd said. God knows, it wasn't me.

Hartwell offered me a ride home, but there was only one place I actually wanted to go. That wasn't an option, so I opted for the next best thing. Shelly had picked me up at the airport, bringing me to the precinct, and since then, I had been staying at a hotel. However, the thought of being alone now made me feel sick. Thankfully, she hadn't moved and, when I knocked on her apartment door, she opened it a second later. I didn't say a word, just couldn't. Just collapsed into my best friend's arms and sobbed. Shelly held me tightly, arms strong and grounding. She had been my rock before I went under, and she still was. She didn't even seem to mind as I soaked her shirt. Instead, she just joked, "Jesus, KitKat. So much for the emotionally suppressed cop you used to be."

I let out a shaky laugh through her tears, the old nickname bringing back fond memories. I hiccupped and said, "I screwed everything up, Shelly. Like, bad."

"Like worse than that one time you forgot to park the shop and it rolled downhill into a roadside fruit stand bad?"

"Worse."

"Well, damn." Shelly raised her eyebrows and pulled me down the hall towards her kitchen. "C'mon. You're a mess. Tell me what's got you all in your head like this."

Ten minutes later, we were curled up on Shelly's worn couch—I had borrowed a pair of sweats and an old Georgia State sweater. With a blanket over my shoulders and a full glass of cabernet in my hands, I tried to figure out where to start. Shelly sat across from me, legs crossed and holding a glass of her own. She waited patiently, not rushing or pressuring me.

Eventually, I decided the best place to start was the most obvious place. At the beginning. I told her everything. Every feeling, every thought, every decision. Every second. Every fucking mistake.

"I loved them," I said quietly. "I still love them. Both of them. So much it hurts."

Shelly didn't flinch, just refilled our glasses with the last of the wine. "I knew that part already. "

I blinked at her. "Huh?"

"I'm your best friend, and I like to think I am of moderate intelligence. The look on your face the first time you mentioned 'the brothers' was practically glowing. I just didn't realize it was *both* brothers. Damn. Go big or go home, huh?"

I gave her a weak smile, then rubbed my eyes. "Well, to be fair, go home wasn't really an option, but it's not like I set out to fall in love with either of them—let alone both of them. There was just something about them… Shelly, I wish you could meet them. You and Dalton are so much alike. But you'll probably never get the chance. 'Cos when they find out who I really am on the news… I didn't even say goodbye properly. I left a note. Like a coward. The thought of facing them, of saying goodbye… Shit, they must hate me. I would. So I ran."

Shelly tilted her head. "Classic emotionally repressed cop move."

I laughed, sounding slightly hysterical, and then immediately started crying again.

Shelly scooted closer and grabbed my hand. "Look, I'm not gonna bullshit you. You broke their trust. But you also risked everything to save kids no one else was looking for. When you left for the assignment, we had been on the case of those poor girls and didn't have a single fucking lead. You took what was basically the only shot we, you, had at taking the DiAngelos down. And from what you told me? You didn't just fall in love while playing a part. You became the part, became *her*, but the real you was always in there."

I looked down. "But I walked away. I chose the badge. Over them. There's no going back from that."

"Did you? Choose the badge?" Shelly said. "Or did you follow the orders and bury your heart like they trained us to? Because, hon… I think your heart's been screaming at you for months. And you've always been a bit hard of hearing."

"What if I go back and they slam the door in my face?"

"Then you keep knocking," Shelly said simply. "Because love like that? That doesn't die so easy. And badge or no badge, you're still the woman who saved lives. Still the woman they fell in love with. Mostly. Ish." She hesitated, her brow furrowed. "Okay, it's complicated and more than a little confusing. But now you've got this opportunity to finally have something real. Something you don't have to… feel guilty about, or whatever. And maybe you could still help people. Sounds like Mac and Dalton aren't the type to just stop being heroes. Be the Robin to their Batman. Their sexy, badass Robin. And maybe, not only help even more than you did before, but also have a shot at being happy."

I swallowed hard, processing her words. "But I wouldn't be a cop."

"No," Shelly said, "but you'd still be you. Just a new and improved version. You always held your tongue, Katie—you followed the rules and did what you were told. But when we were alone or hanging out at the bar, I could see the real you. Maybe being Nicole helped you shake off this idea you had of who society expected you to be. Go back," she said gently. "Tell them the truth. Ask for forgiveness. If they still love you—and I think they do—you build something real this time. Something free."

I looked down at my empty wine glass, then out the window toward the horizon. Maybe it was the alcohol talking, but I was so genuinely tempted by what she was suggesting. Even if it meant throwing away everything I thought I knew. If I did this, there would be no going back. It was them or my badge. I considered it for all of two seconds.

"I think… I think I will. Go back, I mean."

"Well, that's the best idea you've had in a while," Shelly said with a wink. "When you get there, and after the glorious make-up sex, see if they have a cousin or something, would you?"

She dodged the pillow I threw at her head with ease.

After talking to Shelly, I felt a bit more grounded. Was I still losing what little was left of my sanity? Absolutely. But I'd worry about that another time. I wandered around Charleston a bit. Once upon a time, this had been my home, but now I felt like a visitor—and I wasn't sure if I'd ever come back here. I knew I was going to Atlanta, and hopefully staying, but the Feds had been paying for my house. What were the chances I could get it back? There wasn't much I could do until morning, so I got a hotel and spent the rest of the night staring at the ceiling.

As soon as the first rays of morning light hit my window, I packed a small bag and made sure to grab my .45 ACP, safely locked in its hard case. It was the only personal weapon I owned, and I wasn't leaving without it. Downstairs, I flagged down a taxi from the curb. My service weapon was on my hip, my badge hung around my neck, and the taxi driver gave me a skeptical look. I smiled at him, hoping it was reassuring. After a minute, he seemed to decide all was well and headed for the station like I had asked. There was one thing I had to do before I left.

The next two days were going to be tough—not only did I have to face the people I loved and betrayed, but I had to face a man who had been like a father to me, and hope to goodness that he would understand.

The first floor was, as always, a chaotic mess. Perps hollering their innocence, cops on their third or fourth cup of coffee, stray reporters floating around and seeing how long it would take before they got the boot. It was like that in every precinct, a certain kind of elaborate dance. One I knew every step to, one I had devoted a good part of my life to. I had once taken such pride in being a cop, and had busted my ass to become a detective. I was good at it, and, while it wasn't always easy, I had found the work rewarding. But I had to believe what Shelly said—that I could do good in this world even without a badge.

I exited the elevator onto the second floor, and headed for an office I knew like the back of my hand. The morning sun cast long slats of light across the worn hardwood floor, the smell of ink and old coffee. I watched through the doorway for a minute, before knocking. Lieutenant Hartwell, sleeves rolled up and glasses perched low on his nose, was glaring at a stack of paperwork like it had personally offended him. When I knocked, he looked up with a characteristic frown that changed into something softer when he saw me. Not quite a smile. Oh, no—not from that old tough bastard. But I liked to tell myself there was a bit of fondness in his eyes.

"Detective, come in. I could use a break from this bullshit."

My heart was somehow heavy and light at the same time. I took a seat in one of the armchairs in front of his desk and tried to find the words. He raised an eyebrow at me, and I decided not to beat around the bush. So, I took my weapon off my hip and my badge from around my neck, and laid it on his desk. He leaned back in his chair, crossing his arms and waiting for me to explain.

"I'm going back."

"Hm. I assume you've thought about this? *Really* thought about it?'

"Only about a thousand times, sir, and I keep coming back to the same place. My heart's not in the badge anymore."

"Is this about them? The brothers?"

I took a deep breath. It wasn't judgment in his tone, simply a curiosity. I figured I owed him the truth—at least as much of the truth that I understood.

"It's about a lot of things. When I went undercover, I told myself I could keep the lines clean — duty, justice, all of it. You recommending me for the position in the first place, despite my inexperience, that was huge to me. So, I was determined to do right by you. Do right by those kids. But it stopped being black and white a long time ago. I've seen things—helped people—in ways I never could have from behind this desk. I've met some really great people, not just the brothers. But people who want to make this world better. I've come to respect them and, yes, in the case of Mac and Dalton, love them."

"So, you're choosing to… join a motorcycle club?"

I laughed softly, self-deprecatingly. "I'm choosing me."

He nodded, and the silence stretched between us. It wasn't awkward, but I still felt the need to fill it, to justify my decision. "I'm not turning my back on justice. I just… I want to fight for it differently now. With them. On the ground. No red tape. No politics. Just saving lives. Making a difference."

Hartwell finally leaned forward, grabbing the badge I left on his desk, and turning it over and over in his weathered hands. He looked between it and me, and sighed. "You know, when you first walked into this precinct, you were all sharp edges and chip-on-your-shoulder fire. I could see you holding yourself back, never saying what you really wanted to say. Playing the part. But you had more self-control than most people twice your age. Sometimes, I wished you would just let loose and give people what they had coming. But you never did. I never expected you to last six months.

"But you did more than last. You changed people. Hell, you changed me. You devoted yourself to this life and you made a hell of a cop. When you made detective, I had never been so proud of someone under my command. That's why I recommended you for the job. And you did damn good, kid.

"I can't say I understand leaving your badge behind. But I do know that, whatever you decide, you'll be fine. If you want to change the world, you will. Whether you've got a badge or not."

I couldn't help but stare at him, jaw open like a fish out of water.

That was the most I had ever heard the man speak. I sniffled, snapping my mouth closed and staring at the ceiling. Willing myself not to cry again. Not in front of him. Not here. When I looked back at him, it was to find him watching me with a bemused glint in his eye.

"You're not disappointed?" I couldn't help but ask.

"Not even a little. I always figured you'd outgrow this place. Maybe not like this, but old men like yours truly need those curveballs to keep us on our toes." He stood, and I did too. Walking around his desk, he held his hand out to me. "Go. Be happy. Do good. And if you ever need backup, you know where to find it. Good luck."

I reached to shake his outstretched hand, and was surprised when he pulled me into a hug. After a second, he stepped back and cleared his throat awkwardly. "You'll be missed, kid."

I smiled at him, realizing I would miss him more than I thought. His mentorship meant more to me than he realized. I turned to leave and, just before I stepped out into the hallway, I turned around and said, "Thank you. For everything."

He nodded his head and went back to his paperwork, but then looked up at me one more time. "You tell them boys if they hurt you, they answer to me."

I laughed. "Yes, sir."

On the elevator, I wiped my eyes and fiddled with my clothes. My neck felt naked, like a weight missing. But my heart… it felt a bit freer. A chapter closed, so a new one could open. I wasn't really sure how things were going to play out—should I head straight to the clubhouse after getting off the plane, or head to my house that wasn't mine? Speaking of… I grabbed my phone, and called Shelly.

"Are you in Georgia yet?"

"What? No… I'm not The Flash."

"Slacker. Sounds like a bunch of excuses."

"Uh-huh. Listen, I need your help."

"What's up?"

I explained to her about my house, the one I had mentioned briefly the other night.

"I was kinda fond of the place, to be honest. But it was paid for by the Feds, so I'm not even sure how much the rent is. But between the undercover pay and my savings, I got about a hundred-twenty grand stashed away. If I send you my bank stuff and if the house isn't more than like two grand a month… could you get that set up for me? Please."

"Ah, so I get the boring job while you get to go see if you can win your lovers back? You're lucky I love you. But if I do this, I only ask one thing in return…"

I laughed. "What?"

"Tea—every nitty-gritty detail. Short of recording the conversation, I want to hear *everything*. And, once the dust is settled, you fly my poor ass out to see you."

"Deal!"

"Cool beans. Send me the details and I'll see what I can do."

"You're the bomb. Love you."

"I know. Love you, too."

I disconnected the call and sent her everything she would need to, hopefully, get the house worked out for me. Then it was time to grab my bags from where I left them with the desk sergeant, and flag down another cab to head for the airport. I bought the tickets on the drive, and began practicing my speech in my head. What was I going to say? Would they hate me? Forgive me? What if it was too far gone? What about Maria and Holly? Shit, did someone get my Triumph? And my stuffed fox?

My thoughts were going ninety miles an hour, and we were at the airport before I knew it.

After getting through security and checking my Colt, I had about an hour before the plane took off. I had planned on just sitting by the window and waiting but, on my way to the gate, I passed one of the little stores. I stopped, eyeing the travel-sized meds. I really hadn't slept last night and, with my anxiety and adrenaline sky-high, I doubted sleep would come easy. I knew I needed it. I bit my bottom lip, eyeing the Benadryl. "Fuck it," I swore under my breath.

Benadryl in hand, I went to check out, and the attendant asked, "Is that all?"

I opened my mouth to say yes, but what I actually said was, "I'll take two of those mini Jim Beams too." Oops.

I waited until the plane pulled up to the gate, and all the previous passengers had gotten off before tossing back both shots and the Benadryl. Don't try this at home, kids. An older woman watched me and, when I looked over at her, she gave me a judgmental look and said, "Flying nerves, sweetheart?"

I smiled at her, though it was more like a grimace because the fucking Benadryl had gotten stuck in my throat.

"Something like that," I croaked.

When it was my turn to board, I hurried onto the plane. At this point, I was just ready to be there. Ready to be somewhere where it was truly too late to turn back before I lost my nerve.

I found my seat between a guy my age and about three times my size, and a teenager who wore an "unaccompanied minor" lanyard around her neck. The guy basically ignored me, intently focused on his bag of chips, and the teen looked up at me with a look of general distaste and popped her gum. Normally, I would be cursing my luck, but right then, I really couldn't find the time or energy to care. I plopped down between the two of them and pretended I was on a beach somewhere. In my fantasy world, the sun was warm and the water was blue, and the men I loved sat by my side. That must be the Jim Beam talking—I was a lightweight when I had an empty stomach. As my eyelids got heavier, I was happy to note that the Benadryl had started to work too. By the time the flight attendants had finished their safety speech, I was out like a light.

"Excuse me. Excuse me. Helloooo! Wake up. I've had to pee for like freaking years."

I rolled my neck and opened a single bleary eye to find that we had landed, and the strange guy had already gone. The kid next to me frowned. "Oh, great. You're alive. You've kept me from peeing this whole time. Could you maybe get off the plane so that, I dunno, I could get off too? And find a bathroom?"

I stretched and yawned. Snarky teens were the best thing to wake up to.

I eyed her pink hair and hard frown before saying, "Sorry, kid, you should've woken me up."

I stood up, turning to grab my bag as she said, "Trust me, I tried. I thought maybe you were dead."

I didn't bother answering her, just joined the throng of people filing out of the aircraft.

My stomach growled loudly, and the sound must have woken up my brain, which simultaneously said, "Food!" and "Oh shit!" as I realized that I was back in Georgia. I still had no idea what I was going to say.

I turned my phone back on, and was surprised to see a message from Shelly. Damn, the girl worked fast. My house was still on the market. And now it was in my name. My real name. I sent her a heartfelt thank you, and followed my nose towards the smell of food. I sat at the first restaurant I saw and practically salivated at the thought of a big, juicy burger. A waiter quickly came and took my order. Not even fifteen minutes later, he was back with my food, and I burned my tongue in my hurry to scarf it down.

I left money on the table and headed for the luggage carousel. After a minute, I finally located a bored-looking security guard who pointed me in the direction of the baggage services area. I signed for my gun, presented my ID, and then stepped outside to hunt down a cab. Just as I raised my hand to flag one of the waiting ones down, I stopped. I really was just flying along with no plan. Which, cop or no cop, was a stupid decision. I should at least have some idea of what I was doing. Another text to Shelly confirmed that the spare key I had left in the fake rock behind the bushes should still be there.

So, that's where I went first.

The key felt heavier than I remembered. Or maybe that was just my guilty conscience talking. I stood on the porch, just staring at the door, for what felt like hours. Behind that door was a cocktail of memories, and my chest tightened with the overwhelming swirl of emotions—fear, hope, regret, love. I had walked away—I was no longer Nicole Moore. But all those memories were still mine. Still something I cherished. Sighing, I bit the bullet and opened the door which creaked open with an all-too-familiar groan. I stepped inside, and it felt like coming home.

I inhaled the smells deeply. Coffee, cedar cleaning product, the lavender wall plug-in that glowed in the dim light. I flipped the switch, and my smile fell when I saw the mess. My Vans sat by the door, but that was the only thing in place. My footsteps echoed softly against the hardwood as I walked through my home. The overstuffed armchair Dalton liked to read in was on its side; the books he gave me covered the floor. The coffee table in the living room was upside down. My footsteps faltered when I caught sight of the mics mixed into the wreckage. Dalton wouldn't have made this mess. It was all Mac. What were the chances he would forgive me? I steeled myself before making my way to the bedroom.

Our bedroom.

My fox was on the floor, and my cellphone was gone. My mattress leaned up against a wall. The boards in the back of the closet were still loose. I sat on the box springs, reaching for Molly, pulling her close to my chest. If I closed my eyes, I could still see it—the look in Mac's eyes when he let his guard down, Dalton's hand on my bare hip, and that crooked smile. The laughter in the mornings, the gentle sounds of their breathing at night. My heart clenched painfully. The house felt a bit like a tomb, a place full of ghosts. But the ghosts weren't dead. They were just somewhere out there, hurting.

Because of me.

I looked over at my dresser, and at the picture there. One of the many I had been tempted to take with me. We had spent Holly's birthday at the lake house. Maria was on Diego's back, legs wrapped around his waist, and chin resting on his head. Her grin was as bright as the sun shining behind us. Jackson had been tickling Holly, trying to force a laugh out of her, and the camera had caught them mid-tussle. I stood between Mac and Dalton, my arm wrapped around Mac's bicep and Dalton pressing a kiss to my cheek. I loved that picture. I half-expected to see a crack in the glass, a symbolic fracture. But the frame was whole and, perhaps irrationally, that gave me hope.

It was time to face the music. For better or for worse.

# Chapter 25

When I got to the clubhouse, I just stood and stared. I knew that place like the back of my hand. The smell of oil, grease, and a faint trace of cigar smoke. The kitchen I had loved from the second I first saw it. The rooms in the back that I was sure were now empty, and waiting for more survivors. The bay door was half-open, letting in a shaft of morning light that stretched across the concrete floor like a spotlight I couldn't avoid. So, I stepped into the garage with my shoulders back and chin high, every instinct in me screaming to turn around and run. Much to my surprise, my Triumph sat in the corner—half-covered by a tarp, the front peeking out like a secret that wouldn't be hidden.

People started noticing me as I made my way through, and silence fell. My hair was a different color, my eyes no longer green. But they knew who I was. Half a dozen heads turned my way—mid-conversation, mid-wrench-turn, mid-laugh. All of it stopped. The scrape of metal on metal echoed too loud in the sudden quiet. You could've cut the tension in the air with a dull butter knife. I met their stares one by one. There was hostility in their eyes but, at least in some of them, there was a sadness too.

Kaycen's jaw tensed as he stood straighter beside his bike. Henrick crossed his arms. Even quiet Benny, who I once taught how to make scrambled eggs that didn't taste like rubber, wouldn't meet my eyes. Nobody said a word. My hands were shaking, and the garage felt like it had suddenly become the length of two football fields. Shoving my hands in my pocket, I focused on putting one foot in front of the other. If looks could kill, I would've been a puddle on the floor. I tried to remind myself that I had betrayed their trust, and tried to put myself in their shoes. That didn't really make it much easier.

At the far workbench, Cliff stood cleaning a valve cover, pretending to focus on the task in front of him. The tension in his shoulders said otherwise.

"Cliff," I said gently, trying to keep my voice steady even though my stomach twisted. "Where are they?"

For a moment, I thought he wouldn't answer. He just kept wiping, jaw tight, eyes shadowed under his graying brows. Scrubbing the part in front of him with more than a little aggression. I nodded, and turned to go inside. The man who had given me my beloved Molly was closed off to me.

Then, without looking at me, he said, "Upstairs." One word. Gruff, quiet. Like I had dragged it from him. But it was communication, it was a start, and I would take it. He paused, then added, "They've been through hell. We all have been these last few days."

"I know."

Cliff finally looked at me. His eyes weren't angry—just tired. Disappointed. "I don't think you do, young lady. You got a lotta people here feeling like idiots. Me included." He shook his head. "But... I'd be lying if I said I wasn't glad to see you. Place's been too damn quiet. And no one's cooked a decent chili since you left."

I blinked, my throat tightening. "I'll make you some, and I'll chop up some extra onion for you, too. Maybe even make some cornbread."

"You better..." He hesitated. "For everyone's sake, I hope you didn't fuck this up beyond fixing. This club is better with you in it."

Before I could reply, another voice cut in. Rodney leaned back against the far wall, arms crossed, eyes sad. He must have been watching the entire exchange. "They've been messes, both of 'em. Mac's mean as hell, and Dalton is just quiet, which is worse somehow. Last time they were like this was when their daddy passed. They need you, Ni—" He paused, cleared his throat, "Erm, what is your name?"

I turned toward him, surprised he had even spoken up. "It's Kaitlyn, but my friends just call me Katie."

He shrugged. "I think Nicky fits you better. Just sayin'. Anyways, whatever you're here to do… good luck."

I nodded then headed into the kitchen, past the empty motel rooms, and finally to the stairs. Here goes nothing. My boots were nearly silent, but each step reverberated throughout my body. I reached the top and paused, the familiar hallway stretching out before me. I suddenly found the air oppressive and heavy, my lungs seemingly having to work twice as hard to function. Just as I took a step forward, towards whatever fate awaited me, Dalton's door swung open, and he stepped into the hallway. I froze.

He didn't see me at first. His head was down, hand tugging on a hoodie sleeve as he moved toward the stairs. But when he looked up, he stopped dead. My eyes raked over him, taking in the stubble of a beard. The bags under his eyes. The bruise across his jawline. Holy crap, he looked awful. And it was my fault. Those last two words rang in my head over and over. All of it. Mine.

His eyes locked onto mine, wide with shock and something deeper. Something buried. His lips parted like he meant to say my name, but then snapped shut like he thought better of it.

He turned his head slightly, towards his brother's room, his voice calm but low and urgent. "Mac," he called, "You better get out here."

My eyes snapped to the other closed door, and then Mac stepped into the hallway, shirtless, sweatpants slung low on his hips, clearly mid-workout or maybe trying to outrun his own thoughts. His abdomen was slick with a thin sheen of sweat. When he saw me, his whole body stilled. Then the storm hit. His expression twisted, raw fury bleeding through every line of his face.

"What the hell is this?" he snapped. "No one called 911, cop. You're not wanted here."

I didn't flinch. I couldn't afford to. Wasn't sure I had the right to.

"Mac, Dalton… please. I came to talk," I said, voice level despite the ache clawing at my throat.

"Talk?" Mac laughed—a sharp, bitter sound. "*Now* you want to talk? After you lied to us for over a year? After you tore our lives apart and walked away without a goddamn word?"

"Oh, don't discount that bullshit note she left behind."

I glanced at Dalton, then back at Mac. "I had to—"

"You *chose* to," he growled, stepping closer. "Don't twist it. There is no had to. You made a conscious fucking decision. And you chose to leave us behind. To live the lie."

"I'm not here to make excuses," I said quietly. "I know what I did. I know how much it cost. But I'm here because I couldn't stay away. Because I love you. Both of you. And I want, more than anything to explain—"

Dalton guffawed, and Mac's jaw clenched hard enough I could see the muscle tick. Dalton frowned at me. "I'm not falling for you or your bullshit again. You've got some nerve coming back here and talking about love like that fixes anything," he muttered. "You don't just get to drop in and expect forgiveness."

He strolled past Mac into the bedroom, and then Mac turned his back on me too, slamming the door so hard the walls rattled. Damn it all to hell. I knew this wasn't going to be easy. But I had come this far. I walked over to the door they had shut in my face, fists clenched at my sides. My heart thundered against my ribs like it was trying to break free. For a minute, I just stared at the grain of the wood. Willing myself not to tuck tail and run. I was better than that. They deserved answers. Finally, I knocked.

No answer.

I knocked again, harder this time.

"Please," I said, my voice cracking. "Please just… just listen."

Nothing.

"I know I don't deserve it. I know that. But I need you to hear me. I need you to know the truth. I—" My throat tightened, and then I tossed out the only card I had left to play. "Mia Huntington. Anastasia Little. Gabriella Santiago. Kelly MacIntyre. Ruby Johnson."

There was a long pause. Then the latch clicked. The door opened just a few inches—just enough for me to see Dalton's eyes, shadowed with something unreadable. He stepped aside without a word, leaving the door wide enough for me to slip in. The room hit me like a punch to the gut. It was familiar—same paint, same shelves, same bed—but it looked like a storm had rolled through. The same storm that had gone through my house. Clothes were scattered, drawers half-open. The sheets were twisted, the floor littered with half-empty bottles of whiskey and a broken picture frame.

Mac stood in the far corner with his arms crossed and his eyes on the floor. Dalton leaned against the dresser, watching. Guarded. Then he said, "You wanna explain the names you dropped like they meant something?"

I stepped further in, careful not to disturb anything, even though everything already felt broken. My hands still shook, but I didn't try to hide it anymore. "When I was a detective, before I took this assignment, those are the names of the five little girls that went missing in Charleston. My partner Shelly and I were hitting fucking dead ends at every turn. It was like these kids just vanished. You ever have to knock on a mother's door, and tell her that you still haven't found her baby? It's one of the worst feelings in the world. The Feds told me it was the DiAngelos, a name I had only heard in passing before. They gave me a chance, and I had to take it."

I continued in a voice barely above a whisper. "When I first met you both, I didn't expect any of this. It was supposed to be a job. I was supposed to get in, get what we needed to take the DiAngelos down, and leave."

I looked at Mac. He didn't lift his gaze.

"But then I got to know you. The club. Holly and Maria. Everyone. I saw the things you were doing—saving people, protecting them when no one else would. And I saw you. Both of you. And suddenly, the lines I was supposed to follow didn't make sense anymore. Things didn't feel so black and white."

Still nothing. But neither of them had left, so I kept going. "I tried to keep it professional. I tried to remember my mission. But it didn't matter. Every day I spent with you, every time I woke up between you, every laugh at the dinner table, every damn ride on the back of our bikes—I was falling in love. Not with an assignment. Not with the job. With you."

Dalton's jaw flexed, but he didn't interrupt.

"I never meant to lie to you. But I couldn't tell you the truth, either. If I had, I would've ruined everything. I was trapped between duty and my heart, and I made choices I have to live with now. I'll carry that guilt for the rest of my life."

Mac finally looked up, his eyes red-rimmed, his voice hoarse. "And we're just supposed to what? Forgive you? Let you back in like nothing happened? I get why you did it… *Katie*. It's not that. But you used us. You used the people we cared most about."

"No, I know," I whispered. "I can't tell you where we go from here. I don't know what's next. Yell. Scream. Cuss me out. I deserve all of it. But I had to come here. I had to try and explain. Because I love you both. And I couldn't live another day pretending like that didn't matter."

My voice broke on the next words. "This—you two—it was the only real thing I've ever had." I stood there, breathing hard, waiting—bracing for rejection. Waiting to see if love was enough to bring broken pieces back together. "And I know," I said softly, "that technically… you didn't fall in love with me." Dalton looked up at that. Mac's jaw clenched again. "You fell in love with Nicole Moore. A woman who doesn't exist. A name on a file. A lie."

My voice wavered, but I forced myself to keep going. "But the thing is… Nicky is more me than anything I ever was before. Nicky wasn't fake. She was brave and loud and messy. She didn't always play by the rules. She protected people. She laughed too hard, and she cursed too much, and she loved you both with every damn part of her. And yeah—her name was a cover. But everything else?" I touched my chest, placing a hand over my frantic heart. "Everything that mattered… that was real."

My eyes met Mac's, searching for a chink in the armor. "You helped me find her. You helped me find *myself*. For the first time in my life, I wasn't just surviving—I was living. And I can't go back to who I was before I met you. I don't want to.

"I'm not asking you to love Katie McGrady today. I'm not asking for anything at all. But I hope… maybe one day, you'll see that Katie and Nicky aren't that different. That underneath the badge and the lies and the fear,

I'm still the woman who danced barefoot in your kitchen and stole your hoodies and made you laugh when you didn't want to smile."

Dalton's eyes rose from the spot they had been burning into the floor, and I gave him a weak smile. "I just needed you two to know… I never wanted to hurt either of you. But I'd rather you hate me for the truth, than love me for a lie."

I had been talking for so long, my throat was dry. I hadn't planned on making some big ass speech. But, as it turns out, once I got going, I couldn't stop. And there was one more thing I needed to say. I licked my drying lips, rubbed my wet eyes, and said a tad louder than I meant to, "And I really hope, one day, you'll love me just as much as you loved her."

Back home, I sat on the couch, elbows on my knees, fingers laced together, and staring at the floor. My chest still ached from everything I'd just said, from everything they hadn't said back. The silence in the townhouse felt deafening. A knock at the door cut through it, and I jumped about ten feet out of my skin. For a second, I hoped it was one of them. Maybe both. But as I pulled the door open, my stomach dropped.

Holly. And Maria.

Fuck, I had meant to call them.

Holly's hand was flexing like she was resisting the urge to deck me. Her eyes flashed with betrayal and fury. She didn't wait to be invited in. She shouldered past me with enough force that it rocked me back a few steps. Maria followed behind her, slower. Her steps were hesitant. Her eyes… they weren't angry. Just sad. Hurt.

I shut the door behind them, gently, like there was a bomb in the room and I wasn't sure what would set it off. To be fair, the way Holly was looking at me, I had been around bombs that made me feel safer.

"What the hell were you thinking?" Holly glared at me, arms crossed, nostrils flaring. "Do you have any idea what you did to them? To us? You lied. For over a year. You played us."

"Holly," Maria said quietly, touching her arm.

"No. She needs to hear it," Holly snapped, eyes never leaving me. "You don't get to disappear and then come back like this, acting like you're the victim."

I held up my hands. "Hold up, I'm not. I'm not trying to be. I just—just listen for a second. Give me a chance to explain?"

Holly barked out a disbelieving laugh. "You want us to listen? After all the lies?"

My voice cracked. "I was doing a job—"

"A job?!" Holly cut in. "You made them fall in love with a lie! And not just them. Us. *Us.* I trusted you. I let you in. Maria taught you how to make fucking tamales and her kids call you Auntie, and you betrayed us all!"

Maria stepped between us, raising a hand. "Enough." Her brown eyes met mine, and the thought that I had put some wall between us killed me. "Just… tell us. The short version. Please. 'Cos I really don't have the energy for some long-winded bullshit, *chica.*"

I swallowed hard, nodding. "My real name is Katie McGrady. I'm a detective. I was sent undercover to infiltrate the club. I didn't know how far it would go. I didn't expect to care. But I did. I fell in love—with all of you. With this life. With them. I didn't fake that. Not for a second."

Silence settled over the room. Holly turned away, pacing like a caged animal, biting down her next words. Maria's shoulders sagged.

"And now?" she asked. "What now?"

"I turned in my badge," I said softly. "I'm not going back. I want to stay, to still be a part of… everything. If you'll let me." Holly stilled and Maria just stared, eyes misting.

"Time," Maria finally said. "They'll need time. We all will."

I nodded eagerly—that was an answer I could live with. They wanted time? I would give them all the time in the world. Hell, they could ask for the moon and I would do my best to bring it to them. Right now, I was willing to do just about anything to earn their forgiveness.

I glanced between them, then toward the kitchen like it might offer an escape. "Look," I said, voice a little hoarse, "I know nothing I say can fix this. At least not right away. But maybe… maybe I could get us some takeout? My treat. And if you want, I can tell you about me. The real me."

Holly raised an eyebrow. "You think some fucking cashew chicken is gonna fix a year of lies?"

I gave her a half-smile. "No. But it might make it easier to hear about the time I accidentally tasered myself chasing a guy in a Batman costume."

Maria let out a small laugh, surprised, and even Holly's scowl twitched. Just a little.

Forty minutes later, the three of us were settled around my low coffee table, cartons of Chinese food open, the tension slowly fading like fog in sunlight. Maria had helped me pick up the place just enough for us to have seats. I leaned back, chopsticks in hand, telling them about Shelly—who insisted on wearing mismatched socks because it "kept the criminals guessing."

I told them about the time we got stuck in an elevator with a drunk guy who thought we were secret agents and begged us to "take him to space." And, after telling him we were just cops for the millionth time, Shelly finally had enough and started telling him stories about the "great universe", shit she made up for his entertainment and ours while we were stuck in that damn elevator for hours.

Maria laughed so hard she nearly choked on her lo mein. Even Holly, curled into the corner of the couch with her shoes off, started to look less like a lion ready to pounce and more like the Holly that I remembered. Snarky, yes—but a little softer now. I even decided to tell them about Braxton's sleazy ass.

"The guy was obsessed," I said, rolling my eyes. "I thought it was just him being overbearing, but then one day during a debriefing, he went all rabid-puppy-love on me." I told them about the insults and dirty looks when I turned him down, and how glad I was to be rid of his ass.

Holly snorted. "Jesus. He sounds like a real treat."

"You have *no* idea."

We laughed, and for the first time in what felt like forever, I didn't feel like an outsider. Just a very tired woman with two friends who might, just maybe, forgive her one day. As the clock neared seven, Maria glanced at her phone and sighed. "I need to get home. The kids are probably eating cereal for dinner."

"That's my cue too," Holly said, standing and stretching. "I drove."

I walked them to the door. "Thanks for coming. Really. And thank you for listening."

Maria gave me a soft smile. "This doesn't mean everything's okay. But… it's a start."

Holly paused in the doorway. "Still pissed at you," she muttered. "But you're funny. And those egg rolls were solid."

I smiled. "I'll take it."

They left, and as the door clicked shut behind them, I leaned my head against the frame, exhaling. Not forgiven. But not alone either. The apartment was quiet again, the leftover takeout already cooling on the counter. I sat alone on the couch, legs pulled up to my chest, staring at nothing. My mind wandered—not to Mac or Dalton this time, but further back. To the first person who ever truly saw me, badge and all. Shelly.

I could still remember our first meeting eight years ago like it was yesterday.

I had barely been on the force six months when I got assigned a new partner. I was still a rookie, my training office having literally just signed off. I'd been hopeful—maybe even a little eager. That lasted exactly two minutes into meeting Officer Michelle "Shelly" Vaughn.

"I don't do hand-holding," Shelly said, tossing a duffel into the back of her cruiser. "Keep up or get reassigned."

I raised a brow. "Wow. You always this warm and fuzzy?"

Shelly smirked. "Only on days that end in y."

We clashed almost instantly. Shelly was all sarcasm and swagger, a fast-talking city girl with an attitude bigger than her crazy sock collection. Then there was me, still trying to prove myself but not about to roll over and play goody-goody. We bickered about everything— routes, paperwork, interrogation styles. It was oil and water, day after day.

Until that case.

A domestic call turned into a nightmare. A little girl, bruised and terrified, had hidden under the porch while her father tore through the house in a drug-fueled rage. I had found her first, coaxed her out with soft words and trembling hands. It was Shelly who grabbed me by the vest and dragged us both away just as the guy came blazing out with a double-barreled shotgun.

Afterward, we sat side by side on the curb, the adrenaline crash hitting like a freight train. I glanced at her and said, "I think I've decided."

Shelly rolled her shoulders and undid her bulletproof vest. "Decided what?"

"Domestic calls are the fucking worst. Give me gang war gone bad any day over that shit."

Shelly had turned to me, eyebrows raised. "You know, I'm not gonna even disagree with you on that."

I think that was the first thing we had ever agreed on. We didn't talk much more that night. Just got the paperwork done and went home. But the silence between us had changed. It wasn't tense anymore. It was comfortable. Her walls started coming down, and instead of arguing 24/7 in our shop, we got to know each other. And realized we had a lot more in common than we had initially thought.

I smiled softly at the memory, my heart aching a little. After that night, Shelly and I had become inseparable—partners, best friends, sisters in everything but blood. I shot her a quick text: "I'll message you tomorrow. Kinda feel like I've been run over. Gonna try and get some sleep."

Shelly sent back a string of emojis which I didn't even attempt to decipher, knowing from experience the message was one only Shelly would understand. If two stubborn women like us could find a way to understand each other, then maybe there was still hope for the rest of my wrecked life.

Maybe Mac and Dalton could, one day, see me—not the badge, not the lie. Just Katie.

And maybe that could be enough.

# Chapter 26

Time passed—not in days, but in moments. I worked like a woman possessed, doing all the jobs I had done before with a renewed zest. I showed up to every club gathering, cooked every meal until every biker looked a bit more rotund around the waist, and wore my heart on my sleeve. I helped Jackson fix up bikes. I babysat Jewel and Diego Jr., who still called me Aunt Nicky despite my best efforts. I cleaned blood off floors after messy rescue ops, took stitches from Diego with nothing but a wince when things went south, kept the motel rooms ready for anyone who needed one, and threw everything I had into redeeming myself.

At first, no one quite knew what to do with me. Holly still gave me death glares, sharp as a blade, but the venom dulled with every batch of fried chicken and every laugh that slipped out. Maria was cautious, but I caught her smiling during yet another dumb cop story. Baby steps. I would happily take them. I was determined to get my friends back and, with each passing day, the hope that I sheltered like a flame in the wind grew stronger.

The brothers were harder. Dalton barely spoke to me. Mac spoke even less. But sometimes… I caught them watching. A hand brushing mine when passing a plate at the dinner table. A lingering look across the garage. One night, Mac called me "Katie" instead of "her." And I sobbed like a baby in the bathroom the first time Dalton called me "Vixen."

I didn't push. Didn't beg. I just stayed. I kept cooking. Kept cleaning.

Kept helping. Kept loving them from a careful distance. Giving them the time they needed. I could be patient. I owed them that much.

One warm evening, a song drifted from my phone speaker—some old bluesy tune with a beat that made my hips sway and my heart feel light. I was barefoot, spinning around the kitchen, singing off-key, and waving a spoon around like a baton. Dancing like I hadn't a care in the world. It might have been pretend, but it sure felt good. For a moment, I felt like myself again. As the chorus filled the room, I did one last elaborate spin and stopped halfway through, nearly falling on my ass. Dalton stood in the doorway, arms crossed, eyes locked on me like I was the only thing in the room that mattered. I opened my mouth to say something, anything. But he moved first.

Dalton crossed the space in three long strides, took my face between his hands like I might disappear if he let go—and kissed me.

Long. Slow. It felt like coming home. Full of hope and heartache and something that tasted an awful lot like forgiveness. When we came up for air, he rested his forehead against mine and said, "Promise me you'll never leave again, Vixen."

I didn't even have to think—there was no hesitation.

"Never. I promise."

The next few weeks passed by in a blur. The only person who still eyed me with a hint of distrust was Mac. I knew he would come to me when he was ready. So, I lost myself in my work and in my friends. Dalton and I tried to keep everything lowkey. Our relationship was still very much on shaky ground, nothing like it had been when I left. But, for the first time in a long time, I had hope that it would get there. Everything was going right.

Until it wasn't.

One day, I pulled into the parking lot on my Triumph. I knew something was wrong about two seconds later. The club was chaos. Shouting. Guns drawn. Maria crying. Holly pale. I grabbed the first person who ran past me, which just so happened to be Rodney.

"What is happening?"

Rodney looked at me, eyes wild.

"Some guy showed up, he had a gun to Maria's head. Said either Mac went with him or he was going to set the bomb he put on her off. They pulled out not even five minutes ago—you probably passed them on the road."

Holy fucking shit. I had passed a speeding truck, but I didn't think anything of it.

"Where is she? Where's Maria?"

Rodney pointed towards the kitchen and I all but ran that way. Inside, Maria sat at the island, tears streaking her makeup, and Diego doing his best to console her. Holly was on the phone, furiously yelling at someone to do their job. Jackson had apparently already disarmed the bomb vest, or it had been a dud. Dalton whirled in my direction as soon as I walked in. The look in his eyes answered my question. Mac was gone. Holly threw her phone at the wall, cursing angrily. It was pure chaos.

Holly turned to me, and her next words threatened to shatter everything I had rebuilt.

"Your buddy Braxton stopped by for a visit. And we can't fucking find him or where we took Mac."

Dalton snapped at her, "This is *not* her fault."

Jackson stepped in Dalton's face. "Don't you raise your voice at her."

Diego froze, watching his two friends as the tension rose. Holly was pacing, and I knew I had to do something. Where would we take him? Where would they go? Then it hit me. And while everyone was distracted by worry and fear, I slipped out the door.

Holly was right—I had started this, and I damn well was going to finish it.

That bastard had come back from whatever dark corner he'd been hiding in, still obsessed. Still dangerous. Still convinced I belonged to him. I was about to show him just how wrong he was.

I pulled up to the giant storage units, parking several buildings away from the one I knew Braxton had used for a sort of operation base. Most people used these units to store boats and RVs, meaning they weren't here too often. Braxton had taken full advantage of that. I had swung by my house and grabbed my Colt. Swinging a leg over my bike, I pulled it from the holster as I made my way towards Braxton's unit.

The door was just barely open. Inside, Braxton paced in front of Mac, who was tied to a chair and bleeding from the mouth, but smirking anyway. I took a minute to get my bearings and figure out a game plan.

"You think you matter to her?" Braxton sneered. "You think you have what it takes to be the man she needs? I know her. The real her. All you know is a lie."

Mac spat blood at his feet. "Oh, I know her. In ways you never will. And you? You're dead the second my people walk through that door."

"I love her!" Braxton shouted, deranged and shaking. "You and your fucking brother couldn't keep your hands to yourselves…"

Mac's smile was lethal. "Yeah, and neither could she."

Braxton hit him upside the head with the butt end of the gun and, before I could even fully process what I was doing, I was inside. Mac shook his head, clearing the fog from his head. When he opened his eyes, he saw me and his jaw damn near dropped. Braxton spun around, but I had my Colt .45 raised and ready.

"Drop it."

To absolutely no one's surprise, he didn't. Instead, the fucking psycho smiled at me. Like we were old friends, like I didn't have a gun pointed at his chest. Like the man I loved didn't have blood trickling down his face. He opened his mouth, but I didn't give him the chance to speak.

I fired off a warning shot, straight up in the air. Like I had hoped, he flinched from the sudden and unexpected ear-shattering noise. I jumped forward, grabbing his hand and attempting to disarm him. Unfortunately, the asshat was trained too. He bent low, driving his shoulder into my abdomen and taking the breath out of me. I stumbled back but grabbed his hair as I went, taking him with me. My momentum, combined with his weight, caused us both to go down in a tumble onto the concrete floor.

We fought, messy and fast. Ever since Daniel had gotten the upper hand on me, I had made sure to stay in shape. No one was taking me down like that ever again. Braxton got in a few good shots, but I gave as good as I got. His gun went skidding across the floor, and he slammed me into a wall. I grabbed a pipe from the floor and cracked him across the temple.

He hit the floor, groaning, and I hurried towards my discarded gun. Picking it up, I stood above him, breathing heavy. Mac watched us with hooded eyes.

"Give me a fucking reason," I said, sweat and blood mixing on my brow.

Braxton looked up at me and, for a second, I thought he was going to give in. But then he scrambled across the floor like a rat, heading for his own weapon, and I fired two quick shots. One through the head, and one center mass. He stilled, and I exhaled sharply, lowering the weapon. A second later, I moved quickly towards Mac, and untied the knots with trembling hands. He started to rise, and I stepped back instinctively, giving him the space he had made clear was needed.

"I didn't know if I'd make it in time," I whispered, blinking back tears and trembling as the adrenaline wore off. My damn shoulder was hurting like a bitch too from where Braxton had tossed me into the wall.

Mac didn't answer. Instead, he pulled me in, arms wrapped tight around me, like he was afraid I would disappear if he let go. "You made it with time to spare, Vixen. I would always wait for you."

I started crying, and he wiped my tears away with a gentle hand.

"Ready to go home?"

I gave a watery smile. "Probably a good idea. I don't even know if they noticed me walking out."

Mac laughed, and I cherished the sound.

The clubhouse was still a wreck when we got back, but people stilled as they noticed Mac and me. In the kitchen, Dalton barked orders, and Jackson and Diego prepped gear. Guns were checked, phones buzzed with half-formed leads, and tension hung thick in the air like smoke. They were still looking for Mac, still assumed Braxton had him. Maria and Holly were nowhere to be seen, probably having gone somewhere to calm each other down. No one noticed the door open at first. Then Diego went to walk past us and stopped dead. He turned towards us like he couldn't believe what he was seeing.

"Um… Dalton? I think we can cancel all that."

Mac led me to the table, battered but upright, and we stood hand in hand as three heads turned in perfect unison. Dalton was the first to move, his eyes sweeping over his brother, checking for blood, for broken bones, for some sign that what he was seeing wasn't a hallucination born of stress and fear.

"Katie?" Jackson blinked. "What the hell?"

Diego looked like he wanted to sit down. Or pray. Or both.

I held up our joined hands and gave a half-smile. "Yay, we won! Surprise!"

Dalton crossed the room, eyes fixed on Mac. "You good?"

"Nothing a steak and a shower won't fix," Mac said with a wince. Dalton's gaze dropped to our hands. Then rose again, brow lifting. Mac just shrugged. "What can I say? It was kinda hot watching her kick ass."

Dalton looked between us, then finally—finally—smiled. A real one. I let out a breath I had been holding for what felt like years.

Dalton cocked his head at us. "Wait, so… how? You knew where they were and just asked for Mac back nicely or?"

"I used to be a cop, guys," I said, brushing hair out of my face. "Kinda sorta know what I'm doing. I had a feeling Braxton was using a storage unit that he had used during the op, and I went with it. By the way, we're gonna want to send a cleaning crew over there."

Silence fell for a beat. Then Jackson let out a low whistle.

"Remind me never to piss you off."

Diego just shook his head, laughing under his breath as he muttered something in Spanish that sounded suspiciously like *"mujer loca."*

Mac leaned in close, voice low in her ear. "Thank you for coming for me, Vixen."

I squeezed his hand tighter.

"I always will."

The lake house had always been my favorite place. Tucked into the trees, with its creaking dock and wide open view of the water, it was the one spot where everything felt quiet—where the world slowed down enough to let me breathe. Today, though, it was anything but quiet. Laughter spilled from the back deck, where the long table was crammed with food, beer bottles, and more people than the furniture was probably rated for.

A few days ago, Shelly had flown down from Charleston, and now she sat between Maria and Holly, already deep in conversation like they'd known each other for years. I had known they'd click—three smart, stubborn, take-no-bullshit women? It was inevitable. The four of us quickly became a unit, and I believed Maria was doing her damn best to convince Shelly to move down here to Atlanta. I smiled as Shelly laughed her off and sat back, eyeing the men across from her.

Swirling a beer in her hand, eyes sharp as ever, she pinned Mac and Dalton with a look. "I've got one rule. You hurt her? I will make sure you regret it."

Mac raised an eyebrow, grinning. "Yes, ma'am."

Dalton smirked over the rim of his glass. "We know the drill, detective. She's the queen. We're just her loyal subjects."

"Damn right," Shelly said, clinking her bottle against their whiskey glasses.

I watched everything from the patio door, and Mac looked over at me. His soft smile beckoned me closer, and I walked over, taking a seat on his knee. I leaned back, watching them all—the people I loved most in the world, laughing and teasing each other as the sun sank low over the water, setting the lake on fire with gold and rose. Rodney fiddled with the napkins, occasionally stealing glances at Shelly and then blushing crimson when she would catch him staring. The evening was perfect, but then suddenly Mac's phone rang, and he scooted me to his other knee so he could grab it.

He glanced down, looked at Dalton, and grinned. "It's Hartwell."

My eyebrows shot up. "Hartwell? *My* Hartwell?"

"Apparently," he said, then accepted the call and lifted it to his ear. "Hello?"

A muffled voice barked through the line loud enough for me to hear. "Damn thing won't... hold on, I swear this was on speaker—how the hell do I get the *camera* to work on this godforsaken phone?! Where's the button?!"

Mac shook his head and passed me the phone. "Think this one's for you."

Dalton leaned forward, and I glanced between the two of them before looking around at the rest of the table. Everyone was watching me.

I took the phone, confused as hell. "Lieutenant?"

"Katie! Finally. Can you hear me?"

"Uh, yes sir, loud and clear. Just think of it like a very fancy walkie-talkie. What's going on?"

"Give me a second. The tech guy told me this part was simple, but he didn't mention these stupid touchscreen things are possessed... There, got it!"

The screen flashed, and suddenly I was staring at the familiar Charleston precinct. I blinked. "Is that...?"

"Recognize the place?" Hartwell asked, a rare warmth in his voice.

I nodded and teased, "From my worst nightmares. What's going on? Everything—"

I stopped speaking, stopped breathing when I caught sight of a handful of people I never expected to see again. They stood in the background, huddled together. Kelly MacIntyre's aunt. Anastasia Little's mom and dad. Gabriella Santiago's whole family—her brother clutching a pint of cookies and cream ice cream.. My stomach flipped, heart rising into my throat.

"Why are they—?"

A door opened just off-screen. A social worker walked in with a hand resting gently on a young girl's shoulder.

Then another.

Then another.

It was them.

*Them.*

Tiny faces, tired and thinner, but *alive.* Their hair longer, some of their clothes too big or too small, but they were there. *Safe.* Their eyes lit up the moment they spotted their families, and all hell broke loose in the most beautiful way possible. Screams of joy. Tears. The sound of feet running across linoleum as kids launched themselves into arms that had been empty for far too long.

"Mommy!"

"Auntie Mae!"

I covered my mouth with my free hand. If I hadn't been sitting, I would've hit the ground. Tears began to run down my cheeks, and Mac pulled me closer into him. I hadn't realized I was shaking until Dalton scooted closer, reaching for me.

"Katie?" Hartwell said. "They're home. You did it."

I could barely breathe. "I didn't find them. I… thought they were gone."

"No," he said, "but *they* did. Dalton. Mac. They didn't stop. They tracked the last link down. Ran it to the ground. The Feds handled the final extraction, but it was your boys that cracked it open."

In the background, Gabriella's mother picked her daughter off the floor, clinging to the girl like a lifeline. She came closer, until she was right there, and Hartwell handed the phone to her.

I knew her voice, her daughter's face. "I can never repay what you have done for my family. God bless you. God bless you all."

I barely managed a trembly smile as the screen flooded with kids and families all trying to say *thank you* at once.

"We thought you should see it," Hartwell said, a little gruff. "Closure. Not for a case. For *you.*"

I looked over at Mac and Dalton, both watching me with that same look in their eyes. I turned the phone so they could see the screen. They both went still. Mac's grip on me got just a bit tighter. Dalton leaned closer to the screen, and to me. I smiled at them, trying desperately to tell them everything I was thinking with a look.

"Thank you," I whispered.

Hartwell just grunted. "Don't make me sentimental, kid. That's your thing."

The screen went dark. I sat there for a long moment, phone in my lap, heart full to bursting. I looked over at Holly and Jackson, both whom offered me a warm smile. A glance at my friends who had become family. This little slice of heaven that was never supposed to be mine. Cliff was openly crying too, and Rodney handed him one of the napkins that he had been fiddling with.

Shelly met my eyes and winked "You did it. Best damn cop I ever worked with."

I shook my head. "*We* did it. All of us."

They were safe.

They were home.

And so was I.

Thank you for riding with me!

If you loved Katie, Mac, and Dalton's story - don't worry. The ride isn't over yet.

Coming Spring 2026 is Hell of a Ride, book two in the Steel Saints MC series. This story focuses on Holly's and Jackson's story, one you won't want to miss.

A survivor with walls around her heart. A soldier running from ghosts of war. This love story isn't soft. Because some stories aren't just about falling in love.

They're about fighting for it.

Keep reading for a sneak peek…

# Hell of a Ride SNEAK PEEK

I stumbled up the stairs blindly, my stomach in my throat and my heart pounding against my rib cage like a wild animal trying to break free. Swallowing the bile that rose up, I paused at the top, swaying like I couldn't feel the ground under me.

My ears were ringing.

I couldn't breathe.

I heard my mother yelling for me, but her voice was distant. Like it was traveling through water. "Holly, baby, wait! Please! Oh, David… what are we going to do now?" That last bit was directed at my dad, who had remained frozen in front of the TV at the verdict.

Not guilty.

The words echoed around the room like a curse.

How had they found him not guilty?

Almost on autopilot, I made my way down the hall to the trophy room. My mom loved this room, and I had too, once upon a time. Now, standing in the doorway, all I felt was horror. Rage. Disgust. I shuddered at the feel of ghost hands on me, taking what wasn't theirs to take. Greedy, vile, wrong. *His* hands. Robert Lauren. I was a child, and I hadn't been the only one. A sob broke through, my eyes taking in the endless photos and awards. Pictures of me throughout the years, owning the stage like I had been born to it. Pretty dresses. Big smiles. Bright hazel eyes.

I didn't have to look in a mirror to know my eyes weren't so bright anymore.

The last stage I stood on wasn't for a crown—it was for a courtroom. One hand on a Bible, the other clinging to what little strength I had left. I had felt so embarrassed, so ashamed. Despite everyone telling me it wasn't my fault. It was never the victim's fault. I hated that word. Victim. But I sat there and told the truth anyway. Not guilty? After what he did? A sob broke through my throat, I could hear my parents arguing downstairs.

"This is our home, David!"

"It was our home, Ruth. How can you sit here and say you want to stay after what that bastard did?"

I tuned them out, and my eyes landed on the Miss USA trophy, my last and biggest. Tears blurred my vision, and I was moving towards it before I could even process what I was doing. I screamed as I threw it with all the strength my 16-year-old body possessed at the nearest trophy case. The glass shattered—sharp and violent, like the pieces of me I couldn't put back together. As the whole thing came crashing down, both of my parents went quiet. Stopping mid-argument. But the silence just made everything worse. I screamed again as I grabbed another trophy, throwing it at another case. Glass shredded my bare feet, but I didn't notice the pain.

It was nothing compared to the pain inside.

My father made it up the stairs and to me within minutes, but it felt like years. By the time he burst into the room, every piece of glass had been shattered, and I was covered in my own blood. He came up behind me, wrapping his arms around me. I kicked and screamed until my voice was hoarse.

"It's ok, baby. It's ok, I'm here. Daddy's here. It's ok."

He didn't let go, no matter how I thrashed. Finally, I went slack, completely spent.

As I turned into his arms, burying my face in his chest, sobs wracking my body, I caught sight of my mother who stood in the doorway, hand over her mouth as she took in the destruction. Her eyes, just like my own, were wide, and tears left tracks through her carefully applied makeup. My father ran soothing hands up and down my back, not the least bit bothered by the blood. I felt him look over at her, "We're leaving, Ruth. That's final. This town has nothing left for us."

She said nothing, but his tone left no room for argument. We were moving to Georgia.

# Newsletter Sign-Up

Ready for more?

Join the Steel Saints MC.

Sign up for the newsletter today and become one of my VIRs (Very Important Readers, duh) to get access to bonus content, spicy extras, and exclusive Steel Saints MC scenes you won't find anywhere else!

https://BookHip.com/ZXBHXLC

Or scan the QR code below!